MENEHUNE IN KAUAI

PEYTON BROOKS, FBI

Volume 7

ML Hamilton

www.authormlhamilton.net

Cover Art by Karri Klawiter

www.artbykarri.com

MENEHUNE IN KAUAI

This book is for my colleagues at work who support this crazy dream of mine. You don't know how much it means to me when I get your emails, asking me when the next book is coming out. Your encouragement and continued interest in my writing career is something I treasure.

Ku'ia kahele aka na'au ha'aha'a
– *A Humble Person Walks Carefully So As Not To Hurt Others.*
~ Hawaiian Proverb

CHAPTER 1

Marco eased Peyton down to her feet in their room, the whisper of her wedding gown the only sound. Outside she could hear the pounding bass accompanied by the thrum of the guitar from their reception band, but in here there was only silence and the two of them, staring at each other in the dim moonlight shining in the windows.

She faced him, looking up at his handsome features, the patrician nose, the dark hair parted on the side and swept back from the sculpted cheekbones, the large brilliant blue eyes winged by thick, black lashes. The bow of his lips, the jut of his chin, the angle of his jaw – all familiar and in this moment, all foreign.

Her husband.

The thought kept ambushing her, kept pushing out all other thoughts. After all they'd been to each other – partners, friends, lovers, exes, and then lovers again – this was the sweetest thought. He had a part of her that no one else had ever owned. He was hers.

She thought they'd tear into each other as soon as they got alone. Sex had never been a problem between them. They hungered for each other. But as she stood before him, she suddenly felt nervous. There was a level of intimacy here, a level they'd never reached before.

He touched her cheek, just the trail of his fingers along her jaw. She briefly closed her eyes, pressing her face into that touch. His thumb rubbed along her lower lip and she looked up at him again. He was so much taller than she was, so much bigger, but the way he'd always touched her had been gentle. Now it was reverent.

He shook his head in bemusement. "All these years, you'd think I'd know everything about you. You'd think there would be nothing left to discover."

She swallowed and took a step closer to him, not yet touching, but she could feel the heat of his body, smell his aftershave.

"You awe me, woman. Nothing has ever made me feel the way you do."

She smiled. "Frustrated, angry?"

"All those things and so much more." His fingers trailed down her throat to the pulse pounding in the hollow between her collarbones. "You are the most beautiful woman I've ever seen, inside and out. Before I met you, I never gave much thought to marriage and family. It was an abstraction."

She nodded, watching him, wanting to touch him, yet deliberately denying herself that right. She wanted to hear what he had to say and she feared if she touched him, he'd stop talking.

His hand trailed down her arm to her hand. He entwined their fingers. "I could go on about how everything changed the moment I met you, but I didn't know then. I knew I wanted you, but I didn't know about anything else beyond sex." He made a face. "I'm so bad with words."

"No, don't say that. Everything you're saying is perfect. Don't stop."

He smiled, lifting her hand to his lips and kissing it, while maintaining eye contact. It was the sexist thing she'd ever experienced. "Today, saying our vows, standing before our family and friends, it hit me what we were really doing. We were committing to each other, not just for today or tomorrow, but for the rest of our lives. We were committing to have a family, to build a life together. Peyton, I wouldn't have been able to do that with anyone else. I know this. I know myself well enough. You are it. You are the only one that I would have taken that risk for." He shrugged, giving her a gentle smile. "Sweetheart, you are my everything."

She released a shivery breath, blinking back the dampness in her eyes. "After that speech, D'Angelo, you'd better make love to me."

He laughed. "That's my plan, sweetheart. All night long."

She tilted her head to the side, biting her bottom lip. "There's about a million buttons on the back of this dress and they're each the size of a pea."

He quirked one brow. "A million, huh?"

"Two million, a billion. All I know is it took six women and an awful lot of cussing to get me into this thing."

He tugged her to him, their bodies brushing against one another. She looked up at him as he brought his mouth down to hers. "Don't worry, Brooks," he purred against her lips, "those six women getting you into that dress didn't have a fraction of my determination to get you out of it."

A shiver raced down Peyton's spine and she sucked in air as he crushed her against him with a hand in the small of her back. "Oh, boy!" she said, then she kissed him.

* * *

Danté glanced at the time on his phone, after midnight, then looked up at the lone figure sitting in the sand, staring out at the pounding surf. The reception behind him was winding down, people making their way to their rooms, hotel staff beginning their cleanup.

He loosened his tie and strode down the sand until he came to the figure. Bartlet looked up at him, his arms braced on his knees, a bottle of tequila dangling from his right hand. "Heya, partner," he said brightly, but Danté could hear the slur in his words. "Cop a squat."

Danté took a seat in the sand next to him, bracing his own arms on his knees. Bartlet passed him the tequila bottle, but Danté waved it off. He wasn't much of a drinker. The moonlight shone down on the surf, creating a reflection and he sighed, releasing the tension of the day. He didn't do well in crowds, but he'd felt obligated to come to this wedding. After all, it was his captain getting married.

As if Bartlet guessed the direction of his thoughts, he gave a snort of laughter. "Man, it's wild. The captain's married."

"Yep," said Danté. "He seems pretty happy."

"Yeah, but it's wild. Peyton and the captain are finally married."

Danté looked over at him. "It happens. I mean, people get married all the time."

"Yeah, but those two. It's like watching your dad get married."

Danté frowned at that. "Like what?"

"Like going to your dad's wedding, you know? The captain?" He took another swig of his tequila.

"Isn't the captain only a few years older than you are?"

"Yeah, that's not what I mean. I mean, you know, he's special, the captain, to me I mean. We been through a lot, the three of us."

Danté's eyes involuntarily tracked to the scar just visible on Bartlet's throat. "The janitor case?"

"Yeah, Peyton saved my life. She went in after me, and then the captain, he showed up. I mean, if they hadn't been there, that psycho bastard was going to kill me." Bartlet shook his head. "I still see flashes of it. I still hear sounds." He shivered and took another drink. "I wouldn't be a cop still if the captain hadn't fought for me. They were going to can me. They said I almost cost them three lives, but the captain wouldn't agree to take his post if they wouldn't let me stay with him."

"He told you that?"

"Noooo," Bartlet said. "They told me. They said I wouldn't have a job if it wasn't for him, so I'd better do right."

Danté looked back at the surf. "Did you think about leaving the force? I mean, after?"

4

Bartlet frowned. "Huh," he said, considering, "I mean no, I guess I didn't. I mean, I don't think I'd be very good at anything else to be honest."

Danté wasn't sure he was good at this. Bartlet didn't seem to be terribly dedicated to his job. "Why'd you pick being a cop anyway?"

Bartlet looked over at him. "My dad was a boxer."

"Seriously?"

"Yeah." Bartlet laughed, rubbing a hand through his short-cropped brown hair. "Can you believe that? Not a very good one, but he made a living at it."

"Is he…gone?"

"Naw, he's around. He's got Parkinson's now, but he was a tough bastard when I was growing up."

"So you became a cop to impress him?"

Bartlet nodded. "When I was growing up, he always said I was girly, you know, called me princess and cupcake."

"Geez," said Danté, horrified. He had no frame of reference. His own father had been encouraging, always there for him and his brother. "You have siblings?"

"Younger sister. Anyway, he didn't mean it in a bad way."

Danté's brows rose at that. How could calling your son names not be taken in a bad way?

"But I thought he'd be proud of me when I enrolled in the academy."

"He wasn't?" Danté asked.

Bartlet let out a bark of laughter. "No way. He was pissed, let me tell you." He swigged at the tequila. "He said, did I want to get myself killed? And then I almost got myself killed." He fell silent and stared out at the surf.

Danté didn't know what to say. He just sat next to Bartlet in the sand, letting the night deepen around them. He didn't think Bartlet expected him to say anything. Bartlet took another swig, the liquid sloshing in the bottle.

"Funny thing is it changes you."

"Getting shot?"

"Yeah, and almost dying. It changes you." He twisted the bottle into the sand until it stood up on its own. "When I became a cop, I thought it was about saving the damsel, you know? Like in the movies. I ran into that warehouse to save Genevieve without a thought." He looked at Dante. "She was the reporter the janitor abducted."

"I remember."

"I didn't even think. I just ran in there when I heard her scream. And he shot me." Bartlet's voice trailed away and his eyes went back to the ocean. "He didn't even give me warning. He just shot me."

Dante hunched his shoulders. This was getting deeper than he'd thought he'd ever get with Bartlet.

"After, when I recovered, I thought maybe I'd be really cautious, you know? I mean, I'm super cautious at work. I listen to what the captain says and I don't do anything until he orders it."

"Well..." began Dante, thinking that going the extreme opposite of what he'd been before might not be the best idea.

"But in my personal life, I don't know. I just want to take risks, you know? Date all the girls. Get a motorcycle. Just live."

Dante twisted his lips. He couldn't really answer that. He wasn't the adventurous type himself.

"Like right now, you know what I want to do?"

Dante shook his head.

"I want to go skinny dipping in the ocean." He dropped his leg and turned toward Dante.

"You wanna skinny dip in that ocean?" Dante asked in disbelief.

"Yeah!" Bartlet's eyes were wide, his look manic.

"It's the Pacific Ocean, man," Dante said.

"Right. I know what ocean it is," Bartlet said with a laugh.

"The Pacific Ocean will give you hypothermia."

"No, it won't." He waved Dante off.

"It's freezing cold," Danté reiterated, not sure Bartlet knew what hypothermia was.

Bartlet jumped to his feet. "So, where's your adventure? Come on. Live your life a little."

Danté got to his feet again. "It's illegal."

"No one's out here!" Bartlet held out his arms. "Dude, live a little." He shrugged off his suit jacket and started unbuttoning his shirt. "Look at me, I almost died. You gotta grab life by the balls sometimes."

"I'm not going skinny…" His voice trailed off as Bartlet shucked out of his shirt. The scar on his neck went all the way down to his chest, a thick rope of ugly puckered flesh. Holy hell, he wasn't kidding. He'd almost died in that warehouse.

Bartlet dropped his pants and his boxers followed until he was standing nude, his white skin glowing in the moonlight. "Come on!" he shouted. "It'll make you feel alive!"

Danté so didn't want to go into the ocean, but seeing Bartlet's wound, realizing what had almost happened to him, it seemed like a little enough thing to give him. He glanced skyward and cursed himself for ten kinds of fool, then he kicked off his shoes, shrugged out of his jacket and unbuttoned his shirt. Bartlet was racing back and forth on the beach, his naked white body streaking by as Danté dropped his shirt, shivering as the ocean breeze wafted over his bare skin. He toed off his socks and reached for his belt, unbuckling it, then dropped his trousers on the jacket. He was not going in without his briefs though.

"Come on!" Bartlet shouted, turning toward the water.

Danté took a few deep breaths, trying to psyche himself up for this. He knew if he didn't commit fully, he would never do it.

"Come on!" shouted Bartlet again, right at the water's edge.

Clenching his jaw, Danté started running for the surf, keeping his gaze fixed on the horizon. He could do this, he could dive into that brilliantly cold ocean, splash around a little, and get out. Then it would be over and he'd have done Bartlet a solid.

He felt the water strike his bare feet, but he kept going. As soon as the water reached his waist, he dove into it. It sucked the breath from his lungs, sent a riot of pain along every nerve ending, made his heart beat faster. He broke the surface and the cold sent prickles over his skin, making him feel alive in a way he never remembered. A laugh tore out of him – one of pure brilliance and joy. Bartlet had been right. It was invigorating.

He turned and looked back, realizing Bartlet wasn't near him.

Bartlet stood on the shore, his arms wrapped around his naked, pale body, hopping from one foot to the other. "Holy shit! You really did it! You really did it!" he said.

Danté's smile dried as the waves buffeted him back and forth. Bartlet hadn't gone in.

"HOLY SHIT!" shouted Bartlet. "I can't believe you did it!"

Danté had an instant thought of socking him in the mouth as he struggled through the waves back to the shore, but then Bartlet let out a whoop and began dancing around, throwing his arms in the air. The ridiculousness of seeing him carrying on in celebration while naked brought a smile to Danté's lips and he realized he didn't care that Bartlet hadn't gone through with it.

His mother had platitudes for everything when he and his brother were growing up, little nuggets of wisdom she'd imparted to them at every occasion. They sometimes rhymed and they were always ridiculous, but they stuck in Danté's mind and not just because he had an eidetic memory.

She had one for this occasion that kept playing through Danté's head as he made it to the shore and began walking up to his clothes with Bartlet dancing and whooping next to him. "A follower is a foolerer. If you follow others, you will fool yourself."

He bent down and grabbed his shirt, pulling it on, shivering violently with the cold. Bartlet grabbed the tequila bottle and took a swig, then he held it out to Danté. Danté stared at it, hearing his mother's voice, "A follower is a foolerer."

He shrugged and reached for the bottle. What the hell! And he took a swig.

*   *   *

Marco eased the tray onto the bed the next morning, studying the woman sleeping on her stomach, her hands beside her head, her dark curls a riot against his pillow. He felt a catch as he looked at her, her dark lashes lying against her cheeks, the curve of her bare back under the covers, the way a curl draped over her forehead.

He leaned over her, kissing her neck where it dipped into her collarbone. She stirred and drew in air, shifting, her eyes fluttering open. "Wake up, wife," he said, smiling as he said it.

She opened her eyes and stared at the other side of the bed, then she rolled over, holding the sheet to her breasts. "Hey," she said, stretching, then sitting up. He set the tray over her and went around the bed, climbing on it and leaning his back against the headboard.

"What's this?" she asked sleepily, rubbing her eyes.

"Breakfast in bed," he said, lifting the silver lid. He'd gotten her a waffle with strawberries and whipped cream and an omelet for himself.

Her eyes widened when she saw the sweet confection. "A strawberry waffle? Really, D'Angelo?"

He smiled, leaning over to kiss her temple. "A strawberry waffle and fresh squeezed orange juice." He held up the glass and she took it, taking a sip. She shivered in pleasure.

"I could get used to this," she said, setting down the glass and reaching for one of the coffee mugs. She searched over the tray, but he held up a packet of sugar. She smiled at him, her hair mussed from sleep, her eyes dark and tempting. "Anytime you want to spoil me, D'Angelo, I'm all for it."

"How about the rest of our lives?"

"Done," she said, pouring the sugar into the coffee.

He opened the nightstand next to him and took out a box, holding it out to her. She stilled, looking at it, then her eyes rose to his face.

"What did you do?"

"Open it," he said, leaning back against the headboard, his shoulder touching hers.

She took the box, settling herself more comfortably against him, and opened it. She lifted out the plane tickets, her brow furrowing as she read them. "Plane tickets to Kauai?"

"We needed a honeymoon."

She shifted on the bed, rattling the dishes. "We're going to Hawaii?"

"Yep. I tried to get the same place Maria and Cho went to, but they were booked. The travel site said this was their second highest rated resort."

"The Koloa Grove Resort?"

"We have an ocean view."

She stared at the tickets. "How can we afford this? How can we miss work, Marco?"

"The first one's simple. I've been saving up for this. I had a little put away before we moved in together." He kissed her bare shoulder. "And to answer the second question, you have time coming to you after Bodie. Radar can't work for at least another month, according to the doctors, so it was the perfect time to get away."

"What about the precinct?"

"Simons will cover for me. It'll be a good chance for him to see if he really wants to be a lieutenant. And I'm going to have Dante partner with Cho. That also gives Dante some more experience working as a detective before he takes the exam." When she started to protest again, he held up his hand. "Jake has agreed to keep Pickles and I already stopped the mail."

She laughed. "You thought of everything."

"I did. I have Maria on standby to take you shopping for beachwear and bikinis." His eyes tracked over her. "Get a red bikini for me."

"Really? I always thought a one-piece flattered your figure better."

He gave her an arch look. "Cute," he said. "And Abe will take us to the airport on Wednesday. If there's anything you need to shore up at work, you've got two days, and I'll get the sunscreen."

"Abe!" Peyton suddenly gasped. "What about Abe?"

Marco frowned. "Abe's an adult, sweetheart, and he can take care of himself for a week. We can leave some kibbles out if you're really worried."

She nudged his shoulder with hers. "Stop it. I mean, what about his birthday? It's at the end of this month. He's going to be fifty. We need to do something for him. I've got to plan a party or something."

"We'll figure it out when we get home. We'll only be gone a week, Peyton."

She gave him a look that said he was daft. "It's Abe's fiftieth, Marco. You don't just throw together a fiftieth birthday party for Abe at the last minute."

He brushed the hair off her shoulder and pressed his lips to the spot between her neck and her collarbone. "I want to go on a honeymoon with you, Peyton. We'll figure out the party later. Right now, I want to concentrate on us."

She closed her eyes and tilted her head to give him access. "You're right," she said and released a sultry sigh. "Let's go to Hawaii and get away from everything. No cases, no murders, no responsibility for one blissful week."

He slid his hand under the covers, running it along her bare thigh. "Nothing but the two of us in paradise," he purred.

She sighed again and melted into him. "Yeah, I can get on board with that."

CHAPTER 2

Peyton found Jake sitting in a booth at the back of the restaurant. He was twisting a napkin into a rope. As soon as she appeared in front of him, he glanced up through his lashes, looking like a puppy that was being scolded. He rose and kissed her on the cheek, then sat down again, reaching for his coffee mug. She noticed he'd broken about ten coffee stirs into tiny pieces.

She sat down across from him. "Making a Barbie bonfire?"

He swept the pieces and his napkin rope into a pile. A middle aged waitress appeared next to them, giving the mess a jaundiced eye, then forcing a smile for Peyton. "Coffee," she said, holding up a pot.

"Please," said Peyton, turning over the mug and watching her fill.

She and Jake liked to come to this throwback fifties diner for breakfast. The waitresses wore pink suits with their name tags affixed to their left breast. The booths were red vinyl and they had an old jukebox in the corner with playlists in glass cases on their tables. For a quarter, you could hear an actual vinyl record from a bygone era.

She grabbed the sugar and poured, surreptitiously looking at Jake. His brown hair was parted in the middle and feathered back from his face. He had average, everyday good looks, a certain Midwestern wholesomeness about him. He always kept his jaw clean shaven and he wore button up shirts in neutral colors with jeans or slacks. They'd been friends for years now, but it wasn't the time that bonded them, it was the events they'd survived. He was like a brother to her.

"So, what'll you have?" Peyton said, setting down the sugar and reaching for the menu in the metal holder. The menu felt greasy against her fingertips. She opened it and scanned down the offerings, although she already knew what she was going to order. "I'm thinking the vegetable scramble with hash browns."

"Bambi and I slept together!" he blurted out suddenly.

Peyton slowly closed her menu and set it down, staring at him.

He glanced at her and away. "Okay, I know you didn't want that to happen. I know you said she was your partner and you didn't want me messing around in that relationship. I know you think she's out of my league and that she could never care for someone like me. I know you probably think I'm betraying Zoë's memory and I probably am. I know…"

Peyton put her hand on his where he was rolling another napkin. "For God's sake, Jake, shut up!"

He looked up at her, biting his bottom lip.

"I'm happy for the two of you."

He narrowed his eyes on her, then he blinked a few times.

The waitress appeared. "Do you know what you want?"

Peyton flashed another smile at her. "I'll have the vegetable scramble and hash browns. Jake?"

Jake continued to stare at Peyton.

"Jake!" she said firmly.

"I'll have the same," he said, glancing at her.

The waitress gave Jake's pile of trash another aggravated look and walked off.

"You're happy for us?" he said.

"Yes." She picked up her coffee and took a sip. "I'm happy for you."

Bambi was her gorgeous blond, blue eyed partner with a figure that stopped traffic. She was Stanford educated and a damn good special agent. Peyton hadn't been sure about her when they first started working together, but Emma Redford had quickly become one of Peyton's closest friends. She adored her and what's more, Emma had saved her life.

Jake still looked skeptical.

Peyton pushed aside the coffee and took Jake's hands in hers. "I love you, Jake. You're family. I want you to be happy and if Emma makes you happy, then I say go for it."

"I don't know what to say."

"Well, there was a lot to unpack in that diatribe you gave, but let's start with why you feel like you're betraying Zoë."

Jake bit the side of his mouth. "I don't know. I mean I was with Draconia and that didn't feel like betraying her."

"Well, Dragonia…"

"Draconia."

"Dragonia was not from planet Earth."

"True," Jake said, nodding. "Just wish I hadn't gotten that tattoo."

"Yeah, that's another thing we should discuss," she said wryly. "Go on with what you were saying about Zoë."

"I loved her, Peyton. I really did."

"No one doubts that, Jake."

"I was happy married. I like marriage."

"Right."

"Emma's different." He reached for his napkin rope and twisted it. "Already I know Emma's different."

"How so?"

"It's easy with Emma. Being with her, I mean."

Peyton shied away a little. She didn't like discussing intimate details with Jake.

"Not sex. Geez, Mighty Mouse, is that the only thing you think about these days?"

"No!" She thought for a moment, remembering her weekend with Marco and a smile touched her lips.

"Peyton!" scolded Jake.

She laughed. "Okay, so it's not the only thing." She waved a hand airily. "Go on about Emma. What do you mean it's easy being with her?"

"We laugh, we have a good time. We can talk about anything."

"And it wasn't like this with Zoë?"

Jake shook his head, his expression miserable. "It wasn't."

"Okay, well, I think that's all right. Every relationship's different, Jake. They all bring us different things we need. After the nightmare that happened when Zoë died, you deserve easy, Jake. You deserve happy. Take it for what it is."

He considered that, his hands stilling on the napkin rope. "You're really okay with us doing the horizontal mambo."

She made a face. "Please stop."

"The jiggly wiggly."

"Oh for God's sake, Jake, we're going to eat soon."

"Bumping uglies."

She leveled a glare on him. "Stop."

He stopped, but his grin was infectious.

"I'm happy for you," she said.

He lifted her hand and kissed the back of it. "I'm happy for you, Mighty Mouse. No one deserves happiness more than you do."

"Thank you, Jake. So, the reason I asked you here is pretty important actually."

"Okay, what is it?" said Jake, reaching for his coffee.

"We need to plan Abe's fiftieth birthday party!"

Jake sputtered into his coffee, spraying it on the table just as the waitress arrived with their food. She glared at Jake, her jaw setting.

"Seriously, man!" she said, setting their plates down hard.

*   *   *

Danté walked into the precinct Monday morning and found Tag, Holmes, Lee, Cho and Simons all gathered around the front counter listening as Bartlet related what had happened after the captain's reception.

"And then we stripped naked and ran down to the surf!" Bartlet held his arms in the air and pretended to run with mincing steps, while staying in place.

Everyone laughed uproariously. Danté felt his ears heat with embarrassment and he couldn't believe Bartlet was telling them what happened.

"I felt that cold ass water on the bottom of my feet and I figured it would make my winkie shrivel up like a raisin, so I pulled back at the last minute, but Danté...he dove right in, going all the way under!" Bartlet started swimming in the air, making everyone explode with laughter again.

Danté wasn't sure what to do. Part of him wanted to turn back around and get in his car, driving away forever. Part of him wanted to sock Bartlet in the mouth again. He'd never socked anyone in his life and here he was, having a vivid image of punching his partner twice in less than a week.

"I tell you, man, you gotta respect a guy who's got balls of steel!" said Bartlet, barking out a laugh.

Simons pulled open the half door and motioned Danté through. "You got more cajones than I do, kid!" he said, slapping Danté on the back.

Danté stepped into the precinct, looking around in bewilderment. They weren't making fun of him. Tag slapped him in the chest with her tattooed *happy* fingers. "He's right. Respect, man. I have never gotten more than a toe in the Pacific Ocean in my life."

Holmes nodded, throwing an arm around his shoulders and dragging him further into the room. "Man, and here I thought you were a total square. You got balls, man!"

Cho gave him a chin jerk. "Yeah, well, I told you that. Not everyone's a bone-headed Neanderthal like you, Holmes."

Lee held out his hand and Danté took it, letting the huge man drag him in for a chest bump. "I regularly swim in the ocean myself. It makes you know you're alive. Clears the head and gets the blood flowing. Hoaloha!"

Danté found himself smiling bemusedly. He hadn't expected that. A moment later the outer door opened and Captain D'Angelo walked through. The attention immediately shifted and everyone exclaimed over him, coming forward to shake his hand and congratulate him on getting married.

When it was all over, the captain eased through the half door and moved toward his office. "Tell everyone we'll be meeting in an hour in the conference room," he ordered, then he gave Danté a pointed look and walked away.

Danté wasn't sure what to make of the look. The truth was Captain D'Angelo intimidated him. He had nothing but respect for the man, and yet, the captain was particularly hard to read. He kept his emotions in check and didn't offer a lot of praise. Not that Danté expected much, but he wished he knew what D'Angelo really thought of him.

Bartlet threw his arm around Danté's shoulders. "Come on. Let's go get breakfast at the coffee shop across the street before the meeting."

Danté wasn't sure that was okay, but Cho nodded. "Go. Just make sure you're back in time."

Threading through the people, Danté followed Bartlet out of the precinct again. As they crossed the street and entered the coffee shop, an older woman nodded to them. Danté nodded back. The coffee shop was crowded, but as they got in line to place their order, a man in front of them told them to go before him.

"Thank you, sir," said Bartlet, tucking his thumbs in his belt and stepping forward.

Danté wasn't sure he liked the way the people in the coffee shop treated them, just because they were in their uniforms. He didn't expect preferential treatment, never had. His duty was to serve. That was what his parents had always taught him.

"Excuse me!" came a familiar voice. "Sorry. I'm with them."

Danté glanced over his shoulder, seeing Harper McLeod pushing her way through the line to get to them.

"I'm with them," she told a guy who glared at her, then she grabbed Danté's arm, looking up at him. "Hey, Mr. Spock, how's it hanging?"

"Ms. McLeod," he said, looking away from her.

"Hey, Harper right?" said Bartlet, holding out his hand. "Jimmy Bartlet."

"Hey, Jimmy, nice to meet you," she said, taking his hand.

"I'm Danté's partner."

She narrowed her green eyes on him. "You're the cop that got shot by the Janitor."

Danté couldn't believe her insensitivity, but Bartlet laughed. "That's me."

She motioned between them. "You and I should talk."

"No, I learned my lesson. I don't talk to reporters."

She gave him a practiced pout. Danté couldn't deny that Harper McLeod fascinated him. She was gorgeous, long wavy brown hair, big green eyes, wide cheekbones, an intelligent forehead, full red lips. She was tall and slender, but curvy in all the right places and she smelled like vanilla. There was also something lurking behind her eyes that drew him to her, some sadness or unhappiness she tried to keep hidden.

"I promise to play nice. I won't write anything you don't want me to write."

Bartlet exchanged a look with Danté.

Danté shrugged. He couldn't give him advice on this. He was too new to the precinct. He didn't know protocol.

"I gotta talk to the captain," said Bartlet.

"Captain D'Angelo loves me," she said.

Bartlet made a face. "I'm thinking that's not true."

"It is," she said, her eyes going wide. "Ask him. We have a reciprocal relationship, the captain and me. I give him information and he does the same. Tell him," she said to Danté, slapping his arm with the back of her hand.

"You're right, Jimmy," said Dante. "Talk to the captain."

Harper glared at him.

They'd reached the front of the counter, ready to place their order. Harper pushed between the two men. "I'll have a cappuccino with a shot of vanilla and a..." She leaned to the side, looking into the display case. "What's that?" she said, tapping the glass with a long blue fingernail.

Dante couldn't help but notice how her skirt hugged her hips and rear end when she leaned over. He forced himself to look away, but Bartlet caught him looking and nudged him with his arm, nodding. Dante shook his head to stop him from saying anything.

"It's a maple scone."

"I'll take it. Can you warm it up?"

The teenager behind the counter rolled her eyes. "Fine." She shifted her attention to the cops. "What do you want?"

"I want a ham and cheese English muffin," said Bartlet. "We got coffee at the precinct," he told Harper.

"And you?" said the girl to Dante.

"I'm good," he said. "I already ate."

Harper faced him. "Did your mama make you breakfast, Mr. Spock?"

Bartlet laughed.

Dante wasn't going to tell her that his mother often had him over to the house for breakfast before he went to work, so he just leveled a look on her. He didn't have to answer her taunts.

She patted his stomach with the back of her hand. "Got gum."

He narrowed his eyes on her. "You just ordered food."

"For later. I'm gonna want a cigarette after I eat and you know it."

Dante fished in his pocket and pulled out a pack of gum. He wasn't going to tell her he'd bought it for her, for the frequent times they seemed to run into each other. She took a piece and shoved it into the front pocket on her purse.

"Who's paying?" the teenager asked.

"Oh, I will," said Harper, taking out her wallet. "You sure you don't want anything, Mr. Spock. I hear the lattes will bring out your wild side." Then she tittered as she handed the girl her card. "Oh, I forgot. You don't have a wild side."

"He does!" said Bartlet, bursting into a smile. "You should have seen what he did at Captain D'Angelo's wedding!"

Harper placed her elbow on the counter and braced her chin on her fist. "Do tell!" she said, a gleam in her eye.

And for the third time in as many days, Danté had a mental image of his fist connecting with Bartlet's mouth.

*   *   *

Marco called the whole precinct into the conference room at 9:00. He stood at the head of the table as they all filed in, taking seats at the long table. When Simons entered, he motioned him up to the front with him. Simons wedged his way through the people, his bulk making the tight room smaller. Lee didn't bother to come inside, just leaned against the door.

Jake threw himself down in a chair at the other end of the table, giving Marco a piercing look. "What's going on, Adonis? I thought you'd be off getting your honeymoon on by now."

Marco twirled the unfamiliar ring around his finger. He'd never worn jewelry in his life, not even the crosses his brothers had always worn, but this piece of platinum felt so right on his hand. "Captain," he said through clenched teeth.

"Captain Adonis," corrected Jake. "You shouldn't be here. You should be off making little Adonises."

Marco glared at him until Jake finally pretended to lock his mouth shut. When Marco looked around the room, none of his people were making eye contact, but a few were smirking. He drew a breath for patience.

"I called you all here because I'll be leaving on Wednesday for my honeymoon."

Jake's hand shot into the air. Tag reached over and grabbed it, yanking it down.

"Rather than have Deputy Chief Defino cover for me again, I'm appointing Bill Simons as temporary lieutenant. You'll answer to him."

Jake raised his hand again, but Tag swiveled and glared at him. He glanced at her and brought it down himself.

"Since Cho will be without a partner, I'm going to have Price work with him on any cases that come in."

Bartlet patted Danté on the back, but the kid looked wide-eyed.

"Frank," said Marco, focusing on the veteran uniform. "You and Bartlet will work backup for both teams as needed."

"You got it, Captain," said Smith.

Marco turned his attention to Tag and Holmes. "I want to know more about this Renchenko connection with Eduard Zonov and potentially, Victor Maziar. Go out and talk to the business owner. We need to follow up on Wendell's complaint. What was the owner's first name again?"

Holmes pulled out his notepad and flipped it open. "Kazimir, but he won't talk to us and he would only speak in Russian anyway."

"Take Price and Cho with you. Price understands Russian."

They all looked at Danté. The kid fidgeted, looking down. He needed to get more self-confidence. Marco exchanged a look with Cho and Cho nodded. Marco had faith that Cho could bring him around. There were few cops Marco trusted more than Nathan Cho.

"Ryder, I want you and Stan to get whatever information you can on this new Russian gang, the Goblins.

Call Adrian Trejo at CIPAC and talk to Javier Vargas. I want to know what their numbers are, what firepower they have, what their territory is."

"Aye aye, Captain!" said Jake.

"What about the Lowell Murphy murder, Captain?" asked Tag.

"We're still working it. I'm going to see Kurt Foster in the psych facility tomorrow and see if he remembers Murphy having any contact with Russians."

"But you're thinking if we figure out this Russian mob connection, that it'll lead us to Murphy's murderer," said Holmes.

"Exactly," said Marco. "Let's get all hands on deck with this Russian mob thing. If another case comes across our plate, we'll redistribute the manpower as necessary. I'll only be gone a week and I'll be available by cell the entire time."

Jake raised his hand again.

"What?" Marco said with asperity.

"It's your honeymoon. With your wife. Shouldn't you focus on that?" Jake said.

"He's got a point, Captain," said Lee. "You need to concentrate on the missus now. We'll hold down the fort here."

Marco looked around. He knew he had some of the best people in his precinct, people others wanted to poach from him. Just the combination of Stan and Jake alone made other precincts covetous. If any group of people could handle whatever was thrown their way, it was this one. He nodded.

"You're right. I'll focus on that."

Simons patted him on the back, smiling at him.

"Everyone's dismissed," he said and they began filing out, heading off to do their jobs. Marco turned to face Simons. "I'll still be available on cell phone."

Simons chuckled. "I figured you'd say that. I'm gonna set up in your old cubicle and let the kid have my desk."

"Sounds good, but you're welcome to use my office too."

"Naw, wouldn't feel right. Anyway, just enjoy yourself. If you're lucky, you only get one honeymoon in your entire life."

Marco laughed. "I can promise you this will be my only honeymoon, Bill. No way would I ever be luckier than I am right now."

Bill patted his shoulder again and headed out of the room. As Marco reached for his cane, he saw Jake watching him. "What now, Ryder?" he said. "You have work to do."

Jake pushed himself to his feet. "Peyton gave me another job earlier today."

Marco frowned. "What?"

"I have to plan Abe's fiftieth birthday party."

"Sounds like it's in your wheelhouse. Go wild."

"That's just it. I don't know how big I should go."

"Well, the way I figure it," said Marco, walking to the door. "Whatever you're thinking…"

"Yeah?"

"Go bigger."

"What? Like Mardi Gras? Cirque du Soleil? Carnival?"

"Yes." Marco walked out into the precinct, headed for his office.

"Which?"

"All."

"What's my budget?"

Marco paused and looked back at him. "What did Peyton tell you?"

"To run it by her before I made any final reservations."

"There's your answer."

"You're not going to help me, are you?"

Marco shook his head. "I already went on a date with him. Now, it's your turn."

Both Lee and Jake frowned, but Marco didn't wait to hear what they had to say. He just continued on to his office, finding Devan sitting in the chair on the opposite side of Marco's desk. Marco drew a breath for patience.

"What are you doing here, Adams?"

"I thought you were going on your honeymoon," said Devan. "Are you and Peyton already having trouble?"

Marco glared at him as he sank into his desk chair. "No, we're not having trouble. You need to get a new hobby. Peyton's a married woman now."

Devan rolled his eyes. He was the epitome of tall, dark and handsome, and he had a strange obsession with Peyton, even though he'd been the one to call off their relationship when they'd been dating.

"Why are you here? You're like a bad penny I can never get rid of."

"I know your insults don't mean half of what you intend, D'Angelo. Anyway, I came to tell you that Roscoe Butler's coming up for a preliminary hearing in a week."

Roscoe Butler, aka Chicago, was a member of the Mainline Gang, who was in a gang turf war with the Big Block Gang in Hunter's Point. During a drive by, Chicago had shot at a laundromat that was in disputed territory, but he hit seventeen-year-old Jamaad Jones, who was walking home, killing him instantly. With the help of the gang task force and Javier Vargas, Marco's people had brought down the Mainline Gang, arresting Chicago.

"Good."

Devan folded his hands in his lap. "Now hear me out, D'Angelo, before you explode."

"What?" Marco knew he wasn't going to like what Devan was going to say next.

"I need Cashea Thompkins to testify."

Cashea Thompkins had been the terrified young woman who named Roscoe Butler. Her brother, LeJohn, had been part of the Mainline Gang, but some Big Block gangsters had found him, beating him so badly that he had brain damage. He was no longer able to care for himself.

"What?"

Devan quickly held up a hand. "Just hear me out."

"We promised her anonymity."

"No, you told her you would try to protect her identity. Now we can't. She's our only witness."

"We got a confession out of Butler."

"From a rookie cop, D'Angelo. The judge may throw it out."

A horrible thought occurred to Marco. "You're going to need Danté to testify."

"Yes."

"He's green, Adams."

"I know. I'll coach him, but I need him to affirm the confession."

Marco sat back in his chair. "Can you put this off until I'm back from Hawaii?"

"No. I tried, but I was denied. Both Cashea and Danté are essential for this hearing. If I don't have them, Roscoe Butler just might walk."

"Shit!" Marco banged a fist on the desk. "We promised her anonymity. She's never going to agree to this."

"She might. She just might if Danté's the one to ask her."

Marco stared at the picture of Peyton and Pickles on his desk. He wanted nothing more than to go on this honeymoon with her, but no matter what they did, no matter how they tried to catch a few moments just for themselves, their jobs were always pulling them back under.

"Let's see if we can get Cashea in here tomorrow to talk to her before I go."

"Do you want to make the call or me?" asked Devan.

"I'll make it. I just want to talk to Javier and see if there are any programs to help people like the Thompkins."

"Just text me the time and I'll be here," said Devan, pushing himself to his feet. "Let me see what I can do on my end of things. I might be able to find a program the family would qualify for myself."

Marco nodded, feeling horrible about the whole situation.

Devan paused at the door. "I'm sorry about this, D'Angelo, but I have no other choice, especially if we want to get justice for Jamaad Jones."

"I know," Marco said, but it didn't make him feel any better about it.

CHAPTER 3

Gwen opened the door to Peyton Tuesday morning. She was dressed in a pair of pink capris, a sleeveless striped pink shirt, and her red hair pulled up in a messy bun. She was supermodel beautiful, her skin glowing a healthy pink in the late morning sunlight streaming into the room. She had one of the Persian cats in her arms.

"Peyton, it's so good to see you." She leaned over and kissed Peyton's cheek. "Please come in. He's sitting outside on the patio."

Peyton stepped into the pleasant entryway with its earthy terracotta tiles. "How are you, Gwen?"

"I'm doing well, Peyton. Why haven't you left on your honeymoon?"

"We leave tomorrow. I'm just tying up a few loose ends."

"The wedding was beautiful," Gwen said.

"Thank you. Marco planned the whole thing. I had this list of things I wanted and he got me every one of them."

Gwen smiled. "He loves you dearly."

"Well, the feeling's mutual."

"It's a wonderful thing when you find it," she said, then motioned into the great room. "Let me show you the way. Can I get you a cup of green tea? I'd offer coffee, but I'm not letting Carlos drink that yet."

"Green tea sounds nice," said Peyton, reaching out to scratch the white ball of fluff under her chin. The cat immediately began to purr, closing her eyes and pressing her head against Peyton's hand.

Peyton followed Gwen through the great room and to the French doors that led to the patio. Gwen pushed one open and stepped out. Peyton followed her, finding herself in a sunny enclosed brick patio with two lounge chairs, a small bistro set with two chairs, and hanging plants lining the brick wall encircling the yard.

Radar sat on one of the loungers, a throw draped over his legs, the second white Persian on his lap. He wore his sunglasses and a cup of steaming tea sat next to him. Gwen came over and peered into the cup.

"You need to drink that, Carlos. It builds up white blood cells." She set the other cat on his legs and began fussing with the throw.

"I'm fine, Gwen, stop fussing," he said, catching her hand in his. "What's up, Sparky?"

Peyton smiled to see her gruff, no nonsense boss holding the hand of his beautiful wife with two cats on his lap; the cats had started to groom each other. "I just wanted to see you before I leave for Hawaii, old man," she said, taking a seat on the other lounger.

"I'm fine, Gwen," Radar said again, kissing the back of her hand. "I thought you were going to yoga."

"I'll go tomorrow."

"That's ridiculous. I'm perfectly capable of taking care of myself for a few hours. You need to get out of the house."

She waved him off. "I'll just get you that tea, Peyton," she said, heading back into the kitchen.

Peyton reached over and picked up one of the cats, rubbing her chin on her soft head. The cat, Satin she suspected, started purring. Radar ran his hand over the back of the other one. Settling the cat in her lap, Peyton gave Radar a serious once over. He still looked pale, his cheekbones more prominent. He'd definitely lost weight.

"How you doing, old man?"

"I'd be doing better if people would stop asking me that."

Peyton smiled. Radar had a definite place in her heart. "You know I felt the same way Gwen does when Marco was shot. I didn't want to leave him, didn't want him out of my sight. Cut her some slack."

He sighed, his sunglasses shifting away. "I've never been good with inaction."

"Take up a hobby then."

The sunglasses swung back to her. "A hobby, Sparky? What sort of hobby?"

"Crocheting? Needle point?" She pointed a finger at him. "What about pottery?"

He didn't immediately answer, but she could feel the power of his look even if she couldn't see it. Gwen returned and placed a cup and saucer on the table next to Radar's. She bent and kissed Radar's cheek.

"I'll go take a shower if you're sure you don't need anything."

"We're good," he said, giving her a smile. "Take your time."

Gwen touched Peyton's shoulder as she headed for the house. "Enjoy your honeymoon, Peyton."

"Thank you, Gwen."

Peyton stroked her hand down the cat's back. "What about painting?"

"Painting?"

"You could paint the cats. I'll bet people would pay a lot of money for paintings of Satin and Lace. I know I would."

His brows lowered. "You'd pay a lot of money to buy a painting of a white lump with dots of blue in the center?"

Peyton leaned over and looked at Satin's blue eyes. She blinked slowly at her and began purring again. "If you signed it, I would. I could go get you an easel right now and you could get started this afternoon."

"Look, Sparky," said Radar, "can we be serious for a moment?"

"I was serious. I think painting cats would be a good pastime."

The sunglasses stayed fixed on her.

She shifted uncomfortably. "Fine. What do you want to talk about?"

"I know we lost jurisdiction on the Lance Corporal Daws case, but I'm anxious about the messages you've gotten from that anonymous source. I want you to be extremely careful while I'm out of commission. Any strange calls, any strange people you see, I want you to report it immediately. You hear me?"

"Of course, but I'll be out of town for a week. Besides, I haven't gotten any other messages for a long time."

"That may be, but I don't think that's the last we'll hear from your mystery man."

Peyton suspected he was right, but it made her uneasy. She reached over and picked up her tea, taking a sip. The astringent taste washed over her tongue, making her grimace involuntarily. It could really do with a dose of sugar.

"Tastes like feet, doesn't it?" Radar said dryly.

Peyton frowned at him, but she set the tea down again. "Take your medicine, old man. You need to get back in commission."

His brows drew down below the sunglasses. "Listen, kid, I should file a formal reprimand with Sarge over what happened outside the Lucky Boy mine."

"What?"

"I told you to leave, Peyton. I gave you an order."

She didn't know what to say. She felt stung by his words. He held out his right hand. She reluctantly placed her own in it and he covered the back with his free hand.

"But you saved my life. You're a damn good Special Agent, Peyton. You're a damn good cop, and I wouldn't be here if you hadn't done what you did. You have guts and intelligence and compassion. Your daddy would be so proud of you, Sparky."

Peyton's eyes flooded with tears and she blinked rapidly. One slipped out and raced down her cheek.

Radar patted her hand, then released her, leaning his head back against the lounger. "Don't cry. God, I hate when women cry."

"Then you shouldn't be sweet to me," she said, wiping the tears away. She leaned over, disrupting the cat, and kissed his cheek. "I gotta go. I'm meeting Bambi for lunch, but you get well, okay? Drink your feet tea. I need you to come back to work."

He smiled at her as she handed him Satin. "Enjoy the honeymoon and tell Marco I said congratulations."

"I will," she said. "Do what Gwen tells you and send her some flowers. She's been through hell."

He nodded and she turned to go, but he caught her hand at the last second. "Sparky?"

"Yeah?" she said, looking over her shoulder.

"Thank you for my life."

Peyton's eyes flooded again, causing Radar to snort in disgust. "It's your fault, old man," she said, then she blew him a kiss and stepped into the house.

Leaving Radar's house, Peyton drove over to *Molinari's Delicatessen* on Columbus in North Beach. She got lucky and found parking on the street, then hurried down to the small deli with the blue awning over the door. A few tables had been set up on the street and Bambi had secured them one. She rose as Peyton approached, kissing her cheek and hugging her.

"You look so good," she said, holding Peyton off at the shoulders. "You look happy."

Peyton smiled. "I am. You look pretty yourself." But then Bambi always looked pretty with her California good looks, her blond hair pulled up in a ponytail, her blue eyes lined with just the right amount of mascara. She wore a t-shirt and floral shorts, sandals on her feet.

Peyton glanced into the deli, seeing how crowded it was. "Wow, this place is always hopping."

Molinari's was an old fashioned deli with salami hanging from the rafters, warped plank flooring and glass display cases showing the latest cuts of meat. Cheese choked one case, stacked in rounds or rectangular bricks right to the top. A number of workers in white aprons moved behind the counter, making sandwiches for people, and a red number dispenser stood just inside the door. Bambi held up a number.

"I already got one. We're fifty-seven and they're on forty-three. It's gonna be a long wait."

Peyton sat down at the table. "Then we'll have time to talk." She picked up the laminated menu. "Do you know what you want?"

"Salami on rye with Swiss cheese," said Bambi without hesitation.

Peyton considered that, but she hadn't eaten red meat in so long she found she didn't crave it anymore. "I'll have the veggie special."

"Okay. When our number comes up, I'll go order it and you hold the table. Anything to drink?"

"Iced tea," said Peyton, then tilted her head. "And bring me some sugar packets."

Bambi smiled, then her smile dried. "Peyton, I have to tell you something."

Peyton gave her a questioning look, although she already suspected she knew what Bambi had to tell her. "Tell me anything."

Bambi drew a deep breath, then released it. "Jake and I hooked up at your wedding."

"NO!" Peyton said in mock shock.

Bambi gave her a patient smile. "Okay, so you already knew."

"Jake confessed first thing yesterday."

Bambi reached over and took Peyton's left hand, playing with her wedding ring. "I know you didn't want Jake and me to get together. I know you're worried it's going to affect our friendship and working relationship. I'm sorry."

"Emma, listen to me. It's none of my business what you and Jake do. I'm not worried about it affecting us at all. I was worried about Jake."

"Why?" Bambi released her hand. "Is something wrong with Jake?"

"Jake's a family guy, Emma. He liked being married. He likes commitment and you told me…"

"I didn't want that." She nodded. "I get it."

"But to be honest with you, I was wrong. It's your decision. It has nothing to do with me."

"You care about Jake and you don't want him hurt."

"Well, I can't protect him from that, so you two have fun. I'm completely okay with whatever happens."

Bambi fussed with the paper number. "He's not like anyone I've ever dated, Peyton."

Peyton smiled. She could imagine that was true. "He's a good guy, Emma."

Bambi nodded. "He really is. He's funny and sexy. And did you know he has a tattoo?"

"I've heard."

"Of a dia de los muertos skull on his inner hip."

Peyton held up a hand. "I don't need the details."

Bambi gave Peyton a scandalized look. "I didn't know he was that adventurous."

"Right."

She leaned closer to Peyton. "I've got one too."

"A tattoo?"

"A dia de los muertos skull." She licked her bottom lip. "On my right butt cheek."

Peyton let out a laugh. Of course she did. What else would someone as fascinated by death as Bambi get for a tattoo? "Well, then I'd say it was a match made in…" She hesitated. She wanted to say hell, but didn't want to offend her friend.

"Heaven," said Bambi, grabbing her hands again. "I've never felt like this about anyone before, Peyton. I mean, I know we've only spent one night together, but he's taking me on a date, a real date, tonight and he won't tell me where it is."

Peyton felt a rush of warmth for the pretty blond. "With Jake, you can bet it'll be someplace special."

Bambi sat back. "How did you know Marco was the one?"

Peyton reared away. For a woman who claimed never to want a serious relationship, Bambi was moving fast. She'd expected Jake to dive into the deep end, not Bambi. "Well…" she said, dragging out the word. "I guess I knew when I realized no man would ever measure up for me, that I compared all men to Marco, and they all fell short."

Bambi clasped her hands against her breast. "That's so romantic."

Peyton smiled. "Yeah, I guess it is. I hope you find that, Emma. I really do."

Bambi smiled in return.

"Number fifty-seven," shouted a man's voice from the deli.

"That's us," said Bambi, bouncing to her feet and disappearing inside.

* * *

Danté entered the precinct at 8:00 the following morning. He'd spent the night brushing up on his Russian, listening to audio files to get the proper inflection down. He didn't feel as comfortable speaking it as he did reading it, but he wanted to make a good impression on the captain.

Lee looked up from his monitor. "Captain D'Angelo wants to see you in the conference room in an hour," he told the young man.

Danté nodded. "Do you know what about?"

"No, he's at physical therapy, but he called in when I got here and asked me to give you that message." Lee motioned at Danté's tie. "Your tie's a little crooked."

Danté glanced down at it. He hadn't worn a tie very often, except to church, and then his mother had always straightened it for him. "Thank you," he said. He found the police uniform restrictive, but the suit was even more so and he almost would have preferred the uniform. At least then he knew what to wear everyday.

Lee smiled at him and nodded. He was a massive man of Samoan lineage who was even taller than Captain D'Angelo. Danté had never considered himself short, but at six feet in this precinct, he wasn't tall either.

He headed back to his desk, or rather Simons' old desk. He didn't see Cho and he wasn't sure what he was supposed to do while he waited for the senior detective to arrive. Jake Ryder, the precinct's CSI, passed the desk, carrying a mug of coffee.

"Hey, Danté!" he said cheerfully. Jake had always been one of the more welcoming people here.

"Good morning, Mr. Ryder."

Jake paused and smiled at him, saluting him with his coffee mug. "This is why I like you, Danté. You know how to treat a man right."

Danté nodded. He liked Jake, but he thought he could take the job a little more seriously. He called the captain Adonis, which seemed unprofessional, and he was always making quips about *everything*. There wasn't a single conversation that Danté had been part of in the precinct that Jake hadn't made into something silly.

Danté pressed the button to start the computer. He might as well do some more studying while he waited for the captain or Cho to arrive.

"So," said Jake, moving toward the two desks. "You really speak Russian?"

"I read it better than speak it, but I was just going to watch some videos to see if I could get the inflection down."

One brow rose over an eye. "Seriously?"

"I have an eidetic memory. If I listen to it enough, I should be able to reproduce it with no problem."

"So, you know Adonis..."

"Captain D'Angelo," Danté corrected mildly.

Jake rolled his eyes. "Captain Adonis assigned me to research the Goblins, right?"

"With Mr. Neumann."

"Right. Well, if we come across some Russian, can you translate for us?"

Danté nodded. "I don't see why not."

"Good. Well, carry on. You might add Mandarin as your next task."

"Plan on it," said Danté, glancing at the screen. Jake hesitated, shooting a look over his shoulder. Danté resisted the impulse to grin. He actually did plan to study Mandarin as soon as possible, but he knew Jake thought he was kidding. Or maybe he didn't. Either way, Danté wasn't opposed to keeping the CSI on his toes.

At 9:00, Danté headed toward the conference room.

Lee swiveled to face him. "I was just about to buzz you," he said.

"No need." Danté's parents had been adamant that their sons always be prompt. On time was five minutes late, his father always said. Captain D'Angelo and ADA Adams stepped out of the captain's office, both carrying mugs of coffee. Danté had never felt the need for artificial stimulation. If you got a full night's rest, you didn't need anything else.

"Good morning, Danté," said the ADA.

"Good morning, sir," Danté answered. "Good morning, Captain."

Marco jerked his chin at him, but didn't say anything.

"Come inside with us," said Adams, pushing open the conference room door.

"When Javier Vargas gets here, bring him in, Lee," said Marco.

"You got it, Captain," said Lee. "Let me know if I can get you anything."

"Thanks," said Marco, motioning Danté forward.

Danté wasn't sure what this was about, but a flutter of anxiety was working its way through his system. He took a seat at the table and watched both the ADA and the captain sit down across from him. Marco leaned back in the chair, sipping his coffee.

Adams settled his own mug on the table and gave Danté a practiced smile. "How are you liking the job?" he asked.

"I like it," said Danté, shooting a look at Marco. "My parents always told us we had to do something to serve the community. I feel like I'm doing that here."

"Good, good," said Adams.

Javier Vargas appeared in the doorway, motioning Marco back down when he started to rise. He shook hands with all three men, then he focused on Marco. "I heard you got married."

"Yep, this past weekend."

"What are you doing here? Shouldn't you be on your honeymoon?" said Javier, taking a seat.

"We leave tomorrow."

"Lucky bastard," muttered Javier. "That is one special woman."

Danté glanced at him in surprise, but Marco just made an amused grunt.

"Tell me about it," he said.

Lee poked his head inside the room. "Would you like a cup of coffee, Inspector?" he asked Javier.

Javier patted his stomach. He had sleeve tattoos on both arms. "I'm good, Lee. I had so much this morning already."

"Good enough," said Lee and disappeared back out the door.

Marco shifted his attention to Danté, setting his own mug on the table. "You remember Javier Vargas from the gang task force, right?"

"Yes, sir."

"Well, we asked you here because Roscoe Butler is coming up for an evidentiary hearing."

Adams nodded, folding his hands on the table. "An evidentiary hearing is conducted before a judge, no jury, where evidence is presented and witnesses are called. After hearing the case, the judge decides if there's enough evidence to move forward with a full trial."

"I know what it is, sir," said Danté.

"Good," said Adams. "Butler confessed to you. We need you to testify."

Danté lifted his chin. He'd known this would come eventually, but he hadn't expected it to be this soon. "Testify?"

"Yes, I'll coach you, but the judge is going to want to hear how you got a confession out of him."

"I understand," he said, tamping down on his nervousness.

"It's not a big deal," said Marco. "Just tell the truth and you'll be fine."

"I've got it, Captain."

Marco chewed on his inner lip. "That's not all though." He glanced at Devan.

Devan steepled his fingers. "I need Cashea Thompkins to testify also."

Danté's gaze snapped to Marco's face. "We promised her anonymity. She told us about Roscoe Butler because we promised her he wouldn't know about it."

"I know that," began Marco.

Danté leaned forward. "We can't go back on our promise, Captain."

"We can't let Roscoe Butler go free, Danté. He has to pay for Jamaad Jones' murder. We told Cashea we'd try to keep her out of it, but now we can't."

"I told her we would!" Danté said loudly.

Marco looked away.

"You shouldn't have done that," said Devan. "Never promise a witness anything."

"We promised to keep her safe!" said Danté, feeling betrayed and sick at heart. He'd promised Cashea, he'd promised to protect her. "She has to live in that neighborhood. She has to walk those streets to get back and forth to school."

"Maybe not," said Devan, holding out his hand to Javier Vargas.

Javier nodded. "We have programs to help people move out of gang neighborhoods, people who've helped us by informing on the gangs. I put the Thompkins on the list for aid and the odds of them getting it are really good."

"Guaranteed?" demanded Danté.

Javier held out his empty hands. "Nothing's guaranteed."

Danté looked back at Marco. "We promised her she'd be safe from the Mainline Gang."

"And we're doing everything in our power to make her and her family safe, but I also have an obligation to Jamaad Jones to make sure his killer doesn't get back on the street," said Marco.

Danté shook his head, looking away. His jaw clenched. He couldn't believe how angry this made him feel. They'd made a liar out of him, they'd made him go back on his word. He could hear his mother's voice saying, "If you're lying, you ain't trying. Lying is the lazy way of living."

"Danté," said Adams. "There's more. I need *you* to talk Cashea into testifying."

"What?" he gasped.

Marco shifted uneasily.

"You want me to tell her I lied to her, that we can't protect her, but we need her to face a man she fears in court and say he was the one who shot someone dead! You want me to spit in her face and tell her nothing I said had any meaning!"

"I don't appreciate your tone," said Devan.

Marco looked up at Danté, the warning on his face clear. "Slow your roll, son," he said to him.

"Look, I should know in about a week whether we can move Cashea and her family to a new neighborhood," said Javier. "I can be there when you talk to her and tell her what we're trying to do."

Danté stared at his hands on the table. He didn't know what to say and he was afraid if he opened his mouth, he might say something irretrievable.

"This could lead to a whole new life for the Thompkins," said Javier.

"Let me explain how this works, Danté," said Devan.

Marco leaned forward suddenly, touching Devan's arm. "Let me talk to him alone, will you? He'll do it. Go ahead and arrange to transport Cashea into the precinct on a day that Javier can be here."

Devan's gaze shifted between Danté and Marco, then he pushed himself to his feet. "Come on, Javier. Let's grab a coffee in the break room. You ever had this precinct's coffee? It's something special."

Javier also rose. "I have. It's the highlight of my day whenever I visit."

They walked out of the room. For a long time, Marco didn't say anything, just sat and stared at him. Danté couldn't meet his eyes. He felt ashamed for his outburst, but he was also upset that Marco was suggesting he violate his promise to Cashea.

"This is one part of the job that sucks, son."

"You're asking me to go back on a promise I made to her."

"We made that promise when we were trying to get Chicago off the streets. We made that promise to make sure there weren't going to be any more Jamaad Joneses."

Danté met his gaze. "If I don't stick to my words, if I can't be honest with people, how does that make me any better than the criminals we bring in?"

Marco drew a deep breath and released it. "Here's the thing, Danté. Nothing is ever going to be black and white for you again. You've got to weigh the benefits versus the consequences. We needed the information Cashea had, so we promised her anonymity. Now we need her to testify, so we have to take away the anonymity. In exchange, we're going to try making her life better, but either way, I'm not going to apologize for using whatever method we have to use to take a violent criminal off the streets."

Danté's gaze never wavered. "And we wonder why the public doesn't trust us. We wonder why they see us and feel afraid. We're no better than the criminals we catch."

Marco shifted, laying his hands flat on the table. "So, this is your moment of truth, Danté. Every cop reaches it, every person in law enforcement – judge, lawyer, police – every one of them has to make a decision at this point. How far are you willing to bend to keep the public safe? You say you want to serve the community – well, what are you willing to do to serve it? Decide now because there's no going back after this."

Danté couldn't believe how bleak Marco's words made him feel. He couldn't believe how suddenly disillusioned he was. He'd thought being a cop was a noble profession, but here he was, facing a decision he should never have to make.

"You're telling me to compromise my ethics, my morality for the arrest."

"No," said Marco, shaking his head. "I'm telling you that nothing is that cut and dry." He squared his jaw. "Religion and the law tell you that killing another human being is a sin. And I believe it is. I believe in my heart of hearts that it is wrong to take another person's life."

Danté's gaze slid back to Marco, but he didn't speak.

"And yet, I've killed a man. I killed a priest. I had a split second to make a decision and I made it. I shot him."

Danté felt a shiver race over him.

"The minute you put that badge on your chest, son, you made the same decision. You made the decision that someday the time will come when you have to pull the trigger, taking someone else's life. When you find yourself in that moment, and I hope like hell you never do, but when you do..."

Danté didn't miss that he'd said *when* twice, not *if*.

"…you're going to have less than a second to make that decision. We're all walking around doing the best we can. The majority of us don't set out in the morning thinking I'm going to lie to someone, I'm going to hurt someone, I'm going to kill someone." His voice trailed away. "Circumstances force us to make hair-trigger decisions sometimes and when they happen, well, sometimes, the best we can hope for is to minimize the damage we do."

The best we can hope for is to minimize the damage? What the hell? That was the most cynical philosophy Danté had ever heard and he just couldn't accept it.

Marco turned his hands over, palms up. "Here's what I want you to do."

Danté held his breath. If Marco ordered him to force Cashea to testify, he wasn't sure he could keep working here. He just didn't think he had that much bend in him, that much flexibility to his morality.

"Go home. Don't come in until this time tomorrow. I have to be at the airport at noon, so I'll be here until then. When you come in tomorrow, Danté, I want to know what your decision is. I want to know whether you can square yourself with the reality of this career or not."

Danté nodded, staring at his hands.

Marco pushed himself to his feet, but he hesitated. "There's no shame in deciding this isn't the life for you. No shame at all. The shame would be if you continued when you know you can't give it your all." He turned for the door. "But I know you have too much integrity to do that," he said and walked out.

*   *   *

Marco signed in at the desk of the psych facility. The middle aged man who buzzed him through said Kurt would be in the rec room in a few minutes. Marco took a seat in the hard plastic chair, glancing around.

A woman in slippers and a bathrobe wandered the periphery of the room, touching chairs and table tops, counting under her breath. Whenever she passed a person, she touched the person's shoulder as well. No one reacted to the touch, just continued on with whatever they were doing.

A man worked a puzzle before the windows. Another man sat on the couch, reading a book. A woman next to Marco had a coloring book open and was coloring in the pictures so expertly, it almost looked like a painting. She had to be in her seventies with wispy white hair and watery brown eyes.

"Will you be my boyfriend?" she asked him.

Marco's brows lifted, but he didn't know what to say. The question seemed harmless enough, but in here, anything might be a trigger and he wouldn't know it. An orderly strolled throughout the room, checking in with the various patients, but he wasn't paying attention to the old woman.

The room tried to be cheerful with canary yellow walls and chocolate brown accents, but there was an institutional feel to the hard couches and plastic chairs. A few windows looked over a small courtyard, haphazardly filled with more plastic chairs. It didn't look like anyone used it.

"Will you be my boyfriend?" the woman asked him again.

"I thought I was your boyfriend, Jean," said Kurt Foster, appearing before Marco. He took a seat at the table. "You're not trying to upgrade on me, are you?"

She tittered and went back to her coloring.

Marco gave Kurt a once over. He'd recently shaved his head into a crew cut and his face was clean shaven. He was of average height, an army veteran who'd served two tours of duty in Iraq and Afghanistan. He had brown eyes that looked clear and lucid. He held out his hand for Marco to shake.

Marco took it, smiling at him. "How are you, Kurt?"

"I'm better," said Kurt. "This place has actually helped me. How are you, Marco?"

"Good. Got married this past weekend."

"Hear that, Jean. Marco just got married. Guess you're stuck with me."

She tittered again, waving him off.

"Congratulations," said Kurt. "But what are you doing here? Shouldn't you be with your new wife?"

Marco smiled. "I will be. We leave for Hawaii tomorrow." He fingered a scratch in the table. "I just wanted to see how you were. I'm glad you're doing better."

"Yeah, they've got me in a grief group every day here. That seems a lot better for me. And they're giving me some anti-depressants, but they think they'll be able to wing me off those once I get stable again."

"That's real good, Kurt."

Kurt scratched the side of his neck. "I know these things take time, Marco, but do you have any news for me on Lowell's case?"

"Well, that's one of the reasons I wanted to come by. We think we might have a lead on something, but I need more information from you."

"Okay. I'll tell you anything I know."

Marco shifted in the unforgiving chair. "You didn't know who Lowell was seeing before he died, right?"

"No clue. He wouldn't tell me."

"But you suspected it was someone with power?"

"He gave him expensive presents like the watch."

"Did Lowell seem nervous at all? Anxious about this new romance?"

"Lowell played things close to the vest. I think he'd been judged too many times in his life for being gay. It's not easy being gay in the military, even now."

"No, I guess it isn't." Marco considered the situation. "Did Lowell ever mention that someone threatened him?"

"No, Marco, he never said anything."

"Did you notice anything? Did you ever see strange cars in front of your apartment? Hear strange conversations he had on the phone?"

Kurt considered. "I can't remember anything."

"Did Lowell ever say anything about Russians? Mention any dealings with them?"

Kurt leaned back in his chair. "I'm not much help, am I? I don't remember anything like that, Marco. I'm sorry."

"No, it's fine. I just had to ask."

Kurt frowned, his expression going distant. "Now that you mention it, I remember a car parked across the street from the apartment a few times."

"A car?"

"Yeah, it was black with heavily tinted windows. I wouldn't have noticed it, but it was a Rolls Royce. A Phantom."

"A Phantom? That's a cool half a mil," said Marco.

"I know. That's why I remember it. It had the chrome grill on front and the rectangular headlights."

"Did it have the Spirit of Ecstasy on the hood? The flying woman?"

Kurt nodded.

Marco looked over at the old woman coloring. A Rolls Royce Phantom wasn't just any car. Few people would fork over half a million for it, let alone park it across the street of a soldier struggling to make ends meet. The Phantom was a statement car, it was a car men bought who wanted to be noticed. And getting noticed...well, that sounded like Victor Maziar.

CHAPTER 4

Peyton arrived at the FBI office on Wednesday morning. She and Marco were leaving for Hawaii at noon, but she wanted to square everything away with Rosa before she left and she wanted to get in a quick work out. Sitting on a plane for hours would be easier if she physically tired herself. She could have gone to the gym with Marco, but they'd decided it was more efficient if they each separately check in at work and meet back at the house before heading to the airport.

"Hey, Peyton," called Mike Edwards as she crossed the lobby.

She hesitated and forced a smile for him. "Hey, Barnabus, how are you?"

He leaned his forearms on the counter. "Good. I heard Radar got shot. Is he all right?"

Peyton reluctantly crossed over to him. Mike Edwards was an ex-army ranger who Peyton had met in a bar when she and Marco were broken up. He'd needed a job and Peyton had recommended the security position in her building, a decision she found herself regretting frequently. He had blond hair and green eyes and a craggy face that she'd once found interesting.

"He's doing much better," she said.

"It's good to see you back at work. I haven't seen much of you lately."

"I got married this weekend," she said, hoping to head off further conversation.

His face sobered and he straightened. "Really? Well, what are you doing here?"

"I'm just checking in with Sarge, then I'm going to get a workout in the gym before we head for the airport."

"Off on your honeymoon?" he said with false brightness.

"Yes, I am, Mike, and I'm looking forward to it."

"Well, I wish you all the best. It's good you get a chance to have a vacation. You've been working nonstop cases for months now."

Peyton laughed, feeling her tension ease. "That is the solid truth, Mike. It's been one after another. I've done more traveling in the last year than I've done my whole life."

"Traveling gets old, doesn't it? One hotel after another, eating in restaurants. I'm not much for cooking, but man, I've enjoyed being in one place for the last few months."

"You don't miss it at all? Seeing new things, being new places?"

Mike shook his head. "Not even a little. There's only so many deserts you can hike through before every grain of sand looks the same."

They both chuckled.

"Well, all I want is a week without figuring out riddles and motives and looking for evidence."

"You must be glad that the cold case went back to Nevada, huh? That one was getting weird."

Peyton went still. She didn't remember telling him the cold case went to Nevada or that it had anything at all to do with Nevada. "What?"

"You know, the case where your office was broken into. I think Zach told me the Nevada field office pulled it back."

"Zach told you that?"

"Yeah, he said Radar mentioned it when Radar questioned him about the missing minutes on the video feed outside your office."

Peyton nodded. That might have happened, but it didn't sound like Radar, unless he had a plan up his sleeve. "Yeah, well, better it's there than here," she said, backing away from the counter. "I'd better get upstairs."

Mike leveled a look on her, his smile wistful. "Congratulations, Peyton. I really hope you and Marco are happy."

"We are, Mike," she said. "We definitely are." Then she turned and walked for the elevator.

She got off on the FBI floor and headed around the cubicle jungle to Rosa's office. Rosa's assistant, Darren, sat in his desk chair, typing on the computer. He looked up when Peyton arrived.

"Hey, Darren," she said.

"Hey, Peyton, congratulations on your wedding!"

Peyton smiled at him. "Thank you."

"I hear you're off on your honeymoon today."

"Yep, going to Kauai. I can't wait."

"Have you been before?"

"No, have you?"

"Once. I went with my college boyfriend." He gave a wry chuckle. "He fell in love with a fire dancer and I returned home by myself."

Peyton grimaced. "Ouch, that stings."

"Burns," he quipped and they both laughed.

"Hey, Darren, is Sarge in yet?"

"Yep, let me just buzz you." He pressed a button. "Sarge, Peyton's here to see you."

"Send her in," came Rosa's voice.

"Have a good time in Hawaii, Peyton," said Darren.

"Thank you," said Peyton, walking past him and pushing open Sarge's door.

Rosa sat at her desk, wearing her utilitarian black business suit, her dark hair pulled up in a bun on top of her head. Even with the unisex clothes and the severe hairstyle, she was beautiful – high cheekbones, dark eyes, thick lashes, full lips. She always made Peyton feel drab and insignificant in her shadow.

"Hey, Sarge."

"What are you doing here, Brooks? You should be getting ready for your honeymoon."

"I just wanted to check in and get a work out before we leave."

Rosa folded her hands on her desk. "Go enjoy your time off, Brooks. You deserve it."

"I know." She glanced over her shoulder. "Sarge, I just had a weird conversation with Mike Edwards downstairs."

Rosa tilted up her chin. "About what?"

"The Lance Corporal Daws case."

Rosa gave her a stern look. "That case is no longer our problem, Brooks…"

"I know," said Peyton, holding up a hand, "but he knew it went back to Las Vegas."

"What?" Rosa's expression shifted to alarm. "What do you mean he knew?"

"He knew. He asked me if I was glad it went back to Nevada."

"How does he know anything about it?"

"He said Radar told his supervisor, Zach, when we asked for the video feed outside my office after the break in."

"Why would Radar say anything to a security guard about the case?"

"That's my thought, unless Radar was trying to draw them out, get them to give something away."

"He would have cleared that with me. I don't think Radar would have done that without making sure I knew he was going to do it." Rosa rubbed a hand over her chin. "Okay, go on your honeymoon. I'm going to do a little snooping into this Zach, the supervisor."

"Thank you, Sarge."

Rosa nodded.

Peyton turned to go, but Rosa called to her. "Try to enjoy yourself, Brooks. Forget this office even exists."

Peyton smiled. "Oh, I plan to, Sarge, I definitely plan to."

Going to the gym, Peyton puzzled over the conversation with Mike. She tried to remember if she'd ever said anything to him about the case. She didn't think she had. Keeping information about cases to herself had been drummed into her since she went to the police academy.

She spun the dial on the combination lock holding her locker closed and ran through the three numbers to open it, but as the lock clicked in her hand, her thoughts coalesced. Combination. Shit. How had she missed that?

She stared at the lock, her mind seeing numbers, three numbers in particular. It had been right in front of her all this time, right there at the edge of her consciousness, but she'd missed it. Talking with Mike had brought the case to the foreground again and there it was, obvious as day.

She snapped the lock closed again and hurried to the elevator, jamming the button a number of times. She rode up to the FBI floor and hurried to her office, grabbing her keys out of her pocket. She fumbled for the one that locked the overhead cabinet, punching the button on the phone to call Margaret, her assistant.

"Peyton, what are you doing here? Aren't you on your honeymoon?"

"I am, but I just came in to get a workout. Is Tank in, Margaret?" she said, dragging her desk chair over and climbing on it.

"Yes, he came in about half an hour ago."

"Can you get him down to my office as soon as possible?" she said.

"Is something wrong?"

"I think I figured something out."

"Okay, I'll get him," said Margaret, disconnecting the call.

Peyton unlocked the upper cabinet and lifted the door. After the break-in, she'd filled the cabinet with FBI manuals, thinking that the thief would expect her to change her hiding place. She reached behind the manuals and pulled out the file she and Margaret had scanned from the original before it went back to Nevada.

She set the file on her desk and thumbed through it, going to the back where Mark Turner, the Las Vegas Special Agent, had placed the photographs. She found the pictures of the napkins. There were three of them total. Two napkins had two clusters of three numbers on them, twelve numbers total, grouped in threes. The third, however, had just a group of three numbers on it. She stared at the photo. The numbers were 19, 27, 43. A combination?

Tank appeared in the doorway. Thomas Tank Campbell was built like a truck. Six foot three, he filled her door, his crew cut freshly trimmed, his blocky face drawn down into a frown. "Peyton, what are you doing here? You're supposed to be on a honeymoon."

Peyton smiled at him. The Ghost Squad had become like a family to her and she felt happy whenever she saw one of them. "I'm going. I just stopped in to get a workout." She shifted the file, so Tank could see the photo. "You know how we've been trying to figure out these numbers Daws had on him when he died?"

"Yes, I've wracked my brain trying to figure it out. I keep wondering if it's a bank account, but they just don't match."

"I think it's a combination."

Tank's face drew down into a frown. "Combination?"

"I had a weird conversation with Mike Edwards downstairs. He knew the cold case went back to Las Vegas."

"How?"

"He said his supervisor told him, but Rosa's going to look into it. Anyway, I was getting into my locker when it suddenly hit me. Couldn't this be a combination lock?"

"Do you think the other numbers are combinations?"

"No, I think just this one. These three numbers have always bothered me, sitting off by themselves. Lance Corporal Daws has a locker somewhere – gym most likely. We need to contact his parents and his fiancée, and see if they know anything about it."

"Peyton, the highest number a three number combination lock goes to is 35. One of Daw's numbers is 43. It can't be a traditional combination lock."

Peyton felt her excitement dissipate. He was right. She pictured her locker combination and the numbers were all below 35. Tank saw her face, then he pulled out his phone and began typing on it.

"I thought I had something," she said.

"Hold on," said Tank, typing away. "There are some rare locks that have dial combinations with six numbers. Maybe he grouped the numbers to throw people off, but it's still a combination."

Peyton peered at Tank's phone, seeing the locks he was showing her. "That makes sense. Make it harder to figure out what the combination is. Now we just need to find out where he had a locker."

Tank took the file out of her hands. "Tell you what, I'll try to locate the locker. You go on your honeymoon. A honeymoon is a special time, Peyton, and you need to give it your full attention."

She smiled at him. "I agree, but you'll keep me in the loop, right?"

"Right," he said, tucking the file under his arm. "Now, let me walk you to the elevator."

She reluctantly agreed, grabbing the desk chair so she could lock the cabinet, but Tank did it for her, removing the key. Then they headed out of the office, walking around the cubicle jungle toward the elevators.

"Did you know the term *hony moone* was recorded as early as 1546 in England? It's believed the practice started in England when newlyweds would take a bridal tour to visit relatives who weren't able to make the nuptials. Of course, this was mostly an upper class event, since lower classes couldn't afford such a journey."

"I did not know that," she said in amusement.

"As I'm sure you can guess, the idea was primarily for the newly wed couple to establish a physical relationship that would eventually lead to procreation, but the modern practice is more for a couple to get away from the stress of planning an elaborate ceremony."

They reached the elevator and Tank pressed the down button.

Peyton turned to face him. "Where did you and the professor go on your honeymoon, Tank?"

Tank had married one of his professors from UC Berkeley. Of course, as he'd told Peyton many times, they'd waited to date until after he was no longer a student.

"We went to Machu Picchu to see the Inca ruins."

"Of course you did," said Peyton. She kissed his cheek. "You are one of my favorite people, Tank Campbell. Do you know that?"

He smiled at her. "I'm quite fond of you too, Peyton." The elevator doors opened and he nodded at them. "Now go begin the procreation part of your new marriage."

Peyton choked on a laugh and stepped into the elevator. "I'll just get right on that, Tank," she said and the doors closed.

*　*　*

Danté stared at the paper cup in his hands, running his thumb over the emblem inked onto the outside. If he looked up, he could see the precinct across the street, but he was studiously trying to avoid looking at it.

A pair of teal high heels entered his peripheral vision, followed by a shapely pair of calves. He looked up into Harper McLeod's beautiful face, her bow-shaped lips painted red, her dark brown hair in loose waves around her shoulders, her large green eyes lined with black, accentuating the angle of them. She wore a teal skirt that hugged her hips and a teal and pink blouse with no sleeves.

"What's up, Mr. Spock? You look pensive."

He looked back out the window at the precinct. "I'm fine, Ms. McLeod," he said, hoping she would go away.

She sank down into the seat across from him, hanging her designer handbag over the back. "Did your emotional computer chip fry or something?"

He gave her an annoyed look, but she just flashed a white toothed smile.

One of the baristas appeared, setting a coffee down in front of her. "Here you go, Harper," he said, giving her a sultry perusal.

"Thank you, Lucas," she purred, batting her lashes at him. "I love the personal service."

"For you, anytime," he said as if he didn't know Danté was sitting right there.

Danté gave him a narrow-eyed look and he glanced down, noticing the gun hanging from the holster under Danté's arm.

"See you tomorrow, Harper," he said, retreating back behind the counter.

Harper chuckled as she sipped her coffee. "That was very alpha male of you, Mr. Spock. I didn't know you had it in you."

He glanced back at her, but instead of responding, he picked up his cup and took a sip.

"What are you drinking? Not coffee. You don't approve of that."

"What do you want, Ms. McLeod?"

"I hate to see a good looking robot pondering the frailty of human life alone. I want to help you understand humanity if I can."

He didn't respond, just stared at her unblinking.

She leaned forward. "Not up for a little teasing I can see. Let me start over again. What has you looking like you lost your best friend?"

Danté sighed. "Somehow you think that was better?"

She sat back, crossing her legs. Danté tried not to look at the bit of thigh she showed. "So you do have teeth? Well, I can take a little biting. Tell me your troubles and I'll tell you how to fix them all."

"Why do you think you can fix my troubles?"

"That's what women do. Problem is men never listen."

Danté picked up his cup and took another sip. She was right about his choice in drinks. He'd never developed a coffee habit, but when he wanted something hot, he opted for green tea. He hated the taste of it, but he liked to think the antioxidants were chasing free radicals out of his body. "I've got about an hour to decide if I want to stay a cop or not."

Harper blinked her heavily lashed eyes at him. "No shit, Sherlock."

He didn't respond.

She tapped her manicured nails on the table. "Why would that be a consideration?"

He'd been fretting over this whole thing all night, barely sleeping. It made him sick to think of turning in his badge. He liked the challenge of being a cop. He liked being on cases, figuring things out. He liked feeling like he was making a difference. But if Captain D'Angelo made him betray his promise to Cashea, he would be compromising a part of himself to achieve an end and he just didn't think it was in him to do so.

"Come on, boy scout. Tell me. I'm not going to tell anyone else."

He gave her a skeptical look. "Reporter," he said.

"Friend," she countered. "Everything you tell me is off the record. I have my integrity, Danté. You know I protect my sources."

He did know that. Captain D'Angelo had tried numerous times to get her to tell him who gave her the information she had, but she never cracked, not once. And the truth was he could use a friend. He didn't want to confide in his parents. They would tell him this was a decision he had to make himself. *The harder the decision, the deeper the incision*, his mother would say. True, not all of her sayings made complete sense, but he could pull up an applicable one for nearly every occasion. His brother was too young to give him advice and his only real friend anymore was Jimmy Bartlet. Bartlet was not a man you shared secrets with unless you wanted them released into the ether the minute they were spoken.

"Off the record," he said with emphasis.

She crossed a finger over her heart. "Boy Scout's Honor." Then she held up a peace sign.

Danté couldn't believe he was about to trust this woman with something this important, but he'd let her help him buy clothes, so they'd already crossed a weird line with each other. "The captain wants me to talk Cashea Thompkins into testifying against Roscoe Butler."

"Chicago?"

"Yeah."

"Wow, that's some deep shit."

"Yeah," he said again.

She took a sip of her coffee. "What is this? An evidentiary hearing?"

"Yeah."

"Well," she said, dragging out the words. "I can see they need her testimony."

"We promised her anonymity."

"Yeah, but you sure don't want Chicago back on the street."

"That's what the ADA said." Danté flicked the tab on the top of the coffee cup. "I don't want him on the street, but I don't see how I betray my word to Cashea."

Harper considered, biting the inner part of her lip. "That puts her in a bad position," said Harper. "Either way. If she testifies, he knows she turned him in. If she doesn't, he gets out and goes back to her neighborhood. Maybe he finds out she turned him in anyway."

Danté had been agonizing over that all night. "There's a gang task force cop who's trying to get Cashea and her family into a program that moves informers out of gang territory. They'll help her get into that if she testifies."

"Well, what's the problem then? I think that's a good option for her family."

"There's no guarantees."

Harper uncrossed her legs and picked up the coffee. "I think the possibility is far better than the reality of her life right now. She's a sitting duck in that neighborhood. Someone is going to figure out who informed on Chicago one way or another, Danté. The possibility of getting her out should be priority number one and what I know about the hottie captain is this – he gets shit done. He'll do everything in his power to make sure the Thompkins are protected."

Danté nodded. He believed that about Marco himself. "I just don't know if I can compromise my word like that."

Harper gave him a gentle look. "That's admirable. For so many people, their word means nothing. It's nice to meet someone for whom it does, but I don't think this is going back on your word. The circumstances changed and you have a new reality to put before her. You're trying to make her life better and protect the neighborhood. You're trying to get justice for Jamaad Jones. I don't know, Mr. Spock, but I think this is one time when breaking your word might do more good than harm."

Danté stared at her, letting her words sink in. She had a point. She made sense.

She reached over and patted his hand. "Learning how to be adaptable is one of the most human characteristics artificial intelligence will have to master in the future, Mr. Spock. Start here. Don't give up a promising career because your circuits won't redirect when they get new information."

Danté leveled an arch look on her. "You're not as funny as you think you are."

"Ouch," she said, touching a hand to her chest. Then she laughed. "I like this feistier side." She rose to her feet, picking up her coffee and her purse. "You're going to be a real boy someday, Pinocchio, and when that happens, ask me on a date. I'll accept."

She flounced out, her hair swinging against her back. Danté smiled and took a sip of his tea, then grimaced. God, he hated the taste of green tea.

* * *

Marco arrived at the precinct from physical therapy, stepping through the door. He wore a t-shirt and jeans, his suitcase in the Charger. He carried Pickles under his arm, the little Yorkie wiggling the minute he saw Lee. Lee rose to his full impressive height, crossing around his desk and pulling open the half door, taking the dog from Marco.

Pickles began giving Lee kisses under his chin as Lee cuddled him. "It's a good day when Pickles is here," said Lee.

Marco smiled, watching them. According to Lee, everyday was a good day no matter the circumstances. He'd never heard Lee say anything remotely negative. "He's staying with Ryder while we're on our honeymoon. I had to pry him away from Peyton."

"I can bet. I'd be tempted to stash him in my carry-on and smuggle him through the airport."

"Don't give her any ideas," said Marco, pushing through the half door. "Can you get Stan Neumann up here for me, Lee?"

"On it, Captain," said Lee, carrying Pickles behind his desk.

"Is Danté in yet?"

Lee shook his head. He had thick black waves that lay on his shoulders and he always wore Hawaiian shirts and khaki pants. He picked up the phone's receiver, settling Pickles on his lap. Then he pressed the button. Marco made his way to his office, hearing Lee tell Stan, "The captain wants to see you."

Marco sank into his desk chair and booted up his computer. Glancing out his office door, he worried about Danté's decision. He'd actually thought the kid would come in last night and tell him he'd decided to be a team player, but he hadn't. Marco didn't want to lose him. He'd make an exceptional cop at some point, but he had to learn the art of compromise if he wanted to make it in any profession. Being a cop wasn't the only profession where an employee had to understand flexibility.

Jake poked his head inside Marco's office. "Seriously, Adonis? Do you even want to have a family?"

Marco frowned. "What?"

"Honeymoon. Nookie. Making babies."

"Don't. Just don't. I don't need you even thinking about my sex life."

Jake leaned on the back of the guest chair. "You wanna hear about mine?"

"I've known more about yours than any human being should know, including you."

"But I really need to talk about my new squeeze. She's perfect."

Marco shook his head. "Stop. If you want to talk about this, go talk to Abe, not me. I'm here for a few hours and then I'm gone."

"So did you bring Pickles' diet food?"

"It's in the Charger."

"Do I get the Charger?"

"No."

"Can I stay at the house?"

"Nope."

"What about Sunday dinner at Mama D's? Do I still get to do that?"

"Sure."

"So about Abe's party..."

"Nope," Marco said, swiveling to face the computer. "That's between you and Peyton."

"You know, you send me off to other people all the time. It's like we're not even buddies anymore, Adonis."

"We're not."

"Seriously? I helped you go to the bathroom..."

"Out!" shouted Marco, pointing to the door.

60

Stan had just started to enter, but he scrambled out again.

Jake burst out laughing, but Marco closed his eyes.

"Stan, come back. That wasn't for you," Marco said.

Stan eased to the door, peeking inside. "Hey, Jake," he said.

"Hey, Stan. So, if you were going to throw Abe a birthday party, what would be the main thing you'd include in the plans?"

Stan considered that. Today he had on a t-shirt that read *If it moves, it's biology. If it stinks, it's chemistry. If it doesn't work, it's physics.* He also wore his usual jeans and Converse sneakers, his glasses perched on the end of his nose. He pushed them back up and tilted his head.

"I'm thinking glitter. Lots of glitter and booze."

"Glitter and booze," said Jake, holding out a hand to indicate Stan. "Stan just gave me more help in thirty seconds, Adonis, than you have in years."

"Well, consult with Stan," said Marco, leaning back in his chair. "Are we done here, Ryder?"

"I need the keys to the Charger to get Pickles' food."

Marco reached into his pocket.

"You wanted to see me, Captain," said Stan.

"I want you to see if Victor Maziar has a Rolls Royce Phantom registered under his name."

Jake whistled. "That's a seriously expensive car."

"Yep. Kurt Foster remembers seeing one parked outside of their apartment a couple of times before Murphy died."

"I'm on it, Captain," said Stan.

Marco pulled out his keys and tossed them to Jake. Jake didn't even react. They hit him in the chest and fell into the chair. All three of them stared at the keys.

"Really, Adonis?"

"Jesus, Ryder, you didn't even flinch."

"You might have warned me you were sending a missile my way."

"Do you seriously have no reflexes?"

Jake grabbed the keys. "I have reflexes. I just thought you'd be a civilized human being and hand them to me."

Danté appeared in the doorway and Marco's attention snapped to him.

"Come in, Danté."

Jake and Stan turned toward the door, but as Jake passed Danté, he said, "Watch yourself. He's hurling things at people this morning."

Danté gave Marco an alarmed look, but Marco waved it off.

"Don't listen to him. He's an idiot."

Jake gave a wicked laugh as he disappeared into the precinct. "I'll get you, my pretty, and your little dog too!"

Danté stared after them, frowning.

"*Wizard of Oz,*" said Marco, shrugging.

"What?" asked Danté.

"The reference, the *I'll get you, my pretty.*" Marco shook his head. "Forget it. Close the door and sit down. Ryder might come back."

Danté shut the door and moved to a chair, taking a seat. Today he wore a black t-shirt, a black blazer and a pair of jeans. He rubbed his hands on the chair arms. "So, I thought about what you said…a lot, Captain."

"Okay," said Marco, realizing he couldn't read the kid's expression.

"I guess I had an idealized view of what it means to be a cop. I thought I would be helping people. You know, the whole protect and serve thing."

"Right."

Danté turned his hands over, staring at his palms. "I mean, it felt good when we took Chicago off the street and we got his confession. I felt like I was doing what I was meant to do." He looked up, his pale eyes troubled. "But the Boyd Ronaldo confession didn't feel like that. I felt like I was ruining two lives when I got him to admit to murdering Levi Norton."

Marco didn't speak, just waited him out. Danté had to come to his own conclusion. Marco couldn't make this decision for him.

"Still, I told myself that ultimately, Boyd Ronaldo was a murderer. No matter how unfortunate the situation was, he took someone's life. I still felt like I'd done right. That I'd upheld the oath I took." Danté scrubbed his hands on his jeans. "I ran into Harper McLeod at the coffee shop just now."

Marco lifted his head. This wasn't where he'd expected this conversation to go. "And?"

"She said that no matter what, Cashea and her family are in danger, living in that neighborhood. No matter what, someone might figure out she was the one who told us about Chicago. She said that going back on my word might actually be the best thing that could happen to Cashea."

Marco looked down. He hated the disillusionment in the kid's voice.

"I really don't like going back on my word. It makes me feel sick inside."

Marco nodded. He understood that.

"But I can't stand the thought of Chicago being back on the streets again even more."

Marco met his gaze again.

"I understand what you were trying to teach me. I understand what you mean about compromise and flexibility, but I need you to know that I'm never going to be okay with violating my word to someone."

"I understand that, but that doesn't tell me what you plan to do."

Danté's eyes bore into his. "I'm a cop, Captain. That's what I am and I will do it to the best of my ability, no matter what. I will do what I have to do to keep men like Chicago off the streets, but that doesn't mean I have to like the methods."

Marco nodded, feeling a wash of relief. "Here's the thing, Danté, and this is something I've grappled with my entire life. There are the choices we want to make and there are choices we *have* to make, choices that tear at our guts, that leave us sweating in the night. Those are the choices we don't want to make, but we do because if we don't, if we don't make those painful decisions, the consequences are unacceptable. Going back on your word is bad, I know that, but letting a murderer out is unacceptable. Use that for your ballast. Use that for your scale."

Danté nodded, staring at his hands.

"I'll call ADA Adams before I leave and tell him you've made your decision."

"Thank you, Captain," said Danté, pushing himself to his feet. He turned toward the door, but hesitated, looking back at Marco. "I am honored to serve under a man like you, Captain D'Angelo." Then he left the room.

CHAPTER 5

Peyton watched Marco fight his way out of Abe's Mini Cooper. He almost tumbled onto the loading zone in front of the airline, catching himself on the door, then he pushed the seat back to let her out. Peyton smiled at him as she climbed onto the sidewalk next to him, patting his chest.

He gave her a disgruntled look. He'd wanted to take the Charger, but Abe had been adamant that he wasn't driving a "penis compensator". Abe came around the back of the Mini, holding out his arms and gathering them in for a hug.

Kissing each of them on the side of the face, he held them off with a hand on their shoulders. "Do not worry about anything happening here. Go and have a good time. Relax, enjoy the sun and the water, and forget you have careers."

As if to punctuate his statement, Marco's phone rang.

Abe shook a finger in his face. "Don't you dare answer that."

Marco held up a hand. "I'm not. Help me wrangle the suitcases out of your clown car."

A few minutes later, Abe bid them goodbye and they made their way into the airport, waiting in line to check their baggage. By the time they'd worked their way through security with their badges, guns and Marco's titanium filled leg, they sank into the seats before the gate, already feeling like they'd run a gauntlet.

Peyton caught Marco peeking at his phone, but she ignored it. Part of her wanted to call Tank and see if he'd found out whether Lance Corporal Daws had a gym locker or storage facility. When their flight was called, they made their way down the ramp and onto the plane. Marco had opted for first class and Peyton felt a flutter of delight as the flight attendant ushered them into adjoining cubicles.

After stowing their carry-on bags in the overhead compartment, Marco dropped into the seat next to her, settled his back against the edge of their egg shaped enclosure and brushed a curl behind her ear.

"I can't believe we're going on our honeymoon," he said.

She smiled at him, leaning across the center console to kiss him. "I can't believe it either." She gave him a flirtatious look. "You're my husband, D'Angelo. My hubby."

He made a face. "Maybe we stick with husband."

She curled her fingers in his. "Nope. You're my hubby bubby," she said, making them both laugh.

His phone rang again and she sighed.

"Take it. I'll get you all to myself for the next six hours."

He shook his head wryly. "We have to launch ourselves into the stratosphere in order to get any time to ourselves."

"You know you aren't going to relax until you know what it is."

Marco nodded and pulled the phone out, thumbing it on. "Hey, Stan," he said.

Peyton touched the buttons on the console, staring at the large screen affixed to the back of the first class seat before her, but her attention was on Marco's conversation.

"You're sure about that? You checked all of his vehicles?"

Peyton glanced over as Marco's hand tightened into a fist. She covered it with her own and he linked their fingers, his thumb rubbing across her wedding ring.

"Right. Okay. Is there any way to search for people who bought Rolls Royces?"

She glanced at his face. His expression was troubled, a line forming between his brows.

"Yeah, yeah, you're right. People with that sort of money are fiercely private. Okay, can you add your search to the report on Lowell Murphy's murder though? Yeah, thanks. Okay. No, we're waiting for take off. Okay, I'll talk to you later." Marco hung up, but before Peyton could ask him about the conversation, a flight attendant appeared next to them.

He gave them a brilliant white smile. "A little bird told me it's your honeymoon!"

Peyton smiled back at him. "It is."

The flight attendant leaned closer, dropping his voice. "How about a glass of champagne to get this party started?"

Peyton shared a look with Marco. He kissed the back of her hand. "One glass of champagne," he told the flight attendant, "and some ginger ale if you have it."

"Coming right up," he said, hurrying off.

"What was that about a Rolls Royce?" she asked him. They hadn't had much time to talk about anything with getting ready for their honeymoon.

"You know I went to see Kurt Foster yesterday, right?"

"Right."

"Well, he remembered a Rolls Royce Phantom parked out in front of their apartment a few times."

"I'm guessing that's an expensive car."

"Cool half a mil," said Marco. "Not many on the road."

"I guess not and you suspect it belongs to who?"

"Victor Maziar."

Peyton considered that. "And you're pretty sure Victor Maziar has Russian mob ties."

"I'm almost certain of it. Especially after the threats on Wendell Williams."

"For the pawn shop?"

"No, there was another place Wendell was trying to buy and he got a number of death threats when he placed an offer. The man who wanted to sell the building backed out.

His name is Renchenko. He's related to a man that drowned himself in the Hudson River just before he was supposed to testify against Eduard Zonov for assault."

"And you got a threat from Eduard Zonov yourself. The picture of us on the steps came from him?"

"Right. And just before I came up to Bridgeport when Radar was shot, Eduard Zonov had his food truck parked in front of the precinct." He shook his head. "Bartlet bought a piroshky from him."

"Bartlet," said Peyton, also shaking her head. "What's the connection to Victor Maziar?"

"We're still trying to make a definitive connection, but we have a number of witness that say the food truck was parked in front of the San Francisco Buyers Market, the pawn shop Maziar owns. They also come from the same part of Chechnya."

"Huh."

"Adrian Trejo and Javier Vargas came to see me, Brooks, to warn me about this new Russian gang moving into San Francisco."

"Russian gang?"

"They call themselves the Goblins."

Peyton shifted uneasily in her seat. "You may have to get the FBI involved in this, Marco. I don't like where this is all playing out."

He nodded, staring at the screen in front of him. "I know. I don't like it either. Victor Maziar knows you're FBI. When we went to the fundraiser he held for the mayor, he made a particular point of bringing you up to me."

"Like a threat?"

Marco nodded, rubbing his thumb across the back of her hand. "I wanted to take him out right there."

"How is the mayor mixed up in all of this?"

"His wife and son think he's being blackmailed by the Russian mob."

"Which would explain the graffiti on his house."

"*No traitors.* Yep. I don't know, Peyton. This could be really bad. This could light up the entire City if it becomes a gang war."

The flight attendant appeared beside them, carrying a tray with two champagne glasses on it. "One glass of champagne," he said, offering it to Peyton. "And one glass of ginger ale."

Marco took the second.

"Here's to a long and beautiful marriage," he said.

Marco and Peyton touched glasses together, both of them distracted by their previous conversation.

"Drink up. This is a wonderful occasion to celebrate. Your lives together start right this minute," said the flight attendant. "And I predict it's going to be a beautiful adventure."

Peyton smiled into Marco's blue eyes. "You know what, Paul," she said, reading his nametag. "It is. Come on, D'Angelo. For the next week, we aren't going to worry about a damn thing. No cases, no dead bodies, no gang warfare. Just you and me in paradise."

Paul's bright smile darkened a little at her words, but Marco laughed, bringing the glass to his lips. "You got a point, Brooks. Just sun and fun for one blessed week before we burn down the City."

And they drank.

*   *   *

Danté stepped into the conference room with Cho at his side. Devan Adams sat at the table, a file open before him. He motioned Danté into the seat at the head of the table. The ADA wore an expensive suit, a stripped tie, and his cufflinks winked in the fluorescent lights overhead.

Danté felt under dressed in his jeans and plain black t-shirt, but Cho had encouraged him to dress a little less formally when he was working as a detective. The inspector himself wore jeans and a t-shirt with combat boots.

"You can go, Nathan," said Devan, waving him away.

"I think I'll stay," said Cho, taking a seat across from the ADA. "Kid's new at this."

"Suit yourself," said Devan. He pushed the landline and the file over to Danté, pointing with a pen at a phone number on the top of the page.

Cashea Thompkins.

Danté sighed, still feeling conflicted about this.

"Call her and tell her you want her to come into the precinct tomorrow. Don't give her a lot of information. Just say we need to talk to her about it. Keep it on speaker phone, so I can hear and coach you through it."

Danté shot a look at Cho. Cho gave him a brief nod. Pressing the button for speaker phone, Danté dialed the number. It rang a few times, then Cashea's voice came on the line.

"Hello, who's this?"

"Cashea?" Danté said. "This is Officer Danté Price. I worked the Jamaad Jones case."

"Yeah, what'z up, Danté? I'm in school. I gotsta go to class."

"Cashea, Chicago's evidentiary hearing is coming up soon and we need to talk to you about it."

"What'z an evidentiary hearing?"

"The ADA presents evidence to a judge who decides whether we have enough evidence to bring Chicago forward for a full trial with a jury and all."

"Why you need to talk to me?"

"We need to go over the proceedings with you."

She didn't immediately answer.

"This is important, Cashea. We were hoping you could come into the precinct tomorrow."

Devan shook his head. "We want, not hope."

"Who else is there?"

"The ADA's here, Cashea," said Danté, giving Devan a disgruntled look.

"You said it would be over if I give you Chicago's name. You said I didn't need to do nothing more."

"I know, but we still need to talk to you. Can you come to the precinct tomorrow?"

"I don't gots a ride. I don't see how."

Danté looked at Devan.

"We'll get Bartlet to pick her up at her house."

"We'll send an officer to pick you up."

"I don't think so, Danté. You said my part was done. I don't want to come to the precinct."

Danté scrubbed his hands over his face. He didn't want to do this to her, but he had no choice. "It's very important, Cashea. If you don't come here tomorrow, we may not be able to hold Chicago. He may come back to the neighborhood."

She went silent for a long time. Danté shared a look with the other two men. He wasn't sure she was still on the phone. "Cashea?"

"Send the officer tomorrow at 10:00. I'll come in."

"Thank you, Cashea."

"Will you be there?"

"Yes, I'll be here."

"Okay. I'll sees you tomorrow."

"See you tomorrow."

The call disconnected.

Devan smiled at him. "So how about we go over your testimony now?"

Cho rose to his feet. "Sorry, ADA, but we got a date for some Russian translation." He patted Danté on the shoulder. "Let's go kid. Tag and Holmes are waiting for us."

Danté rose to his feet, but he hesitated, meeting Devan's gaze. "Is Inspector Vargas going to be here tomorrow?"

"I'll see if he's available," said Devan.

"Make sure you do," said Danté, not even bothering to hide the menace in his voice.

Devan's brows drew down in a frown, but Danté didn't care. If they were going to make him go back on his word, he was sure as hell going to make sure they didn't go back on theirs.

"Why don't you give him a call right now?" said Cho, grinning at Devan. "Get on his schedule ASAP."

Danté offered Cho a grateful nod and the two walked out of the room, but he fretted over the entire situation on the ride to the stop-and-rob to interview Kazimir Renchenko. He knew Cashea would react badly when he told her what they wanted. He just hoped Javier Vargas came through for them and could figure out a way to get the Thompkins a new apartment to rent.

"It's not easy," said Cho, glancing over at him as he wended his way through the mid-morning traffic. "You can't help but get personally involved in these cases."

Danté nodded. He didn't feel much like talking. He felt betrayed by the entire precinct, even though he knew Cho didn't have anything to do with it.

"I remember a case Bill and I worked once. This kid was going to Balboa High School. He was gay and these boys from the football team, they just tortured him – beat the shit out of him, burned his books in his locker, wrote faggot all over the walls outside his classes. One day they caught him in the locker room and they..." Cho drew a deep breath, holding it. He slowly released it, sighing out. "They did unspeakable things to him in that locker room. I still have nightmares over it."

Danté glanced at him, but he didn't speak. He didn't want Cho to stop talking.

"One night after a football game, as the players were on their way to the locker room, Danny...that was his name...Danny sees them. He's leaving the parking lot in his parents' sedan and he just hits the gas."

Danté stared at Cho fascinated.

Cho slowly shook his head. "He plows into the whole team. They dive to the sides and he clips a few of them. Some broken bones, not much else, but he traps one of the kids, one of the boys who assaulted him, under his wheel. Then he panics and backs over him, speeding away. Kid dies on the way to the hospital, so we get called out."

"Did he deny it?" Danté asked.

"No, no, he didn't deny it. We picked him up and he confessed right away. We talked to the ADA about sending him to juvenile hall instead of prison, but we've got to get him to testify as to what they did to him in the locker room. He's got to tell the judge what happened and he's got to pick them out of a lineup." Cho stopped at a light and looked over at him. "We worked on this kid for days. We hounded him, we pressured him. I knew I was doing the right thing. I knew he didn't belong in prison, so I rode him hard."

Danté felt a sinking in his gut. "What happened?"

Cho stared ahead as if he wasn't seeing the traffic around them, as if he were back in that moment from so long ago. "They had him in juvenile hall, awaiting trial. He grabbed a knife out of the cafeteria line and stabbed himself in the throat, sliced through his carotid artery. He was dead before he hit the floor."

Danté shivered.

"I almost quit. I almost turned in my badge that day." Cho started the car moving again.

"Why didn't you?"

"Another kid at the school came forward after Danny's death, said the same kids that raped Danny in the locker room did it to him too the previous year. He asked us to help him. He asked us to help him get justice for Danny." Cho shrugged and glanced over at him. "So we did."

Danté stared out the windshield and considered what Cho told him.

"This job is compromise and bargain. It's figuring out what you can live with and what you can't. You're going to see depravity like you can't imagine, but then you're going to see a seventeen-year-old kid face down his rapists and you're going to think, there's nothing braver in the world than that. I can't promise you this is the career for you, but I can tell you, kid, this career needs someone like you. We need your moral compass, your integrity, and we sure as shit need your smarts. You'll find your balance. I'm sure of it."

"And if I don't," said Danté, shifting to stare at his profile.

Cho glanced over and his expression was grim. "Then you're gonna be eaten alive, Danté, and no one wants that." He pulled up in front of the stop-and-rob, parking across the front loading zone. The sign over the narrow building said *Moscow Eats*. It was a baby blue building with windows across the entire front that looked out on the street. Display cases showed chips and other snack food.

Cho pushed open his door and climbed out. Danté did the same, stepping up onto the sidewalk. Tag and Holmes strode down to meet them, Tag in her brown leather motorcycle gear, Holmes in a leather jacket, jeans and a ribbed t-shirt. Holmes took off his sunglasses and put them on top of his head.

"Renchenko inside?" asked Cho, facing them.

"Last we saw," said Tag, tucking her hands in the back pockets on her pants. Danté could see the handle of her gun peeking out under her arm. She had her short white blond hair swept back off her face and the skull tattoo on her neck showed starkly in the sunlight. "When we were here last, he just said he knew nothing. Then he'd start talking in Russian."

Danté looked the building over. The siding was warped and it looked like there might be dry rot in the eaves. Tag went to the door first, shouldering it open. It stuck and she had to hit it hard to get inside. A little bell jangled madly as she shoved the door back over the warped wooden floor. Holmes, then Cho followed her inside. Danté entered last, looking around the dim interior.

Rows of shelves filled the little store with nonperishable food haphazardly stacked on the bare metal. Flecks of paint had rusted off the shelves and dotted the hardwood. Two bare bulbs hung from the middle of the building casting circles of light that allowed shadows to lurk in the corners. The place smelled musty and damp. Danté scrunched up his nose in disgust.

A little man with dark hair, a lined face and small dark eyes stood behind a glass counter. An old fashioned iron cash register stood next to him and advertisements for the lottery were plastered all over the dingy grey walls behind him. In a locked case were cigarettes and booze. He had a computer tablet sitting on the counter before him with a credit card reader sticking out of the top of it.

"Hello, Mr. Renchenko," said Tag, leaning a hip against the counter. "How are you?"

His eyes darted around to all of them, then back to Tag. "I know nothing," he said.

"Right," she said, smiling, but on Tag, a smile was intimidating. She danced her *happy* fingers on the counter. Renchenko's eyes fixed on them.

"I know nothing," he repeated, curling his hands into fists next to the tablet.

Tag looked over her shoulder at Danté, then jerked her head at the man.

Danté drew a deep breath. He didn't feel as confident speaking as he did reading Russian, but he knew he had to give it a try.

"Zdravstvuyte," he said. *Hello.*

The man's eyes widened, then he inclined his head. "Zdravstvuyte."

"Kak u vas segodnya dela?" *How are you?*

"U menya vse v poryadke." *I am well.*

"What are you saying?" demanded Holmes.

Danté shot him an aggravated look. "We're just exchanging greetings. Give me a minute, will you?"

Tag moved away from the counter, hitting Holmes in the chest with her *happy* fingers. They wandered down the aisle, pretending to look at the food on display. Danté moved closer to Renchenko, touching himself in the center of his chest.

"Menya zovut Officer Danté Price." *My name is Officer Danté Price.*

"Kazimir Renchenko," said the older man.

Danté nodded, offering him a polite smile. He motioned between himself and the detectives. "My dolzhny zadat' vam neskol'ko voprosov." *We need to ask you some questions.*

"I know nothing," Renchenko said loudly.

Danté held up a hand, feeling the other cops' eyes on him. "Ne boysya. My khotim pomoch'." *Don't be afraid. We want to help.*

Renchenko shook his head violently. "Vy ne mozhete pomoch'. Net nikakoy pomoshchi." *You can't help. There is no help.*

"Kto-to ugrozhayet vam?" *Is someone threatening you?*

"I know nothing," said Renchenko, but he gave an almost imperceptible nod, then his eyes angled up toward the ceiling.

Danté considered that, then he glanced up as well. A camera was just visible, showing between one of the acoustic ceiling tiles and the support beam. They were being recorded and he suspected it wasn't by Kazimir Renchenko. Danté eased his hand into his pocket and palmed his business card, then he laid both hands on the counter, sliding the card beneath the tablet as surreptitiously as he could.

"My khotim pomoch' vam," Danté said again. *We want to help you.*

"I know nothing."

Tag let out a heavy sigh.

Danté gave Renchenko a significant nod and tapped his fingers on the counter near the card. Renchenko inclined his head as well, his eyes boring into Danté.

"Spasibo. Dasvidaniya," Danté said. *Thank you. Good bye.*

"Dasvidaniya," said Renchenko.

Backing away from the counter, Danté turned and headed for the door. A moment later the other three followed him. He stopped when he reached Cho's car and faced them.

"That was a waste of time!" said Holmes angrily. "He said the same thing to you that he said to us."

Danté waited until he'd finished his outburst. "There's a camera above the counter. Renchenko didn't put it there."

Tag whirled and looked over her shoulder. "They're watching the store?" she said in amazement.

Danté folded his arms across his chest. "They're watching the store," he repeated.

*   *   *

Marco and Peyton stepped out of the van in front of the Koloa Grove Resort. Palm trees lined the drive and a fountain sprayed water just before the open air lobby. A woman in a white skirt and shirt with a flower behind her ear greeted them and placed leis over their heads.

"Aloha," she said. "Welcome to Kauai."

"Aloha," Peyton and Marco answered.

A young man in white pants and the same white shirt approached, carrying a tray of drinks. "Mai Tai?"

Marco took one and handed it to his bride. Peyton's smile was infectious and he wanted to kiss her.

"I also have pineapple juice." The young man indicated the glass.

"Thank you," said Marco, taking it.

Pulling their luggage behind them, they approached another young man wearing a black blazer over his white shirt. He had a gold name tag that said Solomon. He beamed a white tooth smile at them. He had coffee colored skin, black wavy hair, and dark eyes.

"Aloha," he said.

Marco returned his infectious smile. "Aloha. Reservation for D'Angelo."

The young man typed on the computer. "Yes, here it is." He looked up at them, his entire attitude giving off good cheer. "You're on your honeymoon."

"Yes, we are," said Peyton, sliding her arm around Marco's waist and leaning against him.

"You have a room that overlooks the ocean." His brows lifted. "Oh, law enforcement, I see. FBI?"

"Just for full disclosure, we have our guns with us," said Marco.

"I'll need to see your badge, Special Agent Brooks," Solomon said to Marco.

Marco shared an amused look with Peyton, then he removed his badge and handed it to the young man. Peyton did the same, slowly setting her FBI identification down on the counter. Solomon's eyes grew round again.

"Oh, my goodness, I'm so sorry, Special Agent," he said to Peyton. "I just assumed."

"I know," she said. "Don't worry about it. It's a bold new world, isn't it?"

He blinked at her in confusion, then he flashed that million-watt smile. "Sure is."

A few minutes later, he handed them their keys, Marco signed for the room and they were on their way to the elevators. Their room was on the seventh floor and they got on the elevator with another older couple. Marco encircled Peyton's waist with his arm and whispered in her ear.

"I like being Mr. Brooks," he said.

She laughed, banding his arms with her own, sipping at her drink. The older couple looked over at them.

"Are you newlyweds?" the woman said. She was short with a jaunty pageboy haircut, round glasses and very pink lips. She wore a pair of lime green capris and a stripped shirt in green and pink. A pair of keds were on her feet.

"We are," said Peyton. "This past weekend."

The woman clapped her hands and the husband smiled at them. "Congratulations," he said. He wasn't much taller than she was with a crown of grey hair circling around his ears and a belly that hung over his khaki shorts. He had on a Hawaiian shirt, white socks, and sandals. "We've been married forty years. We're here celebrating our anniversary."

"Congratulations!" said Peyton enthusiastically. "Forty years?"

"Can you believe it?" The woman held out her hand. "I'm Sally Baxter and this is my husband, Bill."

"Peyton and Marco," said Peyton, shaking hands with them, then the elevator dinged and the doors opened. Sally and Bill Baxter got out on the seventh floor too.

"Can you believe it? We're going to be neighbors," said Sally.

Marco exchanged an amused look with Peyton. "That's awesome," he said as they started down the hallway, dragging their suitcases with them.

Everything in the Koloa Grove Resort was decorated in greens and tans with bright splashes of orange in paintings on the walls or a bird of paradise on a table. They arrived at their rooms. Bill and Sally had the room exactly across the hall from Peyton and Marco. Bill whistled.

"You got an ocean view," he said enviously. "Well, that's probably all right when you're on your honeymoon."

"We're really excited about it," said Peyton.

"Well, don't get too wild and crazy in there," said Bill. "We're right over here."

Sally giggled and swatted her husband on the arm. "You're so bad."

He patted her ass. "Maybe I should warn them about us getting wild and crazy, huh?"

Sally giggled some more as Bill opened their room door, then he pretended to chase her inside. Marco and Peyton watched after them until the door closed, then they both started laughing. Marco slid their key into the door handle and pushed open the door.

The room was decorated in dark wood accents with white linen and pictures of palm trees on the wall. A sink and coffee maker sat on a credenza right inside the entry, to the left was the bathroom and then the king sized bed, a small table and two chairs. The curtains were drawn, but Peyton crossed around the bed and pulled them back.

A sliding door led to a balcony with two chairs on it and beyond that was the crystalline blue of the ocean. Setting her drink on the table, Peyton sucked in a breath and threw open the slider, stepping out onto the balcony. Marco watched her for a moment as she leaned on the railing, crossing her arms, a breeze blowing her long hair back from her face.

The realization that she was his struck him again. He released their bags, set his drink on the credenza, and shut the outer door, crossing the room and stepping out on the balcony with her. She looked up at him, her expression pensive.

"It's gorgeous," she said.

He nodded, sliding the hair off her shoulder. "It sure is," he said, never taking his eyes off her.

She drew a deep breath. "Does it bother you that I'm keeping my last name?"

He blinked. That hadn't been what he'd expected her to say. They hadn't even really discussed it. He just automatically figured she'd keep her name. "No, you have a more important career than I do."

"That is definitely not true, but I think your mother is going to be disappointed if I don't take your last name."

"My mother chose her own path, her own way of living. It works for her and my father, but that isn't our way. You're an independent woman and that's why I love you. I wouldn't ask you to change who you are to adhere to some old fashioned tradition."

She moved into his arms, wrapping her own around his waist. The flowers on their leis compressed, releasing a floral scent. "You know when you're the sexiest to me?"

He gave a small smile. "When?"

"When you talk all progressive like that." She lifted and kissed him on the mouth. "What's say we go get wild and crazy?"

He picked her up with an arm around her waist and she wrapped her legs around him. "Let's go get wild and crazy, wife," he said.

CHAPTER 6

Peyton got a little thrill when she woke up next to Marco, the crash of the waves filtering through the open slider. He slept on his stomach, his hands fisted by his head, his dark lashes resting against his cheekbones. She ran her hand down his spine, feeling the padding of his muscles against her palm. He blinked and opened his eyes, staring at her for a moment before the sleep cleared from them.

"Hey," he said in a husky, sleepy voice.

"Hey yourself," she answered. "Is it weird that I'm still amazed whenever I realize we're married?"

"Nope. I feel the same way." He rolled over onto his back. "Come here."

She scooted over, laying her head on his chest. She ran her hand over his shoulder and down his arm. "I can't believe how happy I am right at this moment."

He kissed the top of her head. "Well, here's to making it last."

The previous night they'd decided not to leave the room, ordering room service. They spent the time making love, talking, and watching a romantic comedy on the television which they got great enjoyment out of mocking. It was the most perfect first night in paradise and Peyton felt relaxed.

"So, what do you want to do today?" Marco said, his fingers running across her shoulder blade.

"I want to take a NaPali Coast Tour."

"Okay. I saw signs for it down in the lobby."

A knock sounded at the door. Peyton looked over her shoulder at it. "What's that?"

"I don't know. Why don't you hop your cute little behind out of bed and find out?"

She gave him an arch look. "Seriously?"

He grinned at her.

She threw back the covers and walked naked to the closet, taking down the fluffy white robe the hotel had left them. She slipped it on and went to the door, peeking out. A man in the white, hotel staff uniform waited on the other side. Peyton unlocked the door and pulled it open.

"Aloha," he said, "Breakfast?"

Peyton looked over her shoulder at Marco. "Did you do this?"

He waggled his brows at her.

"Thank you," said Peyton, stepping back to allow him entry. Giving Marco a nod, he pushed the cart up to the window and began setting out the plates on the table. After it was set, he nodded at them again and wheeled the cart back out.

Peyton lifted the cover off the dishes. A scoop of white rice sat in the middle of the plate topped with what looked like a hamburger patty and a fried egg, covered by a brown gravy. Peyton shot a look at Marco.

"What is it?"

"Loco moco," he said, throwing back the covers. "Traditional Hawaiian breakfast."

Peyton picked up a fork, poking at the meat, but she was distracted watching his taut backside as he went to the closet and took out the second robe, slipping it on. "Is this beef? I haven't eaten beef in months, Marco."

"It's vegetarian sausage. They made it special for us." He came to the table and lifted the cover off the second plate, revealing a vegetarian omelet. "I thought we could split the two, in case we didn't like loco moco."

She smiled at him and reached for the coffee cup, removing the cover. A sugar dispenser sat in the middle of the table and she grabbed it. "Very clever, Captain D'Angelo," she said, pouring sugar into her cup.

He removed the wrapper on two cups of beautifully cut fruit: pineapple, mango, bananas, and set one in front of her. "Eat up. I want to go swimming today and see you in that bikini Maria bought for you."

She sank into the seat and sipped at her coffee, then she picked up the fork, eying the loco moco. With a sigh, she dug in, bringing a bite to her mouth. After chewing, she swallowed, feeling Marco's eyes on her.

"Well?" he said.

"Not bad," she answered and dug in.

After they finished breakfast, took a shower, and put on their swimsuits, they headed down to the lobby to book their NaPali Coast Tour. A number of people milled about the open air lobby, picking up brochures or waiting for the rest of their party to arrive. A man in a business suit stood at the counter, leaning an arm against it. He glanced over at Marco and Peyton, then away.

They found the tour counter and approached. A young man with a friendly smile, dark tan, and black hair greeted them. "Aloha," he said. "What can I do for you?"

"Aloha," Marco and Peyton repeated, then Peyton crossed her arms on the counter, giving him a smile. "We'd like to book a NaPali Coast boat tour."

"Would you like the dinner cruise?"

Peyton glanced up at Marco.

"Sounds good," he said, rubbing a hand down her back over the cover-up she wore.

"Excellent," said the young man, clicking on the computer. "Let me see what's available."

The businessman to their right made an aggravated exhalation, drawing Peyton's attention. A young woman with black hair that fell all the way to her waist came out of the back area behind the counter and approached him.

"I'm sorry, Mr. Meridew. We're working on it."

He straightened, his square jaw clenching. "It's been more than 45 minutes. I need to get some work done."

"I understand, sir…"

"I don't think you understand!" he said loudly. He was in his mid-forties, around six one or six two, trim with dirty blond hair and a heavy brow ridge.

"There are spots available on the 7:00PM cruise. Would you like that?"

Peyton glanced back at the young man. His name tag said Robbie. "That's perfect," she said.

"I have work to do. Do you get the concept of work!" the businessman shouted at the girl. Robbie glanced over uncomfortably.

"Yes, Mr. Meridew, and I assure you we're doing everything in our power to get you internet access..."

"I paid a lot of money for a suite in this hotel. I could have gone anywhere else, but I expressly picked this location!"

"I know..."

"Do you? Do you understand how important it is? You assured me this hotel had all the latest amenities! What am I talking about?" he said, throwing up his hands. "Internet is not an amenity! It's a necessity!" He punctuated each word with a finger on the counter.

The girl held up her hands. "Mr. Meridew..."

"Don't! Don't say it again! I want internet now!"

Marco and Peyton exchanged a look.

"I'm so sorry about this," Robbie said under his breath. "Let me give you a discount on the tour."

"That's not necessary," said Marco. "It's not your fault."

"It's no problem," said the young man clicking some more.

"I want to see the manager now!" shouted Meridew. "Get him out here!"

Robbie looked over, then reached for the phone. "Just a minute please," he told them, then he pushed a button and listened on the line. "Tavis, Mr. Meridew is at the counter. He's really upset and demanding to talk to you."

Peyton watched Meridew as he stepped back and crossed his arms over his chest, glaring at the girl as she frantically tried to get someone on the phone. Peyton hadn't bothered to see if they had internet this morning. She didn't really care. Things happened. Internet went down. Why was this guy getting so worked up?

"Right, right, okay?" Robbie hung up and smiled at them. "Should I charge the tour to your room?"

"Sounds good," said Marco, taking out their room card and passing it to Robbie.

"Who is that man?" asked Peyton, nodding at the businessman, who was tapping his foot, his hands now on his hips.

"Harvey Meridew of Dewdrop Development. They do a lot of building on the islands."

"He lives on Kauai?"

"He has a house here, yes. He also has one on Maui as I understand it."

"Why is he staying at the hotel?"

Robbie shook his head. "No idea. Let me just print your boarding passes."

"Manager. M-a-n-a-g-e-r," spelled Meridew. "English? You know English, right? I want the manager!"

The girl nodded, frantically dialing another number.

Peyton clenched her teeth. She hated bullies. Turning, she started toward him, but Marco caught the back of her cover-up.

"Brooks!" he warned. "I just want to sit in the sand and drink pineapple juice."

She let him pull her to him. He wrapped an arm around her waist, holding her against his side. "You're right," she said, turning back to Robbie. "Do you have any other suggestions for tours?"

"There's…"

"Finally!" erupted Meridew as a man in his fifties, clearly Hawaiian with dark hair, brown skin, dark eyes, wearing a suit, appeared out of the back. "I don't care what you have to do! I want internet now!"

The man held up his hands in a calming gesture. "Mr. Meridew, I'm Tavis Makoa, the manager here."

"Good. Now get me internet! And get someone who understands English!" he spat, sending a venomous glare at the girl.

"Keiki is doing her job, sir. We're trying to restore internet now."

"It's been forty-five minutes!" he shouted in Tavis's face. "Forty-five minutes!"

"I know that..."

"Apparently you don't! I have business transactions to make. I have emails to answer! I don't have time for this prehistoric bullshit! Get off your lazy island asses and get me some internet!"

Marco slid his arm away. "Go," he said with a heavy sigh.

Peyton flashed him a smile and started toward them. "Hey, Meridew!" she shouted.

He looked over at her, his gaze sliding down her body. "What?"

"Calm the hell down."

"Just who the hell do you think you are!"

"Special Agent Peyton Brooks, FBI. Now don't make me go get my badge out of my room."

He visibly struggled with himself to regain control. "FBI?" He gave a sneer. "You?"

"Don't make me cuff your ass, pal!" she said, squaring off with him. "I'm on my honeymoon and my husband wants to sit in the sand, so knock it off. There is nothing you have to do that can't wait until the internet is restored. Or if there is, go to a coffee shop. I'm sure Mr. Makoa can direct you to one."

Meridew's eyes moved beyond her and Peyton knew Marco loomed at her back. Just like old times. Meridew's gaze shifted back to her again. "Fine, Special Agent. I get your point."

"Good," she said, giving him a tight smile. "Here's just a little suggestion. Go put on some shorts and grab a lounger on the beach. Mr. Makoa will make sure you get a Mai Tai, on me." Peyton looked around Meridew at the manager. "Put it on my tab, please, sir."

Tavis inclined his head.

"Then when the internet is restored, Mr. Makoa will let you know."

Meridew held up a hand. "Sounds good," he said, forcing a smile in return. "I'll do that."

"Good."

He shot another look at Marco, then he eased around Peyton and headed for the elevator.

Tavis breathed a sigh of relief. "Thank you, Special Agent," he said.

"No problem," she answered, touching his arm. "Now, I'm going to take my husband and we're going to soak up some sun and surf. Have a good day, Mr. Makoa."

"You too, Special Agent Brooks," he called after her.

She waved over her shoulder and took Marco's hand. He kissed the top of her head. "That's my girl," he said, wrapping his arm around her shoulders and hugging her to him. "That's *my girl.*"

*　*　*

Cashea wore jeans and a white blouse that dropped off her shoulders. She had a pink streak in her hair that ran behind her ear. She sat at the table in the conference room, rocking back and forth, gripping the seat with two hands, her knuckles white.

Danté hesitated, watching her from Lee's desk. She couldn't see him by the angle of the door. "Is ADA Adams here?" he asked.

"He just called. He's on his way," said Lee, following Danté's line of sight. "She's scared."

"Yeah, well, she has reason to be," said Danté, hating this, hating everything about this.

The outer door opened and Javier Vargas entered, his gaze rising to meet the other two men. He pushed through the half door, holding out his hand. Danté and Lee shook with him, then Javier glanced in at Cashea.

"You said she had a brother who has brain damage?" asked Javier.

Danté nodded, marking that Cashea looked over at Javier's voice. He could see her eyeing the Gang Task Force detective.

"That helps things. I have an option to get them in subsidized housing with some potential for medical assistance. It's through a state government program for ex-gang members, many of whom were shot and unable to work anymore."

"That's really good news," said Danté, sharing a relieved look with Lee.

The outer door opened again and Devan stepped inside, wearing sunglasses, his tailored suit accentuating the slim lines of his body. "Good morning everyone," he announced brightly, pushing through the half door.

He shook hands with Javier. "Thanks for coming in again," he said, then he motioned into the conference room. "Let's get this thing going. I just got our date for the hearing."

The three men walked into the room. Danté stood behind Javier and Devan, watching as the ADA offered Cashea his hand. She stared at it a moment, then she carefully placed her slender fingers in his. Danté marked the chipped black polish on her fingertips.

"I'm ADA Devan Adams." Devan motioned to Javier. "This is Javier Vargas, the Gang Task Force Detective."

"Buenos dias," said Javier, shaking her hand.

"And of course, you remember Officer Danté Price."

She nodded, her eyes glued to Danté's face. He wanted to squirm, but he wouldn't allow himself to do so.

"Take a seat," said Devan, motioning to the chairs.

They sank down, Danté to Cashea's right, Devan and Javier to her left.

"What's this about?" she demanded forcefully.

Devan opened his briefcase on the table, taking out a file. Then he closed the briefcase and set it on the floor beside him, flipping back the cover on the file. Finally, he looked at her. "Roscoe Butler is going before the judge on Monday for an evidentiary hearing."

Danté's eyes snapped to his face. He hadn't known it was going to be that soon.

"What's that gots to do with me?"

Devan's eyes shifted to Danté. "Officer Price?"

Danté stared at Cashea, feeling all over again the sense of betrayal. "The evidentiary hearing is for the judge to see if there's enough evidence to hold Chicago for trial. If not..." He paused and drew a deep breath. "If not, Chicago goes free."

"Goes back to Hunter's Point?" asked Cashea, the fear in her eyes evident. She returned to gripping the chair with both hands.

"Yes, Cashea, he goes back to Hunter's Point," said Danté.

Her eyes tracked around the men in the room. "What does that mean? If he goes back to Hunter's Point, he goes back to the Mainline Gang."

"Right," said Devan. "We can't have that, Cashea."

"He gonna come see LeJohn. He gonna come to our house."

Danté could hear the panic in her voice. "That's why you have to testify at the hearing, Cashea."

She reared back. "What?" Then she rose to her feet. The three men rose with her, Danté holding out his hands to keep her from bolting. "You said I had protection. You said you'd keep me out of this!"

Danté closed his eyes. His chest felt so tight, he couldn't hardly breathe. He had promised all of this and more. God, he felt like Judas.

"Please sit down, Miss Thompkins!" said Devan firmly.

She shook her head violently, grabbing her backpack off the floor. "Nope. Screw this. I'm out."

She started for the door, but Danté moved to block her.

"Just hear me out, okay?"

She glared up at him. "You told me I would be protected."

"I'm trying to do that, Cashea. Think for a minute!" he said sharply. "If Chicago goes back to Hunter's Point, someone's bound to figure out how we knew about him. Someone's going to know that he was turned in to the police."

The color drained from her face and she backed up, sitting down in the chair again. The backpack fell from her fingers. Danté hated scaring her like this, but he didn't know what else to do. She looked vacantly at the table.

"He's gonna kill me. He's gonna..." She couldn't finish, just shook her head, her eyes welling with tears. "I knew I shouldna come here. I knew I shouldna gotz involved."

Danté went to her side and hunkered down. "Look at me, Cashea," he said softly.

Her eyes whipped to his face, accusatory, betrayed. "I hate you!"

He nodded. "I understand, but I'm trying to help. We need you to testify to what you know. We need to do anything we can to stop Chicago from getting out again."

"You promised me!"

"I know, but I shouldn't have. I didn't have all the information and I should never have promised you anonymity. I was wrong."

She narrowed her eyes on him, but didn't speak.

Javier cleared his throat. "If you testify, Cashea, I can help you."

"How you gonna help, pig!" she spat, rounding on him.

He pulled his lips back against his teeth in annoyance, then placed his hands flat on the table. "There's a program I can get your family into that will help you move out of Hunter's Point into a new neighborhood, a better neighborhood. They'll help subsidize the rent on a flat and…"

"What you mean subsidize?"

"Help pay for it," said Danté. "They'll help you pay the rent."

She gave the two men a skeptical look. "I don't believe you. I'll never believe you again."

"Then believe me," Devan said. "They're telling you the truth. You help us, we'll help your family."

She made a rude noise.

Javier clasped his hands. "There's more, Cashea."

"Save it. I don't want nothing from you."

"He can get your mother help with LeJohn. Medical help," said Danté.

Her eyes shifted to Danté's face and held. "What?" she said, her hands curling into fists in her lap.

"Testify against Chicago, keep him from getting back on the street, and we can help you move, get LeJohn a nurse to help care for him, give your mother a break."

A tear rolled down Cashea's cheek as she stared at him. "Don't you lie to me no more!"

"He's not lying," said Javier. "Not only do you have my word, but you have the word of the ADA as well. I will make sure you get into this program."

Cashea closed her eyes, tears racing down her face. Devan retrieved the box of tissues from the back shelf and set it in front of her. She took one and wiped her face, blowing her nose. Danté stayed where he was, feeling so many emotions – rage, sadness, shame. She looked around the table, then back into his eyes.

"Swear to me on your life," she said to him.

"Cashea..." began Devan.

She held up a hand blocking him, but her eyes never left Danté's. He stared back at her. If he had to get a second job, if he had to work night and day, he would make sure Cashea and her family got out of Hunter's Point. He would make sure they got help to take care of LeJohn. If Javier failed to provide for her, he would do it no matter what he had to do to succeed.

"I swear to you, Cashea. You testify for us and I will make sure your family gets a new start."

She blinked rapidly a few times, then she released a shivery breath. "Fine, I'll testify," she said.

* * *

Marco and Peyton stepped onto the boat preparing to take them on their dinner cruise to see the NaPali coastline. A young woman in a floral print dress greeted them with leis. "Aloha," she said.

"Aloha," said Peyton. She also wore a floral dress with a halter top that tied around her neck, showing a tempting amount of sun-kissed cleavage. Her hair was in a messy ponytail and she had sandals on her feet, her toenails painted bright red. His locket lay between the valley of her breasts and his ring glistened on her finger. He felt a sudden surge of possessiveness and pulled her to him, kissing her temple.

She gave him a bemused look, but she didn't see the way the other men on the boat tracked her with their eyes.

He, however, didn't miss it and he glared them down until they looked away.

"We have a full bar inside and dinner will be served in an hour. You may choose to eat on the deck or in the cabin," said the young woman.

"Deck," Peyton said.

The young woman motioned to a man standing at a podium. "Just let him know," she said.

Marco placed a hand in the small of her back and guided her to the host. They selected their table and then they entered the cabin, heading for the bar. An older couple turned as they approached and they recognized their neighbors, Sally and Bill Baxter.

"Oh my goodness, look, Bill, it's the newlyweds," said Sally, hurrying forward and hugging Peyton.

Peyton hugged her back, then Sally hugged Marco. Bill shook Marco's hand and kissed Peyton's cheek. Marco wasn't sure they were on such an intimate footing yet, but who was he to argue.

"What did you do today? We took a drive around the island. Oh my goodness, Kauai is beautiful."

Peyton laughed. "We went swimming and spent a lot of time napping on the beach. It was a wonderful day. We don't get much time to relax back home."

"Oh, what do you do for living, Marco?" asked Bill.

"I'm a police captain in San Francisco."

Bill and Sally exchanged wide eyes.

"Seriously? Oh my goodness, that's amazing," said Sally, sipping at her fruity drink. She wore a pair of yellow capris, sneakers and a Hawaiian shirt with parrots on it. Marco suspected Abe would like something like that himself. "What do you do, dear?" she asked Peyton.

Peyton shifted, wrapping her arm around Marco's waist and leaning into him. "I'm with FBI," she said, leaving it at that.

"That's so exciting," breathed Sally. She leaned close and dropped her voice. "I've always been fascinated by true crime."

"What do you want to drink?" Marco asked Peyton, wanting to divert the couple.

"A Mai Tai is fine," she said.

He went to the bar, listening to the ukulele player set up in the corner. The tiny guitar in this man's hands was amazing. His fingers were a blur as they danced over the strings, plucking out a tune that had the people near him swaying.

"What'll you have?" asked the bartender, a large man with his black hair pulled back in a tight bun.

"Mai Tai and a water."

"Coming right up."

Marco took out his wallet, but Bill slapped a card on the bar.

"It's on me. It's your honeymoon after all."

"You don't have to do that," said Marco, not wanting to be indebted to this man. He wanted Peyton for himself and he wasn't in the mood to be socially obligated to these people.

"It's my pleasure."

The bartender set the drinks on the bar and took Bill's card.

"Thanks," Marco said, forcing down his annoyance. He picked up the drinks, but waited for the bartender to give Bill back his card. They headed back to the women and Marco handed Peyton her drink. She smiled up at him and he felt his sour mood dissipate. No woman had ever made his heart beat faster the way this one did with a simple look.

Sally was going on about a true crime reenactment she'd seen on TV. Bill wrapped his arm around her waist and tugged her against him. "Let's go watch the boat leave the dock," he said, saluting Marco with his drink.

Marco smiled at him, giving him a nod. He was grateful Bill got the message. As they walked away, he was left facing his beautiful wife. She sipped at her drink, her dark eyes sultry as she watched him, the flowers around her neck accentuating the curve of her breast, the angle of her jaw. He cupped her cheek.

"Woman, you are so beautiful," he said. "I really enjoyed spending the day with you."

She touched the back of his hand. "I loved spending the day with you. How's your leg?"

"It's fine," he said. He'd been going without his cane more and more now. There hadn't been pain in weeks, but he was also getting more confident that it would hold his weight. He was a little worried about it on the rocking boat, though. "Speaking of that, what's say we find a place at the rail? Not sure how good my sea legs will be."

"You got it," she said, taking his hand. "Sally said the best side to see the NaPali coast is on the starboard side."

Marco quirked a brow as he followed her. "Which side would that be?"

"Right," she said with a laugh.

They took positions just in time for the boat to pull away from the dock. Marco banded Peyton with his arms as they moved out to the open ocean, past other boats with clever names like *Sea Goals* and *DaBoyz Toyz*. The water was a crystalline blue and a light breeze blew over them, sending Peyton's hair back over her shoulders.

A voice came over the loudspeaker, announcing the sights as they motored away from the shore, but Marco breathed in the smell of Peyton's lilac shampoo and rested his cheek against her hair, letting the tension slip from him. She leaned back into him, her body swaying with the rhythm of the boat, her face tilted to catch the final rays of sunlight.

"I could get used to this," she said softly.

"So could I," he answered.

They watched the waves in silence, listening to the guide tell them cute anecdotes. Suddenly Peyton sucked in air and pointed. Marco leaned over, looking at the wake the boat was creating. A school of dolphins were sprinting alongside the boat, breaking the surface and diving back under again.

They laughed at their antics. Marco had never seen wild dolphins before. People crowded around them, trying to get a look, but Marco angled his arms out wider to give Peyton more space. She didn't seem to notice, her delight in the dolphins completely absorbing her attention.

Then a shadow fell over them and Marco looked up and up and up to the rugged emerald green cliffs rising over their heads. A hush fell over the crowd and the guide's voice broke through the silence, speaking in a reverent tone.

"The pali, or sea cliffs you see before you are over 4,000 feet tall. The NaPali Coast State Park is well over six thousand acres with 16 miles of coastline. You can hike in the park to see the waterfalls and the cliffs from above. The first people to settle the NaPali Coast were Polynesian navigators in 1200AD. The coast was used as a trade route between Hanalei, Waimea, and Ni'ihau. After Captain Cook arrived in Kauai in 1778, westerners came to settle the islands. They brought Western diseases with them, which killed off much of the native population. The last known native Hawaiians lived on the NaPali coast in the early 20th century."

Peyton sighed, leaning against him. "It always ends that way."

He didn't know how to respond.

"Now, for something a little more uplifting," the guide said, humor in his voice. "As I'm sure you've heard, Kauai and the NaPali coast is home to the Menehune, little people that inhabited the islands long before colonization. Menehune have many legends, but the one I'm going to tell you has to do with the Menehune Ditch not too far from here. It's a short walk over the Waimea Swing Bridge to the site where a tiny irrigation tunnel is dug into the cliffs, believed to be expertly crafted by the Menehune to bring water to their tiny farms, but lest you believe their diminutive size makes them inferior, you must know the Menehune may be small, but they are very powerful. There is an old saying engraved on the plaque outside the entrance to the tunnel. Uwa Ka Menehune Ma Kanaloahuluhulu Puoho Ka Manu O Kawainui."

Peyton tilted her head, listening. Marco frowned and a few people muttered around them, wondering what it meant. The guide laughed. "You want a translation?" he said playfully.

A number of people shouted, "Yes!"

He laughed again. "The shout of the Menehune at Kauai startle the birds of Oahu."

People frowned at each other or groaned. The guide laughed again.

"I didn't say it was a good saying, just that it was old."

People burst into laughter, then the sound of the ukulele came over the speaker. Marco looked up at the brilliant green of the carved lava cliffs, thinking he'd never seen anything quite so stunning in his life. Pressing his lips to Peyton's hair, he breathed in her scent. She brought so much to his life, made it so much richer than it had been before her.

She gasped and pointed. They rounded a curve in the cliff face and a waterfall spilled over the edge, cascading down in prisms of rainbow light to hit the ocean. He smiled, watching it, hearing the rush of water over the quiet murmuring of the people and the hum of the boat's engine, and he felt awed at this moment in time, this stolen moment when all was right with his world.

CHAPTER 7

Jake's face appeared on the phone screen. Peyton settled it on the table outside their balcony and smiled at him. He smiled back, his brown eyes twinkling. Jake had a smile that lit up his entire face, brought him from pleasantly ordinary to something so much more.

"Heya, Mighty Mouse, how's the honeymoon? You eaten poi yet?"

"No poi, but we've had loco moco and it's becoming one of my favorite dishes."

"What's loco moco?" asked Jake.

Bambi's bright blond head appeared next to Jake's, their cheeks pressed together. "Loco moco is a hamburger patty served on a bed of white rice, covered in gravy. Hey, Peyton! How are you, sweetie?"

"Hey Emma, you're at Jake's?"

"Actually," said Jake, "we're at Bambi's. Her place is a little more upscale than mine."

Peyton frowned. "Where's my dog, Ryder?"

Bambi lifted Pickles so Peyton could see him. "Right here. He's my little snuggle bear," she said, giving him kisses. Pickles gave her kisses in return.

"Hey, save some for me!" said Jake.

"Oh Jakey," she giggled and began spreading kisses all over Jake's face.

Peyton grimaced, shifting uncomfortably. "Wow, you two are sure moving fast."

Jake gave a laugh as Bambi bit his earlobe and hung on. Peyton tried to look away, but it was like watching a car wreck. Marco peered over her shoulder, then he shuddered and went back into their room.

"Ain't nobody got time for that nonsense," he grumbled under his breath.

Jake and Bambi were now giving each other little pecks and laughing the entire time as Bambi squirmed her way onto Jake's lap.

"Okay, could you two just…" She shuddered. "…for the love of God, stop!"

Bambi broke away, her eyes wide. Jake peeled off into laughter.

"Relax, Mighty Mouse, we're just having fun."

"Yeah, I can see that," said Peyton uncomfortably. "Just call me on the regular phone next time," she suggested.

Jake laughed again. "Stop being an old married woman!" he scolded. Then he tickled Bambi and she squirmed, flashing Peyton some skin.

Peyton started to disconnect the call. "Call me when you're done with that," she said, but Jake suddenly grabbed the phone and held it up, setting Bambi on the couch next to him.

"Don't hang up, Mighty Mouse!" he said. "I called you for a reason." He and Bambi giggled at each other and Peyton fought for patience. She didn't think she and Marco had ever been so giddy with each other. It was annoying.

"So, I called about Abe's party. Emma had a great idea. Rather than renting a place that's gonna burn up most of our budget, we can have it in her clubhouse. She can reserve it once a year for free and it's massive."

"Are you sure about that, Emma?" Peyton asked.

Bambi nodded, wrapping her arms around Jake's shoulders. "Of course I'm sure, Peyton. It'll be a blast. Did Jakey tell you the theme?"

"No, *Jakey* didn't tell me the theme," Peyton forced out.

"Tell her the theme, Jakey. It's so brilliant, Peyton, you're going to love it."

"Okay, tell me the theme," she said.

"The 70's," said Jake, raising his brows suggestively.

Peyton frowned. "What? That's it? The 70's?"

"Seriously, Mighty Mouse, the 70's, disco, funk, bell bottoms, polyester. Platform shoes!"

Peyton made a face.

"Don't be like that! Abe will love it."

He had a point. Abe would love it.

"I'm thinking a live funk band. There's a band called *Elements* here in San Francisco. They're a tribute band to *Earth, Wind and Fire.*"

"Okay," she said, leaning back in her chair. She was listening.

"We can rent a fog machine and a disco ball," said Bambi, "and the clubhouse has a marley floor."

"A what now?" asked Peyton.

"A temporary dance floor," said Jake.

"I'm liking it so far," she admitted.

"I found an old music store that has a bunch of vinyl records I can use for table decorations," said Jake.

"And I found some rainbow colored fiber optic floofy things that can go with the vinyl records," said Bambi.

"I located a caterer who will do a 70's themed menu," added Jake.

"What's a 70's themed menu?" asked Peyton.

"Deviled eggs," said Jake.

"Stuffed celery," said Bambi.

"Watergate salad."

"Potato skins."

"Hold on!" said Peyton, lifting her hand. "What's Watergate salad?"

"Pineapple, pistachio pudding, mini marshmallows and chopped pecans." He said it pee-KAHN.

Bambi looked at him. "How do you say that word?"

"What word?"

"Pecan." She said PE-kahn.

"No, it's pee-KAHN," he said, tickling her.

She squealed and fell over onto her back, taking Jake with her. Peyton could see Jake's back and Bambi's feet kicking in the air. She sighed.

"Sounds like you got it," she said and disconnected the call, then slumped back in her chair. Dealing with Bambi and Jake just got a whole lot more complicated and annoying. Very annoying.

Marco leaned against the slider, wearing shorts, a tank top, flip flops and a smirk. "Wanna go for a ride!" he said, dangling keys from his hand.

She jumped to her feet. "Yes, definitely." She grabbed her phone. "How long do you think all that PDA is going to go on for?"

Marco quirked a brow. "The rest of Ryder's damn life," he mumbled. "You better get used to it. And by the way, it's pe-KAHN." Then he turned for the door, heading back inside.

Peyton's eyes lowered to his taut backside. "I don't care what it is, I'm just enjoying this view."

When he gave her a quizzical look, she beamed a smile at him.

"You're a wicked woman, Brooks," he said.

She swiped her tongue across her teeth. "What's say we play a little grab ass ourselves before we take our ride?"

He turned to face her. "You don't have to ask me twice," and he lunged for her.

Sometime later, they were driving across the lush green, tropical Kauai countryside. It had started raining and the windshield wipers made a rhythmic tick tick tick as they whisked the water away.

Because of the NaPali coastline, Marco drove northeast from their hotel in the southern part of the island. They drove through quaint coastal villages, until Marco took a turn on Waipouli Road and headed inland. They passed a number of golf courses, then an area where the trees had been cleared, leaving a gaping wound in the otherwise lush landscape. A sign on the road said, *Dewdrop Development, Making Your Island Dreams a Reality.*

Peyton pointed at the sign. "Isn't that the company owned by that tool I confronted yesterday?"

Marco glanced over. "Yeah, God, that's a mess."

"Yeah, it says a strip mall's going in there. Huh? This seems a little remote for a strip mall."

"You can't stop progress," said Marco, continuing down the road, "or strip malls it would seem."

"I guess." She shifted and looked back at the decimated land. The trees had to have been well over a hundred feet tall, cut down and discarded like so much garbage. It made her a little sad, but she pushed it away. "Where are we going?" she asked, skeptically.

"You'll see," he said, giving her a wink.

Peyton settled back in her seat, enjoying the rain falling on the lush vegetation. Kauai was known as the garden island for a reason and the amount of rainfall it received certainly created a landscape that was green and verdant.

She saw the sign before Marco turned onto a long gravel drive. *Silverweed Farms* had been written in scrolling white letters on a wooden plank with a carved picture of an oblong seed that looked familiar to her, but she couldn't place it.

They pulled into a gravel parking area where a few other cars were also parked and got out. The rain had become a mist, but Peyton had braided her hair, so she didn't care about getting a little wet. Marco held out his hand and they headed for a few buildings they saw through a break in the foliage.

"What is this place?" she asked him.

He kissed the back of her hand. "For you, heaven," he said, then chuckled when he saw her bewildered expression.

"Aloha," said a man wearing a pair of khaki shorts, flip flops, and a t-shirt that said *Silverweed Farms*. "Welcome to *Silverweed*. I'm Will. I'll be your host today." He was Caucasian with thinning brown hair, an affable smile, and large callused hands. He shook Marco's hand, then Peyton's. "I understand you're a chocolate aficionado," he said to Peyton.

Peyton's eyes widened. "Yes, very much so."

He patted her hand and released her. "We usually give a tour in the morning, but it's a three hour walk and your husband said that wouldn't work."

Peyton wrapped her arm around Marco's waist. "Not yet, but someday maybe," she said, looking up at him. He smiled at her in return.

"Well, he asked us to set up a private tasting instead."

Peyton gasped. "Really? A chocolate tasting?"

"So you'd like that?" said the man in amusement.

"Would I ever," she answered.

He motioned toward the interior of a small grass hut. "This way please." A bamboo table and two chairs had been set up before a counter where plastic cups held pieces of chocolate. Peyton's eyes fixated on that counter. She'd never seen so many varieties of chocolate before in her life, some nearly black in color and some a light cocoa that blended almost to white.

"Please have a seat."

A young woman with a thick black braid appeared, placing a pitcher and two water glasses on the table, along with small pieces of bread in a braided basket.

"Lani is my assistant," Will said.

The girl gave a smile, moving to his side. "Aloha," she said.

"Aloha," repeated Peyton and Marco in unison.

"Can we have your names?" asked Will.

Peyton pointed at herself. "I'm Peyton and this is Marco."

"Newlyweds," said Will to Lani.

"Congratulations," she said.

"Thank you," Marco and Peyton answered together.

Will clapped his hands twice. "So let me explain how to properly taste chocolate."

Peyton didn't think she needed a course in chocolate tasting. She'd made it her life's work, but she clasped her hands on the table and gave him an expectant look. The rain had started up again and the sound of it on the tin roof was pleasant.

"We will start with bitter and move to sweet. There's a five step process for tasting chocolate."

Peyton glanced over at Marco. Okay, maybe she didn't know all there was to know about tasting chocolate. She had a one step process. Put it in her mouth and chew.

"Lani will pass out the first chocolate."

Lani placed a small square on a napkin in front of them, then she offered the container to Will. He also took a piece as did Lani. "This one is 35% cocoa, or bittersweet. First we look at it." Lani and Will turned it every which way.

Peyton and Marco shared an amused glance, then they did the same. Peyton wasn't sure what she was looking for, but going through the ritual was fun, a lot more fun than when Devan made her go wine tasting. After that date, she really wondered if she wanted to see him again.

"It should have a glossy appearance without too many bubbles."

"Looks good," said Peyton brightly, wanting to pop it into her mouth.

"Next we hear it."

Peyton arched an eyebrow at that, watching Will and Lani break their chocolate into smaller pieces near their ears.

"You should hear a nice, clear snap," said Will.

Peyton lifted her chocolate to her ear and broke it. Sure enough, there was a clear snapping sound. Okay, so she definitely didn't know thing one about chocolate tasting. Still it was better than hearing Devan discuss tannin levels with the sommelier.

"*Silverweed Farms* was started in the 1990's to bring fine chocolates to the islands. The soil, rain and sun in this tropical paradise are perfect for growing cacao beans," said Will as he held his piece up. "The third step is smelling it. About 75% of your enjoyment in chocolate comes from the aroma."

Peyton had smelled chocolate before. It was one of her favorite things to do. She felt a little vindicated. Clearly she was more of an expert than she gave herself credit. She sniffed at her chocolate, catching Marco's grimace from the corner of her eye. He'd been a good sport about this so far.

"So, Will, if a sommelier is a wine expert, what is a chocolate expert?" she asked.

He considered her question. "I believe it's a chocolate expert."

She felt a little disappointed. She nudged Marco with her shoulder. "I think it should be chocolier."

Lani giggled and Marco gave her a fond smile.

"The chocolate on *Silverweed Farms* is single origin, meaning we source it here and it is made in our own laboratory. You don't find many places that can make that claim," he said. "Now, the fourth step is to touch it. Is it smooth or coarse?"

Peyton stared at her piece of chocolate. She didn't really want to put her hands all over it, she wanted to eat it, but it was his party and she was just the guest. She rubbed it between her fingers, heating it enough to leave a residue on her fingertips. Marco dropped his hand to the table and sighed.

"Come on, D'Angelo. When we retire from the force, maybe we can come to the islands and plant our own chocolate field."

"Grove," corrected Will.

"Grove," Peyton amended. She was getting the impression Will was a chocolate snob. A chocosnob or a snobolate. She giggled to herself.

"And finally, the fifth step is to taste it." Will popped the chocolate in his mouth. "Let it dance on your tongue. Let the flavors bathe your palate. Let your taste buds rejoice."

Peyton let her taste buds rejoice, but the bitter taste made her frown. Marco made a choking sound and grabbed his napkin, spitting the bitter little block onto it and shivering violently. He reached for his water.

Peyton caught Will and Lani's horrified expressions.

"He's a chocolate virgin," she said, beaming a smile at them.

$$*\quad*\quad*$$

Danté received a text message from Simons that they were meeting in the conference room at 8:00. He hurried to finish getting ready, then snagged his keys off the hook by the door. When he'd joined the force, he'd found a rent controlled studio just off Nob Hill that he could afford. He hadn't wanted to get a roommate and the studio suited him just fine. He had a small alcove for his bed, a full bathroom, and a combination living room/kitchen. Although his stove was only two burners, he didn't cook very often and the small fridge, not much bigger than a dorm fridge, suited his needs.

His desk abutted the slider to the balcony and it was covered in textbooks from the night classes he took to get his bachelor's degree. Currently he was taking *Ethics in Criminal Justice* and *Writing and Researching Criminal Reports*. He really enjoyed his studies, but the *Criminal Reports* professor had never been in law enforcement, which made Danté a little skeptical about her expertise.

He jogged down the stairs to the first floor. The garage was just below the main office. He hurried down the cement stairs and pressed the crash bar to let himself inside the darkened interior. The sharp smell of urine filled his nostrils. They were having a problem keeping homeless people out of the parking garage.

He climbed behind the wheel of his battered Honda Odyssey minivan. His parents had given him the car when he moved out, since he couldn't afford a new one with rent as high as it was. Even with rent control, San Francisco's real estate was some of the highest in the world. He knew he looked silly driving a minivan, but he suspected this car would still be running long after he himself was gone.

He eased out onto the street and headed for the precinct. His phone rang as he turned left. He punched the button. "Hey, Inspector Cho," he said.

"Nate or Cho, kid. Knock it off with the inspector crap."

"Fine," said Danté, shifting uncomfortably. Respect had been drilled into him since he was an infant.

"You on your way in? Tag and Holmes have a plan so they can talk to Renchenko without him being worried about the camera."

"I'll be there. Inspector Simons called a meeting in the conference room at 8:00."

"Bill or Simons," corrected Cho. "Okay, I'll see you there." And he disconnected the call.

Danté turned on the music. His parents loved jazz, the more progressive the better, and he'd learned to appreciate it himself. Lately he'd been going through a Duke Ellington phase. As he drove through the early morning San Francisco traffic, he thought of the turn his life was taking. He wasn't sure what to make of it. He liked being a cop for the most part, but there were nuances of the job that bothered him.

His parents had drummed honesty, integrity, and striving for excellence into their two sons. They'd presented a united front his entire life and he never remembered them telling him to compromise or weigh consequences. He was smart enough to know that the odds of him facing such dilemmas was inevitable, but he'd never thought about how he'd respond to it. He'd spent six months working for Captain Alfred Campaña in the Central precinct. He'd been a beat cop, walking the streets. He'd made a few arrests for petty crimes, shoplifting mostly, once for public urination, but he hadn't faced the conflict he was facing in Homicide. And yet he'd felt stifled at Central, itching for something more challenging, something that would test his intellect. He was getting that here.

He pulled into the parking lot and put the Odyssey in park. Bartlet was climbing out of his Toyota Tacoma pickup truck.

"Hey, partner, what's shakin' bacon!" Bartlet said, clapping him on the back.

"Not much," said Danté, giving him a tight smile. He envied Bartlet a little. Things seemed simple for him. You showed up for work, did what you were told, then went home to beer and pizza and playing a racing game on a gaming console. Danté wished he could compartmentalize things the way Bartlet did.

They jogged up the steps and Bartlet pulled open the door. "Maybe we can grab beers at a bar sometime this week," said Bartlet, pushing open the half door.

"Sure," said Danté, following him. He peeked into the conference room and saw Tag and Holmes sitting at the table already. Stan Neumann and Lee appeared, coming from the break room. Lee was carrying a mug of coffee, Stan had a laptop. Stan's t-shirt had two atoms on it with electrons spinning around them. One atom said, "I think I lost an electron." The other responded, "Are you positive?"

Danté smiled. "That's great," he told Stan.

Stan beamed. "Thanks."

Bartlet leaned back and stared at Stan's shirt, then his brow scrunched up. "I don't get it."

Stan started to speak, but Simons appeared around the corner, his bulk moving in their direction. "Jimmy, go scare up a few patrol cars for us. We need them for tomorrow," he ordered.

Jimmy patted Stan on the shoulder good naturedly. "It's okay. I'm sure it's funny to some people." Then he headed off to do Simons' bidding.

Danté and Stan exchanged a look, then Stan walked into the conference room.

"Can I get you anything, Inspector Simons?" asked Lee, settling his coffee cup on the desk.

"Call ADA Adams and tell him I need to talk to him around noon, Lee," said Simons, turning into the doorway.

"Sure thing," said Lee.

Danté followed Simons inside, taking a seat at the table next to Stan. Stan opened his laptop, clicking on the keyboard. A moment later Cho walked through the door, taking the seat on Danté's other side.

"Okay, Tag," said Simons. "Tell us your plan."

She shifted her chair to face the end of the table. "We need to talk to Renchenko at the stop-and-rob, but Danté noticed there's a camera positioned in the acoustic tiles over Renchenko's head," she told Stan. "We're assuming the camera was placed there by Victor Maziar or his minions."

Stan considered that, blinking at her from behind his thick glasses. "Are you sure it's not attached to his security system?"

"He indicated its location to me surreptitiously," said Danté. "He didn't make it obvious. If it was his security system, I don't think he would have said anything about it."

Jake Ryder appeared in the doorway. "Sorry," he said, sliding into a seat. "The Daisy didn't want to start today."

The Daisy was Ryder's purple Dodge Omni with the huge daisies on the doors. Danté thought his Odyssey was bad, but it was nothing compared to the monstrosity that was Jake Ryder's car.

Cho made an aggravated sound in his throat.

"So what'd I miss?" Jake said, looking around the group, then he held up a hand. "Hold on. I need coffee. Anyone else want coffee?" He started to get up.

"Sit, Ryder," grumbled Simons.

Jake slumped in his seat. "Adonis would've let me get coffee," he complained.

"Captain," said Holmes.

"Captain Adonis," amended Jake.

Tag glared him to silence, her happy fingers tapping out an aggravated tattoo on the table. "Are you done?"

Jake made a flourish with his hand. "Go on. I'll catch up."

Tag rolled her eyes. "Anyway," she said, dragging out the word. "We wondered if there was someway you could disrupt the camera, Stan, so that we can talk to him."

Stan nodded. "I'd have to see the setup."

"It's probably on Wi-Fi, wouldn't you think, Stan?" said Jake.

"Probably, but I'd still like to see it. If it's on Wi-Fi, I can jam the Wi-Fi signal, but if it's hardwired in, that might be a little more difficult."

Simon leaned his bulk on the table. "Okay, so if you need to see it, you'll need to go in there on your own. I can go with you, since they haven't seen me on camera before."

"Maziar's seen you though, Bill," said Cho. "I think Ryder and Stan should go in, scope the place out. If you see the camera, can you jam the signal at the same time, Stan?"

"That's easy. I have a device I can carry in my pocket that'll disrupt the Wi-Fi in the area."

"Then as soon as the Wi-Fi's disabled, the camera will be useless?" asked Tag.

"They won't get anything off the feed," said Stan. "They'll just think the Wi-Fi went down."

"Good," said Simons. "Then Danté can go in and talk to Renchenko, see if he's being shaken down for protection money."

"If this is a RICO case, Bill," said Cho, "you know you'll have to turn it over to the feds. Maybe you should get Peyton on the phone?"

"I want to talk to Devan first, then if he thinks we should bring the feds in, I'll make the call to Rosa Alvarez. I don't want to bother Peyton and Marco on their honeymoon."

Danté shifted. He'd never been involved in anything this big. A racketeering case could complicated and involved a lot of moving parts.

"If we get the camera turned off, do you think you can get Renchenko to talk to you?" Tag asked Danté.

Danté shrugged. "I'll do my best."

"You'd better do more than your best, kid," said Holmes. "If this is a RICO case, we gotta have all our ducks in a row. I don't like messing with organized crime and this is the Russian mob we're talking about."

Danté glanced around the room. Everyone's expression had gone grim.

"I'll do my best," he repeated, since there was nothing more he could say.

*   *   *

Marco and Peyton left the *Silverweed Farms* and drove back down the coast toward their hotel. Peyton shifted in her seat and reached over, taking his hand. He smiled at her, enjoying the way the trailing sunlight shot streaks of red through her dark hair. He lifted her hand and kissed it.

"Thank you for this. Thank you for all of this. The wedding, the honeymoon. You arranged everything for me."

He glanced back at the road. "I would do anything for you, sweetheart. To be honest, I enjoyed it and that's not something I thought I'd ever say about such things."

She laughed. "But what can I do for you?"

"Wear the red bikini again," he said, waggling his brows at her.

She laughed once more and he basked in the sound. So often she was tense and worked up. Radar's shooting had brought back the nightmares and he often woke in the night to hear her sobbing. He hated that. He hated that her life had been filled with so much trauma. He'd take it all away if he could, but since they'd been here, she'd started to relax.

She played with the hair at the back of his neck. "I love you, D'Angelo, do you know that?"

He nodded. He knew. He'd never dreamed it would be possible, but it was too hard to deny now.

"I would do anything you wanted me to do," she said and he glanced over at her, his brow furrowed.

"What does that mean, sweetheart?"

"We're starting a new part of our lives and I know you hate my job."

"I don't hate it, Peyton. I hate that it takes you so far away."

"Right. So here's the thing. If you want, I'll go back to work for the SFPD."

He stared at her. He couldn't believe she'd said that.

"Marco, the road!" she said in alarm.

He looked back quickly. Excitement zinged through him. He knew she couldn't come work for him in his precinct. They would never allow that, but the thought of her being back in the City, of not going on business trips, of staying home with him every night, was almost more than he could comprehend.

"Are you serious about that?" he asked.

Her fingers soothed along the nape of his neck. "I'm serious. If that's what you want, I'll do it."

"Where's this coming from, Peyton?"

She sighed and lowered her hands to her lap. "A lot of places. Radar was shot. It could have been me. I just think, looking into the future, one of these times it's going to be me. I don't want to leave you, Marco. I want us, I want our life together. I want to have a family with you."

They'd reached the coast and he turned, heading south. His heart was hammering in his chest. "That's a lot to think about, sweetheart," he said.

"I know. I know it is."

"Have you really given it much thought?"

She shrugged. "No, it just came to me today. I love being with you. I love spending time with you and as long as I work for the FBI, that's going to be a challenge."

They drove for a while, each lost in their own thoughts. Finally he stirred. "Look, we'll talk about this more, okay?"

"Okay," she said.

He gave her a tentative smile. "You hungry?"

"Yeah, I am," she said with a laugh. "I guess the chocolate wore off."

"How about we find a little place and grab something to eat?"

"Sounds good."

A little while later, she pointed out a sign that said *Paolo's Crab Shack*. He turned at the road that led toward the ocean and they arrived at the small hut a few minutes later. The sun had dipped low toward the horizon, shooting out brilliant oranges and reds. The shack itself sat on the beach with outdoor picnic tables for seating.

Tiki torches lined the parking lot and were scattered in the sand around the picnic tables. Someone had lit a fire in a fire pit right on the beach and people sat around it, sipping drinks and eating.

Marco and Peyton climbed out of the car and Marco placed his hand on Peyton's back, directing her to the order window. The shack was made out of bamboo stalks and woven palm mats. A middle aged Hawaiian woman with glorious black hair pulled open an order window and beamed at them, her teeth even and white. Behind her was a massive Hawaiian man, his hair in a bun on top of his head, an apron wrapped around his waist.

"Aloha," they both said.

"Aloha," echoed Marco and Peyton.

"Welcome to *Paolo's Crab Shack*," said the woman. "Have you been here before?"

"No, this is our first time in Hawaii."

She gave them a shrewd look. "Newlyweds, no?"

"Yes," said Peyton with a laugh.

"Let me make a suggestion, okay?"

"Sure," said Peyton.

"Get the crab tacos with my homemade poi on top."

"And a Bikini Blonde Lager," shouted the man, working over a grill.

"Paolo's right. It goes best with the Lager. Made on Maui," she added.

"That sounds great for me, but my husband's vegetarian. Is there anything he can eat?"

"Ah, you let Kana take care of you, honey," she said, giving Marco a flirtatious wink. "I'll make you up a vegan Poke bowl."

"Sounds great," said Marco, taking out his wallet.

"Will that be two Bikini Blondes then?"

"Just one and a water," said Marco, handing her some money.

"Go ahead and take a seat. I'll bring it out to you," she told them.

They made their way over to the picnic tables, but the main group of people seemed to be gathered around the bonfire. A young man with shaggy blond hair and a dark tan motioned to them. "Come sit with us. Nani's telling tales. You'll want to hear them."

Marco and Peyton exchanged a look, then they made their way over to the bonfire, taking two low slung chairs that were open. An old woman sat on the opposite side of the fire, her back to the ocean. She had long grey hair that hung over her shoulders. She wore a floral print dress and flip flops on her feet. Her hands were twisted with arthritis, her face heavily lined, her eyes a faded brown, clouded by cataracts. A string of puka shells hung around her neck.

As Marco and Peyton sank into the seats, the other people smiled at them and nodded in greeting. Nani narrowed her eyes on the two of them and smiled, a few teeth missing in the front. "You were just married," she said.

"Yes," answered Peyton, holding her hands out to the fire. The temperature was still pleasant, but the breeze off the ocean was cool. Marco realized they had a perfect position to see the sun set over the water.

"Aloha," said Nani. "It is good you came here. I see a brightness about you, child," she told Peyton. "You have important work here."

Peyton smiled, reaching over to take Marco's hand. "I like to think that, if you can call making my husband happy work."

The other people laughed, but Nani narrowed her eyes. "That is not what I mean. You have important work on Kauai."

Marco felt a chill race over him. Peyton's smile dried, but she didn't respond.

A strained silence fell over the people. The young blond man shifted in his seat, leaning forward to poke the fire. "Nani has the sight," he told Peyton and Marco, then looked around the group. "She told me she saw me with big teeth." He held up a necklace of shark teeth. "The next day I nearly got eaten by a great white while surfing."

The people gasped.

"Probably saved my life. I saw the fin, remembered what Nani said, and peddled like hell for shore!" He made frantic swimming motions with his arms. "Pissed myself is what I did."

Everyone laughed.

Nani reached over and patted his arm, smiling at him fondly. "You're a good boy, Boomer. You listen to an old woman."

He covered her hand with his. "Damn straight. Otherwise, some shark would be popping me out right about now."

More laughter.

Nani leaned back in her chair. "Tonight, I want to talk about the Menehune," she said.

People exchanged smiles. One man said, "Who are the Menehune?"

"The Menehune are the first inhabitants of the island. They are the little people, who protect the island and all that is upon it," she said.

"They defend the plants and the animals," said Boomer. "You don't want to mess with the Menehune."

"No, you do not. They are not kind to those who would destroy the beauty that is around us," said Nani.

Kana brought them their food, setting their drinks on the lava rocks that ringed in the fire.

"Thank you," said Peyton, her attention turning back to Nani.

"What story are you telling tonight, hālala?" Kana said.

"She's telling about the Menehune," said Boomer.

"Ah, that is a good one," said Kana, touching Peyton's shoulder. She leaned down, speaking so only Peyton and Marco could hear. "My grandmother is ninety-three." She motioned to her own eyes. "She knows many things." Speaking louder, so her grandmother could hear, she said, "You know many things, don't you, hālala?"

"I do, keiki. You know this."

"I do," said Kana, straightening.

The old woman leaned forward, clasping her arthritic hands. "The story I will tell you tonight is this – the tale of Ululani and the Baker man."

Kana walked back to the shack, but no one else moved. The brilliance of the sky deepened and Marco watched the waves come in, lulling him into a relaxed state. This was one of those moments in time that he wanted to etch into his memory. Everything felt right with the world in this instance. For just this moment.

"Ululani was a beautiful Hawaiian maiden. Hair like black velvet, eyes like onyx, skin like the purest honey from the bees. Baker loved her from the moment he saw her. He'd come to Kauai from the mainland to make his fortune, but he never dreamed that he'd lose his heart."

Peyton smiled over at Marco. Marco took her hand.

"Baker wanted to build Ululani the biggest, finest house on the islands with a lanai all around it, so she could follow the path of the sun throughout the day and forever be blessed with his light. He found the land for his hale, his house, and it was a beautiful spot with many coconut and palm trees."

"Baker did not like the trees for they blocked the view of the ocean and he wanted his Ululani to be able to see the waves and the sunset and the white sand of the beach. The first day, he chopped many of the trees, his back ached and his hands bled from the strain, but he was proud of his progress. Soon he would build the hale with the lanai and bring his love to her new home."

"That night he dropped into a deep sleep and did not awake until the sun was very high in the sky. When he looked about the land, he couldn't believe his eyes. Every tree had been returned to its original spot, their branches once more blocking the view of the ocean."

"Baker was perplexed. How could this happen? His hand bore the blisters from his day of work, but the trees had all magically regrown in their original spots, taunting him."

Peyton tilted her head. Marco stared at her. Had she been serious about her offer to quit the FBI? Would she be satisfied going back to being a detective? She hadn't sought the FBI job herself. She'd been pushed into it by Captain Defino and Rosa Alvarez. Maybe it wasn't at all what she'd wanted? Still she thrived in it. She'd solved more cases in the months she'd been with the Bureau than many more seasoned officers. How could he ask her to leave that?

"Since Baker was a wealthy man, he went to town and he hired many men to help him clear the land. They came with their trucks and their trailers, they tore up the soil and beat down the brush. They chopped many trees that day, clearing a wide area where Ululani could see the ocean from the lanai."

Marco shifted his attention back to the old woman, forcing thoughts about Peyton leaving the Bureau from his mind. He wanted to enjoy this moment, be present for once and not let other worries preoccupy him. He realized a lot of the time he and Peyton lost was because they couldn't turn off work when they were together. Maybe the fault wasn't their jobs, but them.

"The next morning the trees stood in the same place again and the ruts in the ground had been covered once more with foliage. Baker was beside himself. He knew he had hired the men. He knew they had cleared much of the land for his home. He went to Ululani and told her what happened."

"Ululani had a wise hālala and she asked her what had caused the trees to grow again, what had made the foliage cover the tracks that the men had made. Her hālala told Ululani to bring her to the spot, so Baker and Ululani brought her hālala to the spot where Baker wanted to build Ululani her house, and the old woman walked the grounds. She touched the earth. She placed her wrinkled palm on the tree trunks. She stood in the spot and looked out toward the ocean where Baker had planned the lanai."

"Baker was an inpatient man. He did not appreciate the pulse of the waves, or the sighing of wind through the trees, or the heartbeat of the volcano. He made things happen with his money and he expected answers from people, but Ululani's hālala was not a woman to trifle with. She took her time, but when she was ready, she turned to the Baker man and she said to him, 'You must stop your work here on this land. You must stop cutting the trees and trampling the foliage. You must stop carving pieces for yourself and destroying what nature has placed here.'"

"Baker said, 'I am a powerful man. I have much money. I want to build a palace for Ululani to honor her, to make her see how powerful I am.' The old woman shook a finger in Baker's face. 'You play with force you cannot understand. The Menehune have taken stewardship over this part of the island. They protect the trees, the earth, and all that lives upon it. Go build your palace on the mainland, but do not attempt to build it here.'"

"Now the Baker man laughed, for he'd heard of the Menehune and knew them to be myth. He did not believe them to be the stewards of the islands, the protectors of

Hawaii. He had money and that was the only akua he knew. 'You talk of nonsense and fairytales, old woman,' he told Ululani's hålala. 'I do not believe you.'"

"Ululani's hålala felt sad for the Baker man's ignorance, but she merely shook her head. 'I fear you will pay for your insolence,' she said somberly. 'If you take what is most precious to the Menehune for yourself, they will take what is most precious from you.'"

"The Baker man laughed. The first thing that came to his mind was his money, for he believed that was most precious to him. He told her that nothing could touch what was most precious to him because it was secured in the white man's bank with the white man's laws."

"Ululani's hålala gave him a grim look, then she left with Ululani. The next morning the Baker man went to town again and hired more men. They came to the land in their trucks and trailers and metal machines and they spent the day tearing at the earth, toppling the trees, ripping the plants from the ground by their roots. When they were done, there was nothing left, but the battered and broken soil. Baker stood upon it, surveying his land with pride. The next day, he would bring Ululani here, so she could see his great work. He knew she would be in as much awe as he was."

Marco stared into the dancing flames. Night had fallen around them and the sun had sunk below the horizon. The fire's light lit hollows in Nani's face, making her features sharp and sinister.

"The next morning, he went to Ululani's house, but she was not there. Her hålala was and she gave the Baker man a sad, searching look. He asked after Ululani, but the old woman's expression grew even more grim and she held out her hands. 'I warned you what would come if you did not respect the Menehune. I told you that what was most precious to you would be taken away. Ululani went out this morning to surf, but she never returned.'"

"The Baker man sat down hard on Ululani's lanai, his legs going weak. She had told him that he would lose what was most precious to him and he had lost it, he had lost his Ululani and his heart. The Menehune do not take offense lightly and they give men many chance to change their ways, but when you have crossed them too many times, they will take their revenge and woe to all who fail to heed this warning."

Nani ended her tale and folded her hands in her lap. The fire crackled and sent a stream of embers into the air. A few people startled. Marco glanced over at Peyton and found her staring into the flames intensely.

Woe to all who fail to heed this warning. Marco heard the words echo in his head and he wondered if that wasn't a bad omen. A chill shivered over his body and he leaned forward, holding his hands out to the flames.

CHAPTER 8

A loud knock brought Peyton out of a deep sleep. Marco was already rolling over, grabbing his jeans to pull them on. She caught up the robe at the end of the bed and glanced at the digital clock on the bedside table. 3:00AM.

Shoving her arms into the sleeves, she rose and tied the robe tight around her waist, then she went to the closet where the safe held their guns and their badges, pulling open the door but not removing the weapons. Marco touched her shoulder as he went beyond her, his chest and feet bare, his jeans unbuttoned. He glanced through the peephole, then frowned back at her before unlocking and pulling the door open.

"Captain D'Angelo," came a familiar voice. "I'm so sorry to bother you this late at night, but Tavis wanted to know if Special Agent Brooks could meet with him."

Marco opened the door wide and motioned inside. "Come in, Robbie. What's going on?"

Peyton pushed the hair back from her face as the young man entered the room wearing khaki pants and a hotel polo shirt. *Koloa Grove Resort* was embroidered on his left breast pocket in yellow with a palm tree.

"Special Agent Brooks, I'm so sorry to wake you," he said, clasping his hands before him, "but Tavis asked me to get you."

"What's wrong?" asked Peyton, pushing the door to the safe closed.

Robbie shifted weight. "He asked me to bring you. We need to be discreet."

Peyton wasn't sure what the hell was going on, but clearly something had happened. "Let us get dressed and we'll be down."

"I'll wait for you in the hall," he said.

Marco shut the door after him, then went to grab his t-shirt off the chair in the corner. Peyton gathered a few things and went into the bathroom. After dressing and using the facilities, she tried to tame her hair into a ponytail, then washed her face and hands. Going into the other room, she grabbed a fluffy sweater from the closet, slipped her feet into her sandals and on second thought, grabbed her gun and badge, affixing the badge to the waistband of her jeans.

Marco reached in around her and did the same, then he gave her a serious look. "This isn't good, is it?"

"Nope. Not if they want a federal agent looking at it." She sighed. "This is what I was talking about earlier, D'Angelo. We can't even get in a honeymoon."

He kissed her. "Let me brush my teeth and use the bathroom, then I'll be ready to go."

She nodded and took a seat on the bed, checking her gun. A moment later they were out in the hall, meeting a pacing Robbie. Peyton gave him a frown. "You sure you won't tell me what it is?"

"Tavis told me it was urgent that I get you. That's all I know, but it has to be bad if he's disturbing a guest."

Peyton nodded and they followed the young man to the elevators. He pushed the button and a moment later the elevator appeared, the doors hissing open. They all stepped inside and Robbie pushed the button for the lobby. He gave them a tense smile as they watched the numbers descend. The elevator let them out in the empty lobby. Another young man worked the counter and an older man washed the windows leading to the lanai, but no one else was around.

"This way," said Robbie, pointing to the glass doors.

The older man opened one and Robbie led them onto the expansive lanai that wrapped around the huge pool in the center of the hotel. He took the radio from his belt and pressed the button on the side of it.

"I have Agent Brooks, Tavis," he said.

The radio crackled, then Tavis' voice came through the speaker. "We're at the hot tub," he said. "Bring them to the gate, then you stay outside. Let no one else in."

"Got it," said Robbie, then he replaced the radio and guided them around the huge pool with a swim-up bar, palm tree islands, and water guns arranged on a platform. The night was cool, the stars brilliant overhead. Peyton sighed, feeling sure their time in paradise was just about over.

Two days was not enough time. No time would be enough, she decided, but this seemed particularly unfair. It was their honeymoon after all. They were supposed to spend it making love, napping, eating too much and getting sunburnt.

They arrived at the secluded gate leading to the hot tub and Robbie pushed the gate open. "Just through there," he said cryptically. "I'll wait here and keep people out."

Peyton nodded and eased through the gate. Potted plants overflowing with ferns marked the outer edge of the enclosure. Planter beds with lush palm trees created a winding path to the hot tub. Peyton came to a sudden stop and took in the scene.

A man lay on his back outside the hot tub, wearing a pair of blue swim trunks with white flowers on them. His hands were out flung, his face mottled and bloated. Beside him stood a man in a grey jumpsuit with water dripping from it and Tavis Makoa, looking like he wanted to be anywhere but here at this moment. The hot tub jets had been stilled.

Peyton sighed. Yep, the honeymoon was over.

"Marco," she said, looking away from the body.

"I'm on it," Marco answered, walking over to the body and crouching beside it. He touched two fingers to the man's throat, then sighed. "Rigor's set in."

So he'd been dead between two to six hours. Tavis Makoa wrung his hands, glancing at her and then back to the body. She approached him. "Do you have a pad of paper?" she said.

Tavis shook his head, then he grabbed the radio at his belt. "Robbie, can you get Agent Brooks a pad of paper from the lobby?"

"Thank you. Have you called the local authorities?" she asked.

Tavis leaned closer to her. "It's Harvey Meridew," he whispered.

Harvey Meridew had been the man Peyton confronted in the lobby just two days before. He'd been demanding and abusive to the hotel staff, shouting at them over the internet, she remembered.

"That doesn't matter. You need to call the local authorities."

"He's a very powerful man on Kauai."

"He's a very dead man, Mr. Makoa. Call the local authorities. Knowing Mr. Meridew, he probably had a heart attack."

Tavis nodded jerkily. "Okay. Okay, I'll call them now." He stepped away, taking his phone out of his pocket.

Peyton edged over to Marco where he was inspecting the body without touching it any longer. She kept her gaze firmly fixed on the potted palm across from them, listening to the distant sound of the surf pounding beyond the hotel.

"Any sign of physical trauma?"

"None on the front. His face is bloated, but that's probably from his time in the water," said Marco. "I don't want to turn him over until a CSI gets here and takes pictures."

"Okay." She turned to the man in the grey jumpsuit, who looked like he wanted to bolt. He was a slight, spare man with a wiry frame and dark black hair. He gave her a panicked look out of dark eyes. She marked his wet jumpsuit again, then smiled at him. "You must have found the body, right?"

"Yes," he said, glancing at Tavis who was talking into the phone, his hand covering the mouthpiece. "I came out here to test the water and he was floating face down. I jumped in and dragged him out, but it was too late."

Peyton wished Robbie would come with the pad of paper. She wanted to take some notes for the local police when they arrived. "After you pulled him out, what did you do?"

"I called Mr. Makoa right away."

"Did you know who the man was?"

"Mr. Makoa said it was Harvey Meridew. I've seen his advertisements around the island."

"Okay."

He shivered, wrapping his arms around himself, his eyes fixed on Meridew. "I've never seen a dead guy before." He glanced back at Peyton. "I mean, I have at funerals, but never...never..."

Peyton touched his wet arm. "I know, Mister? I didn't get your name."

"Peter Akiona."

Robbie came running around the corner of the enclosure, stumbling to a stop, Peyton's pad of paper and a hotel pen held in his hands. His eyes fixated on the body and he made a strange gasping sound. Peyton hurried back to him and took the paper and pen from his hand, pushing him in the shoulder.

"Go back to the gate, Robbie," she said.

"Is that man..." He couldn't look away. "Is he dead?"

"Robbie!" Peyton snapped, drawing the younger man's attention. "Go back to the gate, please, and direct the local authorities back here when they arrive."

Robbie snapped to attention. "Yes, ma'am," he said.

She took the pad and went back to Peter, writing down a few notes. Marco rose and began walking the perimeter of the area, looking around. Peyton found herself distracted, watching him. Seeing him canvass a scene was so familiar, it made her smile, then she remembered the grim task at hand.

Tavis Makoa disconnected his call and came over to her. "They said they'd be here in five minutes."

"Good."

126

Tavis stared miserably at the body. "This isn't good. Harvey Meridew's a very powerful man in Hawaii. He and his business partner own a lot of land."

"What's the name of his business partner?"

"Jackson Hughes. Hughes is the CFO of Dewdrop Construction," said Makoa. "If there's construction on Kauai, they're probably involved. They were just putting in a strip mall out on Waipouli Road."

"We saw it."

Tavis ran his hand through his hair. "This is so bad. So bad. This will be very bad for the hotel."

"How, Mr. Makoa? He most likely died of a heart attack."

Tavis Makoa's eyes shifted and pierced Peyton's. "That's Harvey Meridew."

"Right, we've established that," she said calmly.

"Haven't you watched the news since you've been here?"

Peyton frowned. Marco shifted and looked back at them, hearing the panic in Tavis' voice. "I'm on my honeymoon, Mr. Makoa. News wasn't exactly a priority."

Tavis Makoa swallowed hard and exchanged a worried look with his maintenance worker. "Harvey Meridew has been getting death threats, Agent Brooks. That's why I had Robbie wake you and bring you down here. It's been all over the news. He's been getting letters delivered to him for weeks now." Tavis rubbed his hands over his face. "Yesterday morning, Mr. Meridew came to the front desk, very upset. He was shouting and raving, demanding to see me."

"Why?" asked Peyton, feeling her mouth go dry.

"He'd gotten another letter under his room door."

"A death threat?"

Tavis nodded miserably. "I wanted to call the cops, but he wouldn't let me. He forbade it. He said he wasn't going to take it anymore. He was going to hire bodyguards. He said the cops weren't doing anything about it."

"Did you see the letter, Mr. Makoa?"

"No, he wouldn't show me. He said he'd thrown it over the balcony."

"Did he tell you what it said, Mr. Makoa? Did he give you any idea what was in the letter?"

Tavis nodded rapidly.

Peyton drew a breath for patience. "I need to know what the letter said, Mr. Makoa."

Tavis rubbed his hand over his chin and rolled his shoulders. "It said…" His voice failed him and he made a face.

"What?" prompted Peyton. "What did the letter say?"

"The Menehune were coming for him."

Peyton's eyes rose and met Marco's. Marco looked away, rubbing a hand against his forehead. He knew as well as she did that their honeymoon had just ended.

* * *

Stan pulled his t-shirt down, smoothing it. "I've never worn a wire before. Should I be careful about touching my chest?"

Cho dropped the tape into the black case. "Yeah, don't touch your chest, but don't be overly worried. We've got you wired in an abundance of caution."

Stan's hand hovered over the spot. "What if I start to sweat?"

"Sweat?" asked Cho.

Stan leaned forward, dropping his voice. "Sometimes I nervous sweat. A lot."

Cho and Danté exchanged a look. Tag blew out air, her happy tattoo dancing madly on the conference room table. "Do you want the Preacher to wear it instead?" she asked.

Stan shook his head. "No, no, I can do it. It's almost like I'm a spy or something."

"Or something," said Cho.

"I'll be right there with you, Stan. You got nothing to worry about," said Jake, pushing his chair back on two legs and balancing.

"Are you trying to give him a heart attack?" said Tag.

"What? I'm serious. I'm really cool in a tense situation."

Tag rolled her eyes and Holmes snorted.

"You'll do fine, Mr. Neumann," said Danté. "All you have to do is go in, deploy the device and we'll be in after you."

Stan nodded a number of times jerkily. Then he focused on Cho again. "But what if I sweat and the wire comes off?"

"Don't panic. Just deploy the device and get out of there. Again, the wire's just a precaution. It's just so we know when to go inside."

"I'm telling you, Stan, I'll be right there beside you. You got nothing to worry about," said Jake. The chair tilted backward and he wind-milled his arms to prevent himself from going over. Tag caught the arm, forcing the chair back onto all four legs.

"Idiot," she hissed.

"Okay, let's not waste anymore time talking," said Simons, pushing himself to his feet. "Preacher, try to remember to get some pictures while you're in there, but don't get caught."

"Aye aye, Captain," said Jake, leaping to his feet and saluting.

Everyone else rose and grabbed equipment, moving out to the cruisers.

"Danté," called Simons.

Danté held back, turning to face the giant of a man. "Yes, sir," he said.

"Try to get as much information out of Renchenko, but don't spook him."

"I understand, sir."

Simons put a hand on Danté's shoulder. "I'm not trying to spook you, kid, but this whole thing has got me worried."

Danté frowned. "If it's a RICO case, Inspector Simons, aren't we going to turn it over to the FBI?"

"Of course, but I think this is more than that. These Russian mob guys, this new Russian gang, the Goblins…"

Danté nodded.

"I'm scared they've put a target on Captain D'Angelo's back. We need to get as much intel as we can before he returns."

Danté felt his mouth go dry. "Okay, Inspector Simons, I'll do my best."

Simons patted his shoulder. "I know you will, kid. I know you will."

Danté gave a head nod to Lee as he went through the half-door and down to Cho's waiting car. He slipped into the passenger seat, slamming the door, and Cho pulled away. They were both silent as they followed along behind Stan's Nissan Sentra. Cho messed with the radio until Jake's voice came through the speaker.

"So tell me how this jammer thingy works, Stan," he said.

"Well, it really doesn't jam anything. Okay, so in a way it does, but what it really does is it overwhelms the Wi-Fi signal and…"

Danté watched out the window, letting their words wash over him. He thought about all that he'd heard regarding this new gang, the Goblins. If they were infiltrating areas that had already been fought over by the local street gangs, they had to be well funded and heavily armed. He could understand Simons worry about this, especially if they had targeted Captain D'Angelo.

His cell phone buzzed and he took it out, looking at the display. Frowning, he realized he didn't recognize the number. The message said, *Can you talk?*

He typed back. *Who is this?*

Harper.

Danté didn't remember giving her his number. *How did you get this number?* he demanded.

Reporter came her response.

He felt a little violated, but he forced it out of his mind. *I'm on a call.*

Okay, call me whenever you can, but soon, she said.

Danté shoved the phone back in his pocket, wondering what she wanted now. He forced himself to concentrate on the voices coming through the radio. Concentrating on Harper McLeod was too distracting, he decided.

"Where do you think I'll be able to find some polyester bell bottoms, Stan?" he heard Jake say.

Cho shook his head, his hands tightening on the steering wheel. Danté hid his smile with his fist. He couldn't help it, but he found Jake Ryder amusing.

They pulled around the corner from Renchenko's stop-and-rob, while Stan and Jake went around the front to the tiny parking lot Renchenko had directly in front of the building. They could just see the Sentra, but no one inside the building or watching it could see Cho and Danté. Glancing in the passenger side mirror, Danté watched Holmes and Tag pull up behind them in Tag's Chevy Silverado.

Stan and Jake got out of the car and disappeared into the store. They could hear the bell jangle.

"Hola!" they heard Jake say.

There was a mumbled response, then a crackling noise. Danté looked at Cho.

"He's scratching the wire," said Cho, making a face.

"I'll have a pack of those cigarettes behind the counter there," came Jake's voice. "You want some cigarettes, Stan?"

"Um, s-sure."

"Yeah, we both want cigarettes. The ones there without the filter. Yeah, those ones. Yeah, no, the second shelf, red carton."

Cho let out an exasperated breath. "He's gonna get them both shot, I swear to God."

Danté glanced in the rearview mirror and saw Tag brace her head with her hands, while Holmes had his pressed to the headrest, his mouth hanging open. There was more scratching, then the voices became muffled.

"He dislodged the wire," said Cho, nodding. "Yep, I knew that was going to happen."

Danté leaned forward and looked toward the front of the building. What the hell! It was so simple. Go in, look at the camera, block the signal. Suddenly he heard the car doors slam behind them and he glanced into the mirror again. Tag and Holmes had gotten out of the Silverado. Cho unhooked his seatbelt and got out as well.

"Stan texted me," said Tag, holding up her phone. "The wire came off."

Cho chuckled and Holmes gave a grunt of disbelief.

"Is the Wi-Fi disabled?" asked Cho.

"Yeppers," said Holmes.

Danté got out and stepped up on the sidewalk, but Tag clapped him on the shoulder and turned him toward the store.

"You're up, genius," she said, propelling him forward.

As soon as they got to the store, Stan hurried over to them. "The signal's jammed," he said. "I had to use data to send my text message."

"Good," said Cho as they fanned out across the store.

Danté fixed his gaze on Renchenko. The older man looked like he might bolt. Jake stood at the counter, tapping the cigarettes on the scarred glass surface.

"I've never bought cigarettes before. Did you know these damn things nearly cost me twenty dollars? Do you think the precinct will reimburse me?"

Danté gave him a look, then focused on Renchenko again. "Dobryy den'." *Good afternoon.*

"Dobryy den'," said Renchenko, shooting a look up at the camera.

"My otklyuchili yego," said Danté. *We turned it off.*
Renchenko shook his head. "Oni budut znat'." *They'll know.*

Danté motioned around them. "My otklyuchili Wi-Fi dlya vsego rayona." *We turned off the Wi-Fi for the whole neighborhood.*

Renchenko's shoulders slumped. "Chto, yesli oni vas uvidyat?" *What if they see you?*

"Oni smotryat magazin?" *Do they watch the store?*

"Da, inogda." *Yes, sometimes.*

"Da means yes," Jake told Tag.

Tag glared at him, holding up her right fist. "This means shut up," she said.

Jake looked down, tapping his cigarettes.

"Kto polozhil kameru v vash magazin?" continued Danté. *Who put the camera in your store?*

Renchenko shook his head violently. "Ya ne mogu skazat'." *I cannot say.*

"My khotim pomoch' vam. Oni prosyat deneg? Dlya zashchity?" *We want to help you. Are they asking for money? For protection?*

"Ya ne mogu skazat'." *I cannot say.*

"My zdes' chtoby pomoch' vam." *We're here to help you.*
"Klyanus' tebe na moyem znachke." *I swear to you on my badge.*
Danté touched the badge affixed to his belt.

"Ya ne mogu skazat'." *I cannot say.*

"What is he saying?" asked Holmes, coming up on Danté's other side.

"He's scared. He keeps saying he cannot say."

"Ask him about the Goblins," said Holmes.

At the name, Renchenko's face drained of color and he shook his head. "Ne govorite takikh veshchey. Ne govorite o nikh." *Do not say such things. Do not speak of them.* He waved his hands in front of him. "Ne govorite o nikh."

"What?" said Tag.

"He's really scared," said Jake, watching him.

"He said do not speak of them," translated Danté.

"Gobliny unichtozhat vse!" Renchenko said, leaning forward, his face urgent. "Oni ub'yut vas."

Danté swallowed hard.

"What?" demanded Tag. "What did he say?"

"The Goblins will destroy everything," translated Danté. "They will kill you."

Renchenko nodded violently, pointing at Danté. "Da, da! They will keel ju."

*   *   *

Marco watched the hotel workers spread out, searching the dense foliage under the area where Harvey Meridew had his room. He'd been on the fourteenth floor, but he'd told Tavis Makoa that he'd thrown the letter off the balcony. They needed to find it. It was the only proof they had that Meridew had been getting death threats.

The sun had come up, the clouds a fluffy white, floating by overhead. A slight breeze blew the palm trees, rustling the fronds. Glancing over at Peyton, he watched her talking to the local police constable, a handsome man with sharp cheekbones, black hair, and dark black eyes. He had Hawaiian features and a lean frame. He'd introduced himself as Terrence Kahele, Chief of Police for the island of Kauai. He wore a dark suit, but he'd taken off the jacket and slung it over a lounger, his white shirt sleeves rolled up to his elbows, showing off his toned forearms.

Marco felt a rush of jealousy and resentment wash over him. He'd wanted this honeymoon so much and now it was looking less and less likely. If Meridew had been murdered, which Marco wasn't convinced he had been, he didn't want Peyton dragged into it. The Kauai police department could handle it themselves. Meridew was a resident of the state, this case didn't cross state lines, and there was no reason for the FBI to be involved. Especially since Marco hadn't seen any indication that anything had happened to Meridew except a heart attack like Peyton first suspected. There was no trauma, no indication that anyone else had even been in the vicinity of the man when he died.

Makoa had pulled security footage and it showed Meridew sitting in the hot tub for quite a while, then suddenly acting like he was having trouble breathing before he keeled forward into the water and went still. Men like Meridew had heart attacks all the time – high stress, bad diet, and a type A personality – three things that almost guaranteed he'd be dead by fifty.

Wandering over to Peyton and Kahele, Marco tried to listen in. Peyton gave him an understanding smile.

"Mr. Meridew didn't actually hold residency in Hawaii. He's a Southern California native," Kahele told Peyton.

Damn it, thought Marco. "I thought he lived on Maui," he said.

Kahele put his hands on his hips. "His ex-wife lives in the house he used to own on Maui. Mr. Meridew lost it in the divorce. According to Makoa, he was staying at the hotel while they were constructing the strip mall, but his primary residence is in San Diego."

"I didn't see any sign that this was more than a heart attack," Marco pressed. He could feel them getting sucked into this case and he wasn't going to let it happen. "No stab or gunshot wounds, no blunt force trauma."

"And you are?" asked Kahele, jutting out his chin.

Peyton slid her arm through his and leaned against his side. "My husband, Captain Marco D'Angelo of the SFPD, Chief Kahele."

"Ah!" said Kahele, forcing a closed-mouth smile. "Pleasure to meet you, Captain. Congratulations on your marriage."

"Thank you," Marco said, challenging the man with his eyes. He'd seen how Kahele leaned closer to Peyton when he talked to her, how he studied her when he thought she wasn't looking.

"As I was telling your wife, the problem is the letters. We've been investigating threats against Mr. Meridew for weeks now."

"Any credibility to them?" asked Marco.

"We haven't been able to establish anything yet. Even Mr. Meridew didn't take them seriously. He thought they were a prank by environmentalists on the island who oppose any new building."

"But you thought differently?" asked Peyton.

Kahele shrugged. "To be honest, I agreed with him, but Mr. Meridew's partner, Jackson Hughes, felt they were a little more serious. He insisted we pursue them." Kahele looked out at the workers searching the undergrowth for the letter. "The medical examiner will be able to tell us more."

Peyton nodded, rubbing a hand over Marco's back. "Well, I'm glad you're on the case. It seems like you have everything under control. Hopefully, your ME will have it all cleared up by the end of the day. Now, unless you need anything more from us, I think we'll get back to our honeymoon. I promised my husband we'd learn how to surf while we were here, so we have a lesson at 11:00."

Kahele smiled at her. "Enjoy your stay on Kauai, Agent Brooks, Captain D'Angelo. This is a magical place for romance." He shook hands with both of them. "Aloha."

"Aloha," they said together and turned toward the hotel.

Marco tried to hide his limp as they walked away from the other man. Peyton gave him an aggravated look.

"Seriously, D'Angelo, is this going to be a thing with us?"

"What?" he said, pretending he didn't know what she was talking about.

She stopped, stepping in front of him. "You're my husband."

"I know that."

"Do you? Because you're acting possessive and jealous. You're not threatened by Chief Kahele, are you?"

He gave her a serious look, curving his hand under her chin. "I try not to get like this, Peyton, but I can feel the honeymoon slipping away from us. He's just the closest target for my frustration." He smoothed his thumb along her jaw. "I don't think you realize how men see you."

She curled her fingers in his. "And I don't think you realize that you're my man. You're my only man. I don't want anyone else." She glanced behind them. "We're going to think positive thoughts. Harvey Meridew died of a heart attack. Nothing more. We are not getting sucked into this case. We are not going to investigate anything. We are going to take our surfing lesson. We're going to lay in the sun, and we're going to have a magical dinner tonight at the luau, watching hot men toss fire around."

Marco made a face.

"Repeat after me," she said, wrapping her arms around his waist. "We are having our honeymoon."

"We are having our honeymoon." He kissed her, then glanced up at the hotel. "It's only 7:30. We could head back to our room and..." He waggled his brows suggestively at her.

"Take a nap before our surfing lesson?" she asked hopefully.

He laughed. "Take a nap before our surfing lesson, of course."

They took a nap, but he coaxed her into a little recreation before it. At 11:00, they went down for the surfing lesson. Peyton wore the red bikini and he found himself a happy man, paddling out on the boards to wait for the next wave to come in. He didn't even try to stand up on the board, knowing his leg would never allow for it, but she did and wound up falling off over and over again.

He couldn't remember laughing as much and he pulled her board close, kissing her. God, he loved this woman. Then they played in the surf, splashing each other, before they finally collapsed on the loungers, soaking up the late afternoon sun.

After another "nap", they got dressed for dinner. Somehow Peyton had found a luau that catered to vegetarians. He'd hated to deny her the traditional Hawaiian experience, but he didn't want to see a whole pig roasting on a spit. She confirmed that she hadn't been interested in that herself.

Walking down to the beach, Marco pulled her close. She had on a floral sundress with red hibiscus flowers on it, her hair braided down her back, her skin looking sun kissed and healthy. He'd chosen a pair of linen pants Renee Noir had designed for him with a short-sleeved white Guayabera shirt Peyton had brought him from Mexico.

A young girl in a grass skirt greeted them at the entrance to the luau and placed leis over their heads. "You're at table two," she said, directing them to a spot before the bamboo stage. Another couple already occupied the other two spots at the table, but they had their heads bent together, talking quietly.

As Peyton and Marco approached, the couple parted and looked up with smiles, then they burst into delighted laughs. Marco forced himself to be pleasant as he took Bill Baxter's hand and shook it. Sally jumped to her feet and wrapped her arms around Peyton, hugging her close.

"What are the odds!" she exclaimed.

"What are the odds," repeated Peyton, giving Marco an apologetic look over Sally's shoulder. "I didn't know you were vegetarians."

"Oh, we're not," said Sally, waving Peyton off, "but we were too late to get reservations at the meat luau."

"I'll bet you were hankering for some of that roast pig, weren't you, big guy?" said Bill, patting Marco's stomach. "I hear they roast the whole thing. A suckling piglet. Man, I'll bet that's some good eats."

Marco smiled and nodded.

"Can you believe they sat us next to one another? You think they knew we were neighbors?" asked Sally, hugging Marco next. She smelled of Vapor Rub and sunscreen.

"Maybe," he said, patting her back and releasing her.

Sally grabbed Peyton's hands and dragged her into the seat next to her. "Did you hear about all the excitement at the hotel today?"

Peyton glanced back at Marco as he took his seat, stretching out his bad leg and glancing up at the stage. Tiki torches danced in the breeze on each corner of the platform and Hawaiian ukulele music filtered softly through the speakers affixed to the upper beams.

"What excitement?" asked Peyton, and Marco knew she was hoping Sally had something else to tell her.

"Oh my goodness!" exclaimed Sally, patting Peyton's arm. "A man drowned to death in the hot tub. I'm always telling Bill, those things are death traps. Aren't I, Bill? Aren't I always telling you that?"

Bill leaned forward. "She is. She's always telling me that."

"Drowned! Can you believe it?"

"No, that's awful," said Peyton.

"The cops were here. Apparently the man is a big shot on the island."

"A developer," said Bill. "Yeah, he's a big time developer. He does a lot of construction here, but people aren't happy about it."

"No, they are not. The locals don't want all this development. And I honestly can't blame them," said Sally. "They want to keep Hawaii pristine."

"Yep, it's a damn shame. You know that song, Marco. You know the one about paving over paradise with a parking lot," said Bill.

"Sure," said Marco, giving him a smile.

"It's a shame though. He drowned. Can you believe it, Peyton? He drowned in the hot tub." Sally leaned closer and lowered her voice. "I went in that hot tub just the other night."

Peyton patted her hand. "I know it's a shock, Sally, but I'm sure he wasn't healthy. You know, stress and all that."

"You said it, honey. You said it."

Before Sally could say anymore, a group of young men with bare chests and brightly colored cloth skirts stepped out on the stage, carrying massive drums. Sally made an appreciative noise and fanned herself.

"Oh my goodness," she said. "They are something, aren't they? So lean and masculine and…oh my goodness, so fit."

Peyton laughed and glanced over at Marco, taking his hand. "Sorry, D'Angelo, but I'm gonna need a drink," she said to him.

He kissed her temple. "I completely understand, sweetheart. I completely understand," he answered and signaled for a waiter.

CHAPTER 9

Peyton saw Abe's phone number appear on the screen and she smiled, stepping out onto the balcony to take the call. Marco was in the shower, getting ready for their day of exploration. They planned to hike the trails above the NaPali Coast to see the cliffs from above.

She pressed the video chat button as she settled onto the patio chair, her legs curled under her. Abe's smiling face appeared on the screen, his dreadlocks beaded with orange beads. He wore a shirt that had basketballs all over it.

"Sports phase?" she asked him, a little confused. She didn't remember Abe every saying anything about sports.

"I've been spending a lot of time with Jakey since you've been gone, toots. I wore my baseball ensemble yesterday. The little pants that come to mid-calf are so adorable and I paired them with some orange socks."

"You're wearing basketballs today."

"Well, you can't wear baseballs everyday."

"But it's not basketball season."

"How do you know that, sugar?"

Peyton thought about it. She wasn't sure, but she remembered something about the Warriors being in the playoffs a few months ago. "I don't," she admitted.

"Where's my angel?" said Abe, trying to look beyond her into the hotel room. "I wouldn't be upset if you sent me a photo of him frolicking in the surf."

Peyton smiled. "Have you ever known Marco to frolic?"

Abe braced his chin on his hand. "One can dream, can't one?"

"Yes, one can. How's my dog?"

"Seriously, girl, I call you halfway around the world..."

"Not really."

"...and all you can ask me is how's your dog?"

Peyton gave him a tilt of her head.

"He's awesome. He really likes Jake's Tater. They were all curled up on the couch together yesterday."

"Was Bambi there?"

Abe rolled his eyes. "Good lord, toots, I had to leave. Things were getting X-rated. Do you know what it takes to make me uncomfortable, Peyton?"

"I do. It's a lot."

"I almost took the dogs out of there. I just don't think they should be exposed to that." He shuddered. "Straight sex is really hard to watch, toots. Really hard."

Peyton laughed. "They made me squirm the other morning when Jake called. Bambi was sitting on Jake's lap."

"Yeah, well, she had her tongue in his ear last night."

Peyton made a face. "God, I don't know whether to hope this runs it course quickly or that they shack up together."

"I think the second has already happened."

"Really?"

"We had dinner at her place last night. I don't think Jakey's been back to his apartment since you got married."

"Wow, they're moving fast."

"Mmmhmm, and I don't know, sugar, but I'm not sure this one's ever gonna run its course. They both are gonzo for each other."

Peyton considered that. She couldn't imagine any two people more ill-suited for each other than Bambi and Jake, but if it made them happy, who was she to deny it?

"So, toots, how's *your* sex life?" Abe said, placing his fist under his chin and batting his long lashes at her.

"Seriously? You just said straight sex was not your thing."

"Well, it isn't, but this is the two of you and darlin', you are an epic love story, so your sex life is everyone's thing."

Peyton shook her head. "You're impossible, you know that? I'm not talking about sex with you and you know it."

Abe waved a hand airily. "Fine, fine. Keep all the hot and heavy details to yourself, but I still want a picture of my angel in his swimsuit. You think you can do that for me?"

"I'll think about it," she said.

He smiled at her. "I miss you, little soul sista. You know that?"

"I miss you too, Abe."

A knock sounded at the door. Peyton turned to look back inside the room. Marco stepped out of the bathroom, wearing khaki shorts and a navy blue tank top that showed off the impressive display of muscles in his arms and upper back. Abe let out a whistle.

"I'll tell you, that man gives me heart palpitations," Abe said breathlessly.

Peyton laughed, turning back to him. "Me too, Abe. Me too," she said, fanning herself. "So why don't we talk about your birthday? Maybe you could give me some ideas about what you want?"

Abe was trying to see around her. "You know me, sugar. Something low key and unassuming."

Peyton sputtered. "Low key? You've never been low key in your life. I'm certain when you came out of the womb, you threw your hands in the air and shouted hallelujah!"

"Brooks!" came Marco's voice.

Peyton caught herself and turned around. Chief Kahele and Tavis Makoa stood in the room with a man she didn't recognize. She felt her heart sink, especially when she saw the aggravated expression on Marco's face.

"I gotta go, Abe," she said, glancing back at him.

Abe looked concerned. "Is something wrong, sugar?"

"Yep, looks like we got ourselves a murder."

Abe's face grew grim. "Call me if you need anything."

"I will," she said, then disconnected the call and climbed to her feet, smoothing down her shorts. She stepped into the hotel room and halted before the men. "Chief Kahele, Mr. Makoa?"

"Good morning, Special Agent," said Tavis. "I'm so sorry to disturb you."

"No problem." Her eyes shifted to the third man.

"Thank you for seeing us, Agent Brooks," said the chief. He motioned to the Caucasian man with blond hair, broad shoulders and hazel eyes, wearing a polo shirt and khaki golf pants. "This is Harvey Meridew's partner, Jackson Hughes. He asked to talk with you himself. After hearing what he has to say, I agree that we may need the resources of the federal government on this case. I was hoping you'd be willing to hear him out."

Peyton held out her hand. "Mr. Hughes, nice to meet you. I'm sorry for your loss."

He shook her hand, then rubbed the back of his neck and shifted weight. "I still can't believe it. I've been in shock, I hardly slept all night."

Peyton marked his clothes. "Were you going golfing today, Mr. Hughes?"

He shifted uncomfortably again, glancing at the chief and Tavis. "Business is a strange bedfellow, Agent Brooks. Sometimes the only way to get a meeting with an investor is to agree to a tee-time. Most of my deals are made on the golf course."

"So you were meeting with an investor?"

"State representative, actually. I've been trying to get this meeting for months now. In order to finish the mall we're building, we have to have permits and permits do not come easy on an island, Agent Brooks."

"I can imagine."

"The company was everything to Harvey. I figured he'd want me to keep the meeting since we worked so hard to get it."

"I understand," she said, but she didn't. Still, she wasn't a businessman and she understood they had different priorities from the average person. They had to if they wanted to make their millions. "Do you know if Mr. Meridew had a heart condition, Mr. Hughes?"

"That's the thing, Agent Brooks. Harvey was healthy as a horse. He hardly drank, he didn't smoke, and he ate like a monk – it was all kale and quinoa with him."

"So you don't remember him telling you he was seeing a cardiologist or that he had any concerns about his health?"

"None. Here's what's got me upset, Agent Brooks. Those letters, he didn't believe it was anything, but I told him to take them seriously. They started coming as soon as we broke ground on the strip mall here on Kauai. The environmental groups have been after us since the first shovel was filled, picketing, protesting, trying to get injunctions in court. That's why I had to take this meeting today. I couldn't let it pass me by. The site has even been sabotaged. Scaffolding knocked over, red paint thrown on the equipment."

Peyton shot a look at Kahele. "Have you investigated this?"

"We've investigated and we've put men on it, but we can't watch the building site 24/7. We don't have that manpower here. Besides that, these groups are savvy. They've avoided leaving any evidence or showing any distinguishing characteristics on camera. We finally told Mr. Meridew to hire a security detail to protect the site at night and that seemed to stop the vandalism."

"What about security for Meridew himself?" Peyton asked Hughes.

"He finally went to the police about the letters, but he wouldn't change anything else. He still drove the same car, still went to the same places for dinner. I wanted him to hire a bodyguard, but he refused." Hughes rubbed the back of his neck again. "I should have been more forceful, more insistent. If I had, he might still be alive."

"We don't know what he died from, Mr. Hughes," Peyton reminded him. She focused her attention on Kahele. "Did you find the letter he tossed off the balcony yesterday?"

Kahele shook his head. "But we have the other ones that were delivered."

"When will the ME perform the autopsy?" Peyton asked.

"Today," said Kahele.

"Well then, I have every faith that Chief Kahele is on top of this, Mr. Hughes."

"Harvey was the backbone of our company, Agent Brooks. He worked so very hard for everything he got and he had a vision, but not everyone saw it that way," said Hughes.

"What does that mean, Mr. Hughes?" asked Peyton, sharing a look with Marco.

"Harvey had a number of enemies."

"Enemies?" Peyton repeated.

"I know that sounds melodramatic, but it's true. He and I have been best friends since college. We were college roommates and we got along from the very first day, but Harvey could be a bit..."

"A bit?" prompted Peyton, itching to get this interview over with, so she and Marco could head out on their hike. She still didn't know why they were here. This wasn't an FBI case. It wasn't even a murder case, despite the threatening letters and environmental vandalism.

"Abrasive. He often rubbed people the wrong way."

"Are you saying you're afraid people really wanted to do him harm, Mr. Hughes?" asked Peyton.

Tavis Makoa wrung his hands. This was not doing the manager any good. He looked a little grey and his eyes had bags under them.

"There were a lot of people who..." Hughes sighed heavily and held up his empty hands. "...who wouldn't have minded seeing him dead."

Peyton glanced at Kahele. "Did you pursue the letters at all?"

"We looked into it as much as we could. We couldn't trace them. There were no fingerprints on the envelopes or the paper the letters were printed on, except for the postal workers and Mr. Meridew. They were printed on a computer and mailed from different places according to the postmarks."

"And what did the letters say? Was it different or was it always the same?" asked Marco, the investigator in him getting sucked into it, despite his annoyance.

"The same," said Kahele and Hughes together.

"It's etched in my memory," said Hughes. "They always said, the Menehune are coming."

"The Menehune are coming?" repeated Peyton. "And you took that to be a death threat? It sounds like a prank to me."

"You don't know the legends of the Menehune, Agent Brooks," said Hughes. "They protect the land of Hawaii against any and all invaders. They protect it with lethal force if necessary."

Peyton had had enough. She wanted to go on a hike with her husband and she still saw no reason for these men to be here in her room. "Okay, Mr. Hughes, I understand your concern, but this isn't an FBI matter, I'm afraid."

He reached into his back pocket and took out an envelope, passing it to her. "Really? Not even when a second US citizen is being threatened? I just got this today, this morning to be exact."

Peyton glanced between him and the letter, then she took it and pulled it out of the envelope, unfolding it. Centered in the middle of the paper was one sentence. Peyton scanned it, then looked up into Jackson Hughes' frightened face. The letter read:

The Menehune are coming for you too.

* * *

147

Javier Vargas flatted his palms on the table, his sleeves of tattoos creating an interesting pattern on the wooden tabletop. "Tell me what he said again about the Goblins."

Devan Adams shifted in the chair, curling his hand over his smoothly shaved jaw, but he didn't say anything. Danté glanced at Simons. The huge man nodded.

"He said not to speak of them, that they would destroy everything."

Devan glanced over at the gang task force detective. "What do you know about the Goblins? I mean, I know it isn't much, but remind me again what you've found out."

"They're not like the regular street gangs. They have weapons and money, they're well funded. They don't seem to be territorial and they have links to organized crime."

"When did they start showing up on your radar?" asked Tag, tilting her head so Danté could clearly see the skull tattoo on her neck.

"Less than a year ago. Some of the regular gangbangers we hauled in said they were being crowded out of their regular territory by these well armed Russian mobsters. They were told to get lost or get dead."

"Get lost or get dead," repeated Devan. "How many have gotten dead?"

"Can't really say. They're really good at hiding their dealings, you could say," said Javier. "A lot of their targets go boom!" Javier made exploding motions with his hands.

"That sounds like Eduard Zonov," commented Cho.

Tag and Holmes nodded.

"We'd like to get Zonov on something. We're pretty sure he's one of their suppliers," said Javier.

"Of what?" asked Simons. "Guns, explosives?"

Javier nodded. "All of the above."

"He's probably running all of it through Victor Maziar," said Devan. "Maziar buys the pawn shop and it's the perfect front. So much stuff gets moved in and out of that business, who knows what they're dealing in?"

"Well, we're thinking this stuff with the stop-and-rob might be a RICO case," said Cho.

Devan rubbed his hands over his face. "That means bringing in the feds. I don't want to bring in the feds until we know for sure we've got racketeering going on. Coordinate your efforts with Vargas' office and see if we can get some solid evidence that Maziar or Zonov are running a protection scheme."

"What about Lloyd Murphy's murder?" asked Javier.

"We're still working that in connection with all of this," said Tag. "We think there's a connection, but we just can't make it."

"The blackmailing of the mayor?" asked Javier.

"Could be the case," said Simons. "But the mayor won't admit he's being blackmailed."

The conference room door opened and Lee poked his head inside. "Sorry to interrupt," he said.

"No problem," said Simons, waving him inside. "What's going on?"

"Harper McLeod's here to see Danté. She said it was urgent."

Danté glanced at Cho and Simons. He hadn't called her back the previous day because he felt sure she wanted to know about Renchenko and he wasn't sure how to put her off. He didn't want to lie, but he didn't think Simons would like him discussing the case with a reporter.

"Keep everything off the record," warned Cho. "Don't let her trick you into revealing anything about an ongoing case."

Danté nodded.

"He's serious," said Simons. "If you feel like it's getting away from you, break it off and tell her you'll talk to her another time. Don't let her get you all confused so you reveal more than you should."

"Got it," said Danté.

"In fact," said Devan, stalling him as Danté climbed to his feet. "Just stick to the old standby – no comment – no matter what she wants you to divulge. Just keep saying no comment and she'll get the hint."

"Okay," said Danté, giving them all a nod. "I'll be on my toes."

"You'd better be. Reporters are slippery in the best of times," warned Devan.

Danté thought the same might be said about lawyers, but he kept it to himself.

"Maybe I should come with you?" said Cho.

Lee shook his head. "She said she needed to see Danté alone. She said it was personal."

Cho sat up straighter.

Holmes made a snickering noise. "Getting some journalistic tail…"

Tag slapped him in the stomach with the back of her hand. "Stop being a tool."

Devan leveled a serious look on Danté. "Keep it off the record," he warned sternly.

"I will," said Danté, more confused than ever. What could she possibly want with him? They'd only talked with each other a handful of times. Sure, she'd taken him shopping and he'd escorted her to an art show, but that had all been in the line of work.

He stepped out and found Harper waiting on the other side of the counter. "Ms. McLeod," he said, moving to the half-door.

"I asked you to call me yesterday. Did you get my text?"

"I did, but I was busy."

"I told you it was important."

He opened the half-door. "Let's go talk at my desk."

Lee hesitated by his own. "Can I get you some coffee or something else to drink, Ms. McLeod?"

"Water would be great," she said, walking through the half-door. She wore a pale pink skirt and jacket with a striped pink blouse under it. Her brown hair was caught up in a messy ponytail and her pink heels clicked on the floor as she stepped into the precinct. Danté got a whiff of her vanilla scent and he tried not to breathe it in, but it was hard. She fascinated him, he couldn't deny it.

Usually she was abrasive, but today she seemed agitated. He motioned to his desk, following in Lee's wake as they headed toward the main part of the precinct. When they arrived at his and Cho's desks, he grabbed a chair from another desk and set it up across from his.

She sat down, slinging her purse over the back and smoothing down her skirt. Lee brought her a glass of water and she took it, giving him a tense smile. "Thank you, Lee," she said.

"No problem, Ms. McLeod. Let me know if you need anything else."

Danté sank into his chair a little slower, eying her. He'd never seen her so agitated before. She leaned forward and placed the glass on his desk, then picked it up again and took a sip, setting it down again before she fussed with a loose thread on her skirt.

He swiveled around, bracing his chin on his fist, watching her. She looked up, her green eyes rimmed with mascara and focused on his face. "Do you have gum?"

He opened the top desk drawer and took out a pack, passing it to her. She took the pack, but didn't take a slice, tapping it against her leg. Her fingernails were long and manicured, painted a royal blue.

"How can I help you, Ms. McLeod?"

She held up a hand. "Okay, can we just stop with that? I know you wear briefs, Mr. Spock, so it's ridiculous that you keep calling me by my last name."

He blinked slowly at her. How the hell did she know he wore briefs? He shook away the thought and drew a deep breath. "All right. Before we get started, I have to warn you everything we say is off the record."

She gave him an aggravated look. "Fine. I'm not here as a reporter. God, you're such a Boy Scout. Do you ever loosen up? Do you ever just act like a real human being?"

He continued to watch her, trying to place the vibe he got coming off her. She was clearly agitated, but it wasn't fear, he sensed. It was something else that eluded him.

She touched a hand to the center of her forehead. "Okay, look, I'm sorry. I can be a bit abrasive sometimes."

He arched a brow at that.

"Okay," she said, tapping the gum pack some more. "All the time, but that's the business I'm in. I have to be direct, but I'll be nicer. Boy Scout's honor," she said, flashing him a peace sign.

"That's a pea…" he started to say, then dropped his hand against the desk. It didn't matter. "What's going on, Harper?"

She took out a piece of gum and passed him back the pack. He dropped it on the blotter and watched her run the foil wrapped slice through her long fingers over and over again. It was hypnotizing and he felt a strange flutter in his belly.

"I think you know I come from a very wealthy family," she said.

He forced his eyes to her face. "Right."

"Well, if the McLeods do charitable work, it's to get a tax break or for publicity, but it's all…" She sighed and unwrapped the slice. "…for show."

"I see."

She popped it in her mouth and chewed for a moment, folding the wrapper again and again. "I stopped going to all the charity balls and stuff a long time ago. I got sick of pretending."

"I see," he repeated. Was she going to ask him to escort her to a charity event? He didn't think such a simple thing would make a woman like her into a wreck this way. If she wanted something, she went after it. That had been his experience with her.

"I wanted to do charity work too, but I wanted mine to have meaning, to be something real. I started volunteering at a woman's shelter, *From Hope to Healing*, when I was in college. They help women escape dangerous situations."

"That's very noble of you."

She waved her hand. "Whatever," she said, shaking her head. "Anyway, I run a support group for women who are pregnant and aren't sure how they're going to raise their children. They don't have educations, jobs, they're struggling just to provide for themselves. Some of them are thinking about having abortions, others are thinking about giving the children up for adoption. Some want to keep the baby, but are terrified of the fathers, or they fear they'll end up on the street."

Danté just nodded.

"We meet once a week and the meetings are intense. I mean, sometimes they get really intense. They share things that you wouldn't believe." She messed with the foil and smacked her gum. "I've gotten really close to these women. They're my friends and I care about them."

"All right."

"Luz Gutierrez is one of the women. She's just twenty and almost nine months pregnant. She comes to the group regularly. She wants to keep the baby, but she's so scared of her ex. He's done time for robbery and assault. When she left him, he threatened to hunt her down."

Danté sat up straighter. "And?"

"She didn't come to group two nights ago. She never misses. Never. Usually she's there early."

"Maybe she had the baby?"

"No, I talked with the other girls. They haven't heard from her. I can get her address, but I don't want to violate her privacy."

"If you're worried about her..."

"I am, but I don't want to overstep my boundaries. I mean, I feel really close to these women, but we're not really friends. They have their lives and I have mine."

And her life was a whole lot different from theirs. "Does she have family in the City? Friends she might be staying with since she's so close to giving birth?"

"Her parents are in Mexico. They haven't been able to get back across the border." She made a face. Danté nodded. He understood. "She's an American citizen and she wants the baby to be born here."

"Right." He rubbed his chin. "Where's the father? Do you know?"

"He did time in So Cal. I don't think it was for long. Parole violation or something, but he's out and he could be up here. I just don't know."

"What about friends?"

"She doesn't really have any. Mostly the women in the group and none of them have heard from her." She reached for the water and took another sip. "This is really not like her. She never misses group."

"Maybe she doesn't feel well. I mean, she's at the end of her pregnancy."

Frustration marred Harper's pretty features. "You're not listening. She's going to have this baby and she's all alone. Her ex was abusive to her, her parents are in Mexico, and she lives in some converted hotel room in the Tenderloin!"

"Harper!" Danté said sharply. "I understand. I understand your concern, but I don't know what you think I can do about it. Not showing up for a meeting is her right. It's not a crime."

"What if she's hurt or what if she's having the baby and can't get to the hospital? She didn't even have a cell phone."

"Then she'll have to figure it out herself. There's no crime here. There's no reason for me to intervene."

She stared at him, her green eyes intense, then she grabbed her purse and yanked it off the chair, rising to her feet. "Thanks for nothing, Mr. Spock," she said, turning away.

Danté slumped back in his seat. He didn't know what she wanted from him. Until she had more information, there was nothing more he could do and the truth was Luz Gutierrez was just one woman in trouble in a city filled with them. She took two steps away, then hesitated and turned back around. Coming to him, she held out her hand. Bewildered, he held out his own under hers. She dropped the folded piece of foil into it, gave him a glare, then flounced around and walked toward the front door. Danté studied the piece of foil in his hands, shaking his head. He might have an eidetic memory, but he sure as hell didn't get women, that was for sure.

*   *   *

Marco stared into the laboratory as the medical examiner talked animatedly with Terrence Kahele. Abe would love this set up. All of the equipment was brand new: shining metals, pristine white tiles, gleaming tools. The autopsy room was two rooms actually with a bank of windows splitting the rooms in half. The side he was standing in was for law enforcement to observe the autopsy without contaminating the scene, the other side was the actual autopsy room. The ME had an x-ray and an ultrasound in the same location, so he didn't have to take the body anywhere else and there was a cold storage right next door with an entrance inside the autopsy room. Everything was hermetically sealed.

The medical examiner himself had to be around Marco and Peyton's age, no older, shaggy black hair, Hawaiian features, handsome and muscular. He looked like any surfer dude Marco had ever seen in California.

Behind him, Peyton talked into her phone, pacing back and forth. They hadn't gone on their hike. After Jackson Hughes showed Peyton his letter, she hadn't had any choice. The FBI were now involved and she'd put a call into Radar for advice. Marco was trying not to feel resentful, but it was hard. They'd had just a few days of a honeymoon, but now it was over.

Not that he didn't take death threats seriously. He just wished his FBI wife didn't have to get involved. He knew it wasn't her fault, but that didn't lessen the disappointment any. Since he couldn't be mad at her, he focused all of his rage on the handsome chief of police, Terrence Kahele, but he knew that wasn't fair. Already a high profile one percenter was dead. If another one followed him, Kahele's reputation and possibly his job would be irretrievably damaged.

"I know, Radar, I know," Peyton said. "I will keep you updated every day with developments and if anything happens, I'll call you right away." She shook her head at Marco, then went back to pacing. "I think you should just concentrate on getting well, old man. You know people your age don't heal as quickly as they once did."

Marco smiled and looked back into the autopsy room. Poor Radar. He'd never stood a chance once Peyton had appeared in his life. Much like Marco himself, Radar was wrapped around Peyton's finger.

In the autopsy room, Kahele threw up his hands and turned for the door, the young ME following on his heels. Kahele violently punched the buttons to open the outer door and it made an electronic sound and swished open, then Kahele stepped out.

"I'm just saying, Chief..." complained the young man.

"I can't believe this!" Kahele shouted as Peyton turned to face him, the phone still pressed to her ear.

"Hold on a minute, Radar," she said into the phone. "What's wrong?"

Kahele fixed one hand on his hip and pointed back at the ME with the other one. "He's never done an autopsy before."

The ME held up his empty hands. "That's not completely true."

Marco took a step closer to them, frowning. Peyton's expression sobered and he could hear Radar saying something through the phone. "Hold on, Radar," she told him. "What do you mean he's never done an autopsy before?"

Kahele turned to the younger man. "Tell her!" he ordered.

The young man shifted weight. "I just said, I'd never done one on my own."

Peyton's mouth dropped open and Marco tilted back his head. Yep, there went the honeymoon.

"I've assisted in about a billion autopsies, but the ME on Maui always took the lead. I've just never done one by myself and…" He shrugged his shoulders. "This one's sort of important."

"How long have you been on the job?" asked Peyton.

The young man smiled. "Oh, this is my first week. Yay! It's awesome. I mean, this lab is state…of…the…art!" he said punctuating each word.

Kahele looked at Peyton, his eyes wild. Peyton held up a hand.

"Okay, Doctor…um, what's your name?"

"Haulani Ionakana," he said proudly.

Peyton shot a look at Marco. "Haula—eh…"

"Haulani Ionakana," they could hear Radar say through the phone. Marco hid his smile.

"My friends call me Lani."

Peyton blew out a relieved breath. "Lani, if you've assisted in…um, a billion autopsies…"

"Probably about fifty or so," he said, flashing a smile that could melt any young woman's heart. He rocked on his heels, then glanced at the glowering Kahele and back to Peyton, his smile dimming. "Forty-eight."

"Okay, forty-eight. That's a good number. Surely you're ready…"

Lani started shaking his head no.

"…to perform one on your own."

More head shaking.

Peyton held out a hand, indicating the lab. "You have amazing equipment and state of the art…cutty things."

"Cutty things?" came Radar's voice. "God have mercy…"

"And this isn't your first rodeo, so…"

More head shaking.

"Besides, he probably died of a heart attack."

Head shaking.

Kahele slapped his hands against his thighs. "Why are you shaking your head?" he shouted.

Lani jumped and took a few steps to the side.

Marco felt an affinity for the frustrated chief of police. He'd been here himself many times.

Lani leaned closer to Peyton and pointed over his shoulder. "That man in my cold storage…"

"Right," said Peyton.

"…is Harvey Meridew. He's not only the most hated man in Kauai, but the most powerful."

Peyton's gaze shifted to Kahele.

"He's not wrong," said the chief. "A lot of people didn't approve of Meridew's ventures."

"He also has three ex-wives and I read online that his gardener threatened to smash his face in with a shovel."

Peyton stared hard at Kahele. "Why didn't you tell me these things?"

"Well, you kept saying it wasn't your case and I didn't want to ruin your honeymoon."

Peyton looked at the ground and blew out air, then she lifted the phone to her ear. "Radar, did you get all that?" She turned away, going to the other side of the room for privacy.

Marco felt the ME's eyes on him and he met his gaze.

The ME gave him a broad smile. "How tall are you?"

"Six four."

"Geez, I wish I was six four."

Marco nodded.

"You surf?"

"Tried, but…" Marco shrugged.

"I surf everyday. I'm out catching waves by 5:00AM."

"Of course you are," said Kahele, but Lani ignored him.

Lani continued to study Marco. "You lift weights, don't you?"

"Yeah."

"Yep, but if you surfed, you wouldn't have to do that. Look!" He lifted his shirt and showed Marco his belly. "Six pack, all from surfing. Works every muscle in the body."

"Awesome," said Marco, catching the disgusted look Kahele shot at the ME.

Peyton came back, slipping her phone into her shorts pocket, and stopped before them. "Chief Kahele, the FBI will take the case," she said.

Marco tried not to show his disappointment.

Kahele let out a relieved sigh. "Thank you."

"I'll be your contact in the field and Marco has been authorized to assist me."

"Great," said Kahele.

"I'll need all the information on the case that you've gathered and I'll need a place to work in your precinct."

"Done."

She looked at the ME. "Our Medical Examiner will be flown in tonight or early tomorrow to assist you with the autopsy, Lani."

"Yes!" said Lani with a fist pump.

She gave him a slight smile, then turned back to Kahele. "Now, if you don't mind, I'd like a moment to talk to my husband."

"Of course," said Kahele, motioning for Lani to go into the autopsy room. They went through the door and Peyton turned to face Marco, clasping her hands before her.

"I'm so sorry, Marco."

He shook his head. "It's not your fault."

"I didn't want this to happen."

"I know that."

She came forward and smoothed her hands up his chest. "I promise I'll make it up to you."

He put his hands on her hips and pulled her closer. "You don't have to make anything up to me, sweetheart. This isn't your fault."

She wrapped her arms around his neck. "We get to work a case together again."

He smiled at that. He had missed working cases with her.

"When this is over, we'll talk about me quitting the Bureau. You're right. This is no way to start our life together."

"We can talk about anything you want." But he didn't think she was serious about this. Since they'd gotten up this morning, she'd been filled with a strange energy and he knew it well. She loved solving cases. It was who she was.

"I'm not lying. I hate that this is what our life has become."

"Stop apologizing, Brooks. I'm with you. I'll do whatever you need me to do." He kissed her forehead. "I'm so damn in love with you, woman. If you asked me to jump off the NaPali Coast, I'd do it."

She smiled, sinking her fingers into his hair. "I promise I'll make it up to you," she said in a sultry voice. "And maybe we'll get lucky."

"How do you figure?"

"Maybe it'll turn out that Meridew really did die of a heart attack."

Marco leveled a look on her. "That will never turn out to be the case and you know it."

"Well, I can hope." She kissed him hard on the mouth. "But right now, we need to go shopping."

"Shopping?"

She gave a long suffering sigh. "Oh, yeah, we need orange soda and *Popular Mechanics*."

He frowned. "Why do we need that?"

She patted his chest and eased out of his arms. "Because Igor's coming, D'Angelo, Igor's coming."

CHAPTER 10

Peyton sat in the airport the following morning at 7:00, holding her phone on her knee. Marco had gone to find them coffee and a pastry or something to stave off hunger. Radar's face filled the screen, looking tired. She frowned at him.

"Why do you look so beat, old man?"

He sighed. "I dropped Igor off at the airport at 4:00 to catch his flight at 5:00, which meant I had to get up at 3:00 and get Gwen up at 3:00 to drive us. I'm still not cleared to drive, Sparky."

She frowned. "You're right. What an inconvenience? I mean, of course, you're not on your honeymoon with your hot new husband wanting to spend the early morning hours doing wicked things to him."

Radar made a face. "Please don't give me nightmares, Sparky."

She laughed. "Now you know how I feel when you tell me about you and Gwen getting couples massages."

"But that's sexy, Sparky," he said with a wicked grin. "By the way, we have one scheduled for today."

Now she made a face.

"Is D'Angelo upset?"

"He's not happy, but he's trying to pretend he's okay with this."

"Well, I can imagine this is the last thing he planned to do on his honeymoon. I feel sorry for the big guy."

"But not for me?"

He just stared at her.

"Anyway, can you see if Tank can do his Tank magic and get me anything he can on Harvey Meridew and his company?"

"I'll contact him. Are you sure you're ready for Igor?"

She reached for the shopping bag next to her, opening it. "Orange soda and *Popular Mechanics*."

"His flight leaves tonight at 8:00. Make sure he's on it."

"Are you sure he wouldn't rather spend the night at the hotel and go back tomorrow? That's a terrible lot of hours to go without sleep."

"It's Igor, Sparky. We do not question the method, we just marvel at the results."

Peyton gave him a slow blink of her eyes. "Okay, Gandhi." She shifted on the hard seat. "Look, Radar, I need to talk to you about something serious."

"More serious than murder?"

"Well," she said. Of course, nothing was more serious than murder.

"Just spill it, kid."

"Okay, here goes. I'm not sure this job is going to work with my marriage."

"Why? Did D'Angelo say something?"

"No." She shook her head. "No, I'm saying it. How are we ever going to build a family when all I do is run around, solving cases?"

"I know it's hard, Sparky, but we usually don't get so many cases back to back like we have. Usually there's downtime where we're just glorified paper pushers." He scratched his chin. "Be careful, kid. You're a good agent and you could have a good career here. Right now, you're all caught up in the mystique of being married."

"I don't think that's it."

He arched a brow. "Really? There's a reason it's called a honeymoon…"

"Yeah, Tank told me."

"I mean," he said, enunciating each word. "You're in the glow of being married. You want to spend all your time with him and make him the center of your world."

"He's always been the center of my world, Radar."

"That's cute, but someday, reality's going to set in. You're a crime solver, Peyton. It's in your blood. You aren't going to be able to walk away from that."

"I wouldn't. I'd go back to working at a precinct."

Radar shook his head. "Do you really think that'll be enough for you now that you've got a taste of being in the Bureau?"

"Striker left it. He seemed to have no problem."

"Striker was different. He never had the drive. He was happy being a trainer, but you have an agile mind that wants to figure out the puzzle. You aren't going to be satisfied just sitting on your duff, filling out paperwork anymore."

She shifted uneasily. Some part of her recognized what he was saying, but she couldn't chance losing Marco for a job. "He's the most important thing in my life."

"Then keep it that way. If you give up you, Sparky, you will grow to resent him. You'll grow to resent the marriage. Just as he has to be free to be himself, so do you. The only way a marriage really works is if both people can self-actualize."

She made a scoffing sound. "You're spending too much time meditating."

He shook his head. "On some level, you know I'm right, Sparky."

She looked away, feeling frustrated and worried. Marco had been quiet since yesterday. He'd been attentive, making love to her, walking on the beach with her, but the easy-going fun they'd had had disappeared the moment they saw Harvey Meridew's body outside the hot tub.

"I need to think about it."

"You do that. You think hard and don't make any rash decisions."

"I won't," she said, rubbing the back of her neck.

Radar nodded. "Good. Now, aloha, Sparky."

She smiled. "Aloha, Radar."

"Why even bother?"

"What do you mean?"

"I mean, when a language has only one word, why even bother with it?"

"That's not even a little bit right, Radar. I think there are a lot more words."

"I don't think so. I think I've only heard the one."

She laughed. "I'll get Tank on that for you. I'm sure he has information about the Hawaiian language."

He eyed her again. "I'm sure he does. Aloha!" and he was gone.

She put the phone back in her pocket and sat, staring out at the tarmac beyond the windows. Planes came and went, people hurrying across the asphalt waving lights or moving carts with luggage on them.

She thought about what Radar had said. Would she miss the FBI if she left it? She wouldn't leave law enforcement. She'd still go on cases, but could she go back to being a police officer after she'd been a federal agent? No more traveling, no more seeing strange and wonderful places? She thought of all the things she'd already seen, places she'd never have gone to on her own.

Then she thought of Marco, the man she lay beside each night. The man who she was building a life with, the man who would be the father of her future children. And she wanted those children now. Could she continue on, knowing there would be milestones she would miss, those once in a lifetime experiences that would be gone in a flash? Was her career more important than her family?

She rubbed her forehead, closing her eyes.

"You got a headache?" came Marco's voice.

She looked up. He held a coffee cup out to her. She took it, giving him a smile. "No, I'm fine. Just thinking about everything." She took a sip. Perfect. Just the right amount of sugar. He knew her so well.

He sank down beside her, passing her a muffin. She settled the coffee on the table and pulled open the cellophane bag, breaking off a piece and placing it in her mouth. It was stale, but sweet, so she choked it down. What could you expect at an airport?

"You talk to Radar?"

"Yeah, he got Igor on the plane."

"I looked at the marquee. His flight's on time."

"Good." She shifted and studied his profile. "You know you're my whole world, right?"

He gave her a frown. "Peyton…" he began, then stopped and sighed, sipping at his own coffee, then he shifted to face her. "Look, sweetheart, I'm disappointed. I'm not going to lie about it, but I don't blame you. A man's life is on the line and you had to respond. I get that."

She curled her hand in his. "What if we have a baby, Marco?"

"I hope we do."

"And I miss things like his first word, his first step."

He smiled.

"What?" she said, smiling back at him.

"A son, huh? I like the thought of that. Baseball and basketball and…"

"No football. I won't allow football."

"I played football, Brooks. Look how I turned out."

She leaned her head against his shoulder. "I don't want to miss the firsts."

He leaned his cheek on her hair. "I get that. I don't want to miss them either."

"I never thought about having a family. I never thought about what it would mean, but I don't think you can have it all, Marco. I don't think you can have a career and a family both. Something has to give."

He kissed the top of her head. "Look, you don't have to make that decision now."

She looked up at him, needing more reassurance, and he gave it. He always knew what she needed.

"We'll figure it out. I mean, think about it, Brooks. We already have the biggest family you've ever seen, so we'll figure it out."

"Yeah, there's your brothers and sisters-in-law, and all the nieces and nephews."

"That's not all. There's Abe and Jake and Maria, and apparently, Bambi is now a permanent fixture."

She laughed. "You're right. We'll be fine."

"We'll be fine."

An announcement came over the speaker.

Marco nodded at her grocery bag. "Grab that. Your ME just landed." He rose to his feet and she rose with him, catching up the bag.

"So look, Marco, Igor is a bit eccentric."

He gave her a speaking look. "You think I don't know eccentric," he said and started moving toward the gate.

Peyton followed him, sighing. "Hold that thought," she muttered.

A few minutes later, a young flight attendant led Igor off the plane with a hand on his elbow. Igor waved wildly when he saw Peyton and she waved back.

"Are you here for Dr. Romanowski?" said the young man, passing him over to Peyton.

"Yes, we are. Thank you for escorting him," she said, removing the orange soda from her bag and handing it to Igor.

"Ah, Agent Brooks, you are always so kind to me!" he said, beaming a smile from behind his coke-bottle glasses.

"You're all right now, Dr. Romanowski?" asked the flight attendant.

"Oh yes, I'm in excellent hands. Agent Brooks will take care of me from here."

"Very good. Aloha," said the young man.

"Aloha," said Peyton and Marco together.

Igor looked up at Marco. "Well, you are even larger up close and personal, aren't you?"

Marco held out his hand. "Marco D'Angelo."

Igor took it, shaking vigorously. "Ivan Romanowski, but most people call me Igor. So you're the one that puts the color in Peyton's lovely cheeks. I'm very happy for both of you."

Peyton felt her cheeks color. "I think you'll like this lab, Igor," she said, hooking her arm through his and turning him toward the exit. "They have all the latest equipment."

"That will be something, but you know, my lab is pretty well appointed." He hesitated and looked at her bag. "Do you have anything else for me, Agent Brooks?"

She smiled and took out his *Popular Mechanics*, passing it to him. "It still has that freshly printed smell."

He laughed, a wheezing, asthmatic sound. "You're so clever, Agent Brooks. So clever."

Peyton shared an amused look with Marco, then her cell phone rang. She pulled it out and looked at the display. Tank. Thumbing it on, she held it to her ear. "Hey, Tank."

"Aloha, Peyton!" he said brightly, then his humor faded. "I'm sorry your honeymoon got cut short."

"Yeah, it's okay, Tank."

"Radar just called and said you want any information I can scare up on Harvey Meridew and Dewdrop Construction."

"Yes, anything at all. Also Jackson Hughes, his CFO. He's also getting death threats."

"Oh my," muttered Igor, clutching his orange soda and magazine close.

"On it," said Tank.

"And Tank, while you're at it, Radar needs some information on the Hawaiian language."

Marco shot her a questioning look, but she shrugged innocently.

"The Hawaiian language?" asked Tank.

"Right. The origin, the development, the number of words."

Tank made a curious noise. "Okay, I'll get right on it. When does he need this by?"

"As soon as you can. He's dying to learn," she said.

"Mmmmhmmm," said Tank. "I got you. He made an insensitive comment and you're taking the opportunity to school him in the error of his ways."

"You know me so well," she said with a laugh.

"I'm on it," he answered and disconnected the call.

*　*　*

Danté rose as Bartlet escorted Cashea up to the courtroom. She had her arms wrapped around herself and she was shivering. She wore a skirt and a button up blouse in blue. Danté smiled at her.

"Are you cold?" he asked.

She shook her head jerkily. "Scared."

He motioned to the seats behind them. "Let's sit down. The ADA's in the courtroom."

They took seats, but Cashea sat at the very edge between him and Bartlet. Bartlet gave Danté a commiserate look. Danté felt horrible putting the girl through this.

A moment later, Javier Vargas appeared, striding down the hall in a suit and tie. Danté had never seen the gang task force detective looking so professional before. Rising, Danté shook hands with him, then he motioned to Cashea.

"You remember Cashea Thompkins, Inspector Vargas?"

Javier offered her his hand. "Nice to see you again, Cashea. Did your mother come with you today?"

Cashea shook her head, her dark curls sliding down her back. "She gots to take care of LeJohn. He can't be left alone."

Javier nodded, then passed her a business card. "I want to talk with her and you when this is over. I have good news for you."

Cashea took the card, eying him skeptically. "You serious? Don't play me none."

Javier smiled. "I'm not playing you. With your help today, we are closer to stopping gang violence on the street. I found a couple of programs that promised their support."

Cashea put the card inside her shirt, sliding it into her bra. "Mama will call this afternoon."

"Good," said Javier.

The courtroom door opened and Devan stepped out. "Oh good, you're here," he said. "Come on in."

Javier and Bartlet moved toward the door. Danté followed, but Cashea grasped his arm. He looked down at her.

"I'm scared."

He patted her hand. "I know, but I'll be there and the ADA and Inspector Vargas. We won't let anything happen to you."

She hesitated a moment more.

"I promise, Cashea."

Finally she nodded and walked to the door Devan held open. Stepping inside the courtroom, Danté took in the empty rows of chairs, the spindle barricade between the spectators and the lawyers, the long table with recording equipment on it and the judge's bench. The judge already sat in her seat, an older woman with steel grey hair and a stern expression. Directly below her was a nametag that read Judge Janice Hunter.

With their back to the spectators was a woman and man. Danté recognized the man as Chicago, or Roscoe Butler. Butler was twenty with an afro and scruffy beard on his jaw. He wore a suit, but it didn't look like it fit him very well. Cashea sucked in air and stopped.

Danté took her elbow, helping her into the seat that Devan indicated to the left. They sat down next to Javier and Bartlet. Cashea worried the hem on her skirt with her fingers and her eyes darted around the room.

Devan stopped at the table, straightening his cuffs.

"Call your first witness, ADA Adams," said the judge.

"I call Officer Danté Price," he said loudly.

Danté rose, feeling Cashea's eyes on him. His heart hammered beneath his ribs, but he stepped through the gate and walked to the witness stand, keeping his eyes fixed on the seal of California behind the judge's chair.

The bailiff stepped in front of him. "Hold up your right hand."

Danté did as instructed.

"You do solemnly state that the testimony you may give in the cause now pending before this court shall be the truth, the whole truth, and nothing but the truth, so help you God," said the bailiff.

"I do," answered Danté.

"You may be seated," said the judge.

Devan gave him a closed mouth smile. "State your name for the record please."

"Officer Danté Emanuel Price."

"Officer Price, were you on duty the night the suspect, Roscoe Butler, was brought in for questioning?"

"I was. I was guarding the suspect while we waited for one of the inspectors to question him." He glanced at Chicago.

The younger man glared at him, his expression savage.

"Were you aware of the charges against Mr. Butler?"

"I was. Mr. Butler was being questioned in the shooting death of Jamaad Jones."

"Did Mr. Butler ask for counsel during the time you were in the interrogation room with him?"

"He did and I instructed him to wait for the public defender to arrive."

"Did you question him?"

"Only after he continued to talk to me, despite my warnings."

"Did he seem to understand your warnings?" asked Devan.

"Objection," said the woman sitting next to Butler. She wore a sharp black suit. She was in her forties with short brown hair and she peered at him over the rim of her glasses. "Calls for speculation on the part of the witness."

"Sustained," said the judge.

"Officer Price, how many times did you tell Roscoe Butler to wait for counsel?"

"Objection," said the public defender. "How is he supposed to remember that?"

"Officer Price," said Devan, holding up his hand.

Danté looked at the judge. "I have an eidetic memory."

She gave him a ghost of a smile. "You may answer the question then."

"Twice," said Danté, turning back to Devan.

"Objection, Your Honor, how can we prove Officer Price's claim about his memory?" said the lawyer.

The judge turned to Danté, putting her chin on her fist. "Can you tell Ms. Douglas what her first objection was?"

Danté nodded. "ADA Adams asked if Mr. Butler understood my warnings, Ms. Douglas objected on the grounds that it would force me to speculate, and you sustained her objection."

The judge gave the lawyer a closed mouth smile. The lawyer rolled her eyes.

"Continue, ADA Adams," the judge said.

"Did the suspect, Roscoe Butler, admit to shooting Jamaad Jones?"

"He said the Big Block gang disrespected his gang, the Mainline Gang, that they didn't respect their territory and they beat LeJohn Thompkins, aka Jupiter, so bad he…" Danté hesitated.

"He what?" pressed Devan.

Danté looked at Butler. "He can't even shit for himself."

The judge glanced down to hide her smile.

"Go on," said Devan.

"He said he wasn't aiming at Jamaad, that he didn't mean for him to die, that he didn't mean to shoot a kid, but…"

"But?" asked Devan.

"He did."

Butler dropped his eyes to his bound hands. The lawyer sucked in air and exhaled.

"No further questions," said Devan.

The judge nodded. "Ms. Douglas?"

"Did he seem remorseful?" asked the lawyer.

"Objection. Calls for speculation on the part of the witness," said Devan, taking his seat again.

"Sustained."

The lawyer held up a hand. "Did he say anything to indicate that he felt sorrow for what had happened?"

"He said that what happened to Jupiter, LeJohn Thompkins, was wrong. That his mother couldn't keep lifting him. He said it wasn't right that he had to wear diapers."

Cashea shuddered and curled over on herself.

"What about remorse for Jamaad Jones? Did he tell you he was sorry for shooting him?"

Danté met her gaze steadily. "No, no he didn't."

The lawyer slumped back in her chair. "No further questions, Your Honor."

"You may step down, Officer Price."

Danté rose and walked to the spectators' section.

"Any other witnesses, ADA Adams?"

"I call Cashea Thompkins to the stand."

Danté waited in the aisle for Cashea to rise. She stood and looked at him, shivering violently.

"I can't do this," she whispered.

"You can." He glanced at the judge. "Think about Jamaad and the pictures of the dogs. Think about how badly he wanted to help them."

"Ms. Thompkins," said the judge.

Cashea drew a deep breath, then she walked toward the stand. The bailiff met her and swore her in as Danté took his seat. Her voice trembled as she spoke and when she sat, she sat on the edge of the chair again, her hands clasped tightly in her lap.

"It's all right, Ms. Thompkins," said the judge. "We're not here to hurt you."

She shot a look at Butler. "That's what you says," she muttered.

Devan rose to his feet. "State your name for the record."

"Cashea June Thompkins," she said under her breath.

"You're going to have to speak up, Ms. Thompkins," said the judge.

"Cashea June Thompkins!" she shouted defiantly.

A number of amused smiles filtered through the room. Danté didn't feel like smiling. He knew how terrified she was and it was his fault. He'd promised her this wouldn't happen and yet here she was, facing down a man that terrified her.

"Your brother is LeJohn Thompkins?" asked Devan.

She jutted out her chin. "He is. They calls him Jupiter."

"Who does, Ms. Thompkins?"

"His gang. The Mainline Gang."

"Why do they call him that?" asked Devan.

"He was a big dude. You know, he was 'bout three hunnered pounds, over six feet tall."

"That is big. You said *was*? Why?"

"He lost so much weight after the Big Block Gang gots after him. He gots brain damage, can't walk no more," she said, glancing at the judge.

"I'm sorry," said the judge.

She nodded, chewing on her inner lip. "It's bad at home. My mama, she has to do everthing for LeJohn. He can't even go to the bathroom by hisself."

Devan nodded. He pointed to Butler. "Do you know the suspect?"

She closed her eyes and swallowed hard, then she lifted her chin again. "Yeah."

"Who is he?"

"Roscoe Butler, but they calls him Chicago."

"How do you know him, Ms. Thompkins?"

"He run with LeJohn in the Mainline Gang."

"Has he been to your house?"

She swiped a hand under her nose. "Yeah, he been to our house."

Devan picked up a pen and ran it through his fingers. "Did you know Jamaad Jones, Ms. Thompkins?"

She released a shivery pant. A tear slipped down her cheek. "Yeah, I knew him. We went to school together."

"Did you talk to Jamaad Jones?"

She nodded. "We talk just 'bout everday. He was a nice kid." She wiped the tear away. "He liked dogs. He wanted to be a dog trainer, save them and stuff from the pound." Her bottom lip quivered and more tears rushed down her cheeks. "He wanted to do something good, something special." She looked at Butler, met his gaze directly. "He wanted to do good things!" she said loudly to him. "And you took that away. You took that away from him!"

"Objection," said his lawyer.

"Sustained," said the judge.

"Cashea," said Devan, drawing her attention back to him. "How did you know Roscoe Butler was the man who shot Jamaad Jones?"

She used both hands to wipe away the tears and sat straighter in the seat. Danté marveled at her courage, at her fortitude. She rubbed her lips together, then she took a deep breath. "I knowed because he told LeJohn."

A murmur went through the courtroom. Devan waited for it to pass. "He told your brother?"

"He came to see LeJohn after the shooting. LeJohn don't know people is there, he can't do nothing for hisself, so

Mama told me to keep an eye out. I was looking through the door, I heard him."

"What did you hear?"

"He told LeJohn he made the Big Block Gang bleed." She closed her eyes and shuddered, then took another deep breath. Finally, she looked back at Butler, her eyes hard, sparking with fury. "He told LeJohn he splattered their brains all over the street."

* * *

Marco sat in the viewing room with Chief Kahele, watching Igor and Lani perform the autopsy. Peyton had stepped out to call Tank to get the information on Meridew and Hughes, but Marco knew it was because she couldn't stomach the nightmare that was going on beyond the windows of the hermetically sealed room.

Kahele sat two seats down with his hands clasped between his knees, watching as Igor removed Meridew's heart and weighed it. Marco crossed his ankle over his knee and pulled at a string on his shorts. Watching the autopsy didn't bother him the way it did Peyton, but he didn't love seeing them take the man apart.

"So, honeymoon, huh?" said Kahele.

"Yep," said Marco.

"First marriage?"

"Only marriage."

Kahele nodded.

"You married?"

"Divorced."

"Kids?"

"Two, boy and girl. Kids?"

"Nope," said Marco. "Someday."

"Yep." Kahele leaned back, draping his arms over the two chairs next to him. "So, FBI?"

"Yep."

"Young for Special Agent."

"Yep."

"Young for Captain."

Marco shrugged. "Young for Chief of Police."

"Yep." Kahele looked at Marco's leg. "Shot?"

"Yep."

"Sorry." He pulled back the throat of his shirt, showing Marco a scar on his shoulder. "Pain in the ass."

"Yep."

Peyton opened the door and stepped inside. She studiously avoided the window and stopped in front of Kahele, turning her back to the horror show going on behind her. "So, I had my partner dig up information on Meridew. He's still working on Jackson Hughes and Dewdrop Construction, but as Lani said, Meridew has three ex-wives, all contentious divorces. He's been sued a number of times and an environmental group, *Freedom Kauai*, filed an injunction against the strip mall, but lost in court."

"Like Hughes told you, the strip mall has been vandalized. They threw red paint on the equipment, graffitied a trailer that was left on site, and knocked down scaffolding."

"Do you think it was this *Freedom Kauai?*"

"We couldn't prove it."

"What did the graffiti say?" asked Marco.

"Go home, haole," said Kahele.

"Go home what?"

"Haole. Means white people," said Kahele.

"Anything about Menehune?" asked Marco.

"The Menehune angle was just in the letters, but in legend, the Menehune are believed to be the protectors of the island. There are many fables about them righting trees that were cut down, chasing off or killing people who attempted to take something from the islands. I wouldn't be surprised if the Menehune connection doesn't tie back to the environmental group."

Peyton glanced over at Marco. "Do you remember the story Nani told at the Crab Shack about the Menehune?"

"Ululani and the Baker man, I remember it."

"She said the Menehune protected the land at all costs. Do you think she told that story because of Meridew? Do you think it had anything to do with him or the construction just down the road from their shop?"

Marco shrugged. "She said that weird thing to you before she told it."

Peyton nodded.

"What?" asked Kahele.

"She said I had important work on Kauai. I wonder if she guessed I was law enforcement."

"How?" asked Kahele.

Peyton shrugged. "No idea. Her granddaughter said she had the sight."

Marco's attention was snagged as the two MEs pulled off their gloves and draped a sheet over Meridew's butchered corpse. He glanced at the clock over the autopsy table. It read 4:00 and Igor had to be at the airport by 6:00 for his flight back to San Francisco. This day of their vacation was a waste and they weren't going to get it back.

It suddenly dawned on him that they only had two more days of their vacation left and if it turned out Meridew didn't die of a heart attack, Marco was supposed to be back at work on Thursday. It was already Monday.

"Brooks," he said, nodding at the window as Igor and Lani headed toward the door.

She glanced over her shoulder, then turned as the door opened and they stepped out. Igor gave her a grim smile, but Marco couldn't tell anything from that. "Hey, Igor," she said, smiling back at him. "You've been at it a long time."

"Yes, we have, Agent Brooks, and I'm sorry to say we only have a partial answer for you."

Kahele rose to his feet. "Can you tell if he was murdered or not?"

Igor looked at the young man beside him. "Lani?"

"Poisoned," said Lani, rubbing the back of his neck wearily. "We're just not sure with what yet. We've got to run more tests."

Marco bowed his head. He felt Peyton's eyes on him. Of course the bastard was poisoned, what else?

"How long will that take, Igor?" she asked.

He held up his empty hands. "It's a fascinating puzzle, but the physical examination points us in many different directions. We're going to have to look at blood, prepare tissue samples, do toxicology reports."

"You have a flight out at 8:00," she said.

"I won't be making that flight, Agent Brooks. We're not even sure about the mode of delivery, although I have a theory, but I need more evidence. Lani said he could set up a cot for me in this room tonight and I can shower in the hazard room."

"No!" Peyton said sharply. "I'll get you a room at our hotel."

Igor rubbed a hand over his bald head. "That would probably be best, Agent Brooks. I've been up all night and my eyes are getting blurry. I think I need to get a few hours of rest before I get back at it."

She nodded. "Lani can clean up here. You come back to the hotel with us. I'll get you some orange soda on the way. Do you need anything else?"

"Well," said Igor, moving toward the outer door with her, "a toothbrush might be nice and some pajamas."

"We'll get those for you," she said, taking his arm. Marco followed along behind, trying hard not to let this completely expected change in events sour his mood. He couldn't be the first man to have his honeymoon hijacked by a murder, right? Sometimes the newlyweds decided to off each other. At least he and Peyton didn't feel like doing that. Yet.

"You know what I'd really like to try, Agent Brooks?"

"What, Igor?"

"I've heard of these things called saunas where they have the rocks and the steam."

"Sauna?" she asked.

He nodded. "I've never tried one before, but I think it would be really nice. Really relax me, you know? I get so wound up in a new place. I don't like spending the night away from home, but a sauna might really do the trick."

Peyton glanced over her shoulder at Marco as she pushed the outer door open and led Igor into the parking lot. By the sheepish smile she gave him, Marco just knew he and Igor were going to get up close and personal in the sauna that night. He just freakin' knew it. Good thing he loved that woman something fierce.

CHAPTER 11

Peyton braced the phone against her empty coffee cup and rifled through the documents she'd printed at Kahele's precinct the previous night. On the phone display, Tank and Radar did the same thing, sitting side by side in the conference room at the FBI headquarters in San Francisco.

"Meridew has a civil settlement," said Radar. "He threw a glass of bourbon at the wall, smashing it. His secretary was coming in the door and got cut by flying shards. Guy had an anger management problem, it seems."

"Yeah, I saw some of that with the staff at the hotel," said Peyton. "You said settlement? So it never went to court?"

"No, she left his employment with a nice little chunk of change."

"He had three ex-wives," said Tank, shifting papers. "One on Kauai, one on the big island, and one on Maui."

"He sure got around," said Peyton.

"The company has had injunctions brought against them a few times for environmental violations," said Radar.

"But their financial disclosures look in order. I'll have to go through that with a closer eye," said Tank, "but on the surface it looks clean."

"The ME told me Meridew's gardener wanted to bash his head in with a shovel," said Peyton.

"Awesome," said Radar, rubbing his eyes. "So, instead of no suspects, you've got a whole host of them. What were you telling me about the old woman who told you about the Menehune? Could she be a suspect?"

Peyton shrugged. "No idea. Her granddaughter's crab shack is down the road from the strip mall Meridew was building, but she had to be in her nineties, Radar. I don't think she'd poison anyone."

"Poison is usually a woman's murder weapon. Women are seven times more likely to kill with poison than men," said Tank.

Peyton made a face.

"What about her granddaughter?" asked Radar.

"We can go out and talk to them," said Peyton. "But seven times more likely to kill with poison, Tank?"

"Well, I mean, everything being relative. Men commit 90% of the murders in this country, Peyton, but when women kill they use a variety of methods and poison is one of their most frequent weapons."

"So ex-wives?" said Peyton.

"Good place to start," said Radar.

"Hughes has a squeaky clean record," said Tank. "Not even a parking or speeding ticket. He's been on Kauai for the last twenty years. He came there before Meridew."

"How do you know that, Tank?" asked Peyton.

"There's an article online about their partnership. They were college roommates at the University of Hawaii on Maui. When they graduated, they opened *Dewdrop Construction*. At first it was to build green housing, but then they got into more commercial ventures. That seems to have been Meridew's influence."

"Well, I told Kahele I wanted to talk to Hughes today after we drop Igor back at the lab."

"How's Igor doing?" asked Radar.

She glanced over her shoulder into the room. Marco hadn't come back yet. "Marco took him to get something to eat. Did you know he won't touch eggs?"

"Embryonic chickens," said Tank and Radar together.

"Yep, that's what he said. He wanted fried rice. Fried rice at 7:00 this morning."

"Is D'Angelo about ready to wring his neck?" said Radar with amusement in his voice.

"Marco's been really patient with him. Igor wanted to go in the sauna last night, but I couldn't take him because he didn't have a swimsuit, so Marco had to go."

Radar chuckled. "You gotta do something special for your man, Sparky. I can see if I can locate a vintage Vette."

Peyton gave him an arch look. "I'm not buying him a Vette for going in the sauna, Radar, but I do need you to do something for me. He's supposed to go home tomorrow, back to work. Can you get him on as a consultant again if he agrees?"

"Are you sure he can be away from the precinct that long, Sparky?"

"I'll ask him, but I just can't stand the thought of him going home without me and with this many suspects, I could use his experience here. This Meridew character had three ex-wives and a secretary just waiting to put arsenic in his oatmeal."

"I'll work on getting D'Angelo on as a consultant, but you'd better ask him first," said Radar.

"Thank you." She heard the door open and looked over her shoulder. "Hey, I've got to go. We need to get Igor back to the lab. Call me if you find out anything in the financial records, Tank. Look at the divorce settlements if you can."

"On it," he said.

"Aloha, Sparky," said Radar and disconnected the call.

Peyton rose to her feet and stepped into the room, giving Marco a sheepish look. "Did you find fried rice?"

"Yep," he said. "Third stop."

"I'm so sorry," she said, wringing her hands. She needed to talk to him about staying, but she wasn't sure he was in the mood for more nonsense.

He took a seat on the end of the bed and held out his hand for her. "Come here, sweetheart."

She walked over and he pulled her between his legs, wrapping his arms around her waist. She braced her hands on his shoulders and looked into his blue eyes.

He touched her chin. "Why do you look worried?" he asked.

"Because I have something to talk to you about and I don't want you getting upset with me."

"Okay?" He gave her a speculative look. "I have something to talk to you about too."

She closed her eyes. "You're leaving tomorrow, aren't you? You don't want to stay here with me. You want to get back to work. I understand, it's just we've had so little time together and our marriage is so new and I'm not trying to say my job is more important than yours because it definitely isn't. I would never think that and I know you've already done so much for me with the wedding and the honeymoon, and I've ruined it with this case, but..."

"Brooks!" he said sharply.

She opened her eyes and stared at him.

"God, sweetheart, when you get going, there's no stopping you." He curved his hands over her hips. "I'm not ready to go back yet."

She gave him a surprised look. "What?"

"It's kinda fun being on a case with you again, like old times. I have enough vacation to take another week. I already called Defino and she agreed to check in at the precinct, but Simons seems to have everything under control, so I thought I'd stay. At least another week."

"Really?" She couldn't help the smile that blazed across her face. "Well, don't get mad, but I already asked Radar to look into bringing you on as a consultant again. If he can, you won't have to use your week of vacation."

He smiled, drawing her closer. "Whatever works, just so long as I get another week with you," he said, then he slid his hands up her back and drew her to him, kissing her.

She melted against him, climbing onto his lap and threading her hands through his dark hair. She couldn't believe how happy he made her. He intuitively knew what she needed even before she knew she needed it. There would never be another man like him, ever.

Banging on the door yanked them apart.

"Agent Brooks! Agent Brooks! I've finished my fried rice. I'm ready to go!"

Marco placed his forehead against her chest and groaned.

She sighed. "Let's get him to the lab, so he can finish and go home," she said softly.

Marco nodded. "Please. He saw the list of massages in his room and he wants us to try the hot rocks massage tonight if he's still here."

Peyton couldn't help but laugh. "Ah, you made a friend, D'Angelo."

He gave her a narrow eyed look. "I made a friend? He's half in love with you, Brooks. You got another Stan Neumann on your hands, woman, and you don't even know it."

She slowly slid off his lap. "It's because I'm irresistible, D'Angelo," she said in her sultriest voice.

He gave her a smoky look in return. "That's the God's honest truth, sweetheart," he purred. "That's the God's honest truth."

After dropping Igor at the lab to begin the second leg of the autopsy, they swung by the precinct and picked up Chief Kahele.

"Aloha," he said, sliding into the backseat.

"Aloha," repeated Peyton and Marco.

"Jackson Hughes agreed to meet with us in his office this morning."

"Is this the same office he shares with Meridew?" asked Marco.

"Yes, it's their corporate office in Lihue. Apparently, they have bigger offices on Maui, but they've been working out of this one since they began the strip mall."

"Do we have a warrant to search Meridew's space?" asked Peyton.

"I'm working on it," said Kahele. "I should know by this afternoon."

The drive to Dewdrop Construction didn't take long and Peyton pulled into the parking garage beneath the building that Kahele indicated, parking the rental car, then they got out and headed for the elevator. She didn't have any of her professional clothes in Kauai and she didn't want to go shopping for more of what she had in abundance back home, so she'd opted for a floral sundress and a light sweater. It was the best she could manage out of what she had.

Marco wore a plain blue button-up with jeans, but the humidity of the day was already beginning to make its presence known and she wished they could head to the beach to play in the surf rather than work on a case.

They took the elevator to the eleventh floor and got out. A middle aged woman with long, sleek black hair greeted them in a very generic looking waiting room with blue upholstered chairs, faux wood accent tables, and a tiled floor.

"Aloha, I'm Doreen Kim," she said brightly after they'd all shown her their badges and introduced themselves. "Mr. Hughes is waiting for you." She led them down a short hallway with two doors on either side. One had Meridew's nameplate on it.

"Have you worked for Mr. Meridew and Hughes long?" asked Peyton.

"I've been Mr. Hughes' secretary for the last ten years," Doreen said.

"Who is Mr. Meridew's secretary?"

Doreen hesitated outside Hughes' door and gave Peyton an uncomfortable smile. "He currently doesn't...um, didn't have one." She shook her hair back over her shoulders. "His last secretary, Celia, quit."

"Is she the one who sued him for throwing a glass at her?"

Doreen dropped her eyes.

"Anything you can tell us helps, Ms. Kim," said Peyton.

"Yes. We've tried to hire for the position, but…" She sighed. "You could say Mr. Meridew developed quite a reputation for being…"

"For being?" prompted Peyton.

Doreen met her gaze with her dark eyes. "Unpleasant."

"Thank you," said Peyton. "One more thing, Ms. Kim."

"Please call me Doreen."

"Doreen," repeated Peyton, smiling. "Did you see the death threat Mr. Hughes got the other day?"

"I did. It came through our mail. It scared me to death." Then she flinched at her choice of words.

"Have you gotten any others?"

"Not for Mr. Hughes, but there were a number that Mr. Meridew got. He turned them all over to the authorities." She nodded at Kahele.

"I have them in a file," he told Peyton.

"I need to see them when we get back to the precinct," she said, then she motioned to Kahele. "Can you give her a business card so she can call us if she remembers anything else?"

Kahele took one out of his pocket and passed it over. Doreen thanked him and then knocked on Hughes' office door.

"Come in," came Hughes' voice.

Doreen pushed the door open and poked her head inside. "Mr. Hughes, the police are here to talk to you."

"Let them in, Doreen," he said.

She opened the door all the way and stepped inside. Peyton, Marco and Kahele followed her into another generic space with very basic furnishings – a desk, a rolling desk chair, a table with armchairs situated around it, a credenza behind the desk, and a filing cabinet. The paintings on the walls were generic prints of Hawaiian flowers and there didn't seem to be any pictures of family on his desk. In fact, the only personal item was an ornate wooden box sitting in the middle of the table to their left.

Jackson Hughes rose from the desk chair and came toward them, holding out his hand.

"Aloha," he said.

His grip was firm as Peyton shook with him, but there were bags under his eyes and his hair was disheveled. He'd seemed a lot more polished when he was in her hotel room the other day.

"Have you been getting any sleep, Mr. Hughes?"

"Jackson, please," he said, motioning for them to take seats at the table. "Not much. The letter spooked me and I'm having a hard time relaxing enough to really sleep."

"We have a police detail outside your house, Mr. Hughes," said Kahele.

"I know that, Chief, and I'm grateful, it's just with Harvey's death and everything else, I'm a bundle of nerves."

"Mr. Hughes," said Doreen. "You remember you have that lunch with the county engineer at *Exotica* today at 1:00."

Hughes let out a heavy sigh as he slumped in the chair. "That's right. Confirm the reservation, please, Doreen."

"I already did, sir."

"Thank you, that's all."

She backed out of the room and Hughes glanced at the digital clock behind his desk, then he focused on them.

"Have you been to *Exotica*, Agent Brooks? You really must try it before you return to the mainland. It's amazing. They serve the most exotic dishes you'll ever find. You can try Kopi Luwak, Hákarl, Bird's Nest Soup, Fugu Sashimi, Gnocchi with Truffles…" He laughed. "I can go on and on. Just remember, when you make a reservation, you have to be there on time. If you're late, they give it away and still charge you a minimum for the dining experience."

"What?" said Peyton. "They charge you for eating there when you didn't get to eat?"

"It's very exclusive. If you want to go, I'll make reservations for you, but just understand how important it is to be exactly on time."

Peyton shook her head. "I think we'll pass, but thank you for the thought. My husband's a vegetarian, so it doesn't sound like they have a lot on the menu that he could eat."

"No," said Hughes with a laugh. "I suppose not."

"So, if you don't mind, Jackson, we'd like to get to business," said Kahele. "We have a few questions about Harvey Meridew and your business."

"Of course."

Peyton shared a look with Marco. Usually she had Radar to run interference and explain to the local authorities that this was sort of her specialty, but he wasn't here and she didn't feel right about stepping in and taking over. She set the pad Robbie had given her on the table and pulled the pen out of the binding.

"Do you mind if I take notes, Jackson?" she asked.

"Not at all."

"So, who do you think wanted to kill Harvey?" said Kahele bluntly.

Hughes reared back. Peyton stared up at the acoustic tiles in the ceiling. This was why she preferred to handle the questioning herself. Marco studied his hands, not able to hide his grimace.

"Excuse me, Chief," said Hughes.

"Who exactly wanted Harvey Meridew dead?"

"Dear God, I don't know," said Hughes, clearly alarmed by the question.

Peyton blew out air, reaching over to touch Kahele's forearm. "Do you mind if I try?"

He gave her a *help yourself* look and leaned back in his chair. Peyton offered Hughes a disarming smile.

"When we talked the other day, I got the impression you and Harvey were close? Is that right?"

"We were," he said, his shoulders relaxing. "We were roommates in college. A lot of people thought he was abrasive, but I knew that was just Harvey's way, you know. He wasn't really a people person, but damn, the man had drive."

"The idea for the business was yours though, right?"

"Well, I got my business degree and wanted to go into construction. It was a good time. Real estate was thought to be the safe gamble. Harvey got his degree in civil engineering and it just seemed like a good fit."

Peyton nodded. "Where did you go to college?"

"University of Hawaii, Maui."

"And you stayed in Maui?"

"Right. Harvey went back to San Diego. That's where his parents were."

"Are they still there?"

"They died years ago, one right after the other."

"Did Harvey have any children?"

"Nope."

"Are *you* married?"

"Divorced. Once was enough for me," he said, giving her wide eyes.

She laughed. "Any children?"

"Nope. Always wanted them, but Tricia couldn't have them. I think that's what contributed to the divorce."

"I'm sorry," she said. "When you first opened the business on Maui, you were building green homes, right?"

"Right." Hughes gave a laugh. "You do your homework, Agent Brooks?"

"Thank you," she said, glancing at Marco. She set the pen down on the pad, her eyes falling on the intricately carved box. She could see human figures on the edges and the top. It looked like they were dancing. "Beautiful box," she said, reaching out to trace her finger along a figure.

Marco's eyes followed her touch, but he didn't say anything.

"So, Jackson, it was Harvey's idea to go into commercial building, wasn't it?"

"It was. God, he was a man of vision. He saw the opening and he jumped into it with both feet. I was scared to death, but he said it was the only way for us to really make any money. And did we ever. We're both multimillionaires from his vision."

She tilted the lid on the box and looked inside. Marco shifted uncomfortably. She glanced at him, but he was watching what she was doing. She wasn't going to hurt it. She just wanted to see what was inside.

Cigars.

"You smoke cigars, Jackson?"

"Cubans. It's my one vice. I allow myself one a day."

"Mine's chocolate," she said, setting down the lid. It tilted and the side panel fell off the box.

Marco closed his eyes.

"Oh God, I'm so sorry."

"No worries, Agent Brooks," said Hughes, picking up the side panel and popping it back on the box, shutting the lid. "It happens all the time. I broke it a long time ago, but I haven't gotten rid of it. I like the way it looks."

Peyton shot another look at Marco, then put her hands in her lap, clasping them tightly. "Again, I'm sorry."

He waved it off, not showing a bit of annoyance or anger. "Like I said, it's no big deal."

"It must have been hard, shifting from green building to commercial."

"I liked green building, but I'd never complain about becoming a millionaire, Agent Brooks."

"No, I guess not," she said with a laugh. "Still, you didn't have environmental groups targeting you when you were building green."

He sighed. "No, we didn't."

"Jackson, do you have any idea who might have wanted to kill Harvey? Who might be threatening you now?"

"I wish I did. I'm terrified, Agent Brooks. Do you know how Harvey was poisoned? Did they slip it in his food, his drink?"

"We're working on it."

"Am I safe to come to work?"

She glanced at Kahele.

"We have an undercover officer stationed outside the building and there's one in the lobby. It's best to stick to your regular routine for now."

"Will the officers be there when I go to lunch? Do I dare go to lunch? What if Harvey was poisoned at a restaurant?"

"The officers will be there. I'd only go to establishments where you trust the proprietors, Hughes," said Kahele.

"Is there anyone that both you and Harvey had a disagreement with?" asked Peyton.

"Just the environmental group, *Freedom Kauai*. Their director, Manny Wong, brought a bunch of protestors to the site. They started chanting and blocking our workers from even getting on the location. Our foreman called us and both Harvey and I went out. We got into it with Manny and the cops had to come. They moved the protesters to the other side of the street, but Manny said he'd get back at us."

"Those were his words? He'd get back at you?"

Jackson nodded.

"What's the name of your foreman, Jackson?"

"Teddy Nakamura."

"Is he working today?"

"No, we haven't been able to work. We have a court hearing in a week to start construction again. We had to have new environmental reports filed with the Public Works Department. That's why I have a lunch meeting with the county engineer today at 1:00. I'm hoping to get his approval, so we can move forward. I'll have Doreen give you Nakamura's contact information."

"Thank you. One last question, Jackson."

"Anything, Agent Brooks."

"Meridew's ex-wives?"

Hughes rolled his eyes at that. "Man, they bled that guy dry. Every single time."

"The divorces were contentious?"

"You could say that."

"Would any of them wish him dead?"

"Don't know why," said Jackson shrugging. "That would mean their alimony checks would end."

*   *   *

Danté pulled the Odyssey into the parking space and set the brake. Grabbing his gun off the passenger seat, he climbed out, sliding his arm into the straps. As he rounded the back of the vehicle, he came up short.

Harper McLeod stood in the parking lot, wearing a pair of designer jeans, an off-the shoulder blouse in white with black geometric shapes on it, and black high heeled boots. Her brown hair was curled around her shoulders.

"Harper," he said, shrugging into the other strap and heading for the precinct.

"Is that what you drive?" she asked, stepping in front of him again.

He stopped walking and glanced over his shoulder at the Odyssey.

"Did your parents give it to you?"

"It's paid for and it runs. What do you drive?"

"I don't. I take Uber or public transportation."

His eyes involuntarily raked over her curvy figure. "You take public transportation?"

She placed her hand on her hip, her designer bag hanging from her arm. "I know self-defense, Mr. Spock."

"Of course you do," he said, trying to go around her.

She jutted out her hand, placing her palm in the center of his chest. He stopped again, staring at her hand, feeling a zing of awareness travel up his spine. Her fingers flexed. "Goodness, you work out, don't you?"

He looked up at her and their eyes caught and held. Damn, she was so pretty, so sexy with her full lips and tousled brown hair. Something about this woman captivated him. She parted her lips, then her green eyes shifted away.

"I need your help, Danté," she said.

He quirked an eyebrow at her. "Look, Harper, I've got to get into the…"

"Please," she said, her gaze shifting back to him. "Just help me this one time. I want to do a welfare check on Luz, but I can't do it without law enforcement. I know something's wrong with her. I know it. It's been way too long and she hasn't answered any of my attempts to reach her. I went by her apartment today…"

"You went to her apartment?"

"She didn't answer the door. I asked a neighbor and he said he hasn't seen her either. Please, Danté. Just give me a half hour. That's all I ask."

"How do you know she hasn't left town?"

"I don't. If we find out she's moved on, I promise I'll never bother you again."

He looked up at the clouds floating by overhead. No way would he be that lucky.

She held up a peace sign. "Scout's honor."

He tilted his head, glaring at her as he reached for his phone. "That's a peace sign."

"So you say."

"So everyone says." He pressed the icon for Cho's number.

"What's up?" came Cho's voice. "Tag and Holmes want us to help them run through the footage we got off the camera Stan set up across the street from the stop-and-rob. It's a lot of hours of video. Tag wants you to listen to the voices and see if you can pick up any Russian."

"I've got another issue I need to take care of. It shouldn't take me more than half an hour, then I'll listen to whatever you want me to hear."

"What's going on?" said Cho.

Danté leveled a look on Harper. She had her hands clasped before her in a prayer motion and her eyes were pleading. He could smell the vanilla scent of her hair as the breeze blew past him and he knew he was ten kinds of fool for getting taken in by this woman.

"I'm going to do a welfare check for Harper McLeod."

"Okay, call if you need backup," said Cho and disconnected the call.

Danté stared at the display, wishing he'd gotten just a little more pushback. He didn't think it was wise for him to spend too much time in Harper's company. He was just a little too aware of her as a woman and she made him smile, something that few women had done for him in the past.

"Let's go," he said, taking the keys out of his pocket. "Do you think you can ride in an Odyssey, or do you want to take Muni?"

She gave him an arch look. "Cute. The robot has claws," she said, hurrying to catch up to his longer strides.

He unlocked the minivan and she climbed into the passenger seat.

"Does it have seat belts or maybe a bungee cord to keep me from flying out the windshield?"

He reached behind her head and grabbed the seatbelt, holding it out for her. She snapped it in place and settled into the seat.

"Beam me out, Scotty."

"Beam me out?" he asked.

She bit her inner lip. "Up?"

He shook his head and started the car. "You wanna give me the address?"

"Does this bucket of bolts have GPS?"

"No, but my phone does," he answered, holding up the phone.

She took it and punched in the address, starting the direction app, then she settled into the seat. Despite her banter, as they drove to the Tenderloin she got quiet and stared out the window, watching the City pass by.

"Tell me more about this support group you run. Is it part of *From Hope to Healing*?"

She stared at him.

He glanced over. "What?"

"You remembered the name."

"Eidetic memory," he answered.

"Right. It does run through *From Hope*. It's a group for women who are in difficult positions, usually pregnant or with young children."

"And you got involved with it in college?"

"Right."

"Where did you go to college?"

"Berkeley. Where did you go to college?"

"I'm going to San Francisco State."

"Wait. Why? With your memory, why aren't you in Harvard?"

"I joined the force. In my family, we serve the community."

She rolled her eyes. "Good God, it must be so tedious being a Price. Does your dad fight crime at night in a jumpsuit and cape, and is your mom Florence Nightingale?"

"Let's focus on the support group, shall we?"

She snorted. "Yes, we shall."

"How long have you known Luz Gutierrez?"

"Six months. Since she came to get help for prenatal care."

"And was she still with her boyfriend?"

"No, she left him when she found out she was pregnant. She wanted to keep the baby and he wanted her to have an abortion."

"Was he violent with her?"

He felt Harper's eyes on him. "He beat her, yes. Most of the women in *From Hope* come from abusive relationships. You got a lot of work to do, Superman, if you want to clean this City up."

He sighed. He knew that better than she did. While his family was squarely middle class, he hadn't come from the place of privilege she had. He wasn't going to tell her that part of the reason he hadn't gone to college straight out of high school was that his parents couldn't afford it, even with the scholarships he'd qualified for, and he wasn't having them go into debt for it. He hadn't been opposed to taking that debt on himself, but they'd been adamant they wouldn't allow it.

He'd joined the force to keep them from taking out the loans. They thought it was his calling and he supposed a part of him agreed, but another part of him had really wanted to pursue forensic science, maybe become a medical examiner one day.

While he hadn't experienced the poverty or the racism of some of his peers, he'd seen it. He'd heard of friends being accosted by police, being threatened, getting pulled over for "driving while black". He'd thought that by joining the force he could change some of those systemic problems. Funny thing was it was a lot harder to see the root of the issue when you were on the inside looking out.

They fell silent again as he drove them into the rundown streets that made up the Tenderloin. In a city with one of the highest real estate values in the nation, the Tenderloin was a forgotten, derelict area. The houses were ramshackle, the tenements run down. Young men of every ethnicity lounged on the stoops, children played on the sidewalk, jumping rope or playing street ball. Mothers and grandmothers hurried past, refusing to make eye contact, pushing strollers or grocery carts or walkers.

The address Harper had was a three story walk-up with laundry hanging from the fire escapes, dead plants in the windows, the paint peeling from the aluminum siding. A crack ran from the sidewalk to the stairs, weeds growing through the concrete.

A couple of older men sat on the stairs with a checkerboard between them. Danté looked out at the neighborhood and wondered if he'd have tires on his car when they came back down. He glanced at Harper with her designer clothes and the confident way she carried herself.

"You came here by yourself earlier?"

She nodded, looking up at the building.

"That wasn't smart."

She glanced at him. "I have pepper spray."

"Oh, well, there you go," he said, not even trying to hide the sarcasm.

She frowned. "You can be a judgmental android when you want."

He pushed open the car door. "Let's get this over with before my car winds up in a chop shop."

"And you think that's a bad outcome?" she said, climbing out after him.

They headed toward the stairs.

"Hello, Ossifer," said one of the old men. His skin looked like a paper bag that had been folded too many times. Nearly every other tooth was missing as he smiled up at Danté. "We be keeping an eye on your vehicle for you."

Danté gave them both a nod, placing a hand in the middle of Harper's back and urging her up the stairs. Yep, his car was going to be stripped all right. They entered the dank hallway. A bare bulb lit the way up the stairs.

They climbed to the second floor and walked down a hallway with doors on either side. The carpet had been worn through to threads and the subfloor beneath it was warped. A few lights marked the hallway, some with glass covers over the bulbs, some with just bulbs, and some with nothing in the electrical socket.

A small table sat next to one of the doors with a wilted plant on it. Beneath the plant, someone had draped a lace cloth to brighten the hallway and a welcome mat in bright colors lay before the door.

"Here it is," said Harper, knocking loudly.

Danté looked down the hall as a door on the opposite side opened and a woman with pink curlers in her hair poked her head out. "What you want, baby?" she said to Danté.

"Do you know Luz Gutierrez?" he asked.

"Sure do."

"Have you seen her in the last few days?"

The woman opened the door. She wore a house dress and fuzzy slippers. She scratched her chin. "Can't say as I have."

A man lumbered out of the stairwell wearing a stained white t-shirt and low-slung jeans. His belly hung over his belt, his feet in flip flops. "Pops Walter said a cop come up in here," he shouted as he lumbered their way.

Harper nudged Danté with her elbow. "Show him your badge."

Danté took the badge out of his belt and held it up. "SFPD. Ms. McLeod says she hasn't heard from Luz Gutierrez in a number of days. Are you the manager?"

He jangled a set of keys hanging from his side. "What you think I got these for? Yep, I'm the manager. Ernesto Jimenez." He stopped before them, breathing hard. He had thinning black hair, swept back from his puffy features. His nose had been broken a few times.

"Have you seen Ms. Gutierrez?" Danté asked.

He scratched at the stubble on his chin much the way the old woman had done. "Don't remember the last time. Her rent's paid up until the first of the month."

Danté looked back at the door. He was fairly certain she'd left town, probably gone to live with family somewhere out of the City, but Harper wouldn't be satisfied until he went inside this room. He motioned at the door.

"Can you open it, sir? I need to do a welfare check."

Ernesto continued to scratch his chin. "Yeah, I guess I don't got no choice."

Danté shook his head no. Harper was back to wringing her hands in worry, her eyes glued to the manager's face. He fumbled with the keys, trying one in the lock, but it didn't work. He fumbled some more, the light dim in the hallway. Danté took out his flashlight and shined it on the man's hands.

He grunted a thank you and tried a couple more, then he finally found the right one and the lock clicked open. He reached for the knob, but Danté stopped him, his hand moving to his gun.

"Let me go first, please."

The manager made a noncommittal shrug and backed away. Danté eased to the door and turned the knob, pushing it open a bit. "SFPD!" he shouted into the room, then he took a step inside. The smell struck him as he stepped over the threshold and he gagged.

Harper came in on his heels and started to go around him, but he caught her around the waist and swung her back to the door. "No, Harper!" he said, pushing her back into the hallway. He stepped out after her and closed the door at his back.

Harper had her hands over her mouth, her eyes enormous and filling with tears. He waited for her to explode – scream, cry – but she did neither of those things.

"She's dead, isn't she?" she said in a soft voice.

Danté nodded once and reached for his phone.

"Dead?" said the manager loudly.

The older woman stepped out into the hallway. "Oh no! She was pregnant!"

Danté dialed Cho's number, his eyes shifting to the manager. "I need you to keep everyone away from this end of the hallway. Can you do that?"

He straightened. "I sure can." Then he was moving, pushing the older woman back toward the stairs. Harper's eyes never left Danté's face and a tear raced down her cheek.

"Cho!" came Nathan's voice on the line.

"Cho, it's Danté. I'm gonna need backup. I'll send you the address, and can you bring Mr. Ryder?"

"On it," he said, not asking what was going on. "We'll be there as soon as we can."

"Thanks." He held the phone out to Harper. "I'm gonna need you to coordinate things out here. Send Cho the address and keep him updated."

She grabbed his arm. "What are you going to do?"

"I have to go inside. I have to see where she is."

Harper nodded, shivering violently, but she focused on the phone and began typing in the address. Danté took a deep breath, then he shoved open the door and slipped inside. He carefully made his way through the galley kitchen on the left, the small dining/living room with a small couch and a television affixed to the wall. He peered into the tiny bathroom, pulling aside the shower curtain, but he found nothing. He knew he'd find nothing. The smell of death and decay came from the room right in front of him.

The door was slightly ajar and he paused outside of it, fighting to gain the courage to enter that room. He closed his eyes, said a prayer to a God he wasn't sure he believed in, then eased the door open.

The bed was directly in front of him and Luz Gutierrez, or what was left of her, lay sprawled across its surface. At first he wasn't sure what he was looking at. Flies crawled over her face and out flung hands, her head was turned toward the door, her eyes open and staring. The smell was overpowering, making him gag. He forced it down, but he had to put his sleeve over his mouth to keep from vomiting.

A blanket had been thrown over her body and blood had seeped across the bed, staining the blanket and the sheets beneath her. Pressing his sleeve tighter to his mouth, he stepped into the room, careful not to disturb anything as he eased up beside the bed. Reaching for the blanket with the very tips of his fingers, he pulled it back, then gasped, turning away.

Someone had cut her stomach open and left her to bleed to death, her empty womb lying beside her.

* * *

201

Marco and Peyton stepped into the medical examiner's office after Chief Kahele. Igor and Lani were in the autopsy room, but they waved them to the door. Marco saw Peyton's eyes go to the body on the table, but someone had covered it with a drape.

Lani buzzed them inside, fairly bouncing with excitement. "We've figured out what the poison was."

"Great," said Peyton. "What?"

"Come here, Agent Brooks, and take a look at this." Igor motioned to the microscope.

She leaned over it and looked at the slide. Marco smiled, watching the way Igor stared at her as if she were a rare creature that he was afraid might fly away. He could understand why men became fascinated with her. He was completely enchanted himself.

"What am I looking at, Igor?" she said, straightening, her dark curls sliding down her back.

"That's a tetrodotoxin," he said reasonably.

"Toxin is poison, right?" she said.

"Right," he answered.

"But from what?"

"Puffer fish."

"Puffer fish? He ate it?"

Lani shook his head. "That's what's fascinating. His stomach contents contained no trace of puffer fish. It was in his bloodstream."

"Puffer fish is highly toxic," said Kahele. "If he didn't eat it, how did someone use it to kill him?"

"Injection," said Marco.

Igor's eyes shot to his face. "I knew you were a man of much depth, Captain D'Angelo. Silent men always are."

Marco gave him a grim smile. "Where was the injection site?"

"I'm sorry, Agent Brooks," said Igor, moving to the body. He pulled aside the drape from Meridew's head, then pointed to a mark on his neck. "Someone injected him in the carotid artery."

"What?" asked Peyton, staring at the site. "How can that be? How could anyone get that close to him to inject him without him fighting them off?"

"That is why you are the detective and I am the medical examiner," said Igor.

Peyton's gaze rose to Kahele. "I want the grounds at the hotel closed off, at least around the hot tub. They need to be searched with a fine tooth comb."

"You need to drain the hot tub," said Marco. "And someone needs to take apart the filter."

Kahele nodded. "I'm on it." He took out his phone and moved to the door, stepping into the other room.

Peyton shook her head. "What happens when someone is poisoned by puffer fish?"

"There's a lot of debate about what makes them so toxic," said Igor.

"Most people agree it has something to do with bacteria in the intestinal tract," said Lani.

"Tetrodotoxin is a sodium channel blocker, meaning it prevents the nervous system from carrying messages, causing paralysis of the muscles, even the respiratory muscles. It would begin with paresthesia," said Igor.

"Tingling of the lips and extremities," said Lani.

"Followed by headache, weakness, tremors and then paralysis."

"Which would have made him drown?" said Peyton.

"Exactly," said Lani.

"Why didn't he cry out? No one reported hearing anything," she said.

"He would have suffered aphonia," said Igor.

"A-phone-a-what?" asked Peyton.

"Aphonia, inability to speak," said Lani.

Marco eased closer to the body and looked at the injection mark. A bruise had formed out from the site. "No signs of struggle?"

"None," said Igor.

Marco stared at him. "If someone had used a needle, they would have had to physically subdue him. In order to do that, they'd have come up behind him and wrap an arm around his throat."

"Precisely," said Igor.

Marco motioned to Meridew's neck. "There's no sign of ligature marks, bruising around the throat."

"None."

"And if someone grabbed him around the neck, he would have clawed at them with his fingers. Are any of his nails broken?"

"None," said Igor.

"What are you thinking?" asked Peyton.

He met her gaze. "He was shot with the poison."

"Shot?" she said in bewilderment.

"Like a dart gun or something?" asked Lani.

Marco nodded. "That way the attack could come at a distance. Meridew might not have even understood what was happening to him at the time."

"That's diabolical in its simplicity," said Igor, rubbing his hands together.

"Brilliant," admitted Peyton. "How long would it take before the poison took effect?"

Lani shrugged. "Since it went directly into his bloodstream, seventeen minutes, maybe less."

"He would have felt weak almost instantly, probably too weak to get out of the hot tub by himself," said Igor.

"Meridew didn't stand a chance."

The two medical examiners shook their heads sadly. Peyton stared at Meridew's face. "Someone wanted you dead, buddy, and they wanted it bad."

Igor gave Marco a disappointed look. "It appears you and I will not be getting the hot rock massage after all, Captain."

Marco's eyes whipped to his face and he couldn't believe the rush of relief that swept over him.

CHAPTER 12

Peyton gave Marco a smile as Chief Kahele wheeled in a whiteboard and positioned it at the front of the room. *Just like old times*, she thought. Marco smiled in return, easing back in the chair. She liked being on a case with him again. She liked the way they worked in sync with each other, intuitively knowing what the other was thinking.

Reaching over, she adjusted the laptop screen, so her team could see the whiteboard from their remote location. The chief's computer forensic officer turned on a projector, and a photo of the hot tub appeared on a screen next to the whiteboard.

Kahele faced the gathering. "I thought we could start with introductions," he said. "I'm Chief Terrence Kahele of the Kauai Police Department."

"Special Agent Carlos Moreno," said Radar. "With me are Special Agents Thomas Campbell and Emma Redford."

Kahele shifted his gaze to Peyton.

"Special Agent Peyton Brooks," she said, glancing at Marco.

"Captain Marco D'Angelo of the SFPD."

"Medical Examiner Haulani Ionakana," said Lani, leaning forward to look at the computer screen. He waved. Bambi waved back. He shot a look at the chief, then back to the screen. "Everyone calls me Lani."

"Hi, Lani," said Bambi brightly.

Kahele motioned to the man working the computer. He looked like a Hawaiian version of Stan with thick glasses, mussed black hair, wearing a Hang Ten t-shirt, board shorts, and flip flops. "I'm CSI Willis Akana."

"Give us your report, Will," said Kahele.

Willis picked up a laser pointer and focused it on the screen. "This is the crime scene. Last night we combed every inch of the area. It's been closed off since Mr. Meridew's body was found, but beyond an initial examination, we hadn't taken the scene apart. We were waiting for the report from the Medical Examiner's office." He clicked the mouse and a second photo appeared on the screen. "Upon closer examination, we discovered an area within view of the hot tub in a back corner where the vegetation had been trampled. We believe the assailant hid in this location and shot Mr. Meridew." Another click and a gate appeared. "There is a utility gate, used by the grounds crew, just a few steps away from where the vegetation was trampled. All of this area…" He swept it with his laser pointer. "…is outside of the security cameras range. The assailant could have entered through the gate, concealed himself, attacked Mr. Meridew and escaped without anyone noticing him."

"How would he know that Meridew would be in the hot tub that night?" said Radar through the computer.

"Mr. Meridew had been staying at the hotel for the last three weeks. When we reviewed the video footage of that time, we discovered that he had a habit of going down at around 9:00 each night to relax in the hot tub before retiring to his room. We haven't found a single night that he missed going there," said Kahele.

"So whoever attacked him was close enough to him to know his routine," said Marco.

"Or spent time observing him before plotting the murder," said Kahele.

"Did we find the murder weapon?" asked Peyton.

Willis reached into a manila folder he had sitting next to him on the table and pulled out an evidence bag, passing it to her. Peyton took it, studying the small dart with the red fletching on the end of it.

"Would this be enough to deliver a killing dose of the poison?" she asked, holding the dart in front of the computer for her team to see.

"A lethal dose of tetrodotoxin in humans is between 1 to 2 milligrams," said Tank. "In fact, as little as 0.2 milligrams can cause symptoms."

"Right," said Lani, "and since this was injected directly into his bloodstream, it would have been even more effective."

Peyton studied the small dart. "Was this shot from a gun?"

"An air gun could shoot it," said Tank. "You can buy those online."

"So now that we have method of death, I'd like to list our suspects," said Kahele, picking up a whiteboard marker.

"His three ex-wives," said Marco. "Do we know their names?"

"I did some computer research," answered Willis. "The first wife lives on the big island. Her name's Daisy Meridew. They've been divorced for the last ten years. She got the house and a large alimony settlement."

Kahele wrote Daisy on the board.

"The second wife is Fiona. She's on Maui. She got the house and a large alimony settlement, and the art gallery she and Meridew owned together."

Kahele wrote Fiona on the board.

"The third wife is Phoebe. She's here on Kauai. She got..."

"The house and a large alimony settlement," said Radar. "I think we get the picture. Were any of the divorces contested?"

"All of them were, but Meridew made the women sign prenups," said Willis. "He kept the company separate from the rest of his personal holdings. It's in a trust, managed by both him and his partner, Jackson Hughes."

"Who else?" said Kahele.

"The environmentalist guy," said Peyton.

"From *Freedom Kauai*," said Marco, "Manny something?"

"Manny Wong," said Willis. "He's the director. He filed multiple injunctions against Dewdrop Construction and he was suspected of vandalizing the construction site."

Kahele wrote him on the list.

"Lani mentioned something about a gardener who threatened to bash in Meridew's head with a shovel," said Peyton.

"Dexter Opunui," said Willis. "He took Meridew to small claims court because Meridew refused to pay him for his work. Meridew claimed Opunui didn't show up when he requested and didn't do a good job. The judge threw the case out and Opunui didn't get paid."

"So he threatened to kill Meridew?" asked Bambi. "That's a little extreme."

"Meridew left a negative review on his Yelp page too," said Willis.

"Oh, well, that'll do it," said Bambi, beaming a smile.

Peyton smiled back. She missed her team.

Kahele wrote Opunui on his board.

"What about Jackson Hughes, the CFO?" said Marco.

"He's gotten threats himself," said Kahele.

"He still goes on the board until we get an alibi. Everyone's a suspect…" said Radar.

"…until they aren't," finished Tank, Bambi and Peyton.

"Cute," said Radar.

Kahele wrote Hughes on the board. "So where do we start?"

"Two of the wives are on different islands," said Radar. "We need to figure out if they booked flights between the islands around the time of Meridew's death. That'll cut down on travel until you've eliminated other suspects."

"I'm liking the environmental guy," said Bambi. "He had a motive for wanting Meridew dead."

"I'm liking him too," said Peyton, "but I want to talk to the foreman first. What was his name?"

Willis flipped through some notes. "Teddy Nakamura," he said.

"Can you arrange for us to talk to Teddy? He might have seen something," asked Peyton.

"I'll get on it," said Kahele.

"We'll look into the wives on our end," said Radar.

"Where is the gardener? Is he on Kauai?" asked Marco.

"His business is listed on Kauai, but he doesn't seem to have an office or anything," said Willis. "I suspect he works out of his home."

"Track him down," Kahele told Willis.

"What should I do?" asked Lani.

Kahele held up the dart. "See if you can get anything off this. Blood, fingerprints, DNA."

He took the package. "I'm on it."

Kahele looked around the group. "Let's take a fifteen-minute break and meet back here. I'll see if we can talk to the foreman in the meantime."

Willis and Lani both rose and followed Kahele from the room.

Peyton reached for the laptop, turning the computer to face her. "Hey, guys, how's it shaking?"

"Hey, Peyton," said Bambi brightly. "You look all sun kissed and gorgeous. Are you having fun?"

"Well, I'm investigating a murder, sooo…"

Bambi giggled. "Right. So what did Meridew look like? Was he all bloated from the water?"

Radar gave her an arch look. "Do you mind?" he said, pulling the screen toward himself. "Look, Sparky, you need to get into Meridew's office, search the place. See if there's any clue as to who might have wanted him dead."

"Kahele's working on a warrant."

"It wouldn't hurt to have his computer files too, email addresses, social media logins," said Tank. "I can check to see if anyone has been threatening him on any of the platforms."

"I'll get to work on that, Tank," she told him.

"And get the same for Hughes if you can," said Tank.

"On it."

"Is D'Angelo still there?" asked Radar.

Marco leaned over, peering at the screen. "Here," he said.

"I got you on as a consultant again. Defino will be looking in at the precinct."

"Thank you."

"No problem." Radar focused on Peyton again. "Look, Sparky, if this guy…"

"Or girl," said Peyton.

"Could be a woman, Radar," agreed Bambi. "Women like to use poison."

"Word," said Peyton.

Radar fought for patience. "If this assailant is striking by hiding in the bushes, you better be on your toes. Trust your intuition, okay?"

"Okey dokey," she said. "I'll be careful."

Radar gave a firm nod.

"Hey, Emma," Peyton called.

"Yep!" she said, leaning her head against Radar's.

"How's Jake?"

Her face became besotted. "Oh, Peyton, Jakey is…"

"Nope!" said Radar. "We're signing off now, Sparky. Don't take any unnecessary risks and keep D'Angelo with you."

"Wait, Radar! Wait!" But they were gone.

She looked up at Marco.

He gave her a bemused smile. "You miss them, don't you?"

She remembered what she'd said about quitting and reached over, taking his hand. She brought it to her lips and kissed it. "Not enough that I'm willing to sacrifice us for them."

He gave her a wistful smile and dragged her chair closer to him. Then he kissed her. She returned the kiss, curling her hand around the nape of his neck and tilting her head. Kahele cleared his throat as he stepped back into the room.

"We've got a meeting with the foreman in half an hour," he said, averting his eyes.

Peyton pressed her forehead to Marco's. "Gotcha. Just let me hit the bathroom and I'll be ready to go."

Marco insisted on taking their own car out to the construction site. Peyton knew he was hoping to get in a little more sightseeing while they were working the case. She didn't mind. She hated that their vacation had been cut short. She'd put her bikini on under her shorts and tank top just in case they got a chance to hit a beach during the return trip.

Teddy Nakamura greeted them as they pulled onto the barren land where the strip mall would be one day. He stood not much taller than Peyton, but he had massive arms, well muscled and heavily veined. His face was lined and leathery from sun exposure and he wore a red bandana around his head.

Peyton marked a few protesters lined up on the opposite side of the street, holding signs that read things like *Dewdrop Construction – raping the land of our ancestors, Listen to the sound of our mother dying,* and such.

"Heavy stuff," said Peyton, giving Nakamura a tight smile.

"Everyday they're there, chanting that I am a murderer, a rapist!" he shouted at them.

The protesters gathered together and began a singsong chant. "Hey ho, Dewdrop Construction has got to go! Hey ho, Dewdrop Construction had got to go!"

"Is Manny Wong with them?" asked Marco.

Nakamura shook his head. "He's too busy keeping my men from working by filing motions through the courts. One injunction after another. The last one was for the rainbow-eyed damselfly."

"The rainbow-eyed damselfly? What is that?" asked Peyton.

"A freakin fly!" shouted Nakamura at the protestors. "A freakin damn fly!"

"Is it endangered?" she asked.

He glared at her. Before he could say anything, Kahele intervened.

"Can we go to your trailer and talk? It's a little loud out here."

Nakamura jerked a hand toward the trailer. "It's crowded in there, but sure."

Peyton thought Nakamura didn't seem like a very friendly fellow, but maybe the stress of the constant injunctions, protests, and delays was taking their toll. He led them across the barren ground to the sorry excuse of a trailer in the back corner. The stairs creaked as they climbed up and entered the dank interior.

He was right. There wasn't much room and what room there was had been covered with blueprints and file cabinets. A large desk took up one whole end and a table covered in building plans dominated the middle of the room. As Peyton's eyes adjusted to the dark interior, she made out a copier, a small dorm fridge, a coffee maker, and a microwave.

"Sit wherever," he said.

They looked around and Kahele found some folding chairs stuffed in the corner between a filing cabinet and a wall. He passed them to Peyton and Marco, then took one himself. Peyton and Kahele found just enough space before Nakamura's desk to open them and sit down, while Nakamura sank into his desk chair. Marco wandered around the trailer, looking at photos Nakamura had affixed to the wall or the designs on the table.

Kahele leaned forward and looked at Peyton, jerking his head at Marco.

"It's his style," she said, but when Kahele and Nakamura both gave her skeptical looks, she added, "Hard to sit in a cramped space with his bad leg."

Kahele nodded in understanding, then jerked his head toward Nakamura.

Peyton realized he wanted her to take lead. She was fine with that. It would go much smoother if he just let her do the questioning. She removed her badge and held it up.

"Special Agent Peyton Brooks." She looked at Marco, then smiled, turning back to Nakamura. "And my partner, Captain Marco D'Angelo. I think you know Chief Kahele already."

Nakamura nodded, looking down at the cell phone he'd placed on the blotter. He sent a text message, then looked up. "So you want to know about Meridew?"

"Well, we'd like to ask you a few questions," she amended.

"They said he was poisoned. How?"

"We'd like to do the questioning, if you don't mind?"

"Fine." Nakamura looked at his phone again.

She took out the pad Robbie had given her and made a note of his name. "How long have you worked for Dewdrop Construction?"

He glanced up, considering. "Eight years now."

"You've always been the foreman."

"Yep. They hired me to manage a mall construction on Maui. This'll be the fifth mall I've built for them."

"Do you always run into difficulties like this?"

"Difficulties?"

"The injunctions, the protests?"

"Some, but nothing this bad. These *Freedom Kauai* clowns are a pain in my ass!" he shouted toward the door.

"I don't think they can hear you."

"I don't care," he spat and looked at his phone again.

"I get the impression you're not very happy, Mr. Nakamura."

"Do you see me building anything? No. I can't even get the damn foundation laid. I've gotta be paying my men to sit on their asses. Then we gotta watch the construction site at all times."

"Because of the vandalism?"

213

"They think they're going to run us off, but we're not going anywhere!" he shouted at the door again.

Peyton and Marco exchanged a look.

"How well did you know Mr. Meridew, Mr. Nakamura?"

He shrugged. "He came out, gave orders. Civil engineers," he said with a shake of his head.

"Not a fan?"

"They always got some bug up their ass about something. This beam is too narrow, this footing is too shallow. Frickin' haole."

"Did you know Mr. Meridew was getting death threats?"

"Yeah, he told me. You ask me, it was that Wong character. He was always pushing Meridew's buttons, always doing something to piss him off, making comments on social media, filing complaints with the EPA."

"Mr. Hughes is getting them too."

"Yeah, well, you look at Wong. I'm telling you, he's your man. Frickin protesters!" he shouted at the door. Then he looked back at his phone, picking it up and punching in a text.

"So how would you characterize your relationship with Mr. Meridew?" asked Peyton.

Nakamura shrugged and kept typing. Peyton fought her growing annoyance, but it wasn't working. This space was close and hot and smelled like sweat and mildew.

"Mr. Nakamura, would you please put down the phone?"

He slowly lowered it, his eyes boring into hers.

"How would you characterize your relationship with Mr. Meridew?" she repeated.

"He was a sonuvabitch," he said.

Kahele shifted in the chair, but Peyton ignored him.

"What do you mean?"

"He never asked you for anything. It was always orders. He thought he was superior to everyone, and I mean everyone. He barked orders like he was some frickin general or something. Whenever he was on site, nothing got done because he was always bitching about everything! Frickin haole!"

She took some notes, letting him stew, then she looked up at him. "You didn't like him. Did you have any reason to want him dead?"

He shrugged. "Mr. Hughes runs the company better than he did, so the way I figure it, I don't care one way or another. I just wanna build my malls and move on. No more frickin protesters."

"That's not exactly a denial, Mr. Nakamura."

"I didn't kill him, but if you're asking me if I feel sorry he's dead. Well, I ain't gonna lie about that either. Let's just say I'm not sad." He picked up his phone again.

Kahele made a grunt and looked away.

Marco wandered over to the desk. "You have a permit for the rifle?"

Nakamura's eyes snapped up. "What?"

Marco jerked his chin at the corner behind Nakamura. Peyton couldn't see what he saw from her angle. "The rifle you've got hidden behind the file cabinet."

Kahele rose and eased past Nakamura, grabbing it. Peyton recognized a Winchester when she saw one. "Wow, nice piece," she said.

Kahele broke it and shook out two shells. "Why do you need this much fire power on a construction site, Mr. Nakamura?"

Nakamura pulled open the top desk drawer and rummaged around inside of it. "Really, Chief? How many times you been out here to take a report about vandals?"

"You're going to shoot them?" Kahele said.

Nakamura located something and slapped it on the desk. Peyton picked it up and reviewed it. A gun permit and it was current. She passed it back to the other man. "It's current," she told Kahele.

He nodded and leaned the gun against the desk.

Nakamura rubbed his chin with his hand, then he picked up the phone, looking at the screen.

"Just who are you texting, Mr. Nakamura?"

He gave her a slow look. "Mr. Hughes."

"Why?"

He jerked his chin to the door. "I got a construction site just waiting to go, Special Agent, and I'm wondering how much time this investigation is going to take 'cause I'm way behind schedule."

Peyton gave him a chilling smile. "Any reason you think Mr. Hughes needs to know we're here?"

"I got a construction site just waiting to go," he said, enunciating each word, "and I wanna know when I can tell the protesters to shove it up their asses!"

Peyton was getting a little tired of the shouting. "How about you stop yelling for their benefit?"

"Hughes was meeting with the county engineer yesterday over lunch. I wanted to know if they signed off on the latest permits, so we can get going."

"Did they?"

He shook his head. "They're still waiting for a report from the EPA about the frickin fly!" He half-rose from his chair to shout now.

Kahele gave Peyton an annoyed look, shaking his head slightly. Peyton wrote a note on her pad and closed it, clicking the pen with her thumb, then she pushed herself to her feet. "Thank you for your time, Mr. Nakamura. By the way, you don't plan to leave the island anytime soon, do you?"

"No!" he said in a surly tone.

"Good, don't," she answered and walked toward the door.

Marco and Kahele followed after her, Kahele jogging down the rickety steel steps.

"What are you thinking?" he said, touching her elbow.

She glanced back at the trailer, then shifted to face him. "I was hoping to get some information about the business, about the protesters, even about Meridew himself."

"But?"

"But I wasn't expecting to add another suspect to our list."

Kahele looked back at the trailer, then met her gaze again. "He's a suspect now?"

She sighed and started walking toward the cars. "He's a suspect now," she said wearily.

*   *   *

Danté set a coffee cup in front of Harper in the break room at the precinct. She curled her hands around it, staring at a spot on the table. They hadn't closed up the crime scene until 1:00AM and Harper had stayed the entire time.

"Did you sleep at all?" he asked her.

She shook her head, lifting the coffee to take a sip. She held it away and stared into the cup.

"I didn't know if you liked cream or sugar."

"No, I like it black," she answered, taking another sip. "It's just this is really good."

"Mr. Ryder buys it. He knows his coffee, apparently."

"Does coffee short your circuits, Mr. Spock?"

He didn't rise to the bait. He knew she was hurting. "I try to avoid stimulants and depressants. I avoid things that cause addiction."

She just stared at him without speaking, then she drank some more.

He looked around the room, feeling awkward. It had been a long night and he couldn't get the sight of Luz Gutierrez out of his mind. Someone had cut her baby out of her body and there was no sign of the child. An Amber Alert had been issued, but they'd gotten no leads on the infant.

"You and I are so different," she finally said.

He looked back at her. "What can you tell me about Luz, Harper?"

She shook her head, her eyes drifting away again. "She was just twenty, pregnant. Her mother and father kicked her out of the house when they found out she was keeping the baby. She thought she was having a boy, but she hadn't gotten any prenatal care, so she wasn't sure. We tried to get her in to see the doctor. Her first appointment was supposed to be yesterday."

"You said she left her ex-boyfriend? Was she living with him?"

"She was still living at home, but he lived there too. Her parents wanted her to marry him so the baby wouldn't be illegitimate. They were devout Catholics."

"But she didn't want to marry him?"

"No, not once she decided she wanted to keep the baby. He used to hit her. He didn't even have to be drunk. He'd just come in from work and something would set him off. She knew it was the only way she could keep the baby safe." She shook her head. "Actually it was the only way she could keep the baby."

"Had she seen him since she moved out?"

"She was trying to stay under the radar. That's why she didn't have a cell phone. She didn't want anything that he could use to track where she was. She even subletted that apartment from a friend, so her name wasn't on the lease."

"Where's the friend?"

"I think she's in college, doing a year abroad, but I don't remember where. They met in high school."

"Was she seeing anyone else? Did she have a new boyfriend?"

"No, she was concentrating on preparing for the baby and she'd just gotten a job, working at a grocery story as a cashier." She reached over and clasped his hand. "You have to tell me what he did to her."

Danté didn't pull away. "He?"

Simons appeared in the doorway, his large frame taking up the entire space. "Can I talk to you?"

"Of course," said Dante, rising to his feet.

He followed Simons out into the precinct. Simons motioned him into the cubicle he'd taken when the captain left on his trip. "Be careful what you divulge to the reporter."

"I'm asking her questions about Luz Gutierrez."

"That's fine, but make sure you don't give anything away. Do you want Cho in on this?"

"She's a mess. I don't know if that's a good idea right now."

"That's what Cho thought. He figured you had a rapport with her and might be able to get information on your own, but if you feel at all like it's getting away from you, you step back. Understand?"

"I understand."

"Did she give you anything?"

Dante looked out of the cubicle, but he couldn't see into the break room. He felt anxious about leaving Harper alone right now. "Luz's parents threw her out of the house when they found out she was pregnant. They wanted her to marry the father of the baby, so the baby wouldn't be illegitimate, but the baby's father was abusive. She was subletting the apartment from a friend, who's studying abroad and she was working as a cashier in a grocery story. That's all I've gotten so far."

"New boyfriends?"

"None. We don't even know what sex the baby was. She hadn't gotten prenatal care yet."

"She was how far along? Do we know that?"

Dante chewed on his inner lip. "At least eight months."

"So the baby could have survived?"

"That murder was brutal, Inspector Simons. Her womb was ripped from her body. Could the child have survived that?"

"The ME will let us know what he thinks." He grimaced and rubbed a hand over his face. "God, I just can't stand things like this. Ryder is wading through a sea of blood right now."

"He's still there?"

"He went back this morning, looking for fibers, hair, fingerprints. Anything that'll give us an idea of what happened."

Danté shifted weight. "Is Captain D'Angelo coming back today?"

"No, he's got his own mess. They caught a murder on the island."

"During their honeymoon?"

"Yeah, and the FBI appointed him as a consultant. Deputy Chief Defino will be looking in on us and now we have two murders."

Danté leveled his gaze on Simons. "I want this one, Inspector. I know I'm not officially a detective, but I want this one. I should have listened to Harper when she told me she was worried about the girl, but I didn't and now the girl's dead."

"We don't know when she died yet, kid. Don't go beating yourself up about it. That's not going to solve a damn thing."

"I should have listened to her. A citizen tried to file a concern and I ignored it. I can understand if you want to suspend me, but I would rather try to redeem myself by working the case."

Simons made a grunt. "Cool your jets, kid. You're gonna work the case. You and Cho. He'll be lead and you'll do exactly what he says, you hear me?"

Danté felt an easing in his chest. He hadn't realized how anxious he'd been feeling until then. "Yes, sir. I promise you, sir."

Simons patted his shoulder. It felt like being cuffed by a grizzly bear. Danté braced his legs to keep from staggering. "You'll do all right. Now, see what else Ms. McLeod knows about the girl, then take her home. We're going to work on locating the parents, then..." His voice trailed away.

"Then?"

"You get the miserable task of telling next of kin their daughter's dead."

Danté swallowed hard, the image of Luz Gutierrez forever carved into his memory. Sometimes having a photographic memory was all sorts of curse.

* * *

Marco and Peyton headed back toward the precinct after talking with the foreman, but as they turned onto the Kuhio Highway, Marco glanced at Peyton. "What's say we stop at Paolo's Crab Shack for lunch?"

"Hm, not a bad idea. We could get a little beach time while we're waiting for Kahele to get the warrant to search Meridew's office."

"We could," he said, smiling at her.

A little while later, he pulled into the small parking lot. A few cars occupied the other spaces, but there weren't nearly as many as there had been the last time they came. They got out and walked up to the shack.

Kana leaned on the counter, smiling at them. "If it isn't the newlyweds. How are you, darlin's?" she said.

Peyton smiled back at her. "Excellent."

"I know what you want! A vegetarian Poké bowl and some crab tacos."

"Sounds good," said Marco, taking out his wallet and paying.

"Any drinks?"

"Two iced teas," said Marco.

"Go grab yourselves some seats and I'll bring it over."

They wandered over to the picnic tables, but Marco could see Nani had her chair set up under some palm trees, watching the surfers out on the water. Peyton saw her at the same time.

"Let's go see how she's doing," she said.

Marco nodded, knowing that was code for let's go ask her a few questions. As they made their way across the sand, Peyton kicked off her sandals and picked them up, then reached up and pulled the tie off her hair, shaking it out. It spilled in a wave down her back and he smiled. He loved seeing this side of her. Her shoulders relaxed and she breathed a little more deeply.

Nani grinned up at her as they approached. "Come sit, child. I've been waiting for you."

Peyton hesitated a moment, then sank onto the woven grass mat Nani had beneath her chair. She patted the spot behind her for Marco and he sank down, letting her lean against him. He wasn't looking forward to getting up again.

Nani gave him a commiserate smile. "Getting down, not so bad. Getting up, it's all about the gravity."

He chuckled. "Precisely."

Nani's attention returned to Peyton and she reached out, sweeping Peyton's hair off her shoulder with an arthritic hand. "You have such a brightness in you, child, but I see clouds around your heart." She nodded at Marco. "He chases some of those clouds back though, yes?"

"Yes," Peyton said. She leaned her head against his chest and he rested his chin on the top of it. For a moment, they sat in the quiet, listening to the waves, watching the surfers. "This is peaceful."

"I like to sit here and feel the life of the island around me, like a cocoon. Not much more someone like me can do."

Kana brought them their food and Peyton jumped to her feet to grab it. Kana also had a smoothie for her grandmother. "Drink all of it," she told her.

Nani smiled up at her, taking the drink and placing the straw in her mouth, sipping dutifully. Kana gave a stern nod. "Make her finish it," she told Peyton and Marco.

They nodded in agreement and Kana walked away.

Nani settled the cup into the sand next to her and folded her hands on her lap. Peyton shared an amused look with Marco. For the next few moments, they ate in silence, watching the surfers.

Gathering up their garbage, Peyton took it back toward the shack to throw it away. Nani shifted in her chair. "You are worthy of her," she said.

Marco glanced over. "What?"

"Isn't that what you fear? That you aren't worthy of something so pure, so bright."

Marco felt a chill race up his spine. "Yes," he said honestly.

"You are like a grounding wire for her. You stabilize all that energy."

He nodded. He figured he already knew that. Peyton had told him as much herself. He didn't believe in mystical stuff, he had always struggled with being Catholic, but something about the atmosphere, the moment, held him captive.

Peyton returned, sinking down in front of him, fitting her back to his chest. He nuzzled the wild mane of hair at her back and curled his arm around her waist. How could he ever feel worthy of something so precious, he thought.

He felt Nani's eyes on them. "Death stalks you, child," she said.

Peyton looked over at her, her body tensing. "What do you mean?"

"You disrupt Death's playground. You bring his antics to an end."

Marco felt the hairs on his arms rise.

"I'm…we're both detectives, Nani," she said.

Nani nodded. "You came here to stop him."

Marco wasn't sure who the "him" was in that sentence, but he shivered in the warm, ocean air.

"We've been asked to help investigate the Harvey Meridew death. Did you hear about that?" said Peyton.

Nani went still. "He angered the island. It took its revenge."

"He got letters that said the Menehune were coming for him. Can you tell me anything about that?"

"It is as I said. The Menehune protect the island, the trees, the grasses. He violated that."

"I have to find out who killed him."

Nani nodded, her eyes drifting back to the surf. "I know this too. You cannot rest until you have uncovered the illness, exposed it to the air. To the light. It calls to you, child."

Marco shifted uneasily. He didn't like where the conversation had gone. Nani was voicing the very thing that he feared – Peyton would never be able to stop solving crimes, putting herself in danger to have answers, to get justice.

A figure left the surf and came jogging up the beach toward them. Marco recognized the young man named Boomer from the other night. He stuck his surfboard into the sand, resting it against a tree and held out a fist for Peyton to bump with her own.

"Aloha!" he said. "Nice to see you again."

"Hi. Boomer, right?" said Peyton.

"Right." He offered Marco his fist. Marco bumped it quickly before Boomer's attention shifted to Nani. "You need to drink that, Nani. Kana is gonna yell at both of us."

She waved him off with a scoffing sound. "How are the waves?"

"Ridonculous!" he said loudly, dropping to his knees in the sand. "Man, this sure is the life."

Marco had to agree with him. He could get used to a life that involved sitting on a beach and swimming in the ocean every day.

"What brings you back here?" said Boomer, shaking his blond head like a dog, spraying water everywhere.

"They're investigating the murder of Harvey Meridew," said Nani.

"Whew!" said Boomer. "Man, not surprised by that at all."

Marco could feel Peyton stiffen against him.

"What do you mean by that? You're not surprised we're investigating or not surprised Meridew's dead?" she asked.

"Seriously not surprised he's dead." Boomer shook his head to the side, banging the other side with his hand to dislodge water. "So you cops? Not really surprised by that either." He jerked his chin at Marco. "You look like a cop."

Marco just nodded.

"Why do you say you're not surprised he's dead?" Peyton asked.

"Man, you can't come onto the islands and just start tearing things down. Especially not when you're a haole."

"Haole? White person?"

"Right."

"You're a haole, Boomer," she said.

He held out his tanned arms. "Do you see me tearing shit down? No, you do not. I am one with the surf. I channel the spirit of the great Maui himself."

"Yes, you do, Boomer," said Nani fondly. "Meridew did not and he paid the price."

"Do you know anything about *Freedom Kauai?*" Peyton asked.

Boomer made a face. "Man, I don't hang with that. They're not much better than Meridew and his kind. They're what you call domestic terrorists."

"What do you mean?"

"They vandalize buildings, set fire to construction sites, tamper with equipment."

"They killed someone a few years back," came a voice behind them.

Marco and Peyton shifted to see Kana had returned. "They killed someone?" asked Peyton.

Kana nodded, coming to stand in front of them. "They tampered with some scaffolding, removed the screws that held it together. The worker fell to his death. He was Hawaiian, native to the islands."

"When was that?" Peyton asked.

Kana scratched her neck under her lush hair. "Three years ago. I can't remember the man's name, but he had a family, little kids. He was just trying to support them."

"Did he work for Meridew?"

"I don't remember." Her eyes narrowed on her grandmother. "You promised you'd drink that."

Nani picked up the drink and took another few sips, giving her granddaughter a wide eyed, innocent look.

"Kana, what else can you tell me about Harvey Meridew or *Freedom Kauai*?" asked Peyton.

She considered that. "I didn't know Meridew. I heard about him, but I know Manny Wong with *Freedom Kauai*."

"And?"

"He's a very angry man. He comes here sometimes. He lectures me about using paper products, straws, says we're killing the wildlife."

"He brought protesters one time and they threw water on the bonfire," said Boomer. "Lunatic."

Peyton glanced over her shoulder at Marco. Marco gave her a speculative look.

Her phone buzzed and she pulled it out of her shorts pocket, looking at the display. Marco caught a glimpse of the screen. A text message from Kahele flashed across it. *Got the warrant. Meet me at Meridew's office to search it.*

She climbed to her feet, then held out her hands to Marco. He took them because he didn't want to look weak trying to get to his feet again with his bad leg. "We've got to go." She reached into her back pocket and pulled out one of Kahele's business cards, passing it to Kana. "If you think of anything else, will you call me?"

"Sure," she said.

Nani held her hands out to Peyton. Peyton placed her own in them, letting Nani draw her down close. "Do not be afraid of what the future holds. You hear the calling. Go with it. Everything else will sort itself around that. Turn away and everything falls apart."

Peyton tilted her head in question, considering.

Marco felt a tightness in his chest. He knew she meant Peyton's decision to leave the FBI. She was telling her not to turn away from her calling. Not to give up her career. But if she stayed with the FBI, how would they ever have a family, a life together? How would they work it out?

"Drink the rest of your smoothie," Peyton told her.

She released Peyton and waved her off.

Peyton leaned over, hugging the old woman. "You're still needed here," she said into her ear. "Many people still need guidance."

Nani hugged her back, then held her off, looking into her eyes. "You have such a brightness in you, child. Such a brightness. Don't let them extinguish it." Then she reached for her smoothie and put the straw to her lips.

CHAPTER 13

Taking the elevator to the eleventh floor, they arrived at Dewdrop Construction's generic office space. Doreen Kim met them at the reception desk, smiling brightly. Kahele passed her the warrant.

"We'd like to look over Mr. Meridew's office," he said. "No one's been in there since he died, have they?"

"Not since you sealed the door, Chief," she said, passing the warrant back to him.

"Is Mr. Hughes in?"

"No, he's meeting with the county engineer again. He's hoping they'll get the injunctions lifted today."

"No more issues with the rainbow-eyed damselfly?" asked Peyton.

Doreen shook her head in a gesture that said, *Seriously.* "One can only hope."

"Yes, one can," said Peyton, smiling. "Doreen, can I ask you a few questions?"

"Sure."

Peyton took out her notebook and pen. "You said Mr. Meridew's last secretary was named…"

"Celia, Celia Salazar."

"Thank you. Would you happen to have contact information for her?"

"Sure," said Doreen, turning to her computer and clicking with the mouse. "Here's her number." She rattled off the digits. "And her address." She gave a location in Texas.

"Wait. She's no longer on the islands?"

"No, she left once she got the settlement. Her family lived in Texas."

Peyton turned to Kahele. "Can someone in your office track her down and make sure she was in Texas when he died?"

He took the paper Peyton handed to him. "We can do that," he said, taking out his phone and stepping away from them.

Peyton turned back to Doreen. "Did you like Mr. Meridew?"

"He was a difficult man, Agent Brooks. I'd be lying if I said anything different. He had a quick temper and you never knew what was going to set him off."

"Did he ever yell at you?"

"Frequently, but Mr. Hughes was good at running interference."

"Meaning he stepped in and stopped him?"

"Often."

"How did Mr. Hughes and Mr. Meridew get along?" asked Peyton. "I mean it must have been hard on him to always put out fires."

"I'm sure there were times when Mr. Hughes wished Mr. Meridew wasn't so unpredictable, but he admired him so much. Mr. Hughes never forgot that Mr. Meridew helped him get where he was. Before Mr. Meridew came on board, we were hardly making it. Mr. Hughes was having a difficult time paying the bills." She leaned forward and dropped her voice. "There were a few times my paycheck bounced."

Peyton gave her a wide-eyed look. "Bounced?"

"Oh, he always made good on it, but he was heavily in debt. Even in Hawaii, a lot of people don't want to pay for green construction." She leaned back. "When Mr. Meridew came on board, he changed everything. Jobs were coming in and we started having to turn business away. Whenever Mr. Meridew had one of his outbursts, Mr. Hughes always told me it was a minor price to pay for all that Mr. Meridew had brought us."

Kahele disconnected the call. "I've got a man on it. Should we look at Meridew's office?"

"Of course," said Peyton. "Thank you for talking with me, Doreen. If you think of anything else, will you contact Chief Kahele?"

"Of course I will."

Kahele motioned them into the hall. A strip of crime scene tape had been affixed to the door. Kahele tore it down and turned the doorknob. They entered behind him. The office was similar to Hughes' in the placement of the furniture. They were both so small, there wasn't really much room for variation, but rather than generic floral prints on the wall, Meridew had blueprints for all of the malls he and Hughes had designed and built.

Marco began strolling around the room, looking at all of them, while Peyton went to the desk and took a seat. She tried to open the desk drawer, but it was locked. Swiveling around, she looked about the room, trying to think of where he might have hidden a key.

"Locked?" asked Kahele.

"Yes. Do you remember if they recovered any keys from his hotel room?"

"I don't believe so."

"Did they find anything significant in his hotel room? What about a laptop? I'm not seeing a computer."

"Clothing, but that was pretty much it. Some toiletries, his wallet."

"Could there have been a key in his wallet?"

"No, credit cards, ATM cards, driver's license. That was all. He had very few personal effects."

Peyton thought about that. He'd been living in the hotel for weeks. Where was his stuff? Pictures, souvenirs, private keepsakes. Computer. "Could his stuff still be with his third wife?"

Kahele shrugged.

"He should have a computer at least, shouldn't he?"

"We didn't find one."

"What about a car? Did he have a car?"

"His third wife got the car. I can't find a record of him buying another one."

"Can we get his financial records? Did you ask Hughes for records on the business?"

"We're working on a warrant for Meridew's personal financial records. I haven't asked Hughes for records on the business yet, but I'll do that."

Peyton tried to open the credenza and found it unlocked. A quick search through it turned up zoning manuals, more blueprints, and a bottle of Macallan whisky. She took the bottle out and settled it on the top of the credenza, then she took out her phone and dialed Abe's number.

"Hey toots," came his voice on the line. "What's up, sugar? I hear you got yourself a dead guy in a hot tub."

"I do. I'm in the guy's office right now, staring at a bottle of Macallan whisky. How much would something like that go for?"

"Macallan?" said Abe, giving a low whistle. "This guy was wealthy, huh?"

"Apparently."

"Well, depending on the year of origin, it could go between $250 to $5,000 or so."

"Seriously?"

"Yep, you know what year this bottle was?"

Peyton tilted it, staring at the label. "It says Macallan 30 years old."

"Hold on," said Abe.

While she waited, she opened a white box on the credenza, looking for a key. Kahele came over and watched her, then when she found nothing inside, he lifted the box and turned it in the light. Peyton watched him, trying to place what the box was made of. It was heavy and ornately carved, a yellowed white with an almost waxy feel to it.

"I think this is pure ivory," Kahele said.

Peyton shivered in revulsion. "Ivory?"

Marco looked over, studying it himself.

Kahele nodded, then set it down, pushing it to the back of the credenza. "That must be worth a fortune."

"Hey, little soul sista," came Abe's voice. "That bottle of Macallan?"

"Yep." She reached out and tilted the bottle again, looking at the label.

"It's worth over $7,000."

"What?" She released it suddenly and it tilted, almost toppling off the credenza.

Kahele caught it at the last minute and they both let out a breath. He set it back and Peyton wheeled away from it.

"Are you sure, Abe?"

"Sure as my name is Abraham Frederick Douglass Jefferson."

She paused at that and looked at the phone. "Abraham Frederick Douglass Jefferson?"

"My mama thought I was going to be president. She wanted to make sure I had a name that carried the gravitas of my station in life."

"Well, of course she did. And that name's a doozy."

"Not everyone can be named after football players, toots," he said snidely.

"Why didn't I know that before?"

"Suppose it never came up. Do you know whether I'm a boxer or a brief man, sugar?"

"Boxers, silk."

He chuckled. "I guess you get a pass on the middle name then. So, your dead guy liked expensive things, eh?"

"Seems that way," she said.

"You getting any nookie time, sugar? I mean, you are on your honeymoon and it's supposed to be all about the nookie."

Peyton glanced over at Marco, watching the way he tilted his head to study the drawings on the walls. "Don't you worry about us. Have you been keeping an eye on my dog? I'm a little worried with all the nookie time Jake and Bambi are getting that he's gonna starve to death." She realized both men were giving her alarmed looks. She'd forgotten she was talking on the phone and they couldn't hear the other end of the conversation.

Marco smiled in amusement and turned away, but Kahele frowned.

"Your dog is fine. Stop worrying about that dog. Jakey would never let anything happen to him."

"Okay, I need to go, Abe, but thanks for the information."

"Talk to you soon, little bits."

Once he disconnected the call, Peyton stared at the desk. An ornate letter opener sat in a holder on the surface of the desk and she studied it, then reached for it. The handle was inlaid with shells of some kind.

"What are you going to do?" asked Kahele.

"See if I can jimmy the lock."

"I don't think that's a good idea. What if I get a locksmith in here?" He reached for the letter opener, turning it over in his hand. "I think this is a tortoise shell handle."

Peyton felt a little frustrated. They didn't have time to be waiting for locksmiths and other things. They needed to get this case solved.

"Brooks," said Marco, jerking his head toward the blueprints on the wall to the right of the desk.

She gave Kahele an arch look and pushed back, then rose and walked over to him.

"All of these plans have an address and a date stamp. They're all plans for strip malls Dewdrop Construction has already built."

"Okay," she said, glancing over them.

He pointed to the ones on the wall in front of them. "These don't have dates or stamps or locations. They're just drawings."

"Speculation drawings, maybe? Future buildings?"

"It could be, but there are stores listed that I haven't seen in Hawaii."

"Like what?" she asked.

He looked over his shoulder at Kahele. "Do you have *Backcourt Sporting Goods* here?"

Kahele considered it, then shook his head. "Never heard of it."

"What about *Wine Barrel?*" asked Peyton.

"No, what is it?"

"A big box liquor store," she told him. She thought about it for a moment. "If these are stores that haven't been in Hawaii before, that might be why *Freedom Kauai* is all fired up about Meridew. He was bringing in big box competitors."

"Which will drive out smaller family owned businesses," said Marco.

"I want a meeting with Manny Wong tomorrow, Chief. Do you think you can set it up?"

"I'll do my best," he said.

Peyton's jaw firmed. "If he refuses, we may have to compel him. Everything is pointing at him or someone in his organization."

"Okay, I'll tell him it's imperative."

Kahele's phone rang and he pulled it out of his pocket. "Chief Kahele here," he said. Then his face clouded over. "What? When?" He listened, drawing Peyton and Marco around to face him. "Okay, we'll head out there now." He disconnected the call.

"What happened?"

"Someone tried to drive Hughes off the road. He was coming back to Lihue, when someone forced him off the Hulemalu Road, scraped his back bumper and caused him to get a flat."

"Is he safe now?"

"One of our patrol officers is on the way."

"Did he get a license plate number on the car?" asked Marco.

"I don't know," said Kahele, setting down the letter opener. "We better get out there now."

They hurried for the door, but Peyton stopped long enough to put the crime scene tape back over the entrance.

* * *

Cho pulled up in front of a pleasant ranch style home. The small front yard was fenced in, the grass green and lush, the planter beds against the house bursting with colorful flowers. The house was a pale yellow with white trim and a painted porch. Two metal chairs sat on the porch and two older men sat in the chairs, drinking beers.

Danté watched them, but Cho cleared his throat. "This is the hardest part of our job."

Danté looked over, giving him a speculative look.

Cho shook his head, his eyes drifting to the men. "Of all the things we see and do, this is the one I hate the most, telling someone that their family member is gone. I'd rather be shot at a million times than do this again."

Danté forced his face to be neutral, but he thought this probably was a bit of an exaggeration. Not that he couldn't appreciate how difficult this would be, but these people had kicked their daughter out of their house because she was pregnant. He was having a little trouble making peace with that.

"Let me do the talking on this one, okay?" said Cho.

Danté nodded. "Of course."

"We give them only as much information as they require, no more."

"Are we going to have one of them identify the body?"

"If we have to, but I was thinking Harper might be able to do it for us."

Danté thought it was probably better to make either of her parents do it since they hadn't been concerned with their daughter before now, but he wasn't going to argue.

Cho took a deep breath, held it, then released it and opened the car door, getting out. Danté followed him, heading up the walk. As they approached the two men straightened, tension zipping through their bodies. Both men were Latino with grey-shot black hair and moustaches.

Looking at them up close, Danté figured they had to be related.

"Can I help you?" said the man on the right. He looked like he was a few years older than the man on the left.

Cho removed his badge and held it up. "Inspector Nathan Cho of the SFPD, sir."

Both men rose to their feet and Danté felt the muscles along his back stiffen, but Cho didn't hesitate. He climbed up on the porch and offered the older man his hand.

"This is my partner, Officer Danté Price," he said, motioning at Danté.

Danté shook hands with the two men.

"Are either of you Hugo Gutierrez?" Cho asked.

The older man touched his chest. "I am. This is my brother, Guillermo."

Cho nodded grimly at him, then motioned to the door. "Can we go inside and talk?"

Hugo twisted his lips to the side in consideration, then he nodded and moved behind his brother, pulling open the door. They stepped into a small, but neat living room with a couch and two recliners facing a large flat screen television.

"Have a seat, officers," said Hugo.

"Is your wife here, Mr. Gutierrez?" asked Cho, still standing.

Hugo's dark eyes shifted between the two of them. Danté could almost see the moment he guessed what they were there for. "Elba!" he shouted.

A moment later a woman appeared in the doorway. She had her hair pulled up at the sides, but the rest of it hung far down her back. She looked about Hugo's age and she was wiping her hands on a dish towel.

"What, Hugo? I'm busy," she said, then she stopped when she saw the two strangers. "What's going on?"

Cho stepped forward. "Mrs. Gutierrez?"

"Yes," she said, setting the towel down on a bookcase near the entrance.

"I'm Inspector Nathan Cho and this is my partner Danté Price."

"What is this about?" she said, her frightened eyes shifting to her husband.

"Please have a seat," Cho directed.

The three family members took seats on the edge of the couch. Cho jerked his chin toward one of the recliners and Danté sat down. His stomach suddenly felt fluttery and he wanted to be anywhere else at this moment. The family's fear was palpable, zipping in the air around them. Cho sank into the other recliner and clasped his hands before him.

"I am so sorry to tell you that..."

Elba slapped a hand over her mouth. "Oh God!" she moaned.

"...your daughter was found this morning in her apartment."

Hugo leaped to his feet. "What do you mean found?" he shouted.

"She's dead," said Cho.

Danté watched as the mother collapsed in on herself. She slumped over on her brother-in-law, a dreadful keening sound rising out of her body. Shivering at the impact of it, Danté stared at Cho, willing him to say something, fill the horrible moment with logic and reason. But if there had been any reason to any of this, they wouldn't have been here.

Cho waited until Hugo sat down again, his legs giving out on him. He curled over, pressing his hands between his knees.

"Dead how?" Hugo asked.

"Murdered," said Cho.

"Murdered?" he asked in a strangled voice.

Cho nodded. "We have an Amber Alert out for the baby."

Elba gasped. "Baby? She had the baby?"

Danté didn't want Cho to tell them what had happened. Suddenly it seemed too much.

"The baby was taken from her."

"What do you mean taken from her?" demanded Guillermo.

Cho wiped a hand under his nose and looked at a spot over their heads. "Cut from her womb."

Elba made that animalistic moan again. Her husband gathered her in his arms and they curled into each other as if they could become one person, one person strong enough to survive this. Danté looked away, unable to watch it any longer.

After a moment, Elba forced herself to her feet. "I'm going to be sick," she said and rushed from the room.

Hugo and his brother exchanged looks, then Guillermo nodded for his brother to go after his wife.

Cho waited until the father had left the room. "Please know we are so very sorry for your loss and I promise you we will find out who did this to her."

"The baby was taken from her? She didn't give birth to it?"

"No," said Cho.

"Do you know what she had?"

"We don't. She hadn't gotten prenatal care yet."

Guillermo stared at the table in front of him. "This just can't be happening. This can't be real."

"I understand," said Cho.

"Who found her?"

Cho glanced at Danté. "Officer Price."

Guillermo's eyes shifted to him. Danté felt the weight of his gaze pierce him. "You found her?"

Danté nodded.

"Where?"

"What?" he asked, his heart hammering so hard it was hard to hear over the blood rushing in his ears.

"Where did you find her?"

"Her apartment."

"Where was she living? We didn't know."

"The Tenderloin."

"The Tenderloin?" he said with a strangled sound. Closing his eyes, he fought for composure, then opened them again. "What made you go out there?"

"She'd gone for help at a woman's shelter. She was part of a support group that was run by a woman named Harper McLeod. Ms. McLeod came to me concerned because Luz hadn't shown up for her meeting."

Guillermo nodded slowly.

"I went out with her this morning to do a welfare check."

Guillermo braced his head on his hand.

Danté glanced at Cho. Cho nodded that he'd given the right amount of information.

"We need to ask some questions. Do you think you can answer them for us or should we wait for Luz's parents?"

"I'll answer what I can," Guillermo said, sliding his hand down to his chin.

"Luz was living on her own, according to Ms. McLeod, because her parents had thrown her out of the house."

Guillermo sighed heavily. "It wasn't exactly like that. They were shocked, things were said that shouldn't have been said, and Luz overreacted. It would have blown over, but she grabbed her stuff and took off."

"So they didn't want her to marry the father of the baby?"

Guillermo held out his empty hands. "We're Catholic. Of course they wanted her to marry the father. They didn't want the child to be illegitimate, but they would have accepted Luz's decision."

"She must have thought they were serious," said Danté, unable to help himself. He knew no matter what he and his brother did, his parents would never tell them to leave their house. "Did they know the boyfriend was abusive?"

"Easy," said Cho in warning.

Danté could see the confusion and hurt on Guillermo's face.

"Look, Officer Price, was it?"

"Yes."

"My niece was a beautiful girl." He gasped and let out a sobbing breath. "God, this just can't be happening."

"Go on, Mr. Gutierrez," urged Cho.

"My niece was a beautiful girl, but she was headstrong. She had her ideas and they didn't always gel with her parents. They wanted her to think about all the implications of a twenty-year-old having a baby, but Luz wouldn't hear of it. I don't know if Donny was abusive or not. I never saw anything, but Luz said he was, so I have no reason not to believe her."

"When was the last time Luz saw her parents?"

"It's been months," said Guillermo, "but recently, she and Elba had been talking on the phone. Elba wanted her to come home, but she said she couldn't. She said she'd gotten a job."

"As a cashier at a grocery store," said Danté.

Guillermo shook his head. "The minute she left, my brother regretted what they said to her. They didn't want her to go. They didn't want her to do this on her own, but Luz was so headstrong, so determined to do things her way."

Cho nodded. "A lot of kids are."

"They wanted her to go to college, get a degree, but Luz never liked school. Then she met Donny."

"Did you know Donny well?"

"He lived here. I told my brother after Luz got pregnant that he couldn't have been surprised. I mean, the kid was sleeping on the couch." He made air quotes around *sleeping*. "They let him stay here. They had to know he was sleeping with Luz, but they still reacted badly when they found out she was pregnant."

"What exactly did they say to her? Do you remember?" asked Cho.

"They said she'd violated God's law, that the baby was a bastard. I think my brother called her a whore."

Danté flinched.

Guillermo shook his head, scrubbing his hands over his face. "Oh God, how is he ever going to forgive himself now? How will he ever accept what he did? He didn't mean it, but it doesn't matter now. His daughter died believing her father thought she was a whore."

Cho looked down and Danté felt such a gut wrenching sadness. So much damage done in the heat of the moment. Words had been said that could never be taken back.

"Do you know Donny's last name, Mr. Gutierrez?" asked Cho.

"Ochoa," said Guillermo. "Elba might have his contact information."

"Do you know if Luz was still seeing him?"

"No, I think she broke it off. He wanted her to have an abortion, but she wouldn't hear of it and her parents begged her not to even consider it."

He wanted her to have an abortion? *Had he made sure of it?* thought Danté.

*   *   *

Marco and Peyton arrived at the spot where Hughes had been forced off the road. There was a turnout for cars, but the road was rough and a line of boulders had been placed to keep cars from straying too far off the highway.

Marco pulled in behind Kahele's car and they all got out, approaching the gathering around Hughes' silver BMW. Two more patrol cars and a tow truck occupied the area. Hughes was talking to a couple of uniformed officers, while a tow truck driver changed his tire. He glanced over as he saw the detectives approaching.

"Chief, Agent Brooks!" he said, moving toward them.

"Aloha, Mr. Hughes," said Kahele. "Are you all right?"

"Shaken up, but I'm fine. Your officers got here within minutes."

241

Marco moved away from the group, heading toward the BMW. The tow truck driver jerked his chin at Marco.

"Sup," he said.

"Sup," repeated Marco, studying the car. The tire that had gone flat was on the right rear side. "What happened?"

"Looks like he picked up a nail when he went off on the turnout." He rolled the flat tire around and showed Marco the nailhead.

Marco stored that away, moving around the back of the car. The left rear panel was damaged. Marco found a dent and some white paint that didn't belong there. He touched the paint with the tips of his fingers. "Is this where the other driver clipped him?"

"Yep," said the tow truck driver.

Marco nodded and wandered back toward the group.

"He came out of nowhere and tapped the side of my car. I swerved and drove onto the turnout. I was so scared. When I finally got the car stopped, I just sat there for a minute, shaking."

"What happened with the other car? Did he keep going?" said Peyton, taking her notebook out.

"He just kept driving. He never looked back. I called the emergency number right away."

"How long did you sit in the car before you got out?" asked Kahele.

"I was pretty shaken up. I didn't move for a while, then I got out to see the damage." He motioned to the car. "The tire was starting to go flat and I had the dent on the opposite side."

"Did you get a license plate number on the car?" asked Peyton.

"Not really. Of course, it started with KAB, but I didn't get any of the numbers."

"Did you catch the make and model?"

"It was a white sedan. I didn't think to get any more information. I wasn't sure what I was going to do if he came back toward me. I don't have any weapons or anything to protect myself with."

Peyton nodded, tapping the pen against her lower lip. "Did you get a look at the driver? Any distinguishing characteristics?"

"I saw sunglasses and a ball cap. He was male. That's about all I know."

"Anything about the car? Anything hanging from the rearview mirror?" asked Kahele.

"Not that I saw." He rubbed his forehead. "God, I'm sorry. I'm not being much help, am I?"

"You're doing fine," said Kahele.

"Mr. Hughes, have you gotten any more letters?" asked Peyton.

"No, none."

"Do you have any other cars you can use?"

He shrugged. "I can call a car service. Why?"

"We'd like to take the car and see if we can get any evidence off it. Paint scrapings. Sometimes we can match it to a make and model."

"Sure. Whatever will help," said Hughes. "Do you think this is connected to Harvey's death?"

Kahele shifted weight and looked out over the area. "I think it's concerning, Mr. Hughes, yes. Until we figure out more about Mr. Meridew's death, I wish you wouldn't leave your security detail behind. Keep them with you."

"I can't afford around the clock monitoring, Chief," said Hughes. "With this injunction, we're way behind schedule and I have to keep paying the crew not to work."

"I understand that, but your safety is paramount. My officers can only do so much."

Hughes rubbed the back of his neck. "Okay, I'll see what I can do."

"Come on, Mr. Hughes, I want to arrange for the tow truck driver to bring your vehicle to our impounds lot and then I'll drive you home myself."

"Thank you, Chief. I really appreciate everything you're doing."

As they wandered over to talk to the tow truck driver, Peyton moved back to Marco's side. "What do you make of this?"

"There's damage to the rear panel on the car. They might be able to take a sample of the white paint and figure out make and model."

Peyton studied the road. Since they'd been here, only a few cars had passed down it. Marco knew when something was bothering her.

"What?" he asked.

"If it was the killer, why didn't he turn around and come back for him? He was a sitting duck."

"I was thinking the same thing. Maybe this wasn't related to the murder of Meridew at all. Maybe it was just a traffic accident."

"Maybe," said Peyton, but she sounded concerned.

He tucked a curl behind her ear. "What's really bothering you?"

"That maybe this was a warning. Maybe our killer doesn't want to kill again, but he's warning Hughes that if he doesn't stop fighting the injunctions, something worse will happen."

Marco looked over at Hughes. The man was gesticulating wildly, retelling his story to Kahele and pointing to the damage. "Hughes isn't going to stop, Brooks. He needs to build that mall. These tycoons operate on very narrow profit margins."

"Well, then we'd better figure this out, D'Angelo. Otherwise, we may have another dead body on our hands."

CHAPTER 14

"He wouldn't let me jimmy the desk open. He said he'd get a locksmith," Peyton told her team the following morning, sitting on her balcony. "There's something in that desk. Meridew had these expensive tastes. A bottle of 30-year-old Macallan Whisky..."

Radar whistled in appreciation.

"A solid ivory box, or that's what Kahele said. A tortoise shell letter opener."

Bambi made a face. "He was a sadistic bastard, wasn't he? There's something wrong with a guy who buys ivory and tortoise shell."

"Well, I don't know about that," said Peyton. "But by all accounts he wasn't very pleasant."

"We located Jackson Hughes' ex-wife, Tricia," said Tank. "She's living on Maui, but she was in the South of France when Meridew was murdered."

"At least we can cross one person off the list. I still think we should question her. Maybe she knows something about Meridew. Hughes has his rose-colored glasses on about the guy. He has an excuse for all of his actions."

"I'll take care of that," said Bambi.

"Did you find out anything about *Freedom Kauai*?" asked Peyton.

"Manny Wong's been arrested for vandalism and criminal mischief in the past," said Bambi.

"He was also a suspect in a murder investigation. Three years ago a man fell off some scaffolding at a construction site. He died," said Tank.

"I heard about that from Kana, the woman who owns the Crab Shack. Was it a Dewdrop Property?"

"No, another construction company who tried to do work on Kauai. They went out of business because of the lawsuits when the worker was killed. The cops suspected Wong and his people had removed the bolts holding the scaffolding together," said Tank.

"Was Wong arrested?" asked Peyton.

"They questioned him, but they couldn't find any evidence to make it stick. He probably got away with murder that time."

"Awesome. What happened with the case? Did they look for any other suspects?"

"They ruled the death accidental, the construction company paid through the nose for negligence, and filed for bankruptcy."

"You be careful around this Wong character, Peyton. He sounds like a snake in the grass," said Bambi.

Peyton smiled at her. "You look pretty today, Emma."

"My skin's glowing, isn't it?"

"Sure is."

"It's Jakey."

Radar cleared his throat. "How about you go call Tricia Hughes right now, Bambi?"

"Okay," she said, then waved to Peyton. "Talk to you soon."

"Talk to you soon," Peyton said, waving back. "Tank, can we get the tax filings for Dewdrop Construction for the last few years?"

"I'll get on it," he said and was gone.

Peyton focused on Radar. "How are you feeling, old man?"

"I'm fine," he said with a grumble.

"You sure? You seem a little short tempered."

"You need to start eliminating suspects in this case."

"I know. We're working on it."

"It makes me nervous that someone tried to kill Hughes. If another one of these big shots dies, it's gonna look bad for the FBI. Maybe I should send someone out to babysit that Hughes idiot until you figure this out."

Peyton gave him a shake of her head. "Don't do that yet. We're going to meet with my number one suspect in about an hour."

"This Manny Wong character?"

"Right. He has motive and opportunity. I don't know yet, but all roads seem to point to him."

Radar gave it some thought, then he tilted his head. "You given any more thought to what we were talking about?"

"What?" she asked, frowning.

"You quitting?"

"Yes, I have, Radar. A lot of thought." She glanced over her shoulder into the room, but Marco was taking a shower. "My life with Marco is the most important thing. I have to do whatever I can to preserve it."

"Giving up your life for his isn't the answer, Sparky."

"Giving up a career that makes us both crazy might be, though."

"Whatever you do, kid, just make sure you don't decide while you're in Hawaii. Wait until you get home and get into the domestic part of the marriage. Then decide if you really want to go all traditional or not."

"I will," she told him. "I'd better go, but call me if Tank or Bambi find out anything."

"You know we will."

"Radar?"

"What?" he grumbled.

"I am listening to you, you know? I hear what you're saying and I'm thinking about it, okay?"

"That's all I ask, Sparky. That's all I ask."

"Talk to you soon," she said and ended the call.

A few minutes later, they were headed out to meet Kahele at the *Freedom Kauai* headquarters. Manny Wong's radical environmental group occupied a single story cement building with a hand carved sign above the door reading *Freedom Kauai*.

Kahele pulled in behind them and got out, joining them at the front door. "I made arrangements to meet with Phoebe Meridew, the third wife who lives on Kauai, later today." He shook his head wryly. "Funny thing about that. Phoebe wasn't exactly choked up to find out her husband was dead."

"Ex-husband. The ex part might be the difference," said Peyton.

Kahele nodded and surveyed the *Freedom Kauai* building. "So, Manny Wong has a reputation for being intense and judgmental. Just want you to be prepared for that."

"We can handle him," she said.

"Not sure anyone can handle Manny, but here we go." He yanked open the door and walked inside.

A number of people occupied an open space in the center of the building. The area was bisected by tables, whose surfaces were covered in signs and spray paint cans. Peyton marked that a number of those gathered were of Hawaiian descent, but there were also a mix-bag of other ethnicities present.

A woman detached herself from the group. She had short blond hair and striking features, large eyes, large lips, high cheekbones. She wore a pair of shorts, flip flops, and a yellow tank top. "Can I help you?"

"We're looking for Manny Wong," said Kahele, holding up his badge.

A short, wiry man separated from the group and approached them. He was also dressed in shorts with a t-shirt and collared shirt open over the top of it. He wore sandals on his feet that looked like they'd been braided from grass. His black hair draped over his right eye and he had to shake it back in order to see. A braided band had been tied around his wrist.

"What do you want?" he said, stopping before them. He bristled with hostility. "What are you here to harass me about now?"

Peyton sighed. Yep, Manny Wong was going to be unpleasant.

"We'd like to talk to you in private, if you don't mind?" said Kahele. "I'm Chief Terence Kahele and this is Special Agent Peyton Brooks and Captain Marco D'Angelo."

Manny held out his arms. "You can talk in front of my people. They know everything about me."

Peyton moved up beside Kahele. "And yet we'd still like to talk to you in private." She looked around the building. There wasn't much in here, but she figured she could find something illegal if she looked hard enough. "I don't think you want us to feel the need to search this entire building, do you? Probable cause and all that."

Manny's face grew grim and he looked down. "Fine, let's go to my office."

Kahele gave her an approving nod as they followed Manny across the cement floor to an expansive glass office in the back. He pushed open the door and waved to a set of chairs in front of a desk made out of surfboards.

"Sit," he ordered, shaking back his hair.

Peyton never understood why people chose style over functionality, but then she had a mass of hair that was always getting in her way too and she had no intention of cutting it.

"Interesting piece of furniture," she said, running her fingers across the surface of it.

"Everything in this building is from reclaimed materials. I never buy anything new. Capitalism is destroying the planet and we're just standing around letting it happen." He eyed her clothing, then looked over the desk at her shoes. "Leather. Do you know how much energy and waste there is to produce those sandals that you'll just discard in a landfill at some point to get the new latest fashions."

"Actually, they aren't leather. My husband's a vegetarian, so we don't have leather in our house."

"That's worse."

Peyton arched a brow. This guy vibrated with energy and it wasn't good energy. Marco began wandering around the room, looking at the newspaper clippings on the walls, the display cases that housed...

Peyton frowned and moved toward him.

"Are these weapons?" she asked, tapping a fingernail on the glass.

"I collect primitive artifacts," Manny said. "Bowls, cups, plates..."

"Weapons?" she said, pointing to a wicked looking spear.

"Some weapons."

Marco gave her a speculative look and pointed to an oblong shaped tube suspended by fishing wire. Peyton leaned closer, staring at it.

"Is this a flute of some kind?" she asked Manny, flashing him a smile. The length of the tube had been carved and painted with spiraling lines. The entire surface had been polished to a rich black sheen.

He stared at the case, not answering.

Kahele walked over and peered inside as well. "Did you hear Agent Brooks' question, Manny?"

"It's a blowgun, invented by the Dayak people of Borneo. They used it for hunting."

Peyton turned to Manny. "A blowgun that shoots poisonous darts?"

"In the past."

"Of course," she answered. "How about we sit down?"

Manny eased behind his desk, taking a seat, his eyes roving between the three of them. "This is about Harvey Meridew?"

"You're a quick study, my friend," said Peyton, sitting across from him. Kahele took the chair next to her. "I understand from Chief Kahele that you and Mr. Meridew didn't exactly see eye to eye?"

"He was a capitalist raider that thought Hawaii was his private treasure chest to rape and plunder."

Peyton took out her notebook. "You've filed a number of injunctions against him, protested at the building site and have been arrested for vandalism."

Manny leaned forward, his eyes intense, the whites showing around the iris. "Is it vandalism if you're trying to save your homeland from murderers and rapists?"

"It's vandalism if you destroy property that doesn't belong to you."

He made a slashing motion with his hand. "This is the problem with people like you, Agent Brooks. You think someone like Harvey Meridew has more rights than the rest of us. You think people sitting in the 1% deserve what they have. You're part of the problem. You're just a cog in the system doing what your superiors tell you. You're a fool for the establishment and you'll never even see it. Never even realize how you're being used." He slapped a hand against his chest. "It threatens you that I'm more enlightened, more in tune with what is happening in our world. It scares you that I don't believe in your laws, your enslavement to a false god."

Peyton gave him a patient smile. "Not at all. I'm not denying you have a point, and I admire your dedication to your cause, but if that dedication resulted in the death of a man who was trying to run a business..."

"That business was the business of destroying the natural beauty of this amazing ecosystem. That business was the business of flooding the world with cheap products, plastic and non-biodegradable consumables. That business was the business..."

Peyton held up a hand. "I get your point, Mr. Wong, but I can't condone your practices, especially if they result in the death of an innocent, someone who had nothing to do with capitalism except to provide for his family."

"You mean the scaffolding death? I was never charged with a crime. I had nothing to do with it."

"A man died. His family lost a husband, father, provider. Did his family not matter?"

Manny's gaze never waivered. "There will be collateral damage in the battle to save the planet."

"Was Harvey Meridew collateral damage?"

Manny made a scoffing sound. "Not even close. He was a violator, a murderer…"

"A rapist," interrupted Peyton with a sigh.

"Can you account for your whereabouts on the night of Meridew's death, Manny?" said Kahele.

"We were protesting on Maui. They were breaking ground on another hotel, the *Maui Windjammer*. If you do a little research online, Chief Kahele, I think you'll find I was giving an interview that night on the local news station." He gave Kahele a mirthless grin.

Peyton made a few notes, then looked up. "Did you fly back to Kauai the next day?"

Manny's grin faded. "What?"

"When did you return to Kauai?" she asked sweetly.

Manny pushed back his chair. "I think we're done here. From now on, you can talk to my lawyer."

"But we were having so much fun," said Peyton, giving him a pout. "I have so many other questions."

"Like do you have permits for these artifacts?" asked Marco, tapping the glass on the case.

"Permits?"

"Antiquities that are privately owned should have permits, bills of sale, all those legal documents to make sure you aren't appropriating culturally significant artifacts," Marco continued.

Peyton smiled. His love of art apparently didn't just extend to paintings. Funny how you could still learn new things about someone you thought you knew everything about. It gave her a little shiver of pleasure.

"Tell you what, Manny," she said, rising and placing her hands on his surfboard desktop. "What's say you gather the permits or bills of sale for all those lovely treasures in your cases? Then we'll come back tomorrow and take a look at them."

He swallowed hard.

She leaned closer. "While you're at it, how about you work on where you were the night Harvey Meridew died? And in the meantime, we'll just get a warrant to search this place."

Manny didn't answer, but he glared daggers at her.

She motioned to Kahele and he rose, heading for the door. She started after him, but she turned, giving Manny a smile. "By the way, don't leave town, okay, Manny? I would hate to track you down at your next protest. I mean, I'm sure you'd rather get arrested for exercising your first amendment rights, rather than something more unpleasant."

With that, she left the room.

* * *

Cho turned to Harper outside of the medical examiner's lab. She tilted back her head, shaking her long brown hair over her shoulders, her expression determined, focused, but Danté could feel her trembling.

"Just go in and the ME will show you her face. Identify her and you can leave."

She nodded, a quick jerk of her head up and down.

"Are you sure you can do this?" Cho asked her.

"I'm fine," she said, but her voice trembled.

Danté exchanged a look with Cho, then Cho gave a slow nod and pressed the button on Abe's lab. The door swished open a moment later and Abe motioned them inside. He was dressed in a lab coat, but underneath it Danté felt sure he saw black pants with baseballs running down the legs. He blinked and looked again. Yep, baseballs.

"Come in," Abe said with a flourish that sent the baseballs on the end of his dreads to bouncing.

Danté placed a hand in the center of Harper's back and guided her inside. A body covered by a white drape lay in the middle of the room on a metal table. Abe walked around them and approached it. Harper pressed back against Danté's hand, staring at the table with wide eyes.

Abe gave her a sympathetic look. "Come on, sugar," he said. "Just a quick look and you can leave."

The smell in the room was antiseptic, but underlying it was a smell of rot and decay. Danté swallowed hard. They'd visited the medical examiner's office in the academy, but this was the first time he'd done so on a case.

"Harper, if you can't do this, we understand," he said to her.

She leaned into him. "No, I can do it."

Tilting back her head again, she walked up to the other side of the table, staring down at the body. "Go ahead. I'm ready," she said in that same thready voice.

Abe reached for the drape and pulled it back, exposing the victim's head. Harper stared at her for a surprisingly long time, just stared, not moving, not breathing, but Danté could feel the violent trembling that traveled through her frame.

"It's her," she said. "It's Luz."

Abe quickly covered the face again. "I have things to tell you," he said to Cho.

Cho nodded. "Take Harper down the hall to the break room."

Danté nodded and guided Harper to the door, punching the button to let her out. They walked in silence down the hall to the break room and he eased her into a chair. She clasped her hands between her knees, staring at the floor, shivering violently. Danté wasn't sure what to do, but she looked up at him, her eyes fierce.

"Go hear what the ME has to say. I'm all right."

"Harper."

"Go. You've got to get the bastard who did this to her, so go hear what he has to say. I'll wait for you here."

He hesitated a moment more, but she just stared at him with those unyielding eyes. Then he turned and walked back to Abe's lab. Abe gave him a sympathetic look.

"Is she okay?" he asked.

"She demanded I come back to hear what you have to say."

"She's a strong little cookie." He nudged Danté with his arm. "Pretty too, eh?"

Danté blinked at him.

"Abe!" said Cho in a warning tone.

"Okay, okay, don't get your panties in a bunch. I'm just making an observation."

Danté wasn't sure how to respond. There was a dead girl on the table and he was acting like it wasn't a big deal, but then Danté saw the switch, saw the mask come over his face, the doctor in control now.

Danté approached the autopsy table.

"As I was saying, the excising of the baby happened after she was dead," said Abe.

Danté frowned. "How did she die?"

"Blunt force trauma," said Cho.

"Someone struck her on the back of the head with something heavy. Fractured her skull, caused hemorrhaging," added Abe.

"Wait. She was on the bed. She was on her back on the bed. How did she get there?"

Abe shrugged. "She had to be around 180 pounds when she was pregnant."

"So we're looking at a man, most likely," said Cho. "A woman wouldn't be strong enough to lift her."

"What bothers me is the baby was cut from her womb," said Abe. "Why would a man take the baby?"

"The father of the baby?" asked Danté.

Abe shifted weight. "The blow to the back of the head was violent, so that speaks to someone who wanted her dead. If he didn't want to deal with being a father, then leaving her with the baby makes more sense."

"What do you think the murder weapon was?"

Abe walked over to the light box on the wall and clicked on the light. "Based on the angle of the blow, it came across here." He indicated a line. The blow had hit high on the left side of her head and angled down to the right.

Cho squinted at it. "The direction looks like a stick of some kind swung downward to bludgeon her."

Danté's eyes focused on Abe's pants. "A bat," he said.

"Good," said Abe. "You think like a cop. Probably a bat," he confirmed to Cho. "Makes most sense."

"But why would he take the baby?" asked Cho.

"Revenge," said Danté. "She kicked him out of her life, so he got revenge by killing her and stealing the child."

Cho considered that, tilting his head to the side. He ran a hand over his face. "God, what kind of monster does this?"

Abe placed a hand on Cho's shoulder. "This is the end of the pool we swim in, Nate. This girl was twenty years old. She needs you now. She needs you to get justice for her, and her baby."

"Is there anyway to tell if the baby was alive?" asked Cho, looking up at him.

"If he or she was born alive, no telling what happened after. I just don't know," said Abe.

"Did she have any defensive wounds?" asked Danté, staring at the draped body. "Any signs that she fought back?"

"None."

"Signs of sexual assault?" asked Cho.

"None." Abe frowned. "There was something though." He clicked on the computer at the back of the room. "This bothered me when I saw it. She had undigested pastries in her stomach."

"So she had breakfast just before it happened," said Cho.

"Yeah," said Abe, dragging the word out. "But these were dyed bright colors. Blue, pink, orange."

"Macrons," said Danté.

Abe touched his nose, smiling at Cho. "This one's quick. I like him," he told Cho. "That's exactly what I was thinking." He placed a hand in the middle of his chest. "It's hard being the smartest person in the room, isn't it, Danté? I mean, I've had to deal with this all my life and it just never gets easier. You're always telling people things and they just cannot get on your level."

Danté gave Cho a bewildered look.

"Okay, Einstein, dial it back. The kid's new."

"He's all sorts of adorable is what he is," said Abe, winking at him.

Danté took an involuntary step back. It wasn't the overtly sexual innuendo that surprised him. He'd met Abe before. It was the fact that a dead girl lay on the slab behind him. Then Abe's expression shifted again.

"I took a blood sample and I'll send it out for a toxicology report. I'm also going to swab the head wound again and see if I get anything – fibers, particles, debris."

"Okay," said Cho. "Call us if you find anything else out."

"You know I will."

Cho motioned to the door. "Let's go talk to Harper."

Danté nodded.

"See you, Officer Smarty-pants," Abe called to him.

Danté glanced back over his shoulder at the table with the dead girl on it. Abe went around to the microscope, but as he passed the body, he patted her shoulder.

"We'll figure it out, sugar. Don't you worry none," he heard Abe say to her, then the doors swished open.

Danté followed Cho toward the break room where Harper waited, but he just couldn't get over the strange way Abe dealt with the depravity of his job.

"Nate," he said.

Cho turned and looked at him. "What's up, kid?"

Danté shook his head, looking back again. "I just don't get it. He seems unprofessional, but…"

Cho took a deep breath and released it. "We deal with death everyday, Danté. Not people who have lived a full life and left when it was their time. We deal with people who are ripped from life violently, brutally, unacceptably. How each of us copes with it is different. Don't for a minute think that cutting up a twenty-year-old girl doesn't gut him. I've known Abe Jefferson a long time and there is no more caring person in the world, but he has to compartmentalize what he does or he wouldn't be able to do it anymore. So he uses humor, he flirts, he says inappropriate things." He pointed back at the lab. "There is no one I respect more than that man. He's not just being arrogant. He is a genius and without him, we would be nothing."

Danté nodded. "Okay. Okay. I hear you."

Cho also nodded, then they walked into the break room.

Harper looked up. "Hey, Mr. Spock, you got some gum."

Danté reached into his pocket and took the pack out, sliding it across the table to her. She took a slice and unwrapped it, putting it in her mouth and chewing. Danté couldn't help but wonder if this was her coping mechanism.

Cho sank down at the table across from her. "I need to know everything you know about Luz."

She clasped her hands before her. "I only know her from the support group I ran."

"For pregnant women leaving bad situations?"

"Right," she said, her eyes shifting to Danté. "God, I want a smoke."

"Harper, please focus," Danté said.

"Do you think I'm not focused, Danté? I knew that girl. I held her hand. I told her everything was going to be all right! But it isn't, is it? She's dead! She's dead and her baby is missing!"

"Okay," said Danté. "Okay, I get it."

"You don't get it. This is just about finding a dead girl's killer for you, but I knew her. I sat with her while she talked about what she wanted for her baby. How she wanted things to be better for him."

"Did she know it was a boy?" asked Cho.

"No, she was just going to get medical care. She just called it a boy."

"Did she talk about the father of the baby?" asked Cho.

"She said she left him because he used to beat her. She was afraid he was going to cause her to lose the baby."

"What was his name again?" Cho asked Danté.

"Donny Ochoa," Danté said. "You're sure she wasn't seeing anyone else."

"No, I'm not sure, Mr. Spock," Harper said in a combative tone. "How would I know? We met for the support group, but I didn't know everything about her life."

Danté felt stung by her rebuff, but he tried to let it go. He knew she was upset and responding emotionally.

"Did anyone in the support group know her well? Was she close with any of them?" asked Cho.

Harper thought for a moment, smacking her gum. "I'm just not sure. We could call them all together and ask them if they knew anything."

"That's a good idea. Can you pull them together tomorrow night?" said Cho.

"I'll work on it." She rounded her shoulders and clasped her hands tight between her knees. "Did the ME think the baby was alive?"

"He doesn't know," said Cho.

Harper shook her head. "She wanted that baby so much. He meant everything to her. He was the reason she was trying to change her life."

Danté looked away. He couldn't stand seeing how vulnerable Harper looked right now, how small and sad. He was going to have to find his own coping mechanism or he was never going to make it in this job. Never.

* * *

Phoebe Meridew was younger than Marco and Peyton, a bottle blond with breast enhancements. Or Marco was pretty sure they were breast enhancements by the aggressive way they jutted out like a shelf from her chest. The string bikini she wore barely covered them and showed off an impressive set of toned, long legs ending in a pair of stiletto heels. She lounged on the chaise next to the pool, sipping a cocktail with an umbrella inside, sunglasses covering her eyes.

Marco knew what Peyton was going to say. This was his sort of woman, but it wasn't. It had never been. From the moment he'd met Peyton, he'd known she was his woman, but he'd dallied with women like Phoebe because there would never be any strings attached, any relationship to evolve from them.

Kahele showed her his badge. "Phoebe Meridew?"

"That's me!" she said, beaming up at him with white teeth, full red lips, and a straight, narrow nose. She'd had work done on her face too, Marco noted.

"I'm Chief Terrence Kahele. This is Special Agent Peyton Brooks and Captain Marco D'Angelo."

She ignored Peyton and fixed her gaze on Marco, waving her fingers. "Heya, cutie," she said, then leaned over, patting the chaise next to her. "Take a seat here."

Peyton shot him a half-smile and he shook his head at her, wandering toward the edge of the massive Roman pool. Potted palms lined the mosaic tiles along the edge of the pool and a white arbor ran down the length of it, offering shade. A bougainvillea vine trailed along the arbor, the salmon colored flowers offering a punch of color.

He leaned against one of the Roman columns and glanced back, watching Peyton take the seat next to Phoebe. The blond woman gave a pout in his direction, then she focused her attention on Kahele.

"Can I get you a Mai Tai, Chief?" she said, glazing at him over the rim of her large sunglasses.

"No, ma'am," he said, grabbing a chair from a nearby bistro table and setting it in front of her. "We'd like to ask you some questions about your ex-husband."

She dropped her head back against the chaise. "Oh God, that's so boring. Can't we talk about something else?" The way she slurred her words, Marco knew she was half-drunk.

"How many Mai Tais have you had, Phoebe? Can I call you Phoebe?" asked Peyton.

Phoebe made an airy wave with her hand. "Call me whatever you want. I'm feeling too good to care."

Marco wandered over to the open doorway that led into the house. The mosaic tile ran right up to the French doors. He couldn't imagine how much that must have cost to have installed. The entire house had to be worth more than a couple million.

"So how many Mai Tais?" Peyton asked again.

"Three or four. I'm relaxing."

"Relaxing? You don't seem too broken up about the death of your ex-husband."

"Harvey?" she said, laughing. "No one's sorry he's dead. Well, except poor dumb Jackson."

"Jackson Hughes?" asked Peyton.

"Yeah, Jackson was half in love with the guy."

Marco paused in the shade of the patio cover and glanced over his shoulder at her.

"What do you mean half in love?" asked Peyton.

"Harvey could do no wrong according to Jackson. Harvey made Jackson a millionaire and Jackson never forgot it."

"So you don't mean they had a romantic relationship?"

Phoebe sputtered out a laugh. "No, Harvey was homo…homo…" She waved her hand. "You know what I mean? He was afraid of gays."

"Homophobic?" asked Peyton.

"That!" said Phoebe, jabbing a finger at Peyton. "Harvey liked to collect women."

"What does that mean? Did he have affairs?"

"No…" She caught herself. "I mean, I don't think so. Maybe. Who knows?"

"It didn't matter to you if your husband had an affair."

"We had a marriage of…you know what I mean," she said, laughing.

"No, I'm not sure I do. A marriage of what?" asked Peyton.

"I gave him sex and he gave me…" She made an expansive wave of her arms. "All of this." She leaned toward Peyton and put her finger over her lips. "Don't tell anyone, but I'm a very wealthy woman now."

"Now?"

"Now that Harvey's dead. Oh, man, I have so much money, you wouldn't even believe it. It was in the will. If he dies, I get so much money."

Peyton's gaze rose to Kahele.

"Where were you the night Harvey died, Mrs. Meridew?" asked Kahele.

She slumped back against the chaise. "Phoebe. Call me Phoebe."

"Phoebe, where were you the night your ex-husband died?" he repeated.

"I was here. I was watching about the Kardashians. You know, I think I have as much money as them now." She giggled. "I'm a Kardashian!" she shouted, lifting her arms into the air.

Marco glanced into the house. Terracotta tiles ran throughout the interior and cane backed chairs and sofas were arranged in different configurations, all sporting Hawaiian print fabrics. Something caught Marco's attention in the expansive dining room across from the foyer. He slipped inside, moving silently across the interior.

Between the dining room and living room was a dividing wall, the center of it a massive fish tank. Marco peered inside at the colorful fish in the pristine tank. He wasn't very knowledgeable about fish, but he felt pretty sure the coral at the bottom of the tank and the brilliant colors of the fish meant it was salt water. He took out his phone and snapped a few pictures.

Harvey Meridew had been killed by puffer fish poison. He didn't see a puffer fish in here, but that didn't mean there hadn't been one. He sent a quick text to Peyton. A few moments later, she appeared at his side.

He pointed to the tank. "Take a look at this. Do you think it's saltwater?"

"Hm," she said, peering closely at it. "I would guess so. I'm no fish specialist, but…"

"Ichthyologist," said Marco.

"Ichthyologist? Who are you Tank?"

He held up his phone. "No, I just know how to do a quick search."

She laughed and wrapped her arms around his waist. "You think there was a puffer fish in there?"

"I'm wondering."

"Well, let me go ask Drunken Barbie about her pretty fish tank then. She must have it maintained by someone."

He kissed Peyton's temple. "Can you use anything Drunken Barbie's told you?"

She shook her head. "I don't know. She's completely smashed. I feel a little bad questioning her, but hey, you take what you can get."

"True. Although maybe you want to get her sobered up before you get her to confess to murder."

"You think Drunken Barbie is smart enough to manufacture puffer fish poison?"

"Maybe Drunken Barbie is an ichthyologist. You don't know her life."

Peyton laughed. "You're right. You'd never guess Bambi was an explosives expert, would you?"

"True. You can't judge a book by its cosmetically altered cover, Brooks."

Peyton smiled at him, patting his chest. "And to think I used to judge you for sleeping with all these Barbie dolls when you were just furthering science, weren't you, D'Angelo?" She started back to the lanai, but Marco caught her hand, drawing her back to him.

"Nope, Brooks," he said, sliding an arm around her waist. "I was waiting for you."

She rose on tiptoes and brought her mouth to his. "Oh, that was good, D'Angelo," she said and she kissed him.

CHAPTER 15

"So, one puffer fish contains enough poison to kill 30 people," said Tank, speaking to the entire room in Kahele's precinct.

Willis Akana, Kahele's CSI and tech guru, had set up a projector, so the field team in San Francisco could communicate with everyone on Kauai. Lani, the ME, nodded at Tank's assessment.

"It takes a very small amount to paralyze a full grown male," said Lani.

"How would someone be able to produce it?" asked Peyton.

"The poison is located in the skin, the liver, and the ovaries or gonads. Dry the fish, crush it up into a powder, and you have a lethal recipe," said Tank.

"And yet people eat it? Why would anyone take that risk?" asked Peyton, amazed.

"Thrill seekers," said Radar, making a face.

"A chef has to train for two years in order to prepare puffer fish. Even then, mistakes happen. Between 30 to 50 people a year die from it," said Tank.

"I'll take my thrills at the end of a bungee cord," said Bambi.

Willis' fingers flew over the keyboard. "There are only two places on Kauai that sell tropical fish for fish tanks. *The Fish Palace*. They don't list an address, but there's a phone number." He put it up on the screen.

"I'll call them and see what we get," said Tank.

"And *Kauai Mammals and Mermaids*," said Willis.

"Give me that number," said Marco, pushing himself to his feet and taking out his phone.

Willis flashed it on the screen and Marco punched it into his display as he stepped out of the command center.

"Could you get the third wife to tell you who maintains the fish tank?" asked Radar.

"Phoebe? She was drunk on Mai Tais," answered Peyton. "She said someone just comes once a week and the payment is automatically deducted from her account."

"Does she have a motive for wanting her ex-husband dead?" asked Radar.

"According to the divorce settlement Willis pulled, she and the other two wives each get an extra ten million upon his death," said Kahele.

"So any of them could have a motive," said Radar.

Peyton rose and walked to the whiteboard. "That's the problem. Manny Wong has a motive – his political battle against Meridew over the development. He also had a blowgun."

"So method," said Radar.

Peyton added the blowgun to the list. "Phoebe had motive, the extra ten million, but we don't know if she had method."

Tank appeared on the screen just as Marco stepped back into the room. "*The Fish Palace* sets up and maintains salt water tanks."

"So does *Kauai Mammals and Mermaids*," said Marco, taking his seat again.

"Did they tell you if Meridew was a customer?" asked Radar.

"Not without a warrant," said Tank.

"Ditto," said Marco.

Kahele rose. "I'm on it," he said, taking out his phone and sending a text message.

"I called Tricia Hughes, Jackson Hughes' ex-wife," said Bambi. "I got confirmation she was in the South of France. She sent me her plane ticket and a few credit card receipts. She didn't have much to say about Meridew, except he was a bastard. He treated everyone as if they were inferior to him and she finally had to tell Jackson that she wouldn't go places if Meridew was going to be there. Meridew always made a scene. She said she wasn't surprised someone finally killed him."

"I have something else," offered Willis. "I don't know if it's significant, but I took samples from the threatening letters that Meridew and Hughes both got."

Kahele set down his phone. "And?"

"There was a strange substance inside the envelope, just trace amounts."

"What was it?" asked Radar.

"Ash."

"Like from a cigarette?" asked Peyton.

"Definitely," said Willis.

"So whoever sent the letters likely smoked?" asked Kahele.

"Enough to leave residue behind," said Willis.

Kahele picked up his phone and read the display. "We should have our warrants in the next few hours."

"I want to go back to Meridew's office and open that desk drawer," said Peyton.

"Okay, I've got a locksmith standing by," said Kahele. "By the time we finish that, we should have the warrants."

"We'll work on the other two wives that aren't on Kauai," said Radar. "What were their names?"

"Daisy and Fiona," said Peyton, glancing at the whiteboard.

"Right. We'll try to arrange a time for you to interview them."

"I've got an island hopper ready to take us between islands," said Kahele. "We'll brief each other as more information becomes available."

Peyton stared at the whiteboard for a moment. Usually one person started to become predominant in a case, but they'd been at this for days and nothing was popping. She suspected Manny Wong had the most motive and he had a potential murder weapon, but something didn't feel right about that.

A short time later, they climbed into Kahele's white police issue Ford Explorer and they headed out for Meridew's office. Peyton's phone rang and she pulled it out of her pocket, seeing Jake's name pop up on the screen. She thumbed it on and held it to her ear, curling her hand in the handle over the door.

"What's up? Is my dog okay?" she demanded.

"Wow, no how are you, my dear ex-roomie Jake, no how's your day going, Jake, no how are things in the wonderful new romance you're currently exploring."

Peyton drew a breath for patience. "How are you, my dear ex-roommate?"

"I'm doing really well. In the pink, you might say. I'll tell you I feel like I'm walking on clouds."

"This is why I didn't ask you. I knew you'd have to Jake-it-up."

"Jake-it-up? That is not going to be a thing in our little group, Mighty Mouse."

"Oh, I think it already is. Now h-o-w i-s m-y d-o-g?"

"He's fine. He's really taken to Bambi."

Peyton frowned. "Are you living at Bambi's house?"

"Condo, and we stay there mostly."

"What's mostly?"

"Every night."

"So you're living there."

"No, I still have things in my condo."

"Shack."

"Shack, right."

"Jake…"

"Don't start, Peyton."

Peyton drew a deep breath and released it. She could feel Kahele looking over at her. "You're right. You do you, Jake. I'll stay out of it."

He didn't immediately answer. She looked at the display to see if the call had dropped. Nope. He was still on the line.

"Jake?"

"Sorry. I was in shock there for a minute. You never let me do me. You're always lecturing me."

"Well, I'm on island time now. This is a whole new Peyton. I'm going with the flow, hanging ten."

"Does Adonis know this? That man has never gone with the flow in his life, Peyton."

"Well, he's learning too. So you know what, you're a grown man. You do you. Whatever you want, just go for it."

"Okay." He dragged the word out. "Anyway, what I called for was Abe's birthday party. We have the venue, we have the theme, we even have the menu. What I don't have is the drink?"

"The drink?"

"The pièce de résistance."

"Yeah, okay, that's important."

"Damn straight it is."

"It's gotta be good for Abe's fiftieth birthday – it has to be suave and cultured, but fun and effervescent."

"Now you see my problem. The pièce de résistance." He said it with a heavy French accent. "Oh, and a disco ball."

"A what now?"

"I need a disco ball. Any idea where I can find one?"

"The 1970's."

"Funny," he said. "I'll figure it out. You know you came to the right man, right? The man with the plan. The man with the plan who can. The man with the plan who can use cyan. The man with the plan who can use pecan…"

"I should have just asked Stan," she interrupted.

He laughed. "I miss you, Mighty Mouse."

"I miss you, Jake. Okay, I'll come up with a pez of resistance."

"Pièce de résistance."

"Yeah, that. You find the disco ball. Ask Abe's friends, Misha and Serge. Surely to God they know where to get a disco ball." She again felt Kahele's eyes on her and she beamed at him.

"Good thinking. And they'd be able to help me put the finishing touches on this party."

"Sure they will."

"Okay. Tell Adonis I miss him."

"I won't be doing that."

"Come on, Mighty Mouse, you know it'll get under his skin."

Peyton laughed. "Talk to you later," she said and disconnected the call.

Kahele glanced over at her, his expression troubled. "I'm sorry we're taking you away from home," he said.

Peyton shrugged. "It's the job," she said, staring out the window. She braced her chin on her hand. "It's always taking me away somewhere," she replied wistfully.

She felt Marco's hand on her shoulder and curled her fingers around it. "By the way, Jake says he misses you, D'Angelo."

"Of course he does," said Marco with an aggravated grunt that made Peyton smile.

A few minutes later, they arrived at Meridew's office. Hughes was talking with Doreen, showing her something on a spreadsheet. He looked up as they entered.

"Chief Kahele? I didn't expect you today," he said, smiling.

"We're here to search Meridew's desk. It was locked the other day." Just as he finished, the door opened and a short, round man stepped inside. He wore a ball cap on his head and had a tool belt affixed around his waist. "We hired a locksmith to get it open."

"By all means. You know the way?" said Hughes, motioning them into the hallway.

Peyton stopped by Doreen's desk. "Can you call Meridew's last secretary, Celia, right?"

"Right," said Doreen.

"She's in Texas, right?"

"She is."

"Can you ask her to call into the precinct tomorrow by 9:00AM? I'd like to talk to her about Meridew."

"I'll call her right now."

"Thank you." Then she followed the locksmith, Kahele and Marco to Meridew's office. Nothing had been disturbed. Everything seemed to be in the same place as before. As the locksmith got to work on the lock, Peyton went over to the credenza and searched through it again.

A few seconds later, she heard a click and turned around.

"Got it," said the locksmith, sliding the desk drawer out. He rose to his feet and began putting his tools away.

Peyton walked over and pulled the drawer out all the way, searching inside of it, but it was empty. She then opened the drawers on either side, but they were empty too. Sitting down in Meridew's desk, she stared into the empty drawers, confused. Why had they been locked?

"Is there a false bottom or something underneath the drawers?" asked Marco, his brow furrowed with confusion as well.

Peyton got on her hands and knees and peered under the drawers, then she rapped on them with her knuckles, but she got nothing. "No." Sitting in Meridew's chair again, she swiveled it back and forth. "He has no laptop, no desktop computer, no files in his desk, not even a pencil, and other than the expensive chachkies, there's nothing here."

"Why? Why would that be? Where is a computer of some kind? We didn't find one when we searched his hotel room. He had to at least have a computer," said Kahele. "Who doesn't have a computer?"

Peyton's eyes rose and met Marco's.

"This isn't his real office," they both said.

"What?" asked Kahele, glancing between the two of them. "What do you mean this isn't his real office? Where is his real office?"

"No idea," said Peyton, taking out her phone. She pulled up Bambi's number and called it. Bambi picked up on the second ring.

"What's up, Peyton?" she said brightly.

"I need you to find out if Meridew had any other businesses registered under his name." She hesitated. "Look for businesses he owned by himself."

"On it," she said and disconnected the call.

Marco had wandered back to the blueprints on the wall. "Brooks?"

She rose and moved over to him. "Yep."

He pointed to the drawings that didn't have a date stamp or addresses. "What if these strip malls aren't on Kauai?"

"You mean, what if they're where Meridew's real office is located?"

"Exactly."

"Then we need to locate it because I'll just bet that's where our answer is."

*　*　*

Harper hugged her arms around her body, pacing back and forth in front of the door to the support group. "What about Donny Ochoa? Have you located him?"

Danté wanted to comfort her, but he wasn't sure how and he didn't want to give Cho any ideas that his interest in Harper was anything more than professional. "We're trying to find him. We have some leads. Bartlet and Smith are tracking him down."

"What am I supposed to tell them?" She motioned to the door. "That Luz was murdered in her own home. That someone cut the baby out of her womb."

Cho shook his head. "No, we want to give them as little information as possible. Come on, you're a reporter. You know how to get people talking to you."

She stopped pacing, her eyes fixed on him. Danté admired the way Cho handled her. He was firm, but he knew how to get her to focus, pull herself together. These were skills he absorbed, locking them away. He understood why Marco paired him with a cop like Nathan Cho.

There were so many nuances to this job that he didn't know yet, things that his intellect and photographic memory couldn't provide him. And the truth was, dealing with people hadn't always come easy to him. They often found him aloof, standoffish, intimidating.

He took the pack of gum out of his pocket and offered it to her. She grabbed a piece unconsciously, tearing off the wrapper and letting it fall to the floor. He bent down and picked it up as she shoved the gum into her mouth.

She chomped a few times, her long nails tapping against her upper arms as she hugged herself. "Okay," she said, smoothing her hands down her skirt. "I'm ready."

Danté shared a look with Cho, but they watched as she yanked the door open and walked inside. A group of five women sat in a circle – all of them around Harper's age or younger, all of them in various stages of pregnancy.

They looked over as the two men entered.

An African American woman turned to Harper, her spine straightening. "What's with the cops?" she demanded. "I don't want no cops here."

"Tanisha, let me introduce them," said Harper, taking one of the open seats. "Grab two chairs and join the circle," she told Cho and Danté.

They each grabbed chairs and took seats on either side of the circle, the women moving over to make room for them. Danté clasped his hands in his lap and glanced around at them. The women were all of different ethnicities, wearing either baggy clothes or maternity clothes, their expressions a mix of hostility or apprehension.

"So, these two men are Inspector Nathan Cho and Officer Danté Price of the SFPD."

"Police, so Tanisha's right?" demanded a Latino woman with a Puerto Rican accent. "You brought police here, Harper?"

"They're here about Luz," said Harper, curling her arms around her stomach.

The women leaned forward.

"What happened to Luz?" asked a Caucasian girl with stringy blond hair. She looked younger than the rest.

Harper lifted her chin. Danté knew she did it when she needed to call on her courage. "She's dead. She was murdered in her apartment."

The women gasped and began muttering between themselves. Harper let them talk for a few seconds, then she held up a hand. "Please, listen to me."

They focused on her immediately. Danté was impressed with the respect they showed her. Here she was, clearly of a higher economic class than they were, educated, from a wealthy family, yet they respected her as if she were one of them. Danté studied Harper closer. Something about that surprised him. How had she found a way past their natural defenses, earned their trust?

"Inspector Cho and Officer Price are working the case, but they don't have much to go on. We need your help. You probably knew her better than anyone, even better than her family."

"Her family! Fook!" spat Tanisha. "They threw her out on the street. They murdered her. Arrest *them!*" She jabbed a middle finger in the air.

Danté met Harper's gaze. She shook her head slightly to indicate he shouldn't say anything.

"What about the baby?" asked a woman of mixed heritage. She might have been Phillipino, she might have been Latino, she might have been African American. It was difficult to tell.

"We don't know what happened to the baby," said Harper.

274

"What you mean you don't know what happen to the baby?" demanded Tanisha. "She was more than eight months along."

Cho gave Harper a pointed look. Harper drew a deep breath to compose herself.

"The baby's missing. An Amber Alert has been issued for it."

"She had the baby?" asked the Latino woman.

Harper didn't answer.

"It was that cabrón, Donny Ochoa," the same woman said.

"The officers are trying to locate him," said Harper, crossing one leg over the other. Her shoes must have cost more than any of these women saw in a year. "What we need is the name of anyone else that Luz had contact with. Friends? Men she was seeing?"

"She started working for the grocery store," said the blond girl, rubbing her hand along her protruding belly.

"Right. We'll check there next, but anyone else."

"She make friends with an old woman in her building," said Tanisha. "She bring Luz supper sometimes."

"That's right. I remember her talking about her," said the mixed race woman. "Doolie or Duley."

"Doolie. That was it."

"Do you remember where Doolie lived?" asked Harper.

"Not sure," said the mixed race woman, "but it was in the same building. Different floor."

Cho took out a pad and opened it, writing something on it. "When you say old woman, how old?"

"Sixties, seventies, I think," said the mixed race woman.

"Good, Adele. Do you remember anything else Luz said? Any other people she had something to do with?" asked Harper.

"She was making friends with people at the grocery store," the Caucasian girl said, "but she hadn't worked there long."

"Right," said Harper. "Do any of you know if she was seeing someone romantically?"

"Romantically?" scoffed Tanisha. "Seriously? You think any mens gives us a second look when they seen our bellies." She focused on Danté. "What about you, honey buns? You wan' some of this?"

Danté didn't know what to say, so he looked down.

"Did she talk about anyone else she met? Anyone she associated with?"

"There was the other woman in her building who was pregnant," said another mixed race woman. She looked like she was Caucasian and African American. "They were setting up their nurseries together, going to Goodwill Stores to get baby stuff."

"There was another pregnant woman in her building, Constance?" asked Harper. "I don't remember that. What floor did she live on? Was she a single mother too?"

Danté wasn't sure why that mattered.

"She was married," said Constance.

The Caucasian woman shook her head. "I can't believe she's dead. Does her family know?"

"Fook her family," said Tanisha. "Why you care about them? They kick her out."

"Her family knows," answered Cho.

"Someone murdered her. You should be worried 'bout that," said Tanisha. "Who murders a pregnant woman?"

"Her man," said Adele. "I'll bet her man did her."

"Yeah, he didn't want the baby," said Constance.

"When you say her man, you mean Donny Ochoa?" asked Cho.

"That's the one. He used to hit on her," said Tanisha. "She-et, my man ever lay a hand on me, he draw back a stub. You can put your money on that, fook yeah."

"Did any of you meet Donny?" asked Cho.

"I met him," said the Latino woman with the Puerto Rican accent. "He come to the meeting one night. Say he wanna talk with her. She ask me to stay with her. She afraid of him."

"And what did he say?" asked Cho.

The woman looked away, laying a hand on the top of her stomach.

Harper uncrossed her legs, leaning forward. She clasped her hands together. "Anything helps them, Gertrudis. Any information you can give them."

Gertrudis looked back at Cho and her upper lip twitched. "He offer her money. He say he know someone who could make the baby go away."

"Go away? An abortion?"

"Yeah, but she was already like thirty weeks along. He say he know someone who would get rid of it still."

"What did Luz say, Gertrudis?" asked Harper.

"She slap the money out of his hand. I remember. I seen it just flutter off. He call her a bitch and ran around picking it up. While he do that, I grab Luz and we hurry to the BART station. I seen how mad he get and I was afraid he come after us."

"Did you ever see him with her again?" asked Harper.

Gertrudis shook her head no. "Never again."

The Caucasian girl began to cry, her shoulders shaking, her face buried in her hands. Harper rose to her feet and went over to her, crouching down in front of her and brushing the stringy hair back from her eyes.

"What's wrong, Penny?" she asked her.

Penny shook her head, placing one hand on her belly, the sobs coming faster. "I can't believe she's dead. I can't believe someone killed her."

"I know," said Harper, gathering her into an embrace. "I know."

Danté watched her sob on Harper's designer blouse, but Harper didn't seem to care. She rocked the girl, whispering words of comfort to her.

Tanisha looked over at him. "You needs to find out who did this. You hear me? You needs to lock that bastard so far away, he ain't never getting out."

Danté nodded.

"And find her baby," said Constance. "You need to find Luz's baby. She loved him so much. She wanted him so bad. You need to bring that baby home."

* * *

"Okay, so I have warrants to search the records of each aquarium store. How do you want to proceed?" asked Kahele.

Marco watched Peyton take the documents and sort through them. "Which one is closer to Meridew's mansion?"

Kahele looked over her shoulder at the papers. "*The Fish Palace.*"

"Let's start there," she said, heading for the SUV.

Marco followed, reaching for the door, but she turned to him. "How about I buy you dinner when we get done with this?" she said, curving her hand over his cheek.

He smiled at her. "I'd like that."

She moved closer, sliding her arm around his waist. "And then afterward, how about a couple's massage? Radar swears by them."

"Don't you have to book that in advance?"

"Yes you do," she purred. "Think about that for a moment."

He started to lower his head toward her, but Kahele cleared his throat. Backing up, Marco gave her a pat on the ass. "Hurry up, Brooks. Let's go talk fish, then..." He gave her a sultry look. "Let's not talk at all."

With a wink, she climbed in the car and Kahele started the engine, then pulled out of the parking lot. Peyton shifted to face him. "How long have you been a cop here, Terence?"

"Almost fifteen years. My dad was a cop."

"So was mine," she said. "Is he retired?"

Kahele glanced at her. "Dead."

Marco could see Peyton's shoulders tense.

"I'm so sorry," she said.

Kahele nodded. "He died six months ago. My mom was at him for years to retire, but he just kept putting it off. Then he finally decides he's going to do it and has a massive heart attack three months to the day after his retirement party."

"How's your mom doing now?"

"She's okay. My brother and sister finally talked her into taking one of the trips she'd been planning with Dad. She went with her sister. Still, Dad's death was a shock to everyone. Mom keeps saying how she was afraid he was going to die in the line of duty, but it was quitting that killed him."

"My dad died in the line of duty," she said, looking out the window.

"I'm sorry," Kahele said.

She smiled at him. "It happened a long time ago, but I wish he'd been there for my wedding."

Kahele nodded. "That's hard."

"Yeah."

"So how you like working for the Bureau?" he asked her.

Marco glanced out the window, trying to pretend he wasn't interested in this conversation.

She gave a shrug. "I like it. I mean, I've been quite a few places with them, but it takes me away from home and with a new marriage, I'm wondering if it's worth it." The conversation trailed away and they rode the rest of the way in silence.

Marco just didn't know what to make of this sudden development. Was Peyton serious about wanting to quit the FBI or did she think that's what he wanted? And he did want it? He was selfish enough that he would be secretly happy if this was her decision, except he wasn't sure that feeling would last. His desire for her to quit was his own jealousy rearing its head again. And it scared him – this possessive side of himself. He hated it, but he knew it was there. His possessive side wanted to keep her with him, the way a dragon hoarded its treasure. He knew it was there and he was ashamed that he always had to fight it down. If she gave in, if she quit her job, would he be able to control it? Would having the prize make him want to control it even more?

He was so lost in thought, he didn't realize when they pulled into the parking lot of the *Fish Palace*. Peyton opened the door and jumped out, followed by Kahele. It took him a little longer to get moving as always.

The humidity pressed on him as they crossed the parking lot to the door and he glanced up to see dark clouds floating by overhead. It looked like they might get rain before they got back to the hotel.

A buzzer sounded as they pulled the door open and went inside. The interior was dimly lit, the light coming from the glow of the many fish tanks arranged around the periphery of the room. The floor was concrete, but it had been painted with waves and soft elevator music filtered through the building from speakers over their heads.

A young man with sandy blond hair stood behind the counter, wearing a t-shirt and board shorts. "How can I help you?"

Kahele veered toward him as Marco wandered toward the back of the small shop, peering in at the brilliant colored fish in a pristine tank. Kahele set his badge on the glass countertop and pushed it toward the young man.

"I'm Chief Kahele and this is Special Agent Brooks from the FBI. We're investigating the death of Harvey Meridew."

"Man, I heard about that. Wicked. He drowned in the hot tub, right?"

Kahele deflected that comment. "We'd like to ask you a few questions, if you don't mind?"

"I'll answer whatever I can."

"We actually need some records," said Kahele, placing the warrants on the counter. "Go ahead and look at those if you want."

The young man picked them up and squinted at them in the dim light. Marco moved to another tank, seeing a green boxy fish with brown spots on it. He glanced at the list of fish in the tank, trying to find the name of it as the kid passed the warrants back to Kahele.

"What do you wanna know?" he said, scratching his shaggy head.

Kahele held a hand out to Peyton, indicating it was her turn. She moved to the counter. It came to mid-chest on her. "Your store sets up fish tanks for people, right?"

"Right."

Marco found the name of the fish. A green spotted puffer. Bingo. The store carried them. He turned to say something, but he saw Peyton reach up to spin a display carousel choked to capacity with trinkets for aquariums. He started weaving his way back through the tanks to stop her because he knew what was coming.

"Can you look up a customer for us?"

"Sure." The kid moved over to the computer as Peyton sent the carousel spinning again. "Name?"

"Either Harvey or Phoebe Meridew."

The kid hesitated, looking up at her. "Really?"

"Yep."

He stopped searching on the computer. "I know they have a service account. I service it."

Peyton sent the carousel spinning again. "And your name is?"

"Parker Jones."

"You maintain their tank?"

"Yeah, it's a 300-gallon saltwater tank. I've maintained it the last two years. Mr. Meridew really liked the fish. Mrs.

Meridew doesn't much care about the fish, but she wants the tank kept pristine."

"How often do you go out there?" asked Peyton.

"Once a week. Saltwater's a lot harder to keep balanced. You always got to be fussing with it, and even then there's no guarantee. I don't recommend it for people who've never had a tank before. It's too hard. Even though I come out once a week, the owners still have to check the Ph and stuff between visits."

"What happens if they don't?"

"The fish get sick and die, and then it takes a lot to get it back into balance."

"Did Mr. Meridew keep it balanced between visits?"

"Yeah, he didn't really need me, except for when he was out of town, but once they got divorced, that was a different story. She won't even test the water."

"So is their fish tank out of balance?" asked Peyton.

"Always. I mean, I get it back in balance, but in the meantime, she goes through a lot of fish and they're expensive."

"Do you replace them?" asked Peyton.

"Yeah, I mean Mr. Meridew could keep the more expensive fish, but with Mrs. Meridew, I keep it simple."

"Do you have a list of fish that you put in their tank?"

"Right here in the computer." He clicked on the keyboard. "Mostly now, I keep it stocked with your clownfish, your coral beauties."

"Coral beauties?"

"Two-spined angelfish." He scratched his head again. "Um, yeah, clownfish, coral beauties and you know, a blenny for the algae."

"What about when Mr. Meridew had the tank?" asked Peyton. "Do you have that record?"

"Yeah, he had coral and at one point he had a black long nose tang. Man, he even had a seahorse. It was the cutest little thing."

"What about a green spotted puffer?" asked Marco, moving toward the counter. "Did he ever have one of those?"

"Not while I cared for the tank. I mean, you can't have puffers with other fish. They're aggressive."

"You said you maintained it for the last two years," continued Marco.

"Right."

"Did anyone maintain it before that?"

"Let me look." He clicked on the computer. "Yeah, Angus, he's the other service guy. Hold on a minute." He went to a door in the back of the store and pushed it open, disappearing inside.

Peyton spun the display absently, her attention on the doorway in the back. Her hand hit the packaged items and a number spun off, spilling out into the room. She quickly stopped the display from spinning and Marco retrieved the items, while Kahele gave her a puzzled look. When she reached to put them back on the hooks, Marco shook his head in amusement.

"Let me do it before the whole thing topples over."

She gave him a sexy glare from those exotic eyes of hers and he felt his chest tighten, but she moved aside and let him put the items back on the display. Parker stepped out of the back room with a young man about his age in tow. The young man was Hawaiian with a crew cut and tattoos running up and down his arms.

"Hey!" he said, jerking his chin at them. "You wanna know about Meridew?"

"Yes," said Peyton. "Can you give us your full name?"

"Angus Lokela."

"Did you service Harvey Meridew's tank?"

"Yeah, 'bout two and a half years ago. He had two tanks. One in the living room and one in the bedroom."

"Two tanks?" asked Kahele.

"Yeah, the one in the bedroom was smaller."

"Do you know if he ever had a puffer fish?"

"Yeah, that's what he kept in the bedroom. He had that thing for a long time." He looked at Parker. "He don't got it no more?"

"No, man, he's just got the one tank."

"You can't keep puffers with other fish. That why he was in the other tank."

"How long can a puffer fish live?" asked Marco.

"Oh, man, if you keep them right, they can live damn near forever."

"I'm gonna need a little more specific number than that," said Peyton.

"Ten, fifteen years, easy."

"So could it still be alive?" asked Peyton.

Parker shook his head. "I'm telling you I only maintain the one tank. I never saw no puffer fish in there."

"Then we need to talk to Phoebe again," said Peyton to the chief.

"I'll arrange it," said Kahele.

"Since both of you worked for Meridew, can you tell me how it was?" asked Peyton.

"Working for him?" asked Angus. "I told Rusty, our boss, if he made me go out there anymore, I'd quit."

"Why?"

"Meridew was an asshole. He was always looking over my shoulder, watching what I was doing, telling me I missed something. The bastard would check the Ph himself after I finished and make me redo everything."

Parker chuckled. "Yeah, he did that to me too. And you best not miss a smudge on the glass."

"Did he get upset if any of the fish died?"

They both made derisive snorts. "You shitting me?" said Angus. "I got to hear about how much I was costing him. He'd run down the price of every frickin fish that ever died in that tank."

"We get a lot of difficult clients, but he was a Defcon 1," said Parker.

"Defcon 1?" asked Peyton.

"Total rat bastard," said Angus.

CHAPTER 16

Marco held the chair out for Peyton to take a seat. Tiki torches lit the beach and the sound of the surf made a soothing background music. The sun was just beginning to dip into the horizon. Peyton smiled at him as he took his own seat, shaking out his napkin to put in his lap.

She reached across the table and took his hands in hers. "I'm glad you stayed in Hawaii with me."

He rubbed his thumb across the back of her hand. "So am I." He looked handsome in a collared shirt that nearly matched his blue eyes, his dark hair swept back from his strong features, his face freshly shaven. He made her heart beat faster, made her pulse quicken when she looked at him, and she couldn't believe he was her husband.

A waiter appeared wearing a Hawaiian shirt and khaki pants. "Can I get you something to drink?"

"Water for now," she said.

"Do you want to hear the specials?"

Peyton smiled up a him. "Sure."

"We have fresh caught Mahi Mahi and a wonderful Dungeness crab with garlic butter."

"I'll have the Mahi Mahi," said Peyton.

Marco looked at his menu. "I'll have a vegetarian stir fry."

"Coming right up," said the waiter, taking their menus.

Marco took her hand again, running his thumb over her wedding ring. "Peyton…"

She could feel her back stiffen immediately at his use of her name. She didn't know why she always had that reaction, but she did. "Oh boy."

He looked up, his blue eyes sparkling in the candle light. "What?"

"Nothing good comes out of Peyton."

He laughed. "Okay, sweetheart, let me start again. I think we need to talk about your job."

She nodded. She'd expected this conversation. "You are the most important thing in my life."

"I know that, but…"

"Look, Bill, it's our favorite newlyweds. I thought you were going home yesterday," came Sally's jovial voice as she and her husband appeared beside their table. "Grab a couple of chairs, Bill."

"Sally, maybe they want to have dinner by themselves."

"Nonsense. You don't mind if we join you, do you?"

"Well…" began Peyton, but Sally had already grabbed a chair and placed it next to hers. She gave Marco a sheepish look.

"Sally, you can't just invite yourself to another person's dinner," said Bill.

"You don't mind, do you, honey?" said Sally, patting Peyton's hand.

"No, it's fine," she said, forcing a smile.

"So, how come you didn't go home yesterday?" Sally demanded. "Oh, my goodness, they want you to investigate the death of that man, that Meridew fellow."

"Well, we're looking into it, yes," said Peyton.

"I knew it!" said Sally, touching her hand to the middle of her chest. "Oh, you're here undercover, aren't you?"

"No, we're really here on our honeymoon, but the police have asked for our help on the case," Peyton said, taking Marco's hand again.

Sally slapped her husband on the arm. "I told you he was murdered. Didn't I tell you he was murdered?"

Bill leaned forward. "She did tell me he was murdered."

Peyton glanced at the people sitting around them. She didn't want to alarm anyone. "Well, we're trying to keep it on the down low."

Sally's eyes got wide. "Of course you are. I'm so sorry. Did I blow your cover?"

"We're not undercover," Peyton reminded her.

"Have you ever gone undercover?"

Peyton glanced at Marco. He smiled in amusement. "Once, yes. Marco helped out on that case too. He pretended to be a male model."

Marco's smile turned into a scowl and Peyton laughed despite herself.

Sally and Bill studied Marco closely. "I can see that," said Sally, fanning herself. "I can definitely see that."

Marco looked away.

Sally leaned close to Peyton. "Do you have any suspects?" She dropped her voice, placing her hand at her mouth to conceal her words. "I heard he had three ex-wives who stand to get a healthy amount after his death."

Peyton frowned at that. "Where did you hear that?"

"On the local news. They said he was poisoned. I thought he drowned, but it was really poison. He was getting death threats. Letters. So is his CFO, Jameson Hughes."

"Jackson," said Bill.

"What?" said Sally.

"His name's Jackson, dear."

"Yes, that's right. Jackson." Sally shook her head. "They say that Meridew fellow was an unpleasant man. Well, they didn't say unpleasant, they said demanding and forceful, but it's the same thing. I heard he yelled at employees at the hotel. He was always sending back his food, complaining about something. It wasn't hot enough, it wasn't cooked well enough. I'll bet they poisoned him because he was so mean. Someone just snapped."

Bill shook his head. "Naw, you don't kill someone because they're rude. There's only two types of murder. Passion and personal gain."

Peyton's gaze shifted to Bill's face.

"That's what I mean. He yelled at one too many people and they snapped, putting poison in his dinner," said Sally.

"Naw, that's too premeditated. Poison's not a crime of passion. Poison's a crime of opportunity, of planning. Poison is to get something he had." He rubbed a hand over his chin. "Funny thing though, poison's a woman's method of killing. Now if he'd been stabbed or shot, that would lead me to believe a man."

Peyton stared at the candle in the middle of the table. Meridew had been both poisoned and shot with a dart gun of some kind. Were they looking for more than one killer? Had this been a conspiracy?

"What I say is this," said Bill. "Follow the money. That's always the thing. When you get one of these rich guys dead, you gotta follow the money."

Peyton's phone suddenly rang. She reached for it and looked at the display. Kahele. She thumbed it on and held it to her ear. "Hey, what's up?"

"Hughes was shot at outside his office."

"What? What do you mean?"

"Someone shot at him. He was in his office late and when he left, someone shot at him. The bullet smashed the windshield on his car and embedded in the driver's seat. He was just getting in the car, but he dropped his keys. That's when the shot went through the windshield."

"Okay, we're on our way," she said, getting up and grabbing her shawl off the chair. "Hughes was targeted again."

Marco also rose.

"Wait. What about your dinner?" asked Sally.

Peyton hesitated. "Go ahead and eat it for us. Our treat," she said. "Have the waiter charge it to our room."

"Are you sure?" asked Sally.

"Of course," said Peyton, then hesitated. "Also, there's a couple's massage at 8:00. Go ahead and take that too." She felt the all-too familiar stab of disappointment. Once again this job was interfering with her life and her marriage.

As they headed through the restaurant to the front of the building, Marco's phone rang. He took it out and looked at the display, then he reached into his pocket and took out the rental car keys.

"You're gonna have to drive. I have to take this," he said, thumbing it on and placing it to his ear.

Peyton sighed. It wasn't just her job interfering, she realized, but it meant that one of them was going to have to make a big change if they had any hope of this marriage working out. Problem was she felt pretty sure she was the one who was going to have to make the sacrifice.

* * *

"Hey, Captain, how's Hawaii?" said Stan, peering into the laptop he'd set up in the conference room.

"Good. So I understand you have updates for me? Why are you all there so late? Isn't it almost 10:00?"

"Hold on. I'm gonna patch you onto the screen. I've set up a system where we can all talk to you remotely."

A moment later, Marco's face appeared on the television screen mounted to the wall in the conference room. He was riding in a car and he looked like he was dressed for a fancy dinner or something. Danté felt bad that his honeymoon had been interrupted this way.

"Can you see us?" asked Stan.

"Yeah, I can see you."

"We've been working our cases," Stan told him. "This is the first time we could get everyone together to talk to you."

The people in the room muttered different versions of hello. Of course, Jake Ryder squinted at the screen. "Is my roomie with you, Adonis?"

"Captain, and she's right here. Let's get the debriefing going, so you all can go home and get some rest."

"Is she driving? You let her drive? I thought women were supposed to stop driving after they got married," said Jake, grinning mischievously.

"Ryder," Marco growled and Tag reached over, slapping him with her happy fingers.

He rubbed the spot, but he was still grinning.

"I know where you live, Jake," came Peyton's voice. "Never forget that."

"Not anymore, you don't," he said.

"Can we focus?" snapped Marco. "Everyone must be getting tired."

Simons moved in front of the camera. "Hey, Captain, so we have two cases at the moment."

"Two? When did you get a second one?"

Simons looked at Cho.

"We got a homicide. Twenty-year-old pregnant female, murdered in her home, blunt force trauma, and the baby was cut from her womb."

"Dear God," muttered Peyton.

Cho nodded. "Harper McLeod's involved."

"How?" asked Marco.

"The victim, Luz Gutierrez, was a member of a support group McLeod runs for pregnant, single women. When she didn't show up for the group meeting, McLeod approached Dante and asked him to do a welfare check. Dante found the girl during his check."

"Where's the father of the baby?"

"Bartlet and Smith just located him and they're bringing him in for questioning. His name's Donny Ochoa. He apparently wanted her to have a late term abortion."

"Okay, good. Sounds like your man."

"Mmmm," said Peyton.

Marco glanced over at her. "Mmmm?"

"Well, stealing the baby sounds like a woman," she said. "A lot of these cases are women who have lost children themselves. Did Harper mention if any of the women in the support group stopped coming or had a miscarriage?"

"We didn't ask that. We'll get on it."

"The victim was on her back, on her bed. The ME estimates she had to weigh between 180 to 200 pounds at time of death. We didn't think a woman would be able to lift that much weight," said Danté.

Tag made a grunt of disgust and Peyton laughed.

"Just like women can't drive after they're married, right Jake?"

"I didn't say anything about lifting 200 pounds, Mighty Mouse. I'm sure you could lift a car if you needed to," he said with a smirk. "It's Adonis I question."

"Captain," snarled Marco. "And just watch me throw your ass out of my precinct, Ryder."

The others snickered, but Jake stuck out his tongue at him.

"Fear, rage, any strong emotions can give people superhuman strength when they need it. Also, you might look for someone on PCP or another of those psychotropic drugs," said Peyton. "They've been known to give people unnatural strength."

Danté felt a little embarrassed that he'd dismissed the possibility that it was a woman so easily. He should have asked Harper if there was anyone missing from her support group.

"Could Abe tell if the baby was born alive?" Peyton asked.

"No," said Cho. "But if the baby survived the excision, Gutierrez was far enough along that the baby might be viable."

"Do you have an Amber Alert out for the baby?" asked Marco.

"Yes, but we've gotten no hits."

"Okay, interrogate the ex-boyfriend. What do we know about him?"

"She left him because he was violent with her."

"Have you notified next of kin?"

"We have."

"Could they provide you with any information on her?"

Danté shifted uncomfortably. "They threw her out when she got pregnant. They're Catholic and they felt it went against their religion."

That brought silence. Marco rubbed his forehead. "Okay, work the boyfriend and get back to me." His attention shifted to Tag and Holmes. "Update me on the Wendall Williams case. Did we find a connection to Lowell Murphy?"

Cho glanced at his phone as Tag relayed what had happened with Renchenko in the stop-and-rob, then he jerked his head toward the door. Danté rose and followed him out of the conference room.

"Ochoa's in interrogation."

Lee set his desk phone down. "DA Adams just came in the back door. He'll meet you at interrogation. Just a warning. He's in a crappy mood because of the time. He told me to remind you he has an infant daughter he'd like to see sometime this century."

Cho nodded, then clapped a hand on Danté's shoulder, leading him to the back of the building. "So let me do the questioning, okay?"

"Yeah, of course."

"If he lawyers up, we stop. We can't ask him anything else."

"Okay."

"Simons always uses his size to intimidate, but you gotta find your own style. Just see what feels right for you."

Devan Adams stood in the viewing room when they arrived, staring out at Donny Ochoa where he sat at the table, his arms crossed. He wore a soccer uniform, shorts, jersey, cleats. Cho frowned at the patrol officer, Frank Smith.

"Did you yank him off a soccer field?" asked Cho.

"Pitch. That's what they call them across the pond," said Smith, smoothing his moustache with his hand. "He was playing a match with some guys in the park. They got a lighted field out there."

Danté could see Bartlet inside the interrogation room, standing at the door, blocking it.

Donny Ochoa wasn't a big man, but he was toned, his calves bulging above his socks. He glared at the table with dark, deep sunk eyes. His black hair was long and touched the collar of his jersey. Danté tried to see what team the jersey was for, but he couldn't make it out as long as Ochoa kept his arms crossed.

"Cho, you question him. The kid's too green," said Devan. "Make sure he knows you're just questioning him right now. He's not under arrest. And let's get it done. I want to go home sometime tonight."

"I've interrogated people before," said Cho icily.

Devan gave him an aggravated look. "Just don't screw it up. If he's our prime suspect, we don't want to spook him."

"I've got it," said Cho, turning for the door.

Danté followed him into the interrogation room, watching as Cho took a seat perpendicular to Ochoa. Danté wasn't sure what he was supposed to do, but he couldn't just stand there like he had when he was a uniform. Walking over, he took the seat next to the suspect.

Ochoa's eyes shifted between the two of them, then he sat forward, dropping his arms. Danté marked that he wore an LA Galaxy jersey.

"I'm Inspector Nathan Cho and this is my partner, Officer Danté Price."

"Why am I here? That's all I want to know. It's frickin damn near midnight. I'm tired."

"We understand that," said Cho, "but we need your help on a case."

"What case?"

Cho looked up at him and studied him a moment without speaking.

Ochoa glanced between Danté and Cho again. "What case?"

"The murder of Luz Gutierrez," said Cho.

Ochoa reared away. "What?"

"You know that name?"

"Of course I know that name. What do you mean – murder?"

"She's dead. She was hit on the head with a weapon and killed."

Ochoa's eyes shifted to Danté and Danté couldn't read the emotion he saw there. "Seriously?"

"Seriously."

Ochoa looked at the table. "She's dead? Really? Huh."

"Huh?" asked Cho in surprise. "Huh?"

"Well, she lived in that shithole apartment. I mean, what do you expect?"

Cho braced his chin on his hand. "You don't seem that broken up about it."

"Man, I think it's terrible, but…" He stuck a finger in his ear and scratched. "…you know how it is."

Cho gave him a cold smile. "Why don't you tell me how it is?"

"Bitches be trippin'."

Danté felt a rush of anger. "You didn't even ask about the baby!" he said through his teeth.

Cho shook his head, making a slashing motion with his hand.

Ochoa glanced between them again. "I figured it died with her."

"Actually," said Cho, dragging out the word. "It was cut from her womb."

That got a reaction. Ochoa's gaze fixed on Cho and stayed.

"What?"

"Someone cut the baby out of her womb."

"Seriously?"

"Seriously."

"Oh shit! No f-en' way!"

Cho rubbed his left eye with his fingers. Danté knew he had to be getting tired. "So, Donny, when was the last time you saw Luz?"

He stared at the table, slowly shaking his head. "Holy shit, that's brutal. Are you f'en kidding me?"

"When was the last time you saw the mother of your child?" said Cho again.

"Um…" He scratched his ear once more. "…a few weeks ago. I found a guy who'd take care of the pregnancy, but she wouldn't agree to it. She started screaming at me, swinging at me. I got out of there and never went back. If she was going to be a stupid bitch about it, I wasn't going to argue."

"A stupid bitch?" repeated Cho. "So you weren't concerned about the fact that she carried your child?"

"Why do I need a kid right now? I mean, seriously."

"Did you know she was kicked out of her parents' house for being pregnant?" asked Danté, leaning forward.

"Yeah, they kicked us both out. I was staying there. Damn, those parents of hers are living in the dark ages. Everyone lives together, but they made me sleep on the couch and they'd come out a few times at night to make sure I was still there. Like that would stop me." He gave a disgusted shake of the head.

"Why'd they let you live there if they were afraid you'd get their daughter pregnant?"

"I think they thought they could control us if I was there. I mean, my old man kicked me out at seventeen, so I had nowhere to go. I was grateful and all that, but seriously, how stupid do you have to be?"

"They invited you into their house. They extended you shelter and you violated that by getting their daughter pregnant?" said Danté.

"Easy," said Cho, giving him a strange look.

Ochoa gave him the same look. "Whatever. You can't stop nature."

Cho chuckled. "Then when nature did its thing and she got pregnant, you didn't care?"

"Like I said, what do I need with a baby? I got plans. I got a future."

Cho gave him an amused look. "You were kicked out of your house at seventeen by your father. Did you even graduate from high school?"

"I don't need that."

"No?" Cho shrugged. "Enlighten me. What are these big plans you have that a baby would disrupt?"

"I'm trying out as striker for the LA Galaxy. I leave in two days." He nodded. "You just watch. I'm gonna be big as David Beckham."

"David Beckham?"

"David Beckham was a midfielder," said Danté, "not a striker."

"Doesn't matter. Once I get on the team, I got everything going my way."

"So a baby and child support would hold you back, wouldn't it?" said Cho.

Ochoa's eyes whipped back to his face. "What?"

"That's why you wanted her to have an abortion, isn't it? So there wouldn't be any entanglements, nothing to hold you back."

"Hold on a minute."

Danté had to give him credit. He wasn't stupid. He immediately got where Cho was going with his questioning. "A baby would prevent you from getting a new start. Tie you down," he added.

"No, now wait a damn minute. I never hurt Luz."

"That's not what we heard. We heard you liked to hit her. We heard she was afraid you were going to make her lose the baby," said Cho.

"No, I mean, we got into fights sometimes. She hit me too. She hit back, let me tell you. She gave me a black eye one time."

"Why didn't you file charges against her?" said Cho levelly.

"What? Seriously? No. No way. I file charges against her and everyone would…"

"Would? What? Would they laugh at you because your girlfriend beat you up?" Cho gave him a once over. "I don't know. What do you think, Danté? You think those skinny arms could lift 180 to 200 pounds?"

Danté shrugged. "Maybe if he was a midfielder, but as a striker, I don't think so."

"What are you talking about? I never hurt Luz. Last time I saw her, I told her I never wanted to see her again. Stupid bitch wouldn't even listen to me."

"She wouldn't agree to let you rip her baby out of her womb?" said Cho.

"Hold on. That's not what I said." He held up a hand. "You're twisting my words. You're twisting everything around."

"So she wouldn't agree to an abortion. Did you decide you'd take care of it yourself?"

"No! You're twisting everything." He looked toward Bartlet. "I want a lawyer. You hear me. I want a lawyer. I'm not saying anything else."

There was a knock on the window behind them. Danté felt frustration rush through him. He wanted to keep pressing this bastard. He wanted to break him.

The knock came again.

Cho leaned back in the chair. "Okay, Donny, okay. We'll let you go home."

"Damn straight you will," said Ochoa, looking at everything but the two of them.

Cho rose to his feet and leaned toward Ochoa. "But here's the thing. Until further notice, you stay in town."

"What? I got tryouts with the Galaxy in a few days."

"No, you don't. You're staying right here."

"Are you shitting me? Seriously?"

"Seriously," said Danté with a snarl. He was sick of this punk, sick of his lack of concern for his child. Sick of his completely lack of remorse for the young woman who had carried his baby.

Ochoa shook his head. "You can't do this to me. All I did was talk to her. All I did was try to help her and she started freaking out. She started yelling at me, hitting me, telling me to get out. I didn't do nothing to her. She did it. She hit me." He slapped himself in the middle of his chest. "She assaulted me."

Danté stared at him coolly. "Bitches be trippin," he said, then he rose and followed Cho from the room.

*　*　*

Peyton showed her badge to the uniformed officer who blocked the entrance into the parking lot of the Dewdrop Construction offices. He waved her through. Darkness had fallen and a light rain was beginning to sprinkle the asphalt.

She parked next to Kahele's SUV and they climbed out. An ambulance lay idling a few yards away and Marco could see Hughes in the back, a paramedic taking his blood pressure. Kahele walked across the parking lot to meet them.

"Thanks for coming out," he said, motioning for them to follow him. He had his shirt sleeves rolled up to his elbows.

"Is Hughes all right?" asked Peyton.

"Yeah, just shaken up." He led them over to the Mercedes.

Marco took in the angle of the car, half pulled out of the space, turned toward the exit. Willis, Kahele's CSI, was going through the car, looking for evidence.

"Did he see anyone shoot at him?" Peyton asked.

"No, he was leaving the parking lot, but he remembered he forget something inside, so he threw the car into park and opened the door to get out. He dropped his keys and when he reached to get them, something slammed through the windshield and into the driver's seat."

Peyton tilted her head, looking at the car. Marco knew she wondered the same thing he did. Why was the car parked at such an odd angle?

"Why didn't he pull back into the space? Was he going to leave the car just out in the middle of the parking lot like this?" she asked.

"He was the last one to leave the building."

"I thought you had guys on him at night."

"We're watching his home. We recommended he hire private security when he's at work. I just don't have the manpower to guard him all the time."

Marco moved up to the car and studied the hole in the windshield. It was perfectly round. Willis glanced up at him from inside the car, then waved. Marco moved around the open door and peered inside.

"Hey?"

"Hey," said Willis. "Marco, right?"

"Right. Did you recover a slug?"

The CSI held up an evidence bag. A bullet lay in the bottom corner of it.

"9mm?" Marco asked.

"Yep."

"Just the one?"

"Yeah."

Glancing up, he saw that Peyton and Kahele were headed toward Hughes. Looking around the parking lot, Marco tried to see where the shooter could have stood in order to ambush Hughes as he was leaving the parking lot. He headed in a direct line from the front of Hughes' Mercedes to a point at the edge of the parking lot. A large utility box stood just next to the sidewalk. It was probably the controls for the traffic lights.

He moved behind it, but he didn't have a flashlight. He looked up at the uniform blocking the parking lot entrance. "Can I borrow your light?" he called.

The other man walked over, removing his flashlight from his belt and holding it out to Marco. Marco shined the light on the ground, but the area around the box had been asphalted in as well. A few cigarette butts and some wrappers were the only other things he saw. When he looked back at the Mercedes, he marked that someone hiding behind the box could have a clear shot at Hughes' car from here.

"Thanks," he said, handing back the flashlight.

"No problem," said the uniform, heading back to his post.

Marco returned to the car. Willis had backed out of the driver's seat and was bagging more evidence. He jerked his chin toward the utility box. "You think that's where he stood?" he asked Marco.

"Could be. You might want to see if you can get any fingerprints."

"Gotcha."

"Anything else of significance in the car?"

Willis shook his head. "Almost wouldn't think he ever drove it. It's pristine."

"Huh," said Marco.

"Rich guys," said Willis, shrugging.

"Yeah." Marco wandered toward the ambulance.

"And you're sure you didn't see anything?" asked Peyton.

Hughes' face was pale. "Nothing."

"Did you hear running feet? Did you notice anyone running away?"

"No, I wasn't sure what happened at first. Then I saw the hole in the windshield. I panicked and ran back into the building until the officers got here."

"So, go over it again for me," said Peyton, glancing up from her notepad. "You got in the car and backed it out of the space."

"Right."

"Then you remembered you left what in your office?"

"My cell phone. Since I was the only one here, I just left my car in the middle of the parking lot and turned it off, then I started to get out."

"Right. And you had your keys in your hand."

"Exactly."

"But you dropped them."

"Right. I wasn't even out of the car, so I bent over to retrieve them. Suddenly something broke the glass. I could hear the sound of it, like a whump. At first I just sat there, stunned. He could have shot again because I was stunned for a bit. Then I ran to get back inside." He raked his hands through his hair. "If I hadn't dropped my keys, I'd be dead."

If I hadn't dropped my keys...

Marco frowned, then turned back toward the Mercedes, crossing the parking lot again. Willis smiled at him.

"What's up?"

"Just wondered if I could look at the ignition."

"Sure."

Marco leaned inside the car and studied the interior.

"Sweet ride," said Willis, when Marco straightened out again.

"Sure is. All the bells and whistles."

"Yep. He's got GPS and front, back, and side cameras. Satellite radio."

"Keyless start?"

"Better than that."

"What do you mean?" asked Marco.

"You can start this baby with an app on your phone."

Marco filed that away, turning to watch Hughes sitting in the back of the ambulance, monitors hooked to his skin.

CHAPTER 17

Kahele stared at the whiteboard, hands on hips. Peyton studied it as well, but there were just too many variables. She looked at the screen where the Ghost Squad was crowded around Radar's monitor.

"Tank? Did you get the tax returns on Dewdrop Construction?" she asked.

"I did. Everything looks legitimate. They filed on almost twenty million last year alone. I can't find a recent year when they didn't make a profit."

"So the company isn't in trouble?"

"Not based on their tax returns. We could get a warrant to see their books, but I think something would have shown up through the IRS."

"What about Meridew's personal financials, Emma?"

"I'm still working on that warrant. It's Saturday, so I don't think I'll hear anything until Monday."

Radar rubbed his chin. "So the bullet the CSI pulled out of Hughes' Mercedes was a 9mm?"

"Yeah," said Marco.

"We need to see if any of the ex-wives have a handgun registered to them."

"I'd look at Manny Wong too," said Marco. "And Teddy Nakamura. He had a rifle in his trailer."

Peyton studied the board. "Manny Wong, and the gardener who we haven't talked to yet, Celia his ex-secretary, and Teddy Nakamura, the foreman. There are too many suspects and nothing that's popping yet."

"Well, we know Phoebe had access to the poison since Meridew had a puffer fish at some point," said Bambi.

"Or Angus from the *Fish Palace*, who also didn't like Meridew," said Peyton, bracing her chin on her hand.

"Wong has the blowgun," continued Bambi.

"But does he have access to the poison?" said Peyton.

"There have been two attempts on Hughes' life. What are we doing to make sure we don't have another death? Do I need to send more agents out there?" Radar demanded of Kahele.

Kahele held up his hands. "I don't have that many men to spare."

"We can't have another death on our watch. Not when we know he's been getting death threats," said Radar.

"I know. I told Hughes not to leave his condo until we can figure this out. I've got a man on him right now, but he says he has meetings with the planning board."

"I'll make contact with a field office on Maui, see if we can get a detail to escort Hughes around," said Radar.

"I'd appreciate it."

"Sparky?"

"Yep?"

"We'll work on searching for registered guns. You work on trying to eliminate one suspect. We know what night Meridew died. Let's at least cross someone off that list."

"On it. We have Celia Salazar calling in this morning. She's in Texas. Hopefully we'll be able to eliminate her."

"Good." Radar reached to disconnect the call, but Bambi stopped him.

"We should have a sign off just for us, don't you think?" she said.

Peyton smiled at her. "Like what?"

"Ghost Squad signing off," she said loudly and then saluted.

Radar glared at her, making Peyton chuckle. "Ghost Squad signing off," Peyton repeated and nodded for Willis to end the call. When she glanced around, she found Marco's eyes on her, watching her, an amused look on his face. She gave him a curious look in return, but he just smiled and glanced down at the table.

Kahele turned around. "Salazar should call by 9:00, so we've got a few minutes to talk things through."

"Actually," Peyton said, "I'd like to see the threat letters Meridew turned over to you. Willis, can you get me the file?"

Willis opened a leather folder. "I have them right here," he said, sliding them to her.

She opened the folder and rifled through the small stack. Every letter had been printed on computer paper, centered in the middle of the page, non-descript font. And the threats were all the same.

You'll pay for what you've done.

You owe the people of Hawaii in blood.

Stop or you'll invite the wrath of the islands.

And each letter ended with *The Menehune are coming for you.*

"Whoever it is has excellent spelling and punctuation," she said, glancing at Marco. "No dyslexia. Can you believe it?"

He gave a careless shrug. "It's a burden some of us have to carry."

She laughed and searched through the letters again. "You checked for trace DNA? Hair? Fingerprints?" she asked Willis.

"I did. Nothing but the cigarette ash."

"Right," she said, considering. "But why blame the Menehune?"

"What do you mean?" asked Kahele, taking a seat.

"I mean, that's just a little out there, isn't it? Blaming a fictional people for a revenge crime. If it is a revenge crime."

"I'm not following. The Menehune are the protectors of the island."

"Right. Just like Manny Wong tries to be. Maybe we're looking at this the wrong way. Maybe we're too focused on Meridew and we should be looking at Wong."

"You mean you think he's our top suspect?"

"He is because we were guided to him."

"You mean he could be a red herring?" said Marco.

She held up a hand. "Why not? Meridew and Hughes are contractors making a healthy profit off tearing apart the islands and putting up a parking lot as Bill Baxter said himself. What if all clues point to Manny Wong because we're meant to think it's Manny Wong?"

"So we spend a lot of time focusing on him, while the real culprit gets away with murder."

"Maybe two murders if we're not careful," she said.

Kahele shook his head. "If the reason isn't environmental, what is it?"

"Well, in my experience, there are two things that cause people to commit murder – greed and passion." She set down the letters. "I mean, Bill Baxter's right again. When all else fails, follow the money."

"I'm going to have to meet this Bill Baxter," said Kahele. "Does he work for the FBI?"

Peyton gave an amused laugh. "Maybe he should."

"I got a call coming in from a Texas number," said Willis.

"Patch it through," said Kahele.

A Latino woman's face appeared on the screen. She was in her late thirties, early forties, with short brown hair and wide spaced brown eyes. She sat at a kitchen table and music was playing somewhere in the background.

"Hello?" she said.

"Hello, Ms. Salazar, I'm Chief Terrence Kahele." Then he introduced the rest of the people sitting around the table.

"FBI? Why is the FBI involved?" she asked.

"Well, Mr. Meridew was killed at a hotel where Special Agent Brooks and her husband were staying. I asked for Agent Brooks' help on the case."

She nodded, glancing behind her. "I don't know how I can help you, Chief Kahele. I haven't been on Kauai in more than a year."

"I understand."

"I can prove I was here. I have a timesheet with my current employer and I can send it to you. It was signed by my supervisor."

"That would be excellent," Kahele said.

"Where are you working?" asked Peyton.

"What?" said Celia.

"Where did you get a job?"

"Oh, I'm a secretary for a heating and air company." She glanced over her shoulder again. "Can you turn down the music?" she called.

The music became quieter.

"How do you like being home in Texas?" asked Peyton.

"It's good to be with my family, but I miss the islands. I miss the weather."

"I'll bet. We've enjoyed it so much. Such a beautiful place."

Celia visibly relaxed. "It is. I used to spend hours just walking along the beach, enjoying the sunset. All of the trees and colorful flowers."

"It's like paradise."

"Very much so," she said, a wistful tone creeping into her voice.

"Celia, I know this might be hard to talk about, but I need to ask you some questions about Harvey Meridew."

She looked down, but she nodded. "I heard he died."

"He was murdered."

She nodded again.

"Did you ever get any threatening letters for him when you worked as his secretary?"

She shrugged. "He'd get angry phone calls sometimes. People would put complaints on Dewdrop's social media pages. They weren't really threats. They were just people who weren't happy about a certain build we were doing, or they were complaining about noise at the construction site. Sometimes they complained that we were generating too much debris and dust."

"Those sound like they were directed at the company, not Meridew himself."

"That's right. I didn't get many complaints about him directly."

"But did you hear about complaints?"

She rubbed the back of her neck, clearly uncomfortable. "I sometimes overheard phone conversations he had with people, or once in a while, someone would come to the office for a meeting and storm out."

"Did this happen often?"

"Often enough. It was uncomfortable working for him. People would call and demand to talk to him, but he'd put them off. Sometimes they showed up unannounced."

"He was difficult with you too, wasn't he?"

"He could be intense."

Peyton folded her hands on the table. "Again, I know this might be hard, but can you describe the time he threw a glass at you?"

She shifted her hand to her throat. "He was one of these men who want everything their way. They don't care what you want. They don't care if you can't get something done that they think should be done." She bit her inner lip. "We were bidding for land to build a strip mall on Kauai. It was when we first came over to the island."

"The location on Waipouli Road?"

"No, this was another location. In Lihue. But *Freedom Kauai* got an injunction. The costs were rising and Dewdrop couldn't break ground. Manny Wong found out that the Hawaiian Hoary Bat used that part of the city as its nightly feeding grounds, so the EPA told Meridew they'd have to do an environmental report that could take years to complete."

"I'll bet Meridew wasn't happy about that," said Peyton.

"He lost it. He yelled at Mr. Hughes, he yelled at me. He screamed into the phone at his lawyer. Two lawyers quit on him over it. He threatened to bury Manny Wong in a volcano."

"Hold on a second," said Peyton, lifting her hand. "He threatened Manny Wong's life?"

"Yeah."

"Directly? He told the man he would bury him in a volcano to his face?"

"Over the phone. He called him an…" She drew a deep breath and sighed. "…an f-en patchouli wearing hippy asshole, and he didn't say f-en either."

Peyton smiled. "Then what happened?"

"He came to my desk and swept everything off onto the floor. My computer, my phone…everything." She wrapped her arms around herself. "I was scared. I wanted to leave, but I was afraid he'd fire me if I did. Mr. Hughes tried to intervene, talk sense into him, but he stormed off to his office. I could hear him throwing things around in there. Glass was breaking." She shuddered and closed her eyes. "It was horrible."

"I know, Celia. You're doing great. What happened then?"

"He ordered me to come into his office. I didn't want to go. I wanted to go home, but Doreen said I'd better hurry. I was so scared, I don't know what I was thinking, but I did what she said. I'd just gotten to the door when he screamed for me again, then a glass came hurtling at me. It smashed into the wall and shattered. I turned right around and went to my desk, grabbed my purse and left."

"Did you call the police?"

"No. After I got home, I was scared that he'd black-ball me and I'd never get a job again. I'd been with him for six years. He was the main reference I had."

"When did you decide to file the lawsuit against him?"

"After Mr. Hughes came to see me. He wanted to apologize for Mr. Meridew's actions and he told me he could understand if I wanted to press charges against Mr. Meridew. He promised to write me a recommendation and he did.

That's how I got the job I have now. Mr. Hughes is a good man."

"So instead of pressing charges, you filed the lawsuit?"

She rubbed her hands together. "I went to see a lawyer and he said I'd do better in Civil Court, especially since Mr. Meridew didn't hit me with the glass. I just wanted it to be over, so I did what he said."

"Celia, do you know of anyone that might want to do Meridew some real harm? Was there anyone who hated him that much that they'd want him dead?"

She wrung her hands, taking a deep breath and releasing it. "A lot of people, Agent Brooks. He was a man that brought out the worst in people."

* * *

Cho knocked loudly on the door one floor below Luz Gutierrez. Danté glanced down the hall as other doors opened and people peered out, watching them. He rocked on his heels, then looked back as Cho banged again.

They could hear movement on the other side of the door, then about a million locks turned and the door was pulled open. A very short woman in her early seventies, late sixties looked out. She had her grey hair pulled up in a tight bun, wearing a house dress and holding a tissue to her nose.

Her eyes and nose were red and she sniffled as she peered out at them. "Yes?"

"Are you Mrs. Doolie O'Brien?" asked Cho, showing her his badge.

"Yes," she said, sniffling some more. "Are you here about Luz?"

Cho glanced at Danté. "We are. I'm Inspector Nathan Cho and this is my partner, Officer Danté Price. Can we come in and talk to you?"

She blew her nose into the tissue and opened the door wide enough for them to step inside. The interior of the apartment looked like a florist had vomited all over everything. There was a floral patterned sofa, floral patterned armchairs, an actual flower throw rug under the coffee table. Every available surface was covered in floral teacups and saucers, sitting on top of flower shaped doilies.

"Please sit," she said, motioning for them to sit on the sofa. They perched on either end of it, while she took an armchair, wiping her eyes with the tissue. "I'm sorry. I've been crying for days now. I just can't get over the fact that my darling Luz is gone and her poor baby…" She dissolved into tears.

Cho tapped his fingers on his thighs and waited her out. Finally she pulled herself together, grabbing more tissues to blow her nose and wipe her eyes. "You were close with her?" he asked.

"She was like a granddaughter to me."

"How long did she live here?"

"She was here for about six months. She was such a sweet girl. She would help me carry up my groceries and she'd come over to visit nearly every day. We'd have tea and cookies." She motioned to the teacups. "I can't believe she's gone."

"One of the women in her support group said you brought her meals."

Doolie nodded. "She was trying to work and she'd get home so tired. I wanted to help her out, she was such a sweet girl, so I'd take her dinner or she'd come here." She wiped her eyes. "I live all alone, Inspector. It's nice to have someone around."

"I understand, ma'am," said Cho.

"Please, let me get you something to eat. I have some nice cookies and I just put on a pot of tea."

She rose and disappeared into the kitchen. A few moments later, she returned with a tray. Danté rose and took it from her, setting it on the coffee table. His eyes fixed on the pink, blue and bright yellow cookies on the tray. He looked up at Cho, then nodded at the cookies.

"Are those macarons?" asked Cho, smiling at her.

"Yes, I get them from a lovely little bakery down the street. Luz just adored them." Her eyes filled with tears again and her hands shook as she poured the tea. They'd definitely found the right woman to ask about Luz. Abe had discovered macarons in Luz's stomach during the autopsy. "I don't know how I'm ever going to get over this. Luz meant so much to me."

"Did Luz ever mention anyone that she was afraid of or anyone that she worried about?"

"That good for nothing father of her baby. She said..." The older woman shuddered, passing Cho a teacup. "She said he asked her to have an abortion. She was almost seven months along and he told her he wanted her to have an abortion."

"Did Luz say why he asked her to do that?" asked Danté.

"He had some harebrained scheme that he was going to play professional soccer." She made a snorting noise as she handed Danté a cup. "In the US? Soccer?"

Danté suppressed a smile at her indignation. He could see why a scared young girl would gravitate toward an older woman like this. She reminded him a little of his mother – warm and welcoming, but fiercely protective when necessary. His mother would have a saying for this: *gentle is as gentle does.*

"Was there anyone else she talked about? Anyone else she brought home? A new boyfriend?" asked Cho.

Doolie waved her hand. "No, she was concentrating on the baby. That's all she thought about. She was so excited for him to get here."

Cho leaned forward, setting the cup on a side table and bracing his arms on his thighs. "We heard she was making a nursery, getting stuff for the baby."

Something niggled in Danté's mind, but he filed it away.

"She was. She didn't have much money, poor darling, but she was shopping at consignment shops, looking for clothes and baby paraphernalia."

"Did she buy a crib?" Danté asked.

Both Doolie and Cho looked at him. "No, I don't think she'd found a crib yet."

"Do you remember what she did have?"

Doolie tilted up her head, thinking. "She found some clothes and a car seat, you know one for a newborn. I think she had one of those little baths and some cute bibs with sayings on them like *Mama's Little Darling*. She tried to get neutral colors because she wasn't sure if it was a boy or a girl, but we called it a boy." Doolie smiled sadly. "The baby moved around so much, Luz was sure it had to be a boy." Then the tears started again. "I'm sorry. It's just so hard."

Danté shifted on the couch. He wanted to get back up to the apartment. They'd searched it, but no one had thought to mention the baby stuff and he didn't remember seeing it. He never forgot details like that, but he just didn't remember seeing anything like that. Cho gave him a questioning look, then he refocused on Doolie.

"Did Luz have a car?"

"No, she couldn't afford that. She could barely afford the rent."

"Do you have a car, Mrs. O'Brien?"

"I gave it up. I got to be too afraid to drive San Francisco's streets."

"How did Luz go shopping? Did she take public transportation?"

Danté knew he was trying to get information out of her without asking specifically, guiding her.

"Probably. There was another young woman here who is also pregnant. They started up a friendship." She tapped her lip. "What's her name now? Um, Donna. She's on the same floor as Luz."

A knock sounded at Doolie's door and she frowned. "Who could that be?" she said, struggling to get to her feet.

Danté held up a hand. "I'll go see," he said, placing his cup on the tray again.

"Thank you, young man," she said with a sad smile. "Such a nice young man," she told Cho as Danté went to the door.

He eyed the numerous deadbolts, flip logs, and chains that covered the doorjamb, then he pulled open the door. Harper stood on the other side, her green eyes snapping up to his face. She tried to look beyond him into the apartment.

"What are you doing here, Harper?" he asked her.

"I want to talk to Doolie about Luz."

"We're interviewing her now. You can't start investigating this case."

She pulled the ends of her cardigan around her. "I'm a reporter, Mr. Spock. I can and am investigating it."

He sighed and stepped out into the hall, forcing her to back up. "Cho's questioning her right now. I can't let you in there."

"Well, then I'll just wait out here, but I'm not leaving," she said defiantly.

"Let us do our job. Let us investigate this."

"Luz was a friend, Danté. She came to me for help and I failed her."

"You didn't fail her. You had nothing to do with this." He shut the door at his back. "Let me walk you to the stairs."

"I'm not going anywhere. I'll wait until Cho leaves."

His eyes involuntarily went to the stairs and he itched to go up to Luz's floor. "Suit yourself," he said, "but don't go in there. Cho will not be happy."

"I'm not tangling with him. You know the good cop/bad cop interrogation tactic?"

"Yes," he said, frowning.

"He probably always plays bad cop."

Danté wasn't sure about that. Cho had been a level headed, even tempered partner so far, but if it kept her from disturbing the interview, he'd take it.

"Fine. Stay here." He started for the stairs, but he could hear her heels as she hurried to keep up with him.

"Where are you going?" she asked, grabbing his arm. A rush of awareness tingled up from where she gripped him, snaking across his chest. He could smell the vanilla scent that clung to her. He shook it away and started climbing.

"I want to look at Luz's apartment again."

"Why? Can I come?"

"You have to wait outside. It's a crime scene. You can't touch anything."

She held up her peace sign. "I promise. Scout's honor."

He shook his head, but he didn't correct her. They made it to the next floor and walked down the hall to Luz's door. Harper lagged behind, fussing in her purse.

Crime scene tape was affixed across the opening and the door was closed. He tried the handle, but it was locked. Sighing, he turned to go back down, but Harper stepped up to it, slid a credit card down the door jamb and the door opened.

"Harper!" he hissed at her.

"What?" she said, putting the credit card back in her purse. "How did you think you were going to get in there, Mr. Spock? Teleport?"

He glared at her. "How did you do that?"

She shrugged. "A magician never reveals her secrets."

He shook his head, then pushed the door open, bending to duck between the strips of tape. "Stay here!" he ordered.

She crossed her heart and gave him a sweet smile.

He paused in the entryway. The quiet of the small apartment pressed down on him. Turning into the kitchen, he slipped on a pair of latex gloves and began opening cabinets, searching through them. Then he went into the living room.

Luz didn't have much furniture, so it didn't take long to cover that area. He found a coat closet in the corner and opened it, but besides a few jackets and shoes, there was nothing else inside. Finally he headed for the bedroom. He had saved this room for last because his damn memory could recreate the horror in that room in minute detail.

He found Harper standing before the bed, staring at the red stain.

"Harper!" he hissed at her.

She jumped, her eyes whipping up to his face. She looked so lost and forlorn, he wished he hadn't snapped at her.

"I told you to wait outside!"

She waved him off. "I think you'll find I don't mind too well, Mr. Spock. If you want obedience, get a Golden Retriever."

"Don't touch anything!" He glared at her.

She tilted her head, peering at him without blinking. "What are we looking for specifically?"

"You aren't looking for anything."

"What are *you*, oh mighty protector in blue, looking for?" she asked.

He gave her a sideways look, then went over to the closet and pulled it open, searching through the clothes, taking down boxes on the overhead shelf, and opening bins Luz had stashed in the back. He searched through the dresser and looked under the bed. The only place left was the bathroom.

He slipped inside, pulled back the shower curtain and looked under the sink. When he straightened and turned to go out, he came up flush against Harper. She gave him a slow, sultry smile.

"What are you trying to find, Mr. Spock?"

That same zing of energy spiraled through him, making him aware of the the green of her eyes, the clarity of her skin, the confident way she tilted her head, her mane of brown hair spilling down her back.

"Baby stuff."

"Baby stuff?" Harper's attention shifted immediately. "She should have baby stuff everywhere."

"Doolie said she'd been buying stuff from thrift stores."

Harper's eyes rose to his face again. "This changes everything."

Danté nodded. "Yeah. We're not looking at Donny Ochoa anymore."

Her gaze tracked around the room. "We're looking for a woman." Then she grabbed his arm with both her hands. "And that means…"

"…the baby was alive when he left here," finished Danté.

* * *

"Call the manager of the building and get a list of residents," said Marco into the phone as they drove toward Phoebe Meridew's mansion again.

"Won't we need a warrant?" asked Danté.

"He might give it to you without one."

"What if I just ask for any pregnant residents?"

"You have to think of what the prosecutor will do with any information you ask for," said Marco. "If we focus just on pregnant residents, he could say we were eliminating other possible suspects. Get the whole list, then we can narrow it down. This O'Brien woman told you the woman's name was Donna. That will help focus your search."

"Got it. I'll work on it tonight."

"Danté," said Marco, watching the palms speed past outside the window.

"Yes, sir?"

"You're doing a good job. That was quick thinking to look for baby paraphernalia. Not many men would have thought of it."

"Thank you, sir. I appreciate it. I'm learning a lot from Inspector Cho."

"Good. Cho's an exceptional detective. Absorb all you can. Let me know what you find out regarding the residents."

"I will, sir. Bye."

"Bye." Marco disconnected the call.

Peyton shot him a look. "You're good at that, you know?"

"Good at what?" he said, frowning.

"Managing your people. Mentoring your young officers. He's going to make a great detective because of you."

Marco snorted, but he was pleased with her praise. He'd always admired Peyton's instincts as an investigator and to have her praise his management felt good. Most of the time, he felt like he had no idea what he was doing. It was affirming to think someone approved of his methods.

He ran his hand over her hair and twirled a curl around his finger. "You awe me, woman, you know that? I keep getting ambushed every time I realize we're married."

She smiled and leaned into his touch. "I'm sorry our honeymoon got messed up."

"Don't be. It's kinda fun to be on a case with you again."

That got a full look, then she turned back to the road. "You are so getting laid tonight, D'Angelo," she said, making him laugh.

They pulled up behind Kahele's SUV a few minutes later, both of them climbing out of the car. The late day sun felt muggy and heavy as they walked to the front door of Phoebe's mansion and Kahele knocked. They waited in the sultry air in front of the large doors for a long while, then Kahele knocked again and rang the bell.

Marco thought he heard voices around the side of the mansion, so he wandered down the walkway that led around both ends of the mansion and found a garden gate open, leading to the expansive backyard. The voices were louder on this side.

He motioned for Kahele and Peyton to join him, then they eased through the gate and wandered down a paved walkway through a side yard that looked like it was used to store equipment. Two sheds and some covered mounds that might be furniture – chairs and tables – occupied this area. Another open gate at the end of the walkway led onto the backyard with the pool and the covered patio.

Phoebe Meridew stood in a bikini, her long legs glistening with oil, her hip cocked at an angle, talking to a young man in a tank top and shorts, holding a pair of hedge clippers. Phoebe had a drink in her hand and she laughed, throwing back her head, her hair sliding down her back.

The young man couldn't be more than mid-twenties with toned muscles, deeply tanned, and short cropped black hair. He glanced over as they approached and jerked his chin at them for Phoebe to notice.

She turned and the smile faded from her face. "Chief Kahele, what a surprise?"

"How are you today, Mrs. Meridew?"

"I'm fine, but it's so muggy today, isn't it? My hair must look a fright." She touched the messy bun she had put her blond hair into, shooting a coquettish look at the gardener.

Kahele showed the young man his badge. "You must be Mrs. Meridew's gardener?"

He nodded, not even giving the badge a glance.

"This is Dexter," said Phoebe, smiling at him and tilting her chin down.

He returned the smile, then finally held out his hand. "Dexter Opunui."

"Divide and conquer," Peyton said to Marco under her breath. He nodded.

"I'll take Opunui," he muttered back.

"Got it." Then she stepped forward. "Mrs. Meridew, do you mind if we talk to you inside the house? We have a few more questions we'd like to ask you in private."

She sighed. "Fine," she said and turned, flouncing away. Marco noticed that she didn't walk a straight line into the building, weaving slightly.

When he looked back at Dexter, he found the young man fixated on Phoebe's backside. *So it was like that, was it?* he thought to himself.

"Beautiful, huh?" he said.

Dexter's dark eyes snapped to him. "Huh?" he asked.

Marco jerked his head toward the house, offering a wry smile. "The grounds are beautiful, aren't they?"

"Oh," said the young man, grinning. "Yeah, really nice. I like working here."

Marco rubbed the back of his neck, pretending to take it all in. "How long have you worked for the Meridews?"

"A few years." He opened and closed the clippers. "Just one of my stops."

"Yeah, I get it. Did you know Mr. Meridew very well?"

Dexter's face shifted, a suspicious look entering his eyes. "Why do you ask?"

"We're just trying to get a picture of the guy. Everyone we meet has these stories about what an asshole he was. We can't find one person who has anything good to say about him."

"Well, I try not to speak ill of the dead."

"Yeah, I get that." Marco looked back at the house. "I should probably get inside."

"Yeah, I need to get back to work."

"Right, okay then." He turned to go, but stopped and turned back around. "Did Meridew know you were having an affair with his wife?"

Dexter's clippers snicked shut loudly and his back stiffened.

Marco didn't reach for his gun, but he was ready. "How about you put the clippers down?"

Dexter's eyes rose to his face, then he bent and set the clippers on the ground. "I didn't kill him."

"Okay." Marco motioned to some chairs on the pool deck. "Let's sit down and talk."

Dexter nodded.

They headed to the chairs and took seats. Dexter braced his hands on the table, playing with a leather bracelet on his wrist. Marco leaned back, stretching out his bad leg.

"Do you have an alibi for the night Meridew was killed?"

"I was drinking at the beach with some friends. We had a bonfire."

"Can you give their names and phone numbers?"

"Yeah." He tugged at the bracelet. "Look, I didn't plan on starting up anything with Phoebe. It just happened. I mean, you've seen her." He gave a sheepish laugh.

"I sure have," said Marco. "Did Meridew know about it?"

Dexter shrugged. "Probably one of the reasons he filed for divorce."

"So he filed for divorce, not her?"

"Well, yeah, he filed, but she was wanting a divorce for a long time. He wasn't the easiest husband, you know?"

"I've heard. Do you know if he ever hit Phoebe? Abused her in any way?"

"Verbally, yeah. He was always calling her names. Really awful ones. I heard him shouting at her a lot. I usually had my earplugs in when I worked, but I'd turn off the music and listen. I was worried for her."

"But you don't remember him hitting her? She never told you he was physically abusive?"

"No, but mental abuse can be just as bad."

"True," Marco said. "What about with you? How did Meridew treat you?"

Dexter gave a wry shake of the head. "God, he was a prick. Always bitching about everything I did. If I didn't trim back the plants enough, I was a lazy good for nothing native. If I trimmed them too much, I was a goddamn imbecile."

"He called you those things to your face?"

"Yeah."

"Why didn't you quit?"

Dexter shook his head. "Paid too well, and I was worried for Phoebe."

Marco nodded. "Dexter, I have to ask you something else."

"Go ahead. I ain't got nothing to hide."

"Do you own a gun?"

Dexter went still. "I thought he drowned."

Marco gave a shrug. "I just need to know."

Dexter tugged at the bracelet. "Yeah," he said. "Yeah, I own a handgun. It's just for protection."

Marco nodded. "What size?"

Dexter scratched the side of his head. "Man, do I need to get a lawyer or something?"

"Not right now, no. You've been very cooperative, but I need to know the size of your gun."

"Nine millimeter," he said.

Peyton appeared on the deck, motioning to him. Marco patted the table and rose. "Get me the names of the people you were with on the night Meridew died, okay?"

"Yeah, I'll work on it right now."

"Good," said Marco, then he walked over to his wife.

She looked up at him, her expression tense. "Meridew had the puffer fish stuffed and he kept it as a trophy. When they divorced, Phoebe wouldn't let him have it. She just showed it to us."

"Well, shit."

"Yep. What did you find out? Are they having an affair?"

"Oh yeah, but there's more."

Peyton sighed. "Of course there is. He's a practicing ichthyologist on the side."

"Maybe, but he also has a nine millimeter."

Peyton absorbed that. "Yep, we're never leaving this island, D'Angelo. You better start collecting your coconuts."

He laughed, touching her nose. "Then you'd better learn how to fish."

CHAPTER 18

Kahele met them at the doors to the precinct. "I got us an island hopper to talk to Fiona, Meridew's second wife. We've got to get to the airport ASAP."

Peyton drew a deep breath and released it. She wanted a cup of coffee, but she turned on her heel and followed Kahele out to the SUV. They hadn't gone far before Peyton's phone rang. She dug it out of her sundress pocket and glanced at the display.

Radar.

Thumbing it on, she watched as his face filled the screen. "Hey, old man, how are you?"

"Fine," he said in a clipped tone. She could see he was at home, sitting on his patio. Radar spent a lot of time on his patio when he was home.

"How's Lacy?"

He ignored that and picked up a piece of paper. "I got the information on the search for gun permits."

"Is Gwen there? I want to say hi."

"Sparky!"

She smiled. "It's Sunday. Can't you just give me a few seconds of small talk before we launch into business? I haven't had my coffee yet and I'm being jetted off to Maui. The least you could do is pretend at civility for a half dozen seconds."

Kahele gave her a bewildered look.

"He's crazy about me," she told him. "He just doesn't like anyone to know. He's worried it'll show partiality."

"You might ask Chief Kahele if he has any jobs," said Radar.

"Why? You thinking of coming to Hawaii? Oh my God, you'd love it, Radar. They have a chocolate plantation and you can participate in a chocolate tasting there."

"Did you blow your entire retirement at the plantation, Sparky?"

"Just the amount I was going to use to get you a present."

Radar shook his head. "Is D'Angelo there?"

"Right here," said Marco from the back seat.

"Let me talk to him."

"Why?" she asked.

"He'll listen without all the silly chitter chatter."

"Fine," she said, rolling her eyes, "give me your information."

"Dexter Opunui had a gun permit for a 9mm, just like he told D'Angelo. The foreman, Teddy Nakamura, has a permit for the rifle and a .38."

"No 9mm?" asked Marco.

"Nope. I didn't find a permit for Phoebe Meridew, but Daisy Meridew, the first ex-wife has one and that's a 9mm."

"What about the second wife?" asked Peyton.

"None. I also looked at Manny Wong."

"And?" she prompted.

"Nothing."

"He doesn't have a permit?"

"Nope."

"What about Meridew's past secretary Celia Salazar?" asked Kahele.

"Nothing," said Radar, "but on a whim, I tried someone else."

"Doreen Kim, Hughes' secretary?" asked Peyton.

"Close," said Radar. "I tried both Hughes and Meridew."

"And?"

"Meridew had a 9mm registered in his name. Nothing on Hughes."

Peyton thought about that for a moment. Why hadn't they found the 9mm when they searched Meridew's house and his business? "What happened to that gun?" she asked Kahele.

"We didn't find it and we went through everything."

"So he could have left it with one of the wives?" said Peyton.

"He could have," answered Radar.

"Can you send someone out to go through that office again?" Peyton asked Kahele. "Look for hidden compartments."

"I'll get on it."

"What about the stuff from the hotel room?" asked Marco. "Where's that?"

"Back at the precinct," said Kahele.

"They need to go through all of that again too," said Peyton.

"I think they would have found a gun," remarked Radar. "It'd be a little hard to miss."

"Let's still double check everything," said Peyton.

Kahele reached for the radio affixed beneath his dash.

"Keep me updated, Sparky," Radar said.

"You got it, mon capítan!" she said, saluting him. "Ghost Squad signing out."

He made a hrumph and disconnected the call.

Shortly after that, they arrived at the airport. An officer met them in the drop off lane at the interisland terminal and gave them a nod as he slipped behind the wheel and drove the SUV away. Kahele motioned inside the small terminal and they followed him down to the gate.

The chief flashed his badge and the flight attendant scanned something on his phone, then indicated for them to head through a door. A staircase took them down onto the tarmac where a small jet waited for them. A flight attendant stood at the bottom of the stairs to the jet.

"Chief Kahele, nice to see you," he said. "Agent Brooks and Captain D'Angelo." He gave them polite nods as the three of them climbed the stairs and entered the plane. A number of families and couples occupied the seats, but three seats had been reserved for Kahele in the front of the plane.

Peyton sank down next to Marco and fastened her seatbelt. "You called ahead? That's how the airline knew us?"

"Yes, my superior cleared it," said Kahele.

"How long is the flight to Maui?"

"A little less than an hour."

Peyton settled back in her seat and curled her hand in Marco's. Kahele motioned to a flight attendant, helping people stow their bags, and he came over, bending at the waist to bring himself closer to the chief. "We'd like coffee after takeoff," Kahele told him.

"No problem. Cream and sugar?"

"Sugar," said Peyton. "We like a lot of sugar." She motioned between Marco and herself.

"It'll be ready as soon as we're in the air," he said and moved toward the back of the plane.

Marco gave her an amused look, but he didn't say anything and for that she was grateful. She thought about the case, playing everything over in her mind. Phoebe Meridew and the gardener were having an affair, which led to Meridew filing for divorce. Phoebe had access to the poison, but was she savvy enough to figure out how to concoct it? Was the gardener? Manny Wong had a beef with Meridew and he had the blowgun, but he didn't have a 9mm registered and someone had shot at Hughes. Wong still seemed the most likely suspect and that in itself bothered Peyton.

She only half heard the flight attendant go over the safety protocols for the plane and soon they were taxiing down the runway.

The foreman, Teddy Nakamura, had guns, but what was the motive? He'd had a few run-ins with Meridew, but everyone apparently did. Nakamura had stayed employed with Meridew and he was annoyed with the protestors. Celia, the ex-secretary, had been in Texas, so Peyton excluded her, but no one had looked at Hughes' secretary Doreen Kim.

"What do we know about Doreen Kim?" she asked Kahele as the plane made the stomach dropping lift into the air.

"Hughes' secretary? She's been with him for years."

"Does she have an alibi for the night Meridew died?"

"She says she was home. Her husband confirmed it."

"Her husband?"

"I can see if there's anything else to corroborate that claim," said Kahele.

"Hold off for a while, but file it in the back of your mind."

As soon as the seatbelt sign turned off, the flight attendant brought them their coffee and six packets of sugar, offering three to Marco and three to her. She absconded all of Marco's and poured them into her cup, ignoring the disapproving looks of the two men.

When the plane landed, they were met with an officer from the Maui police force who handed over a vehicle to Kahele. Peyton was impressed by the efficiency of the entire operation.

"Do you do this often?" she asked. "Fly between islands?"

"Frequently enough," he said, climbing behind the wheel.

Then they were off to Kahului, which was the main city on the island. Maui was more developed than Kauai with less green vegetation. Peyton was surprised when Kahele pulled into the parking lot of a business park and set the brakes.

"One of my men texted that Fiona's in her office."

"What does she do for a living?" asked Peyton, opening the car door and climbing out.

"She's a civil engineer. She used to work for Dewdrop before she married Meridew," he answered, pulling open the business's door and stepping into an air-conditioned reception area. No one was at the counter in the front, but a large open space extended beyond the counter and a woman and man worked over a drafting table.

They both looked up, then the woman came toward them. She was Hawaiian with long black hair and high cheekbones. She wore capris and a sleeveless blouse, sneakers on her feet. She held out her hand to Kahele.

"Chief Kahele I presume," she said, shaking his hand.

"Yes, and this is Special Agent Peyton Brooks and her husband, Captain Marco D'Angelo," he said, motioning to them.

She shook hands with them, her grip firm. "Fiona Meridew," she said. "How can I help you?"

"We were wondering if we could ask you a few questions about your ex-husband," said Peyton.

Fiona looked over her shoulder at the man. "Take a break, Sampson," she said and the man wandered off. She motioned to a conference table in the middle of the room and they all took seats around it. Then Fiona regarded Peyton steadily. "Special Agent? Impressive."

Peyton shrugged. "I've only been at it a few months, but it isn't as glamorous as you might think."

"Nothing ever is." She pulled a pencil out from behind her ear and tapped it on the table. "What can I answer for you? I haven't seen Harvey in six months."

"How long were you married to him, Mrs. Meridew?"

"Fiona please. The only reason I kept the Meridew name was for industry recognition. It gets attention, I'll tell you that. Opens doors that would be closed otherwise. Especially to a woman engineer."

"I understand. Fiona, then. How long were you married to Mr. Meridew?"

"Seven years, until he met Malibu Barbie."

Peyton laughed. She liked this ex-wife.

"And if you want an alibi, I was here that whole night. Sampson can vouch for me. We were working on a job and we worked right through until morning. I think we even got takeout around midnight, so the delivery boy can also vouch that I was here."

"We'll confirm that," said Kahele, but Peyton was already sure this woman had nothing to do with his death. She was clearly successful in her own right.

"We've heard Mr. Meridew could be difficult. Demanding."

"Harvey? He was a complete and total asshole. And he knew nothing about business. At best, he was a middling civil engineer, if you ask me."

"What do you mean? He wasn't good at what he did?"

Fiona made a face. "He was good at copying what other engineers did. He never had an original thought in his life."

"Jackson Hughes told us that Meridew made the business what it was. He gave him the credit for making it successful."

"If he did, it was only because Harvey had the ability to surround himself with people who could get things done."

"You don't seem too shaken up by his death," said Marco.

She glanced at him. "Should I be? He used me until he found something better. Harvey Meridew was a user. That's all he was. He took what he could get and he would betray his own mother if he thought it would get him somewhere."

Marco looked away, staring out over the room. Peyton could tell by the way his jaw worked that he had something he was mulling. She'd seen it before.

Peyton shook her head wryly. "No one has anything good to say about Harvey, no one except Jackson."

Fiona sighed. "Jackson's a simple soul. He just wants Dewdrop to be successful and to have financial security. He was one of the few happily married men until Harvey came along."

"What do you mean by that?" asked Peyton.

"Oh, you didn't know?"

"Know what?"

"This was before Malibu Barbie, but we were still married at the time."

"What was?" prompted Peyton again.

"Harvey and Tricia, Jackson's wife? They had an affair and Jackson found them."

"What did he do? Jackson, I mean?"

Fiona laughed, tapping the pencil again. "He forgave them. He forgave them and told them he understood. He said he wouldn't do anything if they stopped, but Tricia filed for divorce a week later." She gave them that twisted smile once more. "That man is either the stupidest man in the world or the most forgiving. Harvey slept with his wife and he continued to work with him for another six years as if nothing ever happened."

* * *

"Yes, I need a list of all the residents. No, just the names," said Danté, glancing up as Cho appeared at his desk with a woman who was almost the same height as he was. She had short hair and wore a sharp business suit. She gave him a severe look. "Right. Right, thank you." He disconnected the call and rose to his feet.

"Danté, this is Deputy Chief Defino."

The woman held out her hand. "Nice to meet you, Danté. Cho has very good things to say about you. So does your captain."

Danté shook her hand. "Yes, ma'am," he said, wishing Cho had warned him he was bringing her by to meet him. He hadn't worn a suit, just a t-shirt and jeans since it was Sunday. "I've heard a lot about you, ma'am."

"I wouldn't believe much of it if I were you, young man," she said in a crisp, no nonsense tone.

"No, no! It's all been good."

She and Cho laughed. "Captain D'Angelo has big plans for you. He thinks you'll make an exceptional detective."

"I'm honored, ma'am," Danté said, ducking his head.

"You know he and his partner, Peyton Brooks, were some of the youngest detectives we had on the force. You might join them in that distinction."

"Thank you, ma'am."

"So where are you on the Gutierrez case?" she asked, squinting at him.

"I called the landlord of the building to see if he would give us a list of the residents. He said he'd email it over by tomorrow at the latest. We're looking for another pregnant woman named Donna."

"She was friendly with the young woman who was killed?"

"They were apparently buying baby things together, going to thrift stores and such."

"But when you went into the Gutierrez apartment, you saw no baby stuff anywhere?"

Danté shook his head. "I even went through the cabinets in the kitchen. There was nothing."

Defino shared a look with Cho. "Good job, Officer Price. I'm impressed."

"Thank you, ma'am."

"Have we confirmed the alibi of the ex-boyfriend?"

"We haven't, but we're working on him. We don't really have enough to hold him right now."

"He wanted her to have a late term abortion," said Cho. "Problem is we don't have an exact time of death, so getting alibis is difficult."

Defino twisted her lips to the side. "Can we get confirmation that there was baby paraphernalia in the apartment?"

"We'll work on it," said Cho, nodding. "Maybe one of Harper's support group members went shopping with her or remembers seeing something. Call Harper and see if she can track the women down."

"Okay," said Danté.

"If there was baby paraphernalia, the person who attacked her took it and the baby. That changes the motive completely," said Defino.

"And likely the sex of the assailant," said Cho.

"Exactly. We need to confirm that Gutierrez had, in fact, purchased something for the baby."

Danté pulled out his phone. "I'll call Harper right now."

Defino gave him the first smile he'd seen from her. "Then go home. You deserve a day off. If we don't revitalize, we'll be no good to anyone."

Danté nodded, but he had a few more loose ends to shore up before he left and his mother didn't expect him until 4:00 for dinner anyway. As Defino and Cho wandered away, Danté took his seat again and pressed the button for Harper's number. It rang and rang, finally going to voicemail. She hadn't bothered to personalize her greeting, so Danté had a moment of worry that he might have dialed the wrong number, but he could remember the moment when she'd rattled it off to him very clearly.

He left a message, asking her to call him, and disconnected, then he pulled up Abe's autopsy report. Abe had estimated Luz's time of death within a twenty-four-hour window. He clicked on the computer and did a search for the LA Galaxy, but no matter how much he dug, he couldn't find a practice schedule. He rubbed his jaw and thought about it for a moment. If Donny Ochoa was planning to try out for the Galaxy, he probably worked out regularly. He'd have to have a gym membership somewhere.

Danté pulled up all the gyms in the City, then located those within a mile of the address Donny had given them when he came in for questioning. He knew they wouldn't just give him information without a warrant, so he'd have to be a little sneaky. It went against his nature, but the memory of Luz's tortured and bloody body haunted him still. Dialing the first number, he tried to think of what he could ask that would give him the information he wanted.

When the receptionist answered, he told them his name was Donny Ochoa and he thought he might have left his cell phone there the last time he was in. After a few seconds hesitation, the receptionist told him she had no one by the name of Ochoa on the list of gym members.

He found the same situation for the next five places he called and he was getting a little discouraged. Figuring out an alibi for someone was easier when they gave it to you. When he called the sixth place, he got lucky.

"Do you remember where you left it?" the male voice asked. "Locker room or weight room?"

"Either of those places. I've been so busy," Danté lied, trying to remember the inflection of Donny's voice. "I'm trying out for the LA Galaxy in a few…"

"Yeah, yeah," the man interrupted. "Geez. Okay, look what day did you lose it? Was it on Thursday when you played with the indoor soccer team?"

Thursday? Danté had found Luz's body on a Tuesday. He clicked back through the autopsy report that Abe had written. Abe estimated time of death to have been between five and six days before Danté had found her. Harper had her support group on Thursday night.

Danté hung up without answering the guy, then rose to his feet and went in search of Cho. He found him talking to Simons in Simons' cubicle, his feet crossed on Simons' desk. Defino was no longer with him.

"I found out where Donny Ochoa goes to the gym."

"How'd you do that?" asked Cho, dropping his feet.

"I looked up all the gyms in the City, narrowed it down to a mile or two radius around his address that he gave us when he was here. Then I started calling."

Cho and Simons exchanged a look. "You started calling the gyms?" asked Simons.

"Yes, I pretended I was Ochoa and that I'd lost my phone until I found the one that he attended."

They both chuckled at that. "That's brilliant."

Danté held up a hand. "Abe estimates Luz was dead between five to six days when I found her. I found her on a Tuesday. Harper reported that Luz didn't attend the support group the previous week and the support group meetings are held on a Thursday, the same night Donny Ochoa plays indoor soccer at the gym."

"So you're thinking that if we can confirm Ochoa was at soccer…"

"We'll have a weak alibi, but it's something. We're starting to piece together his whereabouts at least."

"Okay. Give me the name of the gym and I'll have Adams work on a warrant," said Simons.

Danté rattled the address off from memory.

Cho nodded, obviously pleased. "Good work, kid. Now, go home. We can't do anything without the warrant or the tenant list. Let this go for a while and live your life."

Danté glanced at the display on his phone and was surprised to see how late it was. He had only a half hour to get to his parents and his mother didn't like it when he was late. "See you tomorrow," he said and headed for the door.

The sun was shining when he stepped out into the parking lot. He was surprised to see Harper leaning against his Odyssey as he jogged down the stairs. She was wearing a pair of shorts and a lacy blouse without sleeves, but she still wore her signature heels.

"Hey," she said, straightening.

"Hey, I tried to call you."

She reached into the handbag hanging from her shoulder and glanced at the display. "So you did. What's up?"

"We need to establish that someone saw Luz with baby paraphernalia. Do you think any of the women in the support group saw anything?"

"I know she had baby stuff. We had a shower for her. She had diapers and clothes and blankets."

Danté absorbed that. He wanted to head back inside and tell Cho, but Cho had been adamant that he go home. It could wait until Monday, especially since his mother was waiting on him for dinner.

"What does that prove? That the killer's a woman?"

"No, it doesn't prove anything, except that the stuff is missing. It could just be that she left it somewhere else, at someone else's apartment for storage. Maybe even this Donna woman. Maybe they planned to share everything."

Harper looked away, wrapping her arms around herself. "I did some digging."

"What do you mean?"

She rubbed the back of her neck. "There are places on the web, in the dark web, where people sell things, things they don't want the police to know about."

"Harper!"

She held up a hand. "As a reporter, you use whatever you have in order to get information, Mr. Spock. Don't act all Puritanical with me. You'd do the same."

He liked to think he wouldn't, but he'd just impersonated someone to get information. "What did you search for?"

"Babies. Newborns. People sell them like a commodity to the highest bidder. Usually pedophiles..." She shuddered. "But sometimes to families who really want a baby, who can't have one of their own."

"And?" He could feel his heart pounding.

"I thought maybe Donny took the baby and sold it, so I've got an alert set up if a baby shows up."

"Has one shown up, Harper?"

"No, Danté, no babies have gone on the black market since Luz died."

He released his held breath. "You tell me if you get a ping. You don't contact that person by yourself. Do you understand me?"

She nodded.

"Say it. I need you to say it out loud."

She made an exasperated huff. "Seriously, you treat me like a child sometimes."

"Just do what I ask, Harper. For once."

She held up her peace sign. "Scout's honor," she said. "I'll contact you if I get a ping."

"Okay. Look, I gotta go," he said, taking his keys out of his pocket.

"Oh, sorry. I thought maybe we could go get a drink or something." She looked down as she said it and Danté realized he'd never seen her so uncertain before.

"Actually, I'm on my way to my parents' house for dinner."

"Right, right," she said. "I'll just head out myself." She started walking across the parking lot and Danté remembered she didn't drive.

"Can I drop you somewhere?"

"No, I'm good," she said, continuing toward the street.

Danté started for the minivan, then turned around again. "Harper."

She stopped and glanced back over her shoulder. Danté cursed himself for noticing how her shorts accentuated her long legs.

"Come to dinner with me. My parents would love to meet you."

She hesitated. "I don't want to impose."

"You won't be. Mom always makes way more food than anyone can ever eat and I think Dad's barbecuing tonight anyway. There'll be plenty."

"But this is your family time."

"My parents will find your job fascinating. Come on."

She walked back to him, smiling. "I get to see the whole Vulcan family, do I?"

"Maybe don't call them that to their faces," he said, unlocking the minivan.

She laughed as they both climbed inside, then she looked around, running her hand along the dashboard. "Wow! It's almost like riding in an antique."

"Behave," he told her, starting the van and backing it out of the space.

She smiled at him and he felt a tightness in his chest. He found himself craving those smiles a little too much. Instead, he focused on his driving.

"If Donny took the baby, what would he have done with it?" she said, staring out the window.

"That's what bothers me. If you found a baby available on the dark web, that might be one thing, but Donny doesn't seem like a man who knows anything about caring for an infant."

"If the baby died, wouldn't someone have found its body?"

"Not necessarily," he said. "You'd be surprised what people will do to hide a body."

She shuddered. "I can't talk about this anymore," she said.

Danté let it go. It bothered him too and he'd just as soon put it away for a little while.

His parents had a modest single story home in the Richmond District. He pulled up to the curb and parked. Harper studied the house and he couldn't help but wonder what she thought of it. His father liked to garden, so the front yard was filled with drought resistant plants that were in full bloom this time of year. He got out and walked around, opening her door.

"I don't think this is a good idea," she said, looking up at him.

This vulnerable side of Harper surprised him. He was used to her brash, commanding personality.

"It's a great idea. Come on."

She got out and he placed a hand in the small of her back to direct her up the walkway. He knew his parents' home couldn't be anything like the house where she grew up. She came from money, power, and position.

Before he got to the door, it opened and his mother appeared in the doorway. Roshanda Price was a tall woman with a trim figure. Danté had gotten his pale brown eyes from her. From the time he could remember, she'd kept her hair in braids that touched her shoulders and she wore a pair of shorts and a t-shirt with El Capítan on it. She and his father liked to hike in their spare time.

"Danté!" she exclaimed, opening her arms.

He stepped into her hug, kissing her cheek. She rocked him back and forth for a moment, then her gaze fell on Harper.

"Who is your lovely friend?" she said, easing out of his arms and stepping forward to hug Harper.

"This is Harper McLeod. She's a reporter for the *Emersonian.*"

Harper let his mother hug her, smiling as she embraced the older woman. "Nice to meet you, ma'am," she said.

"Call me Roshanda," his mother said, holding Harper by the shoulders to look at her. "A reporter? What a fascinating job. And the *Emersonian*? I read it all the time. It's quite the subversive force these days, isn't it?"

Harper blinked at her in surprise.

Roshanda leaned close. "I love it."

Harper laughed. "You scared me for a moment."

"Nonsense, we need more rogue journalists bringing the truth into the light." She motioned into the house. "Come in, please."

They stepped into the living room with its comfortable couches and recliners. Danté's younger brother, Virgil, sat on the couch, playing a video game, but he looked up as they entered and then rose to his feet. He and Danté clasped hands and gave each other half-hugs, then Roshanda put her arm around her youngest son.

"Harper, this is Virgil. Virgil, this is Danté's friend, Harper, a reporter for the *Emersonian.*"

"Cool," said Virgil, holding out his fist for Harper to bump. She did and beamed at the younger Price brother.

Virgil was as tall as Danté already, still in that long and lanky teenager's body. He had their father's darker eyes and darker skin, his hair shaved close with a zigzag pattern cut into the side of it.

"Cool hair," said Harper, pointing at it.

"Thanks," he said.

"Virgil's applying to Berkeley in the fall," said Roshanda. "He'll be a senior."

"Really?" said Harper. "That's where I went."

"You went to Berkeley," said Virgil, his eyes lighting up. "You have to tell me everything about it."

"No problem. I can even look over your essays if you'd like."

"Yeah, that'd be awesome."

Danté's father appeared in the opening of the kitchen. "What's this I hear about Cal?" he said.

While Danté took more after his mother's side of the family, Virgil took after their father's.

"Danté," said his father, holding out his arms.

Danté moved forward and let his father grab him in a bear hug. He smelled of barbecue sauce and smoke.

"Hey, Dad," he said, patting his father's back.

Ezra moved away from his son and held out his hand to Harper. "Ezra Price," he said, shaking it.

"Harper McLeod," she answered.

Ezra looked surprised. "Of *the* McLeods?"

Harper nodded sheepishly.

Roshanda hooked her arm through Harper's. "Let me show you the rest of the house," she said, dragging her toward the archway. Harper looked over her shoulder at Danté, smiling in bemusement. Roshanda Price was a force to be reckoned with, but Danté never remembered a time when she didn't bend over backwards to make her guests comfortable.

After the tour, Roshanda deposited Harper in the kitchen where his father was bringing in meat from the barbecue. Roshanda picked up a stack of plates and handed it to Danté. Danté immediately began setting them out around the picnic table that had been their family table for decades.

"No feats, no eats," said Roshanda. "Virgil!" she called and his brother obediently appeared, grabbing the silverware and setting it out.

Roshanda picked up a stack of napkins and passed them to Harper. She gamely took them and began placing them at each place setting without being asked to do so. Soon the table was set and the food arranged in the center.

They all took seats at their regular places, but Danté had set a new place for Harper next to him. As they began passing around the barbecued chicken, the coleslaw, and the corn, Harper helped herself as if she'd eaten with his family a million times.

"Lemonade?" asked Roshanda, reaching for Harper's glass.
"Yes, thank you, ma'am," Harper said, smiling up at her.

No one ate until everyone had dished up their plates and were seated around the table, then they dug in. The minute the first bite was placed in their mouths, Ezra looked up. Danté knew what was coming, but he wasn't sure how Harper would handle it.

"So, I want to discuss a story I recently read in the paper about a pharmacist who refused to fill a prescription for someone due to his religious beliefs. Virgil, you go first. What do you think? Do you think someone should be able to refuse to fill a prescription based on personal or religious reasons?"

From the time of Danté's earliest memory, his parents had posed such moral questions to them and asked them to defend their point of view. His father had always said it was important to hone their ability to argue logically and reasonably. Danté had always believed he just enjoyed a good debate. It had made their family meals lively at any rate.

"I think if you take a job, you take it knowing you may have to do something that goes against your beliefs at some point, but you agreed to take the job, so you need to do what's expected of you."

Harper shook her head. "I don't know," she said, then she glanced at Ezra. "I'm sorry. I didn't mean to interrupt."

"No, go ahead, Harper," said Ezra, waving his fork at her.

"Well," she continued. "In this case, if there are other pharmacists who can fill the prescription for the customer, then both parties can get what they need and no one has to compromise."

"But what if no one else is there to do that? Are you saying the customer should have to go to another pharmacy to get a prescription filled just because someone doesn't want to do their job? If someone has a prescription, the doctor prescribed it, so they need it. That's more important than someone's moral objections," argued Virgil.

"I don't know about that. I mean, our morality is all that separates us from animals and…" continued Harper.

Danté felt his mother's eyes on him and he met her look. She smiled at him, then went back to eating.

Later that night as Danté drove Harper home, he found her unusually quiet. He wasn't sure whether his family had been overwhelming or just too simple for a woman who had been raised with servants and nannies at her fingertips.

"What are you thinking about?"

She glanced over at him, the streetlights playing over her pretty features. "How lucky you are."

"How lucky I am? How so?"

"You have a family that loves each other. Your parents are interesting and you have a brother who means the world to you."

"You have a family too, Harper. And a lot more luxury, I'm sure."

She thought about that, staring out the front windshield. "Yeah, yeah, I do. And summers in Milan," she said wistfully. "That's great too."

He wasn't sure what to say, so he said nothing.

She gave him a strange, pensive smile. "Thank you for letting me come with you, Danté," she said.

"Anytime," he answered, smiling back.

Her smile dried. "Do you mean that?"

"What?" he asked, surprised.

She waved it off, then held out her hand. "Do you have any gum?"

And so the conversation came to an abrupt end.

* * *

Marco sat on a picnic table at the edge of the parking lot, his feet braced on the seat. Peyton waded into the surf, her sundress held in her hands to keep it out of the water. A little boy raced back and forth up the beach, into the waves and out right next to her, his mother a step away on his other side.

Kahele appeared beside Marco, holding out a soda. Marco took it and popped it open as Kahele sat down on the picnic table next to him. Taking a sip of the soda, Marco braced his forearms on his knees and held the can in both hands.

"Thanks," he said.

Kahele set another can beside them and popped open his own, sipping at it, his eyes moving to Peyton where she played in the surf. "You are one lucky man. That is one amazing woman."

Marco smiled, watching as the little boy reached out and took Peyton's hand, holding onto her as the waves wrapped around his feet. Peyton and the mother started talking, laughing with each other and watching the boy.

"Yeah, I know. I've known that for a very long time."

Kahele nodded. "How'd you meet?"

"We were partners on the force for eight years."

"Then you were more."

"Yeah. Man, I never thought I'd be here, I'll tell you that."

Kahele laughed. "I get it. Must be hard with her being an agent though. I mean, you handle it well."

Marco glanced at him. "No, I don't." He drew a deep breath. He didn't like sharing things with other men, but Kahele was tapping into the worry that had been niggling at the back of Marco's mind for their entire trip. "She's thinking of quitting."

"Why? She's a damn good agent. Her team really respects her and her stats are incredible."

"Yeah, I know." Marco ran his thumb over the label on the can. "She thinks her job will affect our marriage."

"Ah, well, I get that too. It's hard when even one of you is a cop, but both of you…" He drank, then stared into the top of the can. "My marriage didn't survive it."

"Was your ex-wife a cop?"

"Yeah. Damn good one too, but we just never had any time together and I was always afraid I was going to get that call one day."

"Yeah, I know the feeling. I'm also discovering some very unpleasant flaws in myself throughout all of this."

"What do you mean?"

"Jealousy, possessiveness."

"Yeah, I know that too. Man, some of the fights we had. When I think back on them, I feel so ashamed of some things I said, some accusations I hurled."

Marco stared at the surf, watching Peyton and the young mother swinging the little boy back and forth, his feet skimming the waves. Peyton was laughing, completely at ease and enjoying herself in the moment. He smiled, watching her.

"The thing is I want her to quit the Bureau. I'm not going to lie. It would make me happy."

"But? I hear a but in there," said Kahele.

"Then it wouldn't. If she quit for me, quit something she loves, she would eventually resent me for it. Or if she didn't, the knowledge that I could get her to give in to my wishes would make the jealousy and possessiveness worse. She thinks it would save our marriage, but I know…I know it would destroy it."

CHAPTER 19

Peyton and Marco stepped into the precinct the next morning at 9:00. Willis met them in the reception area, his face lit with excitement. "Chief Kahele asked me to escort you back to his office as soon as you arrived today."

"Is something up?" asked Peyton.

"Harvey Meridew's first wife, Daisy, is here. She came on her own to talk to the chief."

"Interesting," said Peyton, exchanging a look with Marco.

Willis guided them through the busy precinct and to Kahele's frosted glass door. He knocked twice, then they heard Kahele call, "Enter."

Willis pushed open the door and poked his head inside. "Agent Brooks and her husband are here."

Peyton gave Marco a bemused smile. A man like Marco probably wouldn't like being called her husband. He winked at her though, making her heart beat a little faster. How could he still do that to her after all this time? She wanted to hug him, but she kept her professional persona in place.

Willis opened the door wide and they stepped through. A woman in her early fifties sat in a chair before Kahele's desk. She was Caucasian with a deep tan, brown stylishly cut long hair, wearing an expensive skirt and suit jacket in pale pink. The heels on her feet made Peyton catch her breath, and Peyton wasn't one to swoon over shoes that would be particularly punishing. When she crossed her legs, Peyton caught the iconic red soles. Louboutins. Of course.

Kahele rose to his feet. "Mrs. Meridew, this is Special Agent Peyton Brooks and her husband, Captain Marco D'Angelo of the SFPD."

Daisy Meridew held out her hand with her fingers curved downward. Peyton wasn't sure if she expected someone to kiss her fingers or what. She gripped her hand briefly and released it. Then Daisy presented her fingers to Marco, but her gaze traveled over him languidly. Peyton bristled at the familiar twinge of jealousy as Marco took her hand.

343

Kahele motioned to the chairs closest to him. Peyton sat so that she could watched Daisy, but that forced Marco to sit next to the older woman and a flirtatious smile touched the corners of Daisy's mouth.

"As I was saying, Chief, I wanted to save you the trouble of having to come after me. Besides, I do so like to take a break from my other duties." She spoke with a rather regal British accent. Peyton couldn't help but wonder if it was fake.

"I appreciate it, Mrs. Meridew," said Kahele, then he gave Peyton a pointed look.

Peyton beamed a smile at Daisy Meridew. "Do you prefer Daisy or Mrs. Meridew?"

Daisy's eyes rolled toward the ceiling in a dismissive expression. "Mrs. Meridew, of course. I'm the original."

"I see," said Peyton, taking her pad from the pocket on her sundress. "How long were you married to Mr. Meridew?"

"Seventeen years."

"How did you meet? I'm detecting a British accent."

"I was on vacation in Hawaii. Harvey was working at the hotel where I was staying. He was a student at the time."

Which explained why she seemed older than Harvey.

"Seventeen years? You lasted quite a bit longer than your followers."

Daisy's supercilious smile dried. "That's a very crass way to put it."

"Well, I'm with the FBI. We're pretty much known for being straight shooters." She flipped back a few pages. "Which brings up an interesting question? You have a 9mm registered to you, Mrs. Meridew."

"Yes, I do. It's properly licensed. I use it for protection."

"Can you tell me what happened that a seventeen-year marriage ended?" said Peyton, sidestepping the gun permit. She sensed Daisy Meridew was not a woman easily thrown off her game.

"Fiona happened. Harvey was a man who easily fell in love, but he never stayed in love for very long."

"That must have been hard. Such a betrayal."

Daisy laughed. "Oh, goodness, aren't you sweet?" she said in that annoying superior accent. "Harvey was a tomcat, always messing with his latest acquired toy. I didn't mind as long as he didn't bring it home, but then he thought he fell in love with Fiona and decided he had to divorce me to marry her."

"Aggravating."

"Definitely, however, he paid me so well, I forgave him."

"You forgave a man who cheated on you and dumped you for someone younger?"

Daisy's smile broadened. "How charming. You think that my ego is so easily bruised. I'd become very disenchanted with Harvey over the years and I actually felt a sense of relief. After all, I wouldn't have to kill him when he made the inevitable mistake of striking me." She laughed again, touching Marco's arm.

Peyton bristled at that, but she fought it back under control. *Black widow,* she thought. "Interesting you should put it that way since he's dead now."

"Yes, but as I said, I didn't have to kill him. I figured someday he'd upset the wrong sort of person."

"You hated him?"

"Hate is such a strong word, Agent Brooks. I loathed him."

Peyton smiled slowly. "Ah, vast distinction." She made some notes on her pad. "It helps that you also got a ten-million-dollar payday upon his demise."

Again the rolling of the eyes toward the ceiling. "Do you think that paltry amount is enough to make me give up my very enjoyable life? I've learned how to invest well and I will never want for anything, which is more than I think you can say, working on a police officer's salary."

Peyton wasn't about to take the bait. She shrugged. "I don't know. Money buys very little that pleases me, to be honest." She gave Marco a sultry wink. He smiled in return.

Daisy gave Marco a slow once over again. "I can imagine," she said, clasping her hands on her knee. "Anyway, I came to help you in your investigation. I think you'll be very interested in what I have to say."

Peyton's focus shifted back to her. "By all means. You have my undivided attention."

"As I was telling Chief Kahele, you may not realize all the interconnections between people in Harvey's life. Not only did he have three wives, but he had no problem keeping side pieces around."

"We know he had an affair with Jackson Hughes' wife," said Peyton.

Daisy smiled a cunning smile. "Do you now? Did you know that he also had an affair with Jackson Hughes' secretary Doreen?"

"Doreen? Really?"

The smile remained. "At the same time that Jackson was…how do you Americans say it…banging her."

That took Peyton by surprise. She glanced over at Kahele. Kahele himself had gone still.

"Did this happen when Hughes was married to Tricia?"

"Goodness no. Dear Jackson believed he was in love with his wife. He wouldn't have cheated on her. Jackson is a darling simpleton."

"Does Doreen's husband know she was having an affair with two men?"

Daisy gave a cheeky shrug.

Damn it. That would add another suspect to the list.

"When were they all having this affair?" asked Marco.

"You should do more of the talking, darlin'," Daisy said, petting him. "So here's the really juicy part."

Peyton didn't want this woman's information, but they needed it. She ground her back teeth and forced herself to listen.

"Doreen was sleeping with Jackson and Harvey at the same time, but neither one of the men knew about the other one. Then one day Jackson asked Doreen to go on a business trip with the two of them. He figured Doreen would share his room, but Harvey had the same idea. Doreen had to tell them both what was going on. Of course, Harvey had a temper and flew into a rage, saying he would never sleep with the same woman that Jackson was tipping. According to Harvey, he said this right in front of Doreen and Jackson, then he called Doreen all manner of names that begin with whore and…" She leaned close to Marco, petting his arm again. "Here's the part that's going to get your little wife out of her chair." She drew a deep breath and released it, smiling the entire time. "…he threatened to tell her husband."

Peyton did want to leap out of the chair, but she restrained herself. Damn, this woman was good. "How do you know this, Daisy?"

"Harvey told me himself. You see, we've remained on speaking terms all these years. To be honest, I think I was the only one he trusted." She picked up her purse from the edge of Kahele's desk. "And because I know what your next question will be, I took the liberty of printing this out. I was in New York when Harvey died. I attended a showing of *Hamilton* and spent the three nights at the Ritz-Carlton." She extracted some papers and passed them to Kahele. "My plane tickets, my play stub, and my hotel bill."

Then she rose to her feet and turned toward the door, laying her hand on Marco's shoulder, but she hesitated at the last second and turned back around. "Oh, and one more thing..." The corners of her lips turned up in a smile the envy of any Academy Award winner. "...Doreen apparently threatened to kill Harvey if he told her husband."

Peyton could feel every nerve in her body vibrating, ready to spring into action as Daisy Meridew sashayed out of the room, letting the door close behind her. Then she said through gritted teeth, "Bring Doreen Kim and her husband in for questioning right away."

"I'm on it," said Kahele.

* * *

Danté printed off the list from Luz's landlord and picked up a highlighter from his desk, scanning down the names. Cho set a cup of coffee on his desk blotter and looked over at him. "Is that the list?"

"Yes, there's no Donna here, but there's a Dana. Dana Veres. She lives on the same floor as Doolie, opposite end of the hall."

Cho grabbed his travel mug, yanking the top off, then he poured the coffee into it. Once he had the top in place again, he grabbed his jacket off his desk chair and swung it around his shoulders. "Let's head out there and talk to Dana Veres, then."

As they moved toward the front of the precinct, Cho slipped his other arm into his jacket sleeve. "Lee, tell Simons we're heading back out to Luz Gutierrez's apartment building."

Harper was stepping through the precinct's outer doors as Cho pushed open the half-door. "The apartment building? You got the tenant list?"

Cho eased around her and caught the outer door. "Nice to see you again, Ms. McLeod. Let's go, kid," he called to Danté.

Danté eased around Harper also, but she placed a hand on his arm. "Did you get the list, Danté?" she pressed.

"I've got to go," he said, looking out at Cho.

Her eyes went hard and she released him. "Fine."

He shot her one final look, then jogged down the stairs and into the parking lot. As soon as he had his seatbelt buckled, Cho wheeled out of the parking lot and headed down the street. Danté felt guilty for ignoring Harper, but he understood that Cho didn't want her knowing about an active case.

They drove to Luz's apartment building in silence and parked the sedan, climbing out. The same men lounged on the stoops up and down the street, watching with idle interest as they climbed the stairs and entered the building. Danté tried to ignore the peeling paint, the worn spots on the carpet, the water stains on the ceiling. He tried to ignore the poverty around him, but it was difficult. It always amazed him what people did to survive.

He could hear voices raised in loud conversation, babies crying, a barking dog. The smell of urine permeated the hallways, but underlying it was a smell of cooking and mildew and decay.

They arrived at the door to Dana's apartment. She'd put a welcome mat out and a holiday wreath hung from the center of the door. Cho rapped loudly, setting a dog in the next door apartment to barking.

They waited in the dim light of an exposed bulb, staring down the other end of the hallway, but no one opened the door. Cho rapped again, even louder this time. The door directly across the hall opened a crack and a little old man poked his head outside.

"Ain't no one there," he said, his brown skin stretched taut over too much bone.

Cho showed him his badge. "We're looking for Dana Veres," he said.

"She ain't been here for about a week."

Cho and Danté exchanged a look. "Where did she go? Do you know?"

"I don't ask her where she's getting to. I ain't got her to study 'bout." He pointed over his head. "Ask the girl upstairs. They close."

"Can you tell us what the upstairs girl's name is?" asked Cho.

"One of them fancy Spanish names. Don't remember what it was."

"Do you know Dana Veres?" asked Danté.

"Enough to say hi. She and the other girl were friendly though. Go ask her." A crafty look entered his face. "What she do? She do something bad?"

"We just want to ask her a few questions," said Cho. "That's all."

"We were told Dana was pregnant, same as Luz, the girl upstairs. Can you confirm that for us?" asked Danté.

The old man held up a hand. "Whoa, I learned a long time ago that you ain't supposed to be asking about them things. You get some of these girls and they got themselves a belly, but you don't ask. You get your face slapped if you do. I know this. I surely do."

Cho fought the smile that tugged at the corner of his mouth, but Danté was feeling edgy. He wanted answers and they just weren't getting anywhere. He exhaled in frustration, but Cho gave the guy a nod.

"You can tell us. We're not going to tell anyone. Bro code, you know?"

Danté shot Cho an aggravated look, but the old man eased out of the door, shuffling toward them. He put his hand to the side of his mouth and leaned close to them. Danté could smell sweat and unwashed clothing. His hair smelled of cigarette smoke.

"This one here," he said conspiratorially, "was one of them big girls."

"Heavy?" asked Cho.

"Big," said the old man. "Tall and built like a man."

Danté felt his heart begin to pound a little faster. It would have taken someone with some upper body strength to drag Luz to the bed after bashing in her skull.

"Do you know if she was pregnant?" asked Cho.

"She had a big belly, now didn't she," he said.

"Thank you. You've been helpful." Cho took a card out of his wallet and passed it to the man. "If she comes back, will you call us right away?"

"You need my help, doncha?"

"Very much so. Without the help of citizens like you, we'd have a hard time doing our job."

"Okay. I'll call ya."

"Don't confront her yourself or tell her we were here. Just call me if you see her."

"Got it," said the old man and he shuffled back to his apartment, closing the door behind him. Cho jerked his chin down the hallway.

"Let's go."

"Where?" asked Danté.

"Back to the precinct. Let's see if Stan Neumann can scare up some information on Dana Veres."

Danté followed him down the hallway, feeling frustrated. If this was their person, they were losing precious time when they could be searching for the baby. If this wasn't their person, they needed to get out there and hunt the perp down. Or they had to find a way to make Donny Ochoa sing.

When they got in the car, headed back to the precinct, Cho looked into the rearview mirror, glancing at the traffic behind them. A few seconds later, he cleared his throat. Danté glanced over at him.

"You know the saying you get more flies with honey," Cho said.

Danté blew out air. His mother used that all the time and he'd always wondered why the hell anyone wanted to get flies. "Yes," he said. He didn't know why he was feeling cantankerous and rebellious, but he was.

"You never know where information might come from. The man you dismiss because he's old or he's a slow talker, or he's lonely so he rambles, might actually have seen something important. It's sometimes worth it to let someone talk for a while. If they're nervous or afraid, they might just tell you something if you're patient with them."

Danté rubbed a hand over his face and back over his short hair. "I understand. I'm sorry. I'm just feeling anxious and frustrated."

"It's understandable. We all feel that way at times."

"Harper's checking the dark web to see if the baby winds up on the black market, sold to a pedophile." He could hardly say the word without wanting to punch something.

Cho shot him a look. "That was actually good thinking. Huh, she might be an asset to us."

"What sort of sick…" He caught himself before he swore. His parents had always told him to find different ways to communicate.

"Sonuvabitch? You can say the word, kid. Better to swear than to sock someone in the throat and I know that's probably what you want to do."

Danté thought about that for a moment. Cho had a point. Swearing was definitely preferable to the feelings he was fighting presently.

"I just keep thinking we need to move quicker. We need to solve this faster, so we can get that baby before the unthinkable happens."

Cho sighed. "Look, kid. We're going to work this case. We're going to solve it, but you may have to reconcile yourself with the fact that it may already be too late for this baby. He may already be dead."

Danté looked out the side window, unable to process that. It just couldn't end that way. It couldn't. If they found out the baby was dead, Danté wasn't sure how he'd accept that level of failure.

They arrived back at the precinct, heading toward the back and Stan Neumann's office, when Lee held up a hand. "You should probably know that Harper McLeod's still here."

"What?" said Cho, giving him a stern look. "Why?"

"She ran into Stan on his way in this morning and she cornered him, telling him she wanted to get as much information on Dana Veres as she could. They've been in Stan's office for the last hour."

Cho gave Danté an aggravated look and headed toward the back at a brisk pace. They found Stan and Harper huddled over one of Stan's laptops. Stan Neumann's office was a converted closet with shelves to the ceiling holding action figures and comic books in glass cases. He had a table across the door with just enough room to squeeze through and a number of monitors and hard drives arranged around his U-shaped workspace.

Harper looked up with a closed-mouth smile, her arms crossed on her knee. "Hey, Mr. Spock, how's it hanging? Got gum." She held out her hand.

Danté didn't know how to answer her, but Stan blinked at her owlishly from behind his thick glasses. "I have gum," he said, then he pulled out a drawer and took out a pack, passing it to her.

She took a piece and placed it in her mouth, her eyes never leaving Danté's face. "Thank you, Stan," she purred.

Stan got a goofy look on his face and blushed.

Danté scowled at her. "What are you doing, Harper?" he asked.

"Exactly," demanded Cho. "You have no business being back here."

"I'm trying to help you locate Dana Veres."

"How do you know about Dana Veres?" demanded Cho.

She picked up a paper from the tabletop and waved it at them. "You really should shred important documents instead of leaving them in the trash."

Cho shot a furious look at Dante.

"It wasn't in the trash. It was on my desk."

She shrugged, smacking her gun. "Reporter."

"Actually, Inspector Cho," said Stan, ducking his head, "she found something I didn't."

"What?" snarled Cho.

"Dana Veres' husband is in the army. He's currently deployed in Afghanistan. I found his unit and placed a call to his superior officer. We're just waiting for him to call us back," said Harper.

"How did you do that?" demanded Cho.

"I told his superior officer that the SFPD was investigating the murder of a pregnant woman, therefore, we were doing a welfare check on any other pregnant women in Dana's building. Since we couldn't locate Dana, we were concerned."

Cho turned to Stan. "Did you find out anything else about her?"

"No. She has no criminal record. She doesn't have a driver's license, and I couldn't find a marriage certificate on file in California."

"What does that mean?" asked Dante.

"Since her husband is in the military, they may have gotten married in another state or overseas," said Harper.

"Can't you find that out?" asked Cho.

"I can, but I'll need a warrant."

Harper held out her hands. "My way was faster and I didn't need a warrant."

"How did you do it?" demanded Cho. "You could compromise my case...'

"Cool your jets, Scary Spice," she said, leveling a look on him. "I went on her social media pages. Thankfully she hasn't changed them to private."

"Could you see if she was pregnant?" asked Danté.

"She talked about it and she had pictures." Harper's face clouded over. "Pictures of Luz too. They must have been close."

"So you found her husband's name that way?" said Cho.

"Yeppers. Then I called in a few favors and found out where he's deployed."

Cho gave her a grudging nod of approval.

"Why isn't she living in military housing?" asked Danté.

"Some people do, some people don't," said Harper.

"But she's living in the Tenderloin? Why?"

"The military gives a set amount for housing. Maybe the rents are just too expensive in San Francisco and that's all she can afford."

"Where do you think she's gone?" Danté asked Cho.

"Maybe she's in the hospital, having the baby. We'll just have to wait until we hear back from her husband."

Harper braced her chin on her hand. "Maybe she got spooked when Luz died and took off. Maybe she was afraid she might be next."

Danté shifted uneasily. It was bad enough to think of one young woman being murdered and her baby stolen, but if this was a serial attacker, he didn't like to think what might happen next.

* * *

Doreen Kim sat at the table in the Kauai police department's interrogation room, her hands clasped tightly in her lap, her eyes darting around the room. Marco watched her, thinking that she looked guilty, but then a lot of people did when you brought them in and forced them into one of those austere, intimidating rooms.

Something bothered him about the whole thing, but he couldn't put his finger on it. He felt like they were missing some relatively minor piece of information that would change the direction of this case. He'd felt this way before, but he knew if he just left it alone, he'd eventually pull together what wasn't fitting properly.

"Okay," said Kahele, coming in the room with a folder in his hand. Peyton trailed in after him, giving Marco a tired smile. This was supposed to have been a relaxing trip, but she looked like she needed a vacation from their vacation. "We've got her husband, Donovan, in another room. He's demanding to talk to a lawyer, so we're dead in the water until one gets here. Doreen hasn't asked for a lawyer yet, so I thought we'd take a crack at her."

"Sounds good," said Peyton, studying the woman sitting on the other side of the two-way glass from them. He knew she was assessing the situations, figuring out the best way to proceed. He'd always been awed by her instincts. She was born to solve cases.

Kahele tapped the folder against his hand, then he motioned to the door. Peyton turned to face him. "What if you let me go in first? Let me talk to her woman to woman. Maybe I'll get somewhere?"

Kahele considered that. "Works for me."

Peyton took the folder he held out to her and moved into the interrogation room. Marco and Kahele stepped up to the glass, watching as she appeared on the other side and took a seat. Kahele glanced at Marco.

"Her superiors said this was her expertise," he commented.

"Interrogation?" asked Marco. "You better believe it. I've never seen anyone better."

"Interesting," Kahele said, crossing his arms.

Marco reached over and turned up the speaker.

Peyton set the folder on the table and gave Doreen a gentle smile.

"Why am I here, Agent Brooks?" Doreen said. Her eyes darted to the armed police officer at the door. "Where is my husband?"

"He's fine. He's in another room, so I can talk to you. I just want to ask you a few questions, if that's okay, Doreen."

"I guess. Is this an interrogation room?"

Peyton made an airy wave of her hand. "It's a room like any other."

"I don't know what you think I know. I didn't work for Mr. Meridew."

Peyton tilted her head, the smile still in place. "But you were sleeping with him."

Doreen reared away. "What?"

"He told his ex-wife, Daisy, that you and he were having an affair. Did he lie about that?"

Doreen's eyes lowered and a blush painted her cheeks. "No, he didn't lie. It was a mistake. It shouldn't have happened." She looked up at Peyton. "It only happened a few times. That's all. Just a few times. Donovan and I were going through a rough patch and..." She closed her eyes briefly. "I shouldn't have done it."

Peyton nodded. "I get it. People make mistakes. I see it all the time." She played with the folder, opening it and closing it. "Funny thing is I can't tell you how many murder investigations I've done where the person said they didn't mean for it to happen." She crossed her legs, folding her hands over her knee. "You know, it's so interesting. People, I mean. There's such a vast difference between men and women. They kill for very different reasons."

"Kill?"

"Mmmhmmm. Take men, for instance. They often kill out of passion or greed or a vague sense that someone has wronged them. Sometimes it's premeditated, but often it just happens in the spur of the moment, a moment of pure rage."

"Okay," said Doreen, looking confused.

"Women, on the other hand, kill for three reasons, or at any rate, that's my experience. They kill to protect themselves, to protect someone else, or to get revenge. The first two happen spontaneously. The woman is forced to react to protect herself or someone she loves, usually a child. There really isn't rage. It's more desperation and fear. The third though, the third are women who premeditate, who plan and execute their plan with precision. Those women are hard to break. They've been baked in a crucible of pain and suffering a lot of their lives and they aren't afraid of anything."

"Why are you telling me this?" asked Doreen.

Peyton shrugged. "Just trying to figure out what sort of killer you are."

"Me!" Doreen shrieked, placing her hand against her chest. "Me a killer! How could you think that?"

"Because, Doreen, you weren't just having an affair with Harvey Meridew, you were also sleeping with Jackson Hughes at the same time. Meridew found out and threatened to tell your husband."

Doreen reared away. "No, you don't understand!"

"Oh, I think I do. It was a scandal you couldn't afford and then Meridew rejected you..."

"He didn't reject me!" she spat. "He wanted me to leave my husband and Jackson."

Peyton smiled. "Did he now? That's not what he told Daisy. He told Daisy he was disgusted by you. He told Daisy he called you horrible names. Whore, slut..."

"Stop it!" shouted Doreen, covering her ears. "Stop it!" She wrapped her arms around herself and curled over, a sob escaping her.

Peyton sat still, watching her for a long moment. Finally Doreen regained control and looked up, tears streaming down her face.

"He was a cruel man."

"Harvey Meridew?" Peyton asked.

"Yes. I don't know why I slept with him. I didn't even like him as a person, but we were drinking one night and it just happened." She wiped at the tears. "Then it happened a few more times." She drew a breath and slowly released it. "Donovan and I were talking divorce and I was so lonely."

"But you were sleeping with Hughes at the same time?"

Doreen shrugged. "We've been sleeping together on and off for a few years, since his wife left him. He's a sweet, sweet man and I feel sorry for him. He just needs someone to treat him kindly."

"I'm confused, Doreen," said Peyton. "Were you actually in a relationship with Hughes?"

"No, no." She shook her head, brushing her hand under her nose. Peyton motioned to the guard to grab the tissues and he placed them before Doreen. "I think the world of Jackson, but he's so timid, so..." She sighed. "Weak. He reminds me a lot of Donovan and I guess I felt sorry for him."

"But it wasn't that way with Meridew?"

"No," she said with a scoffing laugh. "He took what he wanted and he let you know he was in charge." She leaned forward, dropping her voice. "It was kinda exciting." Then she sat up straight. "Until it wasn't."

"Was he an abusive lover?"

She shrugged. "He liked to play rough, but I was fine with that. It was after, when he found out I was sleeping with Jackson too. You should have heard the way he talked to me. The things he called me."

"I can imagine. He was a brutal man."

"It wasn't even that so much, but it was the things he said to Jackson. The way he belittled him, talking about his penis size, implying that he couldn't perform, saying he couldn't even get his wife pregnant because he didn't have balls. Jackson just stood there and took it, looking like a lost little boy. I hated Harvey for that." Her eyes rose to Peyton's. "God, I hated him so much."

"Enough to want him dead?"

"Oh, I wanted him dead. And then he threatened to tell Donovan. I love my husband, Agent Brooks. I truly do love him. I would do anything to protect him from this."

"So the only thing you could do was…"

"Tell Donovan myself."

Peyton sat back, her shoulders slumping. "What?"

"I told Donovan about all of it. Everything. I just came clean. That way Harvey couldn't do me any damage. I had to face what I'd done. I had to accept I was responsible and I couldn't keep trying to hide it." She gave a grim smile. "You should have seen Harvey's face when I told him what I did. It was worth it. Just to see the disappointment on his mug." She gave a laugh. "I'd do it all over again. He thought he would ruin me, but I took that satisfaction away from him. I won."

Peyton tilted back her head and sighed.

Marco looked down. He knew what she knew. He knew it as surely as he understood the slump of her shoulders, the slight tilt of her head. She curled her fingers around the folder and rose to her feet, heading for the door.

Kahele turned as she walked into the room. "Well?" he asked.

Peyton's eyes went beyond him to Marco. They weren't going home yet.

"She didn't do it," she said.

CHAPTER 20

Peyton and Marco returned to the hotel in the early evening. Walking to the slider, Peyton threw it open, stepping out on the balcony and watching the waves crash in the distance. She could see families still on the beach, children playing in the surf.

Marco stepped out after her and leaned on the rail beside her. "What's up?"

"This case. This tangle of people all sleeping with each other, cheating on each other. Is no one faithful anymore? What the hell's the point of being married?"

He nudged her with his shoulder. "I don't know, Brooks. I never thought I wanted to be married, until I met you."

She smiled wistfully at him. "But is that our future? Is that what we get to look forward to? I mean, we have so many strikes against us already. We're both in crazy difficult careers, we've both never been able to make a relationship work before this, and we've already broken up once."

He put his arm around her waist and drew her to him, kissing her temple. "I can't tell you what the future holds, but I can tell you this, sweetheart. I have never loved anyone the way I love you and I've loved you for a very long time. That's not changing."

"Is that enough? Is that enough to keep us together, Marco? With our jobs and our history?" She couldn't deny that the thought kept ambushing her over and over again. One of them needed to make a sacrifice, one of them needed a new career. If they had any hope of making this work, one of them needed a *normal* job. And since she was the one whose career took her away from him, she was the one who had to make that change.

He turned her to face him, clasping his hands together at the small of her back. "Peyton, I'm never going to give up on us. I'm never going to walk away. You've got to believe me in this. I know we've had our problems before, but maybe that made things clearer for me, made me realize what we have. So, I guess the thing that remains is this, are you going to get bored with me? Are you going to want something dangerous?"

She laughed, laying her head on his chest and wrapping her arms around him. "You're about as dangerous as I can handle, D'Angelo," she said. "I got my hot tamale the first time out."

His laugh rumbled under her ear, then he patted her on the ass. "Come on. Let's find someplace special for dinner. I'm buying."

She eased back and looked at him, then she rose on her tiptoes and kissed him under his jaw. "You know what it means to me that you're always reassuring me."

He slid his hands up her back and under her hair. "Baby, I will do that for the rest of my life, but right now, my stomach is touching my backbone."

She laughed again and eased out of his arms. "Just let me take a quick shower. While I'm doing that, why don't you pick some place for dinner and maybe we can ask the Baxters? Sally texted me that she wanted to have dinner before they left the islands."

"Sounds good," said Marco. "I actually find the Baxters amusing."

"I'm sure they'd love to hear that," she said, then she gathered some clean clothes and went into the bathroom, letting the water run. Stripping out of her dirty clothes, she let them fall on the bathroom floor, climbing into the tub under the hot spray. If they didn't solve this case soon, they were going to have to do laundry. She was running out of things to wear.

She thought about Doreen Kim and her husband, Donovan. Could the husband have killed Meridew in a jealous rage? Somehow that didn't make sense. Meridew's death wasn't one of rage. It was premeditation, especially with the Menehune angle. That was designed to point directly at Manny Wong and his *Freedom Kauai* group.

She shampooed her hair and rinsed it off, then poured a large dollop of conditioner in her hand. All this hair was expensive to keep up and the amount of product she had to buy felt like the national debt. She knew it would be easier to cut it all off, but her hair was her one allowance to vanity.

Her thoughts went back to the case as she soaped her body, letting the conditioner soak into her hair. Could framing Manny Wong be the motive? Could Meridew's death have nothing to do with him, but everything to do with getting Manny Wong out of the way?

Who benefited if Manny Wong was charged? Dewdrop Construction, which could be Jackson Hughes, his secretary Doreen Kim and her husband, and his foreman, Teddy Nakamura. It could also benefit all of their shareholders. Fiona Meridew might benefit by removing Manny Wong, since her projects had also drawn the scrutiny of *Freedom Kauai*.

Ducking under the spray again, she washed the conditioner from her hair.

That didn't add up, though. It would be easier just to kill Manny Wong. The Menehune angle could still work. Eliminate him and say the Menehune were tired of his interference in the development of the islands. Flip the script. No, Manny Wong couldn't be the target.

That brought her back to Harvey Meridew. Someone wanted him dead and if they could frame Manny Wong at the same time, it was an added bonus. So many people wanted Meridew dead, it might be impossible to figure it out.

She wasn't seeing this case clearly. That was the problem. She needed to eliminate suspects, but no one had a clear alibi and they all had motives to want him dead. Many of them actually said they wanted him dead. So go back to the murder weapon. A number of them had access to that as well.

Turning off the shower, she towel dried and climbed out, then she smoothed lotion on her body, dressed and fussed with her hair. Finally, she swiped a little mascara on her eyes and opened the bathroom door, her thoughts preoccupied by the case. She rounded the corner into the room and found Marco at the table, a folder open beside him, his thumbs frantically typing on his phone.

He looked up at her. "Look at this, Brooks," he said.

She felt that rush of excitement she got whenever they'd been on a case together, that moment when one of them had found a piece of the puzzle that had been eluding them. He held up the leather bound folder and she recognized the *Things to Do* from the hotel.

"I was looking up places to eat in here and I came across this." He pointed to a name.

Peyton peered at it. *Exotica*. "Isn't that the weird place Hughes told us to try?"

"Exactly. I pulled up their menu to remind myself of the things they have there. A lot of the names I don't recognize, so I started looking up what they were. And I found Fugu Sashimi." He leaned back in his chair. "You know what Fugu Sashimi is, Brooks?"

A smile slowly curved Peyton's lips. "I can hardly contain myself, D'Angelo. I'm about to jump your bones."

He smiled as well, then he turned his phone display around so she could see it. A brown, bloated fish stared back at her. "Fugu is…"

"…puffer fish," she said.

He nodded. "Now we just need to know what happens to the parts of the puffer they discard."

She gave him a sultry look. "Do you suppose Bill and Sally Baxter would like to go to *Exotica* for dinner, D'Angelo?"

"I don't think it would hurt to ask."

* * *

Cho, Simons, Stan Neumann and Harper gathered around a laptop in the conference room. Danté glanced at the clock on the wall above the table. In San Francisco, it was 8:56PM, which meant it was 9:26AM in Afghanistan. He scrubbed his hands across his face. He was so damn tired.

Cho patted his shoulder. "It's the all-nighters that give you grey hair," he said, sitting down next to him and placing a cup of coffee in front of him. "You gotta start drinking coffee, man. No way around it."

Danté stared at the cup, then picked it up, taking a sip. The bitter flavor ambushed him, followed by a milky sweetness. He grimaced and forced himself to take another sip. He found Harper watching him in amusement.

"You'll get used to it, Mr. Spock," she said. "It's one way to appear like you're human."

"Enough," said Cho. "Look, reporter, you think this is a game to us. We're here working twelve to eighteen hours a day on this case. I haven't seen my wife in two days."

"You think I don't take this serious, Scary Spice? You think I view this as some kind of joke? The little woman playing at being a reporter?" She held out her arms.

"Harper!" said Danté firmly. She was out of line. She was the one who kept poking at them, trying to get a reaction. Well, she'd gotten one from Cho and now she needed to realize not everyone could take the caustic nature of her personality.

She stopped, her eyes snapping to his face. She took a deep breath and released it. "Fine. Fine," she said, then she crossed her arms.

At precisely 9:00PM, Stan got a video call on his computer. He connected it and turned the laptop to face Cho and Danté. A moment later, a soldier's face filled the screen. He had a crew cut and wore his military uniform, his features clean shaven, his eyes dark.

"Good morning, Private Veres," said Cho. "I'm Inspector Nathan Cho of the San Francisco Police Department. This is my partner, Officer Danté Price."

"Inspector Cho, I was told by my CO to contact you. Is something wrong, sir?"

"We're trying to locate your wife, Dana, Private Veres. When was the last time you talked with her?"

"I talked to her a few days ago. Has something happened to Dana?" The panic in his voice made Danté sit forward.

Cho held up a hand. "No, no, we don't believe anything has happened to her. We're trying to reach her in connection to another case we're working." He glanced at Danté, then motioned for him to take over.

"Private Veres, we understand your wife was friendly with a woman in her building, a woman named Luz Gutierrez. Were you familiar with Luz?"

"I've been stationed in Afghanistan for the last five months. I'm not sure who she was friendly with."

"Your wife was pregnant, right?"

A smile touched his face. "She was. Our first. I'd planned to be home for the birth, but the baby came early. A beautiful baby girl."

Harper made a noise and covered her mouth with her hands. Danté glanced at her, then back to the screen. "She had the baby already?"

"Yes, about two weeks ago." He gave a laugh. "It was touch and go there for a bit. Dana said it was a hard birth, but little Angelica pulled through."

"Where did your wife give birth? Do you know?"

"San Francisco General."

"How long was she in the hospital?"

"Oh, I don't know. I think a couple of days. She didn't contact me until after she was released."

Cho and Simons exchanged a look. Danté caught it and replayed over in his mind what Private Veres had said. "Wait. She didn't let you know you were a father until after she left the hospital."

"She didn't want to distract me, she said. She's worried about what I'm doing out here, so when she went into labor early, she was afraid to call and let me know. My girl is so brave. She did the whole thing by herself. Got to the hospital, had the baby, then got herself home. Her folks didn't even know until after it was over."

Danté stared at the table. He had a sinking feeling he knew why she did all this on her own.

"Is something wrong, Officer?" asked Private Veres.

Danté looked up, but he didn't know what to say. Cho pulled the laptop over to him, forcing a smile. "We'd just like to contact your wife and ask her what she knew about Luz Gutierrez. Do you know where she is? We went by the apartment and she wasn't there."

Private Veres visibly relaxed. "Oh, yeah, she went up to Santa Rosa to see her parents. She's staying with them until I get out in another three weeks. I'm gonna be deployed to Fort Benning in Georgia and Dana will come join me there with the baby."

"Congratulations, by the way. You must be excited to see your wife and daughter."

"I am."

"Have you seen pictures of the baby?"

"I sure have. Give me a second. I've got one here." He looked down as he fumbled with his wallet.

Cho gave Stan a significant look. Stan nudged Danté out of the way and took over the keyboard. As soon as Private Veres lifted the picture before the screen, Stan clicked on a few keys, then ducked back into his seat.

Cho's eyes followed him and Stan nodded, then Cho smiled at the private. "She's beautiful. You said her name's Angelica?"

"Angelica Serena Veres. My sweet darling. I can't wait to come home to her in a few weeks, I can tell you."

"I'll bet. Thank you for talking with us, Private."

"My pleasure. If there's anything else I can do for you, just let me know."

"We'll do."

"Oh, Inspector Cho," said Veres.

"Yes," answered Cho.

"Is this friend of my wife missing or something?"

"We're trying to find out what happened to her," said Cho.

"Man, that's scary. I hope you locate her."

Cho just gave him a nod. "Again, thank you for your time." Then he disconnected the call. Sliding the laptop back to Stan, he said, "Get me the address of her parents, Stan, and print out copies of the baby's photograph."

Simons pushed his bulk to his feet. "Danté, get on the horn to Devan Adams and tell him we need warrants for Dana Veres' apartment."

Danté nodded, but his attention was snagged as Harper rose and started walking for the door. He rose as well and followed her out into the precinct. She didn't stop, but started walking for the outer door, letting the half-door swing open.

"Harper!" he said, but she kept going.

He knew she had no way to get home, except for public transportation, and the thought of her taking BART or a taxi at this time of night worried him. He jogged after her.

"Harper!" he said, stopping at the top of the steps.

She whipped around. "You think I don't care what happens in this case!" she shouted at him.

He took a step back, surprised by her anger. "I never said that."

"No, but your partner did! He implied I didn't care!" She jabbed a hand at the building. "You think this isn't tearing me apart! You think I'm not half sick over this!"

"I never implied you weren't."

She hesitated, staring at him. "Luz was my friend. I listened to her tell me all of her dreams, her fears, her hopes, everything."

"I know."

"And her little baby, her precious little baby was ripped from her body."

"I understand that."

She made a slashing motion. "No, you don't! You can't! You will never experience it! So don't pretend you have more empathy than I do, all you men sitting around a table. You don't have any idea what Luz experienced in those moments before she died because you can never understand!" She placed particular emphasis on the word NEVER.

He narrowed his eyes on her. He couldn't help but feel confused by her sudden fury. He didn't know where it came from. "Okay, you're right."

She swiped a hand under her nose. "God, I want a damn cigarette."

"Look, let me take you home."

"No, I'll just call Uber. I don't really want to talk to men right now."

He came down the stairs and reached out to touch her elbow. "Harper, please."

She looked up at him, then before he could react, she launched herself into his arms, wrapping her own arms around his neck. He didn't know what to do, but the scent of vanilla enveloped him and he curled his arms around her back, pulling her closer.

After a few blissful moments, she eased back, sliding her hands down to his chest. He looked into her eyes. He didn't have a whole lot of experience with women. He'd gone with a few girls in high school and he'd had a rather intense relationship when he was nineteen, but other than that, he had no experience with a woman like Harper McLeod.

"Sorry. I just needed a hug," she said.

He nodded. "No problem. Let me make a phone call, then I'll drive you home."

"Okay," she said, stepping away from him.

He hesitated a moment more, studying her face. He wanted to say something suave and cool, he wanted to joke off the hug as if it happened to him everyday, but he couldn't. It had probably meant nothing to her, but it meant something to him. It meant a lot to him.

He turned back to the precinct, taking his phone out of his pocket. When he got to the door, he looked back, feeling a wave of protectiveness swell inside of him. She looked small and vulnerable, standing in the parking lot, but he knew that was an illusion. There was nothing small or vulnerable about Harper McLeod and yet, for the first time, he thought he understood how someone could become so obsessed with another person.

* * *

Exotica was a small restaurant hanging on the edge of a cliff, backed up to the ocean. Peyton wore a long, red dress with a white shawl draped over her shoulders. Sally had opted for a black sheath dress and sensible sandals, while Bill wore slacks and a jacket. Marco had opted for his Guayabera shirt and slacks. The night was still a little warm for anything more.

When they'd asked Sally and Bill to dinner, the couple had been excited. They were leaving the island two days from now and had seen about everything there was to see. Of course, Peyton hadn't told them why they wanted to go to the restaurant, but Sally had peppered Peyton with questions the whole ride over, wanting to know how the investigation was progressing.

The interior of *Exotica* was dark with heavy wood paneling, slick black tables and black napkins. A young woman greeted them, wearing a black dress and heels, guiding them to their table in the middle of the busy restaurant. Dim light filtered down from a chandelier overhead and candles in the middle of the tables provided dim task lighting. They took seats and the waitress passed out the menus.

"Can I get you anything to drink?" she asked.

"What wine do you recommend?" said Bill.

"I would recommend our lovely lilac wine, made from flower blossoms. It's delightful."

Marco glanced at Peyton. She always smelled of lilacs. "We'll try that. Three glasses, please."

"Very good. I'll be right back," she said and left the table.

Sally shook her head. "You don't know how expensive the wine is."

"It's our last night going to dinner with you. Don't worry about it. I've got this covered," said Marco, touching Peyton's back. She gave him a sexy smile. God, this woman made his pulse pound.

She opened her menu, scanning it, then she looked up and met Marco's gaze. He'd seen the Fugu Sashimi on there as well. Below it was a description that read: *Our fugu sashimi is specially prepared by Chef Max, who trained at the Tokyo Sushi Academy for three years. You can be assured that our fugu sashimi is prepared with our diners' health and safety always a top priority.*

"I have to try the Kopi Luwak," Bill said to Sally, but Sally wasn't paying any attention to him, she was reading her menu. He looked up at Marco and laughed. "Can you imagine drinking coffee from beans shit out by a cat?"

A few diners next to them look over, frowning. Peyton smiled and lifted her napkin, laying it in her lap.

Bill went back to reading his menu. "Dear God, did you see this Hákarl? It's fermented shark. They let it rot for three months." He shook his head, his mouth hanging open. "I've got to try that."

Sally glared at him, leaning close. "Stop it!" she hissed. "Look!" and she pointed to something on the menu. Bill studied it, then both of their eyes lifted to Marco and Peyton.

"They have fugu here," said Bill.

"Hush! Don't you get it?" Sally scolded him.

"Get what?" He looked around the group. "What am I supposed to get?"

"We're on a recon mission," said Sally.

"No," said Peyton quickly. "We're just here for dinner."

Sally gave her a quelling look. "You can be honest with us. We're like family now. We're here investigating the murder case."

"You think this is where the blowfish poison came from?" said Bill in a loud whisper.

"No, no," said Peyton.

Sally's expression grew even harder. "Seriously? I wasn't born yesterday. I've seen movies."

Peyton shared a look with Marco, then she leaned forward. "Okay, we want to ask a few questions. See how they dispose of the dangerous parts of the fish."

Sally nodded rapidly.

"We want to figure out how they prepare it before we disrupt their business with a warrant."

"You know someone who came here to eat?" said Sally.

"Well…"

"We're in," she said without waiting for an answer.

"What now?" Peyton sputtered.

"We're with you. Just tell us what you want us to do." She looked at Bill, then back to Peyton. "We need code names."

"Code names?"

"Yes, I'll be Yellowtail. Bill can be Flounder and you'll be…" She gave Marco a pointed look. "…you're definitely an Angel Fish."

"Oh, Abe's gonna love this," Peyton said under her breath.

"And you, you're an Anthias," said Sally.

"What's that?"

"A lovely little colorful fish that welcomes everyone to her tank."

"That's nice," said Peyton, "but we're not really going to do anything."

"I can create a distraction," said Sally.

"No."

"And I can ask to talk to the chef. I'll tell them I'm something of a sushi expert," said Bill.

"No again."

"We need to get you into the kitchen," said Sally. "We should have a warning sound if someone's coming."

"We don't need that."

"What are you thinking? I can do the call of the American bittern," said Bill, then he made a strange bloop bloop sound that drew the attention of the diners next to them.

Marco put his fist over his mouth to hide his smile.

"That doesn't work," said Sally, "I've got a fish theme going here."

"Right, right," said Bill. "What about blub blub, then?"

"That might work," said Sally.

Peyton drew a deep breath and slowly released it, then she leaned forward, lowering her voice to a conspiratorial level. "Okay, here's what we're going to do."

Bill and Sally leaned forward as well. Marco bit his lip to keep from laughing out loud.

"When the waitress comes over, we're going to ask her how they dispose of the dangerous blowfish parts."

Bill and Sally glanced at each other, then back to Peyton. Finally they both slumped back in their seats. "Yeah, yeah, if that's the way you want to play it," said Sally in clear disappointment.

Peyton glanced up at the chandelier. Marco wondered if she was counting to ten, then she leaned forward again. "And while you're questioning him," she said, giving them significant looks. They leaned forward once more as well. "I'm going to slip around back and look in the dumpster."

Sally nodded vigorously. "That's a good plan."

"Right," said Peyton, then she touched a finger to the side of her nose.

Bill and Sally followed her movement, touching fingers to the sides of their noses. Everyone looked at Marco. "Come on, Angelfish," Peyton hissed at him. "Get with the program."

Marco shook his head, then he touched the side of his nose as well.

The waitress returned, beginning the whole wine tasting ritual. Marco eyed Bill and Sally. They fairly vibrated with excitement, but they contained themselves.

"Lovely vintage," said Bill, taking a sip. "You can really taste the lilies in there."

"Lilacs," corrected Sally.

"Lilacs, you can really taste the lilacs," said Bill.

The waitress smiled at them. Peyton took a sip, settling her glass by her plate and giving Sally a significant look. Sally touched her finger to the side of her nose. Peyton mimicked her, then Sally opened her menu.

"My husband has a few questions," she said in a conversational voice. She gave the waitress a closed-mouth smile. "Bill?" She nudged him.

He glanced up, then looked around the table. He clearly hadn't realized the recon was going to land on him. "Um, yes, yes, I do. The fugu sashimi. I read your disclaimer here, but I'm still concerned. How can I be sure I won't be poisoned? I hear it's a terrible way to die."

"Yes, but rest assured, we have a highly trained staff that has been extensively instructed in the proper preparation of fugu," said the waitress.

"So what exactly is so deadly about eating puffer fish? Can you explain that to me?"

Sally groaned, then she smiled up at the waitress. "He's gonna go on all day," she said, causing the waitress to give her a panicked look. "I'm gonna go to the little girl's room. Peyton dear, will you join me?"

Marco frantically looked at Peyton.

"No problem," she said, rising and setting her napkin at her place.

"Brooks," Marco said.

She kissed him. "We'll be right back. Ask about the Bird's Nest Soup."

Marco's eyes followed her as she left the table.

"So, I understand it's a neurotoxin. Good lord, do you realize how awful that death is? First is numbness and tingling in the mouth," Bill said loudly, looking at his phone screen.

The waitress looked around in alarm. They were drawing attention from the other diners.

"Then you start salivating and feel nauseous. Next is the vomiting. Ha!" laughed Bill to Marco. "That'll ruin a date."

Marco gave him a weak smile.

"Finally, you become paralyzed, including your breathing. Wow, what a way to go!" He put his chin on his hand.

"Right," said the waitress, forcing a smile. "Is there anything I can answer about the preparation of our fugu?"

Marco looked down the hallway toward the bathroom, then he squinted, trying to see into the dark interior. Was that Sally's head peeking around the corner? What the heck were they doing? Leave it to Peyton to get him into some mess like this.

"Yes," said Bill, looking at his phone. "It's says here the poison's mainly in the liver, the eyes, the skin and the ovaries or..." He burst out laughing. "The gonads. Oh, dear lord, toxic balls!"

Marco clenched his jaw to keep from laughing. The poor waitress made a couple of short mincing steps in anxiety and Marco resigned himself to giving her the biggest tip of her *or* his life. His attention was snagged by a busboy, turning into the hallway. What he thought was Sally's head disappeared and although the restaurant was loud, he swore he could hear her calling frantically, "Blub blub. Blub Blub!"

Marco realized the waitress and Bill were both looking at him. He glanced around, not sure what had transpired in the last few seconds. Holding up his hands, Bill gave him an "I'm done" look.

"Do you have any questions about the menu?" asked the waitress with a miserable expression.

Marco drew a breath and released it. God, his woman got him in such messes. "Can you tell me about the Bird's Nest Soup?" he said.

A few seconds later, he'd learned everything he ever wanted to know about exotic dining. Peyton and Sally appeared out of the hallway, hurrying over to the table and taking a seat. Finally, they placed their orders and the poor waitress moved away. Marco noticed that Sally's cheeks were flushed, but Peyton seemed relaxed.

He leaned toward her. "Well?"

She gave Sally a conspiratorial look. "We found a fish spine in the dumpster outside. If it proves to be puffer fish, we may have found our source."

"Did you touch it with your bare hands?" he asked in alarm.

"No, D'Angelo. I pulled a plastic bag out of the garbage can in the bathroom. They put clean ones in the bottom for ease of disposal. Then I wrapped the spine up in paper towel before using the bag to pick it up. You know how we clean up after Pickles during his walks."

He nodded, bewildered. "Where is it?"

Peyton never carried a purse or bag of any kind.

"It's in Sally's clutch," she said, looking over at the other woman and placing her finger beside her nose.

Sally winked at her and did the same, then Bill followed suit.

Marco glared at his wife, but she just stared at him with an expectant look on her face, so he lifted his hand and placed his finger beside his nose as well. Man, he used to be so cool.

CHAPTER 21

Peyton's phone rang as they were driving to the precinct. She glanced at the display and pressed the video feed button. Bambi's pretty face filled the screen. A moment later, Pickles popped his head up, making Peyton smile.

"Are you in your office?" she asked.

"Yes," said Bambi. "Pickles wanted to come with me. I hope that's okay."

"It's fine. How is everything?"

Bambi beamed at her. "It's really good, Peyton. Jakey's so wonderful. He really makes me happy. Do you know what he did today?"

"I can't imagine," said Peyton, feeling a flush of warmth that her two friends had found each other. She just prayed it lasted and didn't burn out. They were both moving so fast on this.

"He made me pancakes shaped like little hearts. It was the sweetest thing I've ever seen and butter in the shape of a flower. I almost didn't want to eat them. He served me breakfast in bed. Who does that?" she said, laughing.

"Jake Ryder. He's a great guy, but don't you tell him I said that."

Marco made a snort of agreement next to her.

"Never." Bambi rested her chin on her fist. "How are you and Marco?"

"We're good. Driving into the precinct."

"Tell Marco I said hi."

Peyton shifted the phone so she could see him.

"Hello, Emma," he said.

"Hey, Marco. You look all tan and gorgeous."

He laughed. "Thanks."

"So I actually called for another reason, Peyton," said Bambi.

Peyton turned the phone back to her. "What's up?"

Bambi shifted Pickles to the side and opened a file on her desk. "I did the research on Harvey Meridew that you asked me to do. Just last month, he filed an llc under the name of *Meridew Construction* in California."

"He did. A partnership?"

Bambi shook her head. "That's the thing. It's a sole proprietorship. Just Meridew."

"Interesting," Peyton said.

Marco made a noise of agreement.

"You said last month?" Peyton asked.

"Yep."

Another call came in to Peyton's phone. "Emma, can you send me all the information you've uncovered?"

"Already did."

"Perfect. I've got another call to take. It looks like Chief Kahele."

"I'll talk to you later then." She lifted Pickles and made him wave at the camera.

"Talk to you later," said Peyton, waving at both of them, then she connected over to Kahele's call.

"Good morning, Agent Brooks."

"Good morning, Chief."

"I'm calling because I want to use our warrant for Meridew's office to search Doreen Kim's desk. Can you meet me at their office instead of here?"

Peyton nodded. "I have information on Meridew too."

"What?"

"He filed an llc under a sole proprietorship in California last month."

"Interesting. A sole proprietor. So that means he was cutting Hughes out of this new venture? I wonder if Hughes knew?"

"I'm wondering that as well. Hughes didn't say anything about it?"

"No, he didn't. Hm, that is interesting."

Marco made another noise of agreement.

"You seem to be stewing on something," she said to Marco.

"I'm working it out in my mind, but yeah, I've been stewing on something for a while now."

"What's that?" asked Kahele.

"Just remarking that Captain D'Angelo seems to be chewing on something in his mind."

"Is he thinking we need to take a look in Hughes' office as well? 'Cause that's where I'm leaning," said Kahele.

"I think that might be a good idea."

"Okay. I'll bring Willis with me. Maybe he can take a look at the computers in *Dewdrop Construction.*"

"Can you call the FBI detail on Hughes and tell them to have him stay put today? I'd rather not have him in the way as we search."

"Got it," said Kahele. "I'll also bring the coffee. Any preferences?"

Peyton glanced at Marco. "We both take sugar, so bring about six packets."

Marco gave an amused shake of the head. "Brooks," he warned.

"Make that eight. We like it sweet," she said before she hung up.

They arrived at Meridew's office a short time later. Kahele met them at the car with his CSI Willis Akana.

"Good morning," said Kahele, handing Peyton a paper cup of coffee and four sugar packets.

"Good morning, Terrence, Willis," she said, setting the cup on the hood of the rental car and opening it to pour in the sugar.

"Good morning, Agent Brooks," said Willis.

"Where's Doreen Kim?" Peyton asked.

"We let her and her husband go last night once his lawyer arrived. I told her to lay low for a few days and not come into the office."

"Did you talk to Hughes?" asked Peyton, stirring her coffee.

Kahele handed Marco his coffee and sugar. Marco passed the packets directly to Peyton. She tore them open and added them to her own coffee. Kahele's brows lifted, but he didn't say anything. "Yes, I told him we'd brought Doreen in for questioning."

Marco sipped at his coffee. "Not sure that was a good idea."

Kahele's attention shifted to him. "Any particular reason?"

Marco pointed the coffee cup at the office. "Let's go take a look first. Something's been bothering me."

"Oh!" said Peyton, hurrying to the trunk and popping it open. "I almost forgot. I have something for you, Willis." She pulled out a small cooler. "Tavis Makoa, the hotel manager, gave me the cooler. You can keep it."

Willis took it from her, looking skeptical. "Thanks?" he said.

She laughed. "There's a fish spine in there. We got it from the dumpster outside of *Exotica*."

"*Exotica*?" said Kahele.

"We ate there last night. We need to test it to see if it's fugu."

"You're thinking it might be the source of the poison?" asked Kahele.

"It's possible," said Peyton. "We need to confirm it."

"I'll have it analyzed," said Willis.

"Shall we?" said Kahele, motioning to the office building.

An officer stood outside of the *Dewdrop* main door. "Has anyone been by?" asked Kahele.

"No one," said the officer.

379

ML HAMILTON

"Have you had an officer here since last night?" Peyton asked Kahele.

"As soon as we released the Kims. I didn't want to chance having anyone tamper with the office in case we missed something."

"Good job," said Peyton.

Kahele stood up a little taller, then he opened the office door. "Let's search everything today."

"I'll take Kim's desk," said Peyton.

"I'll search Hughes' office," said Marco.

"And I'll do another pass through Meridew's," offered Kahele.

"Willis, do you think you can get on the computer and see if you can scare up anything?" said Peyton, taking the latex gloves Willis held out to all of them.

"Not a problem," said the CSI and they dispersed to their various locations.

She slipped the gloves on her hands, watching Marco do the same as he disappeared into Hughes' office. Kahele followed him and turned into the doorway across from Hughes' office.

Doreen Kim's desk contained the usual paraphernalia. Pens and pencils in the top drawer. Peyton pulled out a number of paper pads, leafing through them, but they were blank. A side drawer contained lotion, bandages and antacids. She didn't seem to keep any files in her possession.

Willis sank into Doreen's chair and began working on her computer. Peyton watched him for a second. He opened the top drawer again and found a list tucked under a pencil holder that showed Doreen's passwords.

"Clever," she said to Willis.

He smiled at her. "You'd be surprised how many people do that."

"Can you look at her internet search history too?"

"Always do," he answered. "What are you looking for specifically? Hoping to find a search for how to poison your boss?"

"You never know," she said.

He laughed. "Exactly."

She went to the other side of the desk, pulling open that drawer. It contained a few magazines, mostly fashion and tabloid. She took them out and shook them to see if anything was caught inside.

Marco appeared in the doorway to Hughes' office. "Brooks?"

She looked up. She could tell by the tone of his voice he'd found something.

"Get Kahele."

Kahele appeared in the doorway to Meridew's office and he exchanged a look with Peyton, then they walked to Hughes' office together. Marco stood at the table where they'd interviewed Hughes.

"What's up?" Peyton said, noticing once more how utilitarian Hughes' office was compared to Meridew's with his expensive artifacts. In fact, the only thing on the table was the box she'd broken the last time she was here.

Marco pointed to the lid of the box. Peyton and Kahele approached the table and peered at it, seeing a number of very small men carved into the lid, frolicking through a grove of palm trees.

"Menehune?" she asked, looking up at Marco.

He nodded gravely, then he lifted the lid. Inside the box were cigars, stacked one on top of another. Peyton felt her stomach drop.

"Wait. Willis found..." began Kahele.

"...ash in the envelope the threat letters came in," finished Peyton. "Why didn't we make the connection before this?"

"Because Hughes was getting threats himself. Twice someone has tried to kill him," said Kahele.

"Have they?" asked Marco. "He says he was forced off the road. No witnesses, no evidence."

"He had the paint on the side of his car."

"That could be from anything. Scraping a pole, the side of a building. Maybe he smashed the door into another car himself," said Peyton.

"That's not the only things that's bothered me. The night he got shot at he said he bent over because he dropped the keys," said Marco.

"Right," said Kahele.

"I looked inside the car. It had a push button start. You just need the keys in your pocket. Why would he have them in his hand?"

"What's his motive?" asked Kahele.

"There are a number of them," said Peyton. "Meridew slept with his wife, causing their divorce, then he slept with Doreen Kim, who Hughes was also sleeping with."

"We just found out Meridew applied for a sole proprietor llc," added Marco.

"Where did the gun come from?" asked Kahele. "We don't have a 9mm registered to Hughes."

"But Meridew had one and you don't know where that gun is," said Peyton.

Kahele thought for a moment. "He knows we questioned Doreen Kim."

"I know," said Marco. "I wish he didn't know that."

"Okay, but we've got him under FBI security watch."

"Call them and make sure they know he can't leave," said Marco.

Kahele took out his phone, punching buttons. Peyton shared a tense look with Marco, then her eyes landed on Hughes' computer. She moved to the door and looked down to the reception area. "Willis, can you come here, please?"

He appeared a moment later.

"See if you can get into Hughes' computer."

He went over to the desk and began messing with it as Peyton walked back to Kahele. She took out her own phone and dialed Radar's number. He picked up on the fourth ring.

"What's up, Sparky?" he said. By the color of the walls behind him, she knew he was home.

"We think the murderer is Hughes."

"Really? Why?"

She laid out what they knew, but she was distracted by Kahele's conversation. "Hold on, Radar," she said.

"How long has it been since he answered?" said Kahele.

All eyes shifted to Kahele and Willis stopped typing.

"Last night? You haven't checked on him this morning?" Kahele's eyes widened. "What do you mean that isn't protocol? Yes, check on him immediately."

Kahele looked around the group, shaking his head.

Peyton motioned to Willis. "Get us into that computer," she said and he went back to typing.

"What's going on, Sparky? Put me on speaker."

She did what he asked and set the phone on Hughes' desk.

"Yes," said Kahele. "What? No, break down the door. I repeat, break down the door!"

"They're checking on Hughes," said Peyton to Radar.

Marco leaned on the desk, looking at the computer as Willis typed.

"I'm in," Willis said.

"Go to his email first," said Marco.

Willis clicked on the mouse a few times.

"Yes!" said Kahele, listening intently on the other end of the phone. "Have you searched the whole apartment?"

"There!" said Marco, pointing at something on the screen.

Willis clicked.

The color blanched out of Kahele's face. "Hughes is gone."

"How?"

"I don't know. They're going to question the agents on duty last night."

Peyton closed her eyes.

"He's at the airport," said Willis.

Peyton and Kahele's gaze snapped to him. "How do you know that!" demanded Kahele.

"He electronically checked into his flight," said Marco. "They sent him a boarding pass through his email."

"Where's he flying to?" asked Peyton.

"New York," answered Willis.

"What time?" Peyton demanded.

"Two hours," said Willis.

"We've got to stop him!" Peyton said to Kahele.

"Send me all the pertinent flight information, Will, then go through that computer and get me whatever you can," ordered Kahele. "Get on the horn to the lab and see if they've processed the paint on Hughes' car, get someone down here to pick up the cigars and see if they match the ash you found, and have them analyze that spine Agent Brooks brought you."

"On it," said Willis.

Peyton snatched up her phone. "I'll keep you updated, Radar," she said.

"Sparky?"

She put the phone to her ear as she followed Marco and Kahele out of the office. "Yep?"

"If you corner him at the gate, remember there are a lot of innocents around."

"I know."

"Use your talent. Stick to your strengths. Bring him in alive."

"Got it."

"And Sparky?"

"Yep?" she said impatiently, jogging out the doors of the building into the parking lot.

"Be safe."

She smiled, feeling a rush of emotion for him. "I will," she said.

* * *

Danté followed Cho to the door of Dana Veres' apartment. The super was waiting for them, wearing his flip flops, his belly showing beneath the too-small t-shirt he wore. He jangled the keys and gave them a grim smile.

"You think there's another dead body in my building?" he said.

"No, not a dead body," said Cho, holding out the warrant.

The man waved it off. "I don't need to see that. Your badges is good enough for me."

Good to know he protected his tenants' privacy, Danté thought.

As he began the ritual of trying to find the right key, Jake jogged up to them, encumbered by bags.

"Nice of you to join us, Preacher," said Cho.

"Sorry I'm late," Jake huffed, bending over and placing his hands on his knees, struggling to catch his breath. He jerked a thumb over his shoulder. "You don't think the Daisy will get stolen, do you?"

"One could hope," grumbled Cho.

Jake straightened and beamed a smile at Danté. "Hey, Danté!"

"Hey, Mr. Ryder."

Jake nudged Cho with his arm. "You could take lessons from this kid," he told him.

Cho glared at him. There was something terrifying about a Cho glare and Jake sidled over, closer to Danté, placing Danté between him and Cho. Danté wondered how Cho managed to convey all that menace with a look.

The super finally found the right key and the door opened. He started to step inside, but Cho laid a hand on his shoulder, drawing him back. "Let Officer Price and I go through first," he said.

"You wait out here with me," said Jake. "I think I can help you with the key situation. Have you seen these color coded bands you can put around the top of the key to distinguish them from one another?" He took out his own keys, showing them to the baffled super. "This one is for my car. It's purple because the car's painted purple." He held up another key. "This one's blue for my apartment door. I picked blue because it's a soothing color and I feel soothed when I go home. This one is for my personal lockbox where I keep all my personal papers. I chose red because..."

Cho made an aggravated sound. "Stop it!" he hissed.

Jake snapped his mouth closed.

Danté realized he really wanted to know why Jake had chosen red for his lockbox and why he felt he needed a lockbox.

"Idiot!" Cho hissed at Jake, drawing his gun.

"Cop," Jake muttered under his breath, then ducked behind Danté when Cho shot another glare in his direction.

Danté fought a smile as he drew his own gun. Positioning themselves on either side of the door, Cho pushed it open and they rolled into the dark apartment. It was an exact duplicate of Luz's apartment upstairs.

Cho spun into the kitchen, while Danté took the bedroom. A moment later, they'd made sure the place was secure. Danté marked that the air was close as if it had been shut up for a long time. He came back into the main room and holstered his gun, then pulled out a pair of latex gloves and slipped them on. Cho went to the door and motioned Jake inside as he also pulled on a pair of gloves.

The super eased into the entrance, peering around. "No dead bodies?"

"No dead bodies," Cho remarked.

"I need some light," said Jake, so Danté went over to the windows and drew back the curtains.

Sunlight flooded the room and Jake set down his case, taking out his camera. Danté wandered back to the bedroom, searching for baby paraphernalia. In a drawer, he found baby clothes, folded neatly and arranged by size. The clothes were all in shades of blue and green with trucks and sports equipment on them. In the bathroom, he found an entire cabinet dedicated to baby shampoos, diapers and a plastic newborn bathtub.

Cho appeared in the doorway. "Find anything?"

Danté pointed to the cabinet. "She bought things for a boy."

"But her husband said she had a baby girl, didn't he?"

Danté nodded. "Maybe they got the sex wrong?"

"Maybe."

Cho moved back into the bedroom and opened the closet. Clothes had been ripped off hangers and thrown on the floor. "Someone was trying to get out of here in a hurry."

Danté nodded, then a thought struck him. He moved back into the bathroom and stared at the hamper next to the shower. Opening the lid, he peered inside. Clothes filled the wicker basket, so he started lifting them out, carefully setting them on the floor. As he reached the middle, he hesitated.

Taking out the flashlight on his belt, he shined it into the hamper. The brown stains covering a garment could only be one thing. He sighed and lifted it out. It was a maternity blouse covered in blood.

"Cho!" he said.

Cho appeared in the doorway, focusing on the item in Danté's hand. "Well shit," he said. "I'll get the preacher."

Cho started to leave the room, but as he moved, Danté caught sight of the dust ruffle on the bed. One edge of it was wedged into the bed frame. He eased past Cho and into the bedroom, kneeling beside the bed. Bending down, he peered under it, shining the flashlight in the dark space. A tubular piece of wood lay in the middle of the floor, directly under the bed.

He straightened and glanced at Cho.

"The murder weapon?" Cho asked.

Danté nodded.

"Don't touch it. Let's have the preacher start photographing in here."

Danté rose to his feet and studied the carpet for traces of blood. "Mr. Ryder needs to shine a black light all over this room. I'll bet it'll light up with blood stains."

Cho nodded, placing his hands on his hips and looking around himself. "I have a really bad feeling regarding the motive for this attack."

"What do you think it is?"

"Cho?" came Jake's voice in the other room.

Cho briefly closed his eyes. "I think we're about to find out."

They headed in Jake's direction. He was sitting on the floor in the kitchen, going through Dana's garbage can. He held up a coffee stained and crumpled piece of paper. Cho took it, laying it on the counter and smoothing it out.

It was a discharge paper from the hospital with instructions for further care. Danté scanned the document, feeling his heart sink. Cho ducked his head and sighed, but Danté couldn't help but fixate on the word emblazoned across the top of the paper: *Stillborn.*

* * *

Sirens wailed as they drove toward the airport. They pulled up before Hawaiian Airlines terminal as the SUVs and patrol cars fanned out, blocking the entrance. Police swarmed out of vehicles as Peyton and Marco climbed from Kahele's car and stepped onto the sidewalk.

Peyton fussed with her flak jacket. She always fussed with her flak jacket, she hated wearing it, but Marco felt so much better seeing her bundled inside the thing. He knew she thought it looked silly over her Hawaiian print shorts and tank top.

He drew his gun and checked it, then looked up as Kahele rounded the front of his vehicle. "Ready?" he said.

"Tell your men to fan out, but hold back. If we can take Hughes without a fight, I'd feel better," Peyton said.

"We don't know where the 9mm is," reminded Marco.

"He couldn't have gotten it past TSA," said Kahele. "No way."

"Stranger things have happened," said Marco.

"And there's an entire terminal of innocents inside. I don't want anyone getting hurt if Hughes spooks," added Peyton.

"Okay." Kahele pressed the button on his radio and conveyed the message.

Peyton's dark gaze swung to Marco. "I love you," she whispered.

He felt his stomach lurch. He hated this. He hated putting her in danger of any kind. She was his life, had been his life for so long. The protectiveness rose inside of him and he had to fight it back under control, reminding himself she was a better cop than he was.

"I love you, sweetheart," he answered.

She gave a short nod, then they faced the terminal doors. "Let's do this," she said and they headed inside.

Stopping before the marquee, they searched for the gate Hughes' flight was departing from.

"Gate 10," said Peyton, glancing up to see which direction the gate was.

Marco pointed to their right. It was the last gate on that end of the terminal. Kahele nodded to his men and they disbursed, moving throughout the building, their guns drawn. Marco saw a number of people sidle away, their worried gaze following the large police presence filtering through the terminal.

Peyton took the lead as they came to the TSA line. She held up her badge, threading through the people. "FBI," she said and the people parted like the red sea before her.

The TSA agent at the kiosk studied her badge. "Where are you headed?"

"Gate 10," she told him. "This line needs to be held here until we've secured the suspect."

He picked up a walkie talkie on his kiosk and began talking into it, but they didn't wait to hear what he said, moving past the security checkpoint. Kahele directed men to block the inspection area and the walkway headed toward gates 1-6. He left some more men to secure gates 7-8 and the corridor leading between them.

Marco searched chairs around the remaining two terminals for Hughes. A murmur had begun to filter through the area as people became aware of the tension snaking from one end to the other. Peyton moved toward the desk in front of Gate 10, but someone gave a muffled cry behind Marco and he heard something crash to the ground.

He whipped around as fast as his leg would allow and saw Hughes sprawled on the linoleum, having tripped over a couple dragging their suitcases. He must have just come out of the bathroom behind them. As Marco raised his gun, Hughes leapt to his feet and people screamed, trying to get away.

A number of uniforms approached from gates 7 and 8, blocking his escape and Marco could feel the tension rise, knowing that Hughes was about to become completely unpredictable.

"Jackson Hughes!" shouted Peyton, moving into Marco's peripheral vision on his right. She also had her gun trained on the man. "Put your hands on your head and get on your knees!"

Hughes' eyes darted around. Kahele moved to flank him, but he caught the motion. At the same time, a teenage girl and her mother left the bathroom, oblivious to what was happening. Hughes lunged for the girl, grabbing her around the neck. Her mother tried to reach for her, but Hughes hauled her against his chest, his forearm tightening.

"Hold your fire!" shouted Peyton.

"Hold your fire!" echoed Kahele.

Marco ground his back teeth. This was the very thing that every cop feared – the innocent bystander taken hostage.

"I'll break her neck!" Hughes shouted, shaking the girl.

The girl whimpered and her mother moved toward Hughes, reaching for her daughter. "Please don't hurt her," she begged.

"Stay back!" shouted Hughes, tightening his grip on the girl. The girl gagged, raking at his arm to loosen it, but he braced his wrist with his other hand, hauling her head back.

Marco was closest to the mother. He could tell by her agitated movements that she was about to rush Hughes. He had to stop her.

"Hughes!" he shouted, then he held up both hands, letting the gun dangle from his thumb. "Let me help you. Let me get the mother out of your way."

Hughes nodded jerkily and eased his hold on the girl. She gasped in air and Marco moved to the side, grabbing the mother and shoving her behind him. Hughes glanced over his shoulder.

"Get out here where I can see you, Chief!" he ordered.

Kahele moved around until he was next to Peyton, his gun still pointed at Hughes' head. "You've got nowhere to go."

"I have a flight in a few minutes. You're going to let me get on the plane."

"And then what?" said Peyton. "You know we'll have the terminal cleared in New York and SWAT will be waiting for you. They'll take you out as soon as the plane lands."

"I'm getting on the plane!" Hughes shouted.

Peyton held out her left hand, keeping her gun trained on him. "Listen to me, Jackson. You're a reasonable man. You know there's no way out of this. Look around you."

"Don't speak!" he shouted, shaking the girl. She gave a sobbing half-scream and the mother strained against Marco, wanting to get to her.

Marco could see the moment Peyton made her decision. She lifted the gun above her head as he'd done and straightened from her shooting crouch. "We can talk this out, Jackson. It doesn't have to be like this. We can talk it out and come to a decision."

He laughed. "There's no talking. Don't you get it, Agent Brooks? Don't you understand?"

"No, I don't. Help me understand. Help me figure it out."

Hughes jabbed a finger at himself, making the girl whimper. "I played by the rules. I was the good guy. I wanted to build green. I wanted to design useful things. I never wanted the money or the fame. I never wanted it."

"But Harvey did?" She lowered the gun to her side.

"Yeah, he did. It was never enough. No matter how much we made, it was never enough. He took and took and took…" He tightened his hold on the girl and she gagged again.

Peyton held up her empty left hand. "Okay, okay, Jackson. I get it. He betrayed you over and over again."

Hughes laughed. "Over and over and over. He slept with my wife. He slept with Doreen, then you know what he did!"

"He created a new company without you."

"He created a new company without me! That's right!" He made a slashing motion with his hand.

Peyton took a step closer to him. "You were clearly the brains of the operation. Everyone knew that."

"You're right. I was. He had plans, but he never knew how to execute them. But I executed them."

"Right. I mean, you had us stumped all this time, spinning our wheels, coming up with so many suspects. It was a stroke of genius to make us think it was Manny Wong."

Hughes laughed. "That bastard was a thorn in my side. I just figured I could eliminate two birds with one stone."

"And it almost worked. When we saw the blowgun in Manny's collection, I was sure he did it."

When Hughes laughed again, he eased the tension on the girl's throat. She tugged at his arm, trying to dislodge it, but he didn't seem to notice. "I thought maybe you'd suspect Phoebe, but that stupid twit can't get her head out of the bottle long enough to properly dress herself, so I figured you wouldn't spend a lot of time on her."

Peyton shook her head, taking a step closer. "I don't know. The stuffed puffer fish threw us. That was also clever. You knew Meridew had it?"

"Yeah, isn't that sick? He was so impressed with his money that he stuffed a damn fish. God, he was such an asshole."

"That's what everyone said. No one was sorry to see him gone. In fact, a lot of people were relieved. Is that how you felt, Jackson? Were you relieved?"

His expression grew thoughtful and his arm eased a little more. "No, I actually felt sad. I actually regretted it after it was done. We'd been together for so long, he was like a part of me. No matter what he did, I forgave him."

"You did. You forgave him so many times. You were the better man, Jackson. You always were."

Hughes nodded. "That's true."

"So, that's why I don't get this. I get Meridew. I get why you did that. In fact, some people might say you did the world a favor, but this…" She motioned to the girl and took another step closer.

Marco wanted to warn her to stop, but he didn't want to break the spell she'd created around the two of them. It was like she'd put up a bubble with her words, narrowing the situation down to just the two of them, ignoring everything else around them. This was her superpower, her gift, the reason she was such an exceptional cop. He'd always been in awe of her and he could see it on the faces of the people standing around them.

"This isn't you, Jackson. You would never hurt an innocent."

He glanced at the girl, studying the tears that streaked down her face.

"And let's be honest, you're too damn smart to think there's a good end to this situation, unless you surrender."

He took a shuddering breath. "I'm getting on that plane…"

"No, you're not, Jackson. Eventually, you're going to make a move and one of these officers is going to fire, causing untold damage and injury, but you can stop that. You can save everyone from having to be part of this. Just surrender and it'll be over."

"I'm not surrendering," he said stubbornly, but Marco thought his resolve seemed to be wavering.

"There's only one good alternative, Jackson. All others have the potential to do so much harm. You don't want that. That's not the man you are. You are a man of honor, integrity. Be the man I know you are, Jackson. Let the girl go."

He looked at the girl again. She whimpered and closed her eyes. Marco pushed the mother back.

"Let her go, Jackson. See how scared she is. Don't do this. Don't terrorize her for no reason. You know there's only two options here and one is so very bad. Please, Jackson, please remember who you are, what you wanted to do with your life. Remember the man who launched a green company because he cared about the world, about people. Remember that man. He would never do this."

Jackson looked around, then his eyes fixed on the gate. Marco glanced over at it. The plane was sitting on the tarmac, but it hadn't taxied the rest of the way to the gangway. They weren't going to unload until the situation in the terminal was secure and Marco knew Jackson understood that.

"I forgave everything."

"I know you did."

"I forgave what happened with my wife."

"I know."

"Doreen."

"Yes."

"Everything. Then he went and started a business without me. Without *me*!"

Peyton stepped closer still. "I know, Jackson."

"The world's better off without Harvey Meridew."

"I'm certain it is," said Peyton, holding out her free hand.

"Much better. I did the world a favor."

"Many people would agree with you."

He glanced at the girl again. "Do you?"

"What?" asked Peyton.

"Do you agree with me?"

Marco held his breath. If she answered wrong, this could all go south immediately, but Marco wasn't sure what the right answer might be. If she said yes, he might think she condoned everything he did. If she said no, he might be provoked to take action.

"Answer me!" he shouted.

Peyton squared her shoulders and sighed heavily. "No, Jackson, no I don't agree with you. I don't...I can't condone murder, but...but Jackson, I understand you. I get why you felt you had no other choice."

He studied her a moment in silence, his jaw working. Then he shifted and...

...shoved the girl away from him.

Peyton caught her in her arms as Hughes lifted both arms into the air.

"Down! Down!" shouted Kahele, grabbing Hughes' shoulder and shoving him to his knees.

Peyton turned the girl and hurried her away, placing herself between the girl and Hughes as her mother ran, throwing her arms around her daughter.

Marco watched as Peyton was engulfed in the mother/daughter reunion, but he didn't speak. He couldn't speak. Once again, Peyton had proven she had a gift, a gift that had once more saved lives.

CHAPTER 22

Peyton and Marco dragged their suitcases to the checkout desk. Robbie greeted them with a beaming smile, holding out a piece of paper to Marco. Marco took it, looking at the contents, then his blue eyes snapped to Robbie's face.

"What's this?"

"Your bill, Captain D'Angelo."

"No, this isn't right."

Peyton looked over his arm. The total at the bottom was zero. "Robbie, what's going on?"

The door behind the counter opened and Tavis Makoa, the manager, stepped out. "It's our gift to you for all you've done for us. You've saved the reputation of the Koloa Grove Resort."

"We can't accept this. It's too generous," said Peyton. Marco nodded.

"Nonsense," said Tavis, waving her off. "It's already done. Consider it our wedding gift to you."

Peyton felt a rush of warmth for the people of this island. She knew she and Marco would be coming back. There was so much more to explore, especially laying on the beach and playing in the surf.

"We can't thank you enough," said Marco.

"Nonsense," said Tavis again. He leaned forward and dropped his voice. Peyton, Marco and Robbie also leaned forward. "You solved a murder. Do you know what bad press that would have been? Come to the Koloa Grove Resort and get offed!" He shook his head, straightening. "We couldn't have that."

Peyton smiled. "I guess not," she said.

He held his hand over the counter and she took it. He clasped it in both his own. "Mahalo, Agent Brooks."

"Mahalo, Tavis Makoa," she repeated.

Tavis shook hands with Marco. "Mahalo, Captain D'Angelo."

"Mahalo, Tavis," said Marco.

Tavis looked at Robbie. "See that their bags are put in the shuttle."

The younger man ran around the counter and took their bags, hurrying toward the front drive. Peyton and Marco turned to follow him, but came up short as Bill and Sally Baxter appeared in front of them.

"You're leaving!" Sally said dramatically, coming forward and clasping Peyton in a bear hug. "I can't believe it."

"Yep, it's time to go home."

Bill shook hands with Marco. "We got our man, didn't we?"

Peyton laughed. "We sure did, Bill. You both were instrumental in helping us."

Sally clapped her hands. "That's so exciting, isn't it? You know, Bill and I have been talking."

Peyton felt a drop in her stomach. That couldn't be good.

"We had so much fun solving this case with you."

"So very much fun," echoed Bill.

"That we think we're going to take PI classes."

"What now?" said Peyton, tilting her head.

"PI classes. You know, get certified as Private Investigators," said Bill.

"I told Bill I think we'd be exceptional at that."

"She did. She told me that."

"Private Investigators?" repeated Peyton.

"Yes, dear, they call them PI's in the business." She patted Peyton's hand. "I signed up for a gun safety class." She made a gun out of her hand. "Can't you just see me? Pow, pow, pow…"

Peyton pulled her hands down, cupping them in her own. "Sally, don't you think that's a little dangerous?"

Sally gave her a patient smile, squeezing her hands in return. "Oh, aren't you sweet, but you know what, Peyton dear?"

"What?"

"When you get to be our age, danger has a whole new meaning. What's the point of living to 90 if it isn't fun? Isn't that what I always say, Bill?"

"She's right. That's what she always says."

Peyton gave her a warm smile. "You're right." She leaned over and kissed the older woman's cheek. "You are completely right." Then she released her.

Sally hugged Marco next and Peyton was engulfed in a hug by Bill, then the older couple turned for the exit, discussing what type of gun they each figured they should get. Peyton leaned her shoulder against Marco's chest.

"You think that'll be us in 50 years, D'Angelo."

He slid his arm around her waist and kissed her temple. "God, I hope so," he said.

They headed toward the front drive and found Robbie talking to Chief Kahele. Marco and Peyton's bags were in the trunk of his cruiser. Robbie waved at the Chief, then hurried back toward the building.

"Aloha, Agent Brooks, Captain D'Angelo," he said, rounding the corner.

"Aloha," they called after him.

Kahele went around to the passenger side and opened it. "I thought I'd give you a ride."

"Thank you," said Peyton, sliding into the seat.

Marco climbed in behind her and Kahele hurried around to the driver's side, climbing behind the wheel.

"Did you talk to Jackson Hughes today?" asked Peyton as Kahele pulled out of the driveway and onto the road.

"Late last night. He made a full confession."

"What do you think will happen to him?"

Kahele shrugged. "He'll serve the rest of his life in prison." He shook his head. "I just don't get why. He had a whole life ahead of him."

"A life he felt was ruined by Harvey Meridew." She sighed and looked out the window at the beautiful scenery, the green palm trees, the waxy flowers, the lush vegetation. Hughes had paradise at his fingertips, but it hadn't been enough. It was never enough, no matter what you had, no matter how fortunate you were. Humans always wanted something more. It was their greatest flaw. She was guilty of it herself.

Here she was with everything she'd ever wanted – the perfect husband, family and friends surrounding her, and she wanted a career too, a career that made her feel alive, made her feel purposeful, but she didn't think she could have that and the rest. She had to make a choice and the choice was making her miserable.

She rolled her head on the seat and stared at Kahele's handsome profile. "We never know what we have until we've lost it," she said wistfully.

Kahele glanced at her, his brow furrowed. Then he reached into his jacket pocket and pulled out something wrapped in a leaf. "This is for you. A woman came to the precinct and left it for you yesterday."

Peyton took it, frowning, and unwrapped the small bundle. A necklace lay in the bottom, the pendant hanging from a piece of twine. A silver star lay in her palm, glistening in the sunlight. Peyton turned it over in her hand, then saw the note lying beneath it.

You have a brightness in you, child, it read. *Don't let it go out.*

She smiled and slipped the star off the twine, reaching for the locket necklace Marco had given her so long ago. Unhooking the necklace, she slipped the star onto the chain so it lay behind the locket, then she ran her thumb over the surface of it.

For once, she had her answer. It was clear to her and she felt an easing in the center of her chest. She could have it all, and damn it, she was going to take it.

Aloha.

*　*　*

Danté and Cho pulled up to the Veres' house in Santa Rosa just as the local police force drew up behind them. Cho glanced in the rearview mirror and then over at Danté.

"Let me do the talking. We don't want anyone getting territorial," said Cho.

Danté nodded. That was fine with him.

They climbed out of the vehicle and headed toward the two officers who climbed out of their own vehicles. The driver was a woman with lieutenant stripes on her shoulder.

"Morning. Inspector Cho, right?"

"Right," said Cho, shaking her hand. "This is my partner, Officer Price."

"Lieutenant Anders and Sergeant Bond," she said, pointing between them. She glanced at the house. "You think your suspect's inside."

Cho shrugged. "We're not sure. Her husband said she was staying here, but we haven't seen any sign of her yet."

"How can we help you?" Lieutenant Anders said, hooking her thumbs in her belt. She was around Cho's age with her brown hair pulled back in a ponytail.

The sergeant was a heavyset man with light hair and blue eyes.

"There's an infant. We want to try to talk the suspect down without anyone getting hurt. We were hoping you could help us secure the street, so no one can interfere until we have the suspect in custody."

Anders surveyed the street. "We can do that. We'll just go knock on doors, while you go to the house."

"Thank you." Cho looked down the road to their left. "Is that the way out of the subdivision?"

"One way. You want one of us waiting down there in case she runs?"

"That might be a good plan."

"I'll call for backup too," said the lieutenant.

"Perfect," said Cho, removing his badge.

Sergeant Bond got in the vehicle and drove it off to the north, while the lieutenant started across the street, talking into her radio for backup. Cho nodded at the walkway and they started toward the front door. The house was a single story with a well maintained front yard, neatly trimmed grass and shrubbery. A Kia Sorento sat in the driveway, but the spot closest to the front door was empty.

Cho climbed up the single stair and rapped on the door. A dog began to bark inside. A few moments later, they could see the curtain flutter and a face peered out. Cho held up his badge.

"SFPD," he said loudly.

The locks on the door turned and the door opened a crack. A small dog poked his head out between the legs of an older woman. "SFPD?" she said. "What in the world are you doing here?"

"Is your daughter home, ma'am?" asked Cho. "We'd like to ask her a few questions."

"My daughter?"

Danté could hear the fear in her voice. The little dog growled.

"Shh, Brutus," she ordered.

Brutus, huh? He looked like a dust ball, Danté thought, but Brutus settled down, going back to snuffling at them.

"Yes, we need to ask her a few questions about a friend of hers. Can we come in?"

"Well, I don't know. She isn't here right now. She took the baby to the pediatrician for a checkup."

"Do you know when she'll be back?" asked Cho.

The older woman shook her head. At the same time, Danté heard a car pull up on the street, but it didn't pull into the driveway. He glanced over his shoulder, but it just parked across the street. A black Jeep Wrangler, he noted, then turned back to Dana Veres' mother.

"Is this very important?" asked the woman.

"Very," said Cho. "Do you remember your daughter ever talking about a friend named Luz Gutierrez?"

"No, no I can't say I do. We don't get to see our daughter very often. Her husband's in the military and they move around a lot. He's in Iraq right now."

"Right. Is your husband home, ma'am?"

"My husband?"

"Dana's father?"

"He's not here. He goes to the lodge in the mornings now that he's retired. I'm afraid he's having a hard time dealing with the baby being in the house. The poor little thing cries all the time. I think she's got colic. I told Dana I thought she should be breastfeeding, but she doesn't listen to me. She's never listened to me, so now she's at the pediatrician to find out what's wrong."

A second car could be heard coming down the street.

"That's the problem with young people today," said Cho. "They never listen, do they?"

She gave a small laugh and Brutus barked as if in agreement. "I guess it would be all right if you came in and waited for Dana. She should be back any minute now."

Danté heard the car pull into the driveway. He reached out and caught Cho's arm, stopping him from crossing the threshold. "Cho?" he said, jerking his chin toward the driveway. They could see the backend of the car from where they stood.

"That'll be Dana," said the older woman, opening the door wider.

Cho gave Danté a significant nod and laid his hand on the handle of his gun. At the same time, the driver's side door on the Wrangler opened and Harper McLeod got out, running across the street in high heels.

"Shit!" grumbled Cho, making Brutus bark.

Danté moved to head her off, but Harper reached the driveway at the same time as Dana Veres' lifted the car seat and backed out of the car. Danté and Harper both stumbled to a stop with Dana trapped between them. Danté could just see a tiny head covered in a pink cap lying in the car seat.

Dana's eyes shifted between Harper and him, then she started to put the baby back in the car.

"Dana!" said Harper.

Dana stopped moving, staring at her.

"I'm Harper McLeod of the *Emersonian*."

"The what?" asked Dana.

"I'm a reporter for the *Emersonian* newspaper. We're doing an article on military mothers. I was wondering if we could talk to you."

Danté and Cho didn't move, watching as Harper eased up the driveway, standing behind the vehicle.

"Who are they?" Dana said, jerking her chin at the two men.

"My photographer and an apprentice. The cute one's the apprentice," said Harper. "He's gonna take notes while we talk. Can we go inside?"

Dana considered it a moment. "Why aren't you with them?"

"The little mean looking one has a lead foot. He beat me here," Harper said, giving a forced laugh.

"How did you know I was here?" asked Dana, her back straightening.

"We contacted your husband. We're doing stories on all the men in his division and he told us you'd just had a baby. Can I see her?"

Dana took a step back, turning the baby away. "I don't know. I think I should talk to Anton."

Harper reached into her bag and pulled out some papers. "I have his signed agreement right here. Would you like to see it?"

Dana frowned. "He signed an agreement for you to talk to me? Anton signed an agreement?"

"Right here," said Harper, holding out the papers. "Can we come in and I'll show you everything?"

Dana waivered. Danté held his breath, hoping she'd buy this story, but a moment later Sergeant Bond's patrol car pulled down the street and parked across the driveway. Harper glanced over her shoulder and Dana's face lost color. She backed toward the front of the vehicle as if she were going to go around it for the house next door.

Harper held up her hands. "Dana!"

Her gaze whipped back to Harper. "You lied!"

"I'm sorry," Harper said.

Danté flexed his muscles. He wasn't letting this woman get away with the baby.

"Easy," muttered Cho. "Easy."

"Dana!" said her mother, coming up behind them. Cho caught her and held her back by his side.

Dana's eyes moved from her mother to Harper to the patrol car. Sergeant Bond rose out of the driver's side door, bracing his gun on the top of it and pointed it at Dana.

"Freeze!" he shouted.

"Shit!" snapped Cho as Lieutenant Anders came running, her gun drawn.

Dana made a stutter step as if she'd run, but she had the baby in the car seat in front of her.

"Hold your fire!" Danté shouted. Not only would Dana drop the baby, but Harper was between her and the cops.

"Hold your fire!" echoed Cho.

Harper held her arms out to the sides. "Dana, please put the baby down. There's nowhere for you to go."

"She's mine."

"I know. I know she is."

"You have no business being here. I've done nothing wrong."

"Of course not, but they aren't going to go. Let me have the baby and we'll get it all worked out. I am a reporter,

Dana. I'm here to make sure nothing happens to either one of you."

"She's mine!" Dana shouted, her voice cracking. "I gave birth to her."

"I know," said Harper. "And I know you'd do anything to protect her. Anything."

"She's mine!" Dana sobbed. "Mine."

The baby started to cry, a high, plaintive wail.

Harper held her hand out. "Give me the baby, Dana. I promise I'll take care of her until we can work this all out. I will protect her with my life. I swear to you."

"I gave birth to her!" sobbed the woman, bowing over the car seat. "I gave birth to her."

Danté could hear Dana's mother sobbing behind him, but he kept his attention fixated on Harper. The look on her face was arresting. She dropped her purse on the driveway, then started forward, holding out her hands to receive the baby.

"I know you want to do what's best for her, Dana. I know you want to protect her. I promise you I'll do the same. One mother to another," she whispered. "One mother to another."

Danté caught his breath, wanting to shield Harper, afraid the cops in the street might open fire or Dana might lash out. She curled over the car seat, sobbing, one hand holding the handle, the other over her mouth.

"I gave birth to her."

"I know," said Harper in a soothing voice. "I know."

"She's mine."

Harper reached Dana and curled her hand around the handle on the car seat. The baby's cries increased in volume, echoing back from the houses. "Let me have her, Dana. Let me have her."

Dana released the handle and Harper pulled the car seat to her as Dana crumpled to her knees. Danté moved then, getting between Harper and Dana as Harper hurried down the driveway toward the Wrangler and beyond the police standing in the street.

A moment later, Lieutenant Anders holstered her gun and came up the driveway, taking her cuffs out of her belt. "Dana Veres, you have the right to remain silent," she began, reaching for Dana's arms.

Danté stepped back to let her work and saw Cho escorting the mother into the house, his arm around her shoulders as she sobbed brokenly. Danté blew out air, closing his eyes briefly, letting the tension slip from his shoulders, then he headed down the driveway and across the street.

Harper had the car seat in the back of the SUV, but she had the baby in her arms, rocking her back and forth, crooning to her. Danté leaned against the panel of the vehicle, watching the two of them.

Harper looked up, tears glistening in her eyes.

"Where did you get the car?" he asked.

"It belongs to my father. One of a dozen. I borrowed it."

"You shouldn't have come out here."

"Luz was my friend."

"You still shouldn't have interfered with police business."

"You gonna arrest me, Mr. Spock?" she asked. The baby had stopped crying and was watching with wide, dark eyes.

Danté couldn't help but think how natural Harper looked holding her. "You said from one mother to another."

Harper leveled a look on him. "That memory thing is annoying," she said.

He smiled. "Is it true?"

"That I had a baby?"

"Right."

"Yes."

"Where is it?"

"The baby?"

"Yes."

Harper sighed, smiling at the small body in her arms. "You haven't earned that information yet, Boy Scout. Take me on a date first and we'll talk."

He felt his smile widen. Taking Harper on a date scared the hell out of him, but it also thrilled him. "Any idea what a proper date with you would be?"

She gave him a sultry look. "Come on, Mr. Spock. I'm certain if you search your databases you'll be able to come up with something appropriate. I'm an old fashioned kind of girl. I like romance."

He laughed. Old fashioned. He didn't believe that for a minute.

*　*　*

Peyton stared out of the plane window. Marco watched her, enjoying the way the light played over her features, caressing the curve of her shoulder. Her hands lay clasped in her lap, her wedding ring shining in the sunlight.

"Peyton," he said softly. "We need to talk, sweetheart."

She rolled her head on the chair cushion and studied him, her expression unreadable. "I love you, Marco. You know you mean more to me than anything or anyone."

"I know that."

"And I know how hard this job is for you."

"It is."

"It takes me away, puts me in danger, consumes my attention."

"It does all of that."

She sighed. "I want nothing more than to make our marriage work."

"I know that, but I also know that you wouldn't be you without the job."

She frowned. "What?"

He gave her a closed-mouth smile, shaking his head. "Sweetheart, you were born to solve crimes. It's in your

DNA. Working with you again on this case has only solidified what I already knew. If I were to ask you to quit, you'd do it for me, but you'd be miserable. I'd lose the woman I love."

She shifted in the seat toward him and took his hand. "Are you serious?"

"I am. I watched you talk Jackson Hughes into surrendering and I knew then that you have to do this. I love you because of who you are, and who you are is an investigator. So, we'll figure it out. We'll figure out how to make things work between us."

"I promise I'll work on being here more."

"I know. I know you'll try, but the job will make demands that we're just going to have to weather. I fell in love with who you are, woman. I went in fully aware of who you are and loving you for it."

"What about having a family?"

"We'll have one. That isn't going to change no matter what job you have, but you wouldn't be any kind of wife or mother if you weren't doing what you love to do, what fulfills you."

She lifted his hand and kissed the back of it. "You're my best friend, D'Angelo. You are my partner in everything. I couldn't love you more if I tried."

He curved his hand under her chin. "God, Brooks, you got me so bad, I can't remember anything before you came into my life."

She laughed, bringing her mouth close to his. "Well, fifty years from now when we're sitting on a plane headed home from our anniversary trip, I hope you'll say the same thing."

He slid his hand around the side of her face, curving his fingers around her neck. He kissed her, deeply, pouring all of his emotions into it. "In fifty years, sweetheart," he said against her lips, "I'll say this was the greatest adventure of my life." Then he kissed her again.

EPILOGUE

Peyton and Marco stepped through the security checkpoint and into the main part of SFO. The fog blanketed the City, rolling in from the bay. People bustled about, dragging children behind them, some of the children crying. A dog barked.

"Peyton!"

Peyton looked up just before she was engulfed in a hug by a blond whirlwind. She laughed and hugged Bambi in return. "Wow! How are you, Emma?"

Jake strode up, his hands in his pockets, a grin on his face. He reached up and punched Marco in the shoulder, then shook his hand as if he'd hurt his fingers. "Welcome home, Mighty Mouse, Adonis."

"Captain," growled Marco.

"Captain Adonis," said Jake, then he pulled Peyton to him for a hug. "So you pregnant yet?"

"Jake!" said Emma, scandalized.

Peyton glared at him. "Did you take some personality lessons from Drew Holmes? Why are you being an ass?"

"I've spent the last few weeks trying to find a disco ball, Mighty Mouse. My generally good nature has been soured."

"Really?" said Peyton, hooking her arm in Bambi's. "And here I thought you were all giddy with your new romance."

Jake's gaze shifted to Bambi and grew besotted. "Oh, I'm giddy all right. Emma is the illumination in the darkness of my existence. She is the beacon drawing me out of the wilderness. She is the sunlight in the desolation of my soul."

"Oh dear God, you had to go and wind him up, didn't you?" Marco grumbled.

Bambi and Peyton giggled.

"Can we go now?" Marco said, starting for the baggage claim.

"You know I brought the Daisy right."

"Of course you did. It's my punishment for leaving paradise," Marco said.

Peyton's phone buzzed in her pocket. She figured it was her mother, wanting to know if they'd landed safely or not. She wasn't sure how she was supposed to respond in the case of "or not", but she'd text her when they got to the car.

As she and Bambi followed along behind Jake and Marco, Peyton realized she was glad to be home. She'd missed these crazy people and in a few days, they'd have Abe's fiftieth birthday party, which was bound to be filled with the most intriguing people Jake could find.

Her phone buzzed again and she reached for it, knowing her mother wasn't going to wait for her to reach the car. When she stared at the screen, she realized she didn't know the phone number. A text message flashed at her and she thumbed it on, pulling it up.

A picture spread across the screen. She stopped walking and stared at it, then expanded the picture so she could see it more clearly. Three men stood in the middle of a desert. She immediately recognized the man on the left – Isaac Daws. She felt pretty sure she recognized the man in the middle as well. Senator Theodore Lange. But the third man was unfamiliar. She saw the bubble indicating someone was typing something.

She waited, staring at the picture.

Did you figure out the first riddle?

She typed back, *No, who is this?*

Let me refresh your memory. North, south, east, west. That which clears the evidence shows the best.

What does it mean? Who are you?

Here's a new one. Once there were three, then there were two. One plus one now makes none. Soon, soon, soon.

WHO ARE YOU?

I am the Enigma, came the response. *Figure out this riddle and you'll have something.*

"Peyton?" said Bambi, moving back to her side.

Peyton shoved the phone in her pocket. She didn't want to deal with this right now. She'd handle it when she got back to work. This was part of what she'd promised Marco. When she was off duty, she was going to stay off duty, completely focused on those around her.

Still, she could feel the weight of the phone in her pocket and the need to work the riddle pressed at her as she hurried to the baggage claim where her husband waited, but tomorrow would be here soon enough. Tomorrow she would handle it.

*   *   *

Danté strode to the front of the precinct where the social worker and Harper waited for him. Harper held the baby in her arms, smiling at the bundle wrapped in a pink blanket. The social worker held out her hand.

"I'm Lucinda Hernandez."

"Nice to meet you, Ms. Hernandez," said Danté, shaking her hand. "Are we ready to go?"

"Yes, I talked with the Gutierrez family this morning. They're very excited to meet their granddaughter."

"Good," said Danté, but his eyes focused on Harper. "Harper?"

She blinked up at him, her expression far away. "What?"

"You ready to go?"

"Yes," she said, but he could hear the reluctance in her voice.

He pushed through the half-door, but as he did so, the outer door opened and Cashea Thompkins stepped inside. She glanced around the gathering, then focused on Danté.

"Hey," she said.

"Hey," repeated Danté, "what's up?"

411

She shot a look at the other two women again, then tugged at her t-shirt. "I just wanted to come talk to you."

"We're just heading out, but do you want to come in for a moment?" he said.

"No." She held up a hand. "This'll just take a second. I wanted to tell you I gots a job."

"A job?"

"Yeah, with the public defender's office. You know Angela Douglas?"

"I've heard of her."

"Yeah, well, that gang guy, Javier Something or Other…"

"Vargas?"

"Right. He introduced us. I'm gonna be working for Angela two days a week, doing filing and stuff like that. Answering phones, but it's work."

"That's fantastic, Cashea."

She gave him a ghost of a smile, then looked down. "I just wanted to tell you. Thaz all. I think I might wanna become a lawyer myself. You know, go to law school and all that."

Danté shook his head in amazement. "I'm so happy for you," he said. "I think that's a brilliant plan."

"Well, I better go. Mama's waiting in the car. Talk to you soon," she said, turning for the door.

"Talk to you soon," Danté called after her.

Cho appeared from the back. "Let's get this show on the road," he said, jangling his keys.

They left the precinct and headed for Cho's patrol car, climbing inside. Harper strapped the baby into her car seat between herself and the social worker, then Cho headed the car in the direction of the Gutierrez house. No one said much as they went, but Danté could hear Harper in the backseat, singing a lullaby under her breath. It was the sweetest sound he'd heard in a long time.

A short time later, they pulled up in front of the Gutierrez's house and got out. The social worker carried the car seat and Harper held the baby in her arms. Danté and Cho hung back, letting the women go first.

Before they reached the first step, the door opened and the three Gutierrez family members walked out. Elba caught sight of the baby and gasped, covering her mouth with her hands. Harper walked up to her, smiling, and placed the baby in her arms.

Hugo put his arm around his wife's shoulder and stared down at his granddaughter, then the two grandparents looked at each other, their eyes swimming with tears, their smiles broad and joyous.

Guillermo shook hands with Harper and the social worker, repeating over and over again, "Dios mio, gracias, muchas gracias."

Cho nudged Danté with his shoulder. "You still think you want to quit, kid," he said.

Danté watched the family, torn apart by violence, now brought together by a tiny baby. He shook his head. "No, no I don't," he said.

*   *   *

Abe's fiftieth birthday party was a disco nightmare come alive. There were strobe lights, there were rotating colored bulbs, there was a disco ball. A DJ, wearing an afro and polyester pants with a satin jacket, played funk and drawled out the song names like Wolfman Jack. An open bar was set up in the back, serving Harvey Wallbangers, Tom Collins, and Piña Coladas.

Marco had agreed to wear a brown shirt with geometric patterns on it and a collar wide enough to land an airplane. He had no idea where Jake had found brown corduroy bell bottoms, but he had. Peyton wore white bell bottoms with a silk shirt tucked into them and a belt with silver medallions affixed to it. She'd teased out her curls and put them into pigtails, then she'd put gold eyeshadow on and orange lipstick. Added to that, she wore four-inch platform shoes. She ought to look ridiculous, but Marco thought she looked sexy as hell.

As they wandered through the room, they found Jake wearing a white leisure suit with a black shirt and shiny black platform shoes. Bambi had on an orange and brown mini dress, her blond hair in a high ponytail.

"This is amazing, Jake," said Peyton, looking around.

Jake put a drink in her hand. "Have a Harvey Wallbanger."

Peyton laughed and took a sip. "Where's the man of the hour?"

"Dancing with Misha and Serge," said Jake, pointing over his shoulder.

Abe wore a turquoise faux fur suit with a turquoise faux fur fedora on his dreadlocks. His spats were patent leather, shining in the light from the disco ball as he shimmied and shook his body in a loose limbed shuffle.

Before they could head over to him, Maria threw her arms around Peyton's neck. She wore go-go boots over a slinky leopard print catsuit. Cho wore a black and white zoot suit with the words Disco King scrawled across his back in sequins.

"Can you believe how fun this is?" said Maria, hanging on Peyton. She clanked her drink against Peyton's glass. "Drink up and let's dance." She grabbed Peyton's hand and dragged her onto the dance floor.

Peyton looked over her shoulder at Marco, but he just smiled at her.

"Come on, Sex Kitten," said Jake to Bambi, curving his arm around her waist.

She giggled. "Oh, Jakey, you're so funny!" she said, letting him guide her onto the dance floor.

Marco made a face and looked around for Bill Simons. The large man was sitting with Danté in a corner, sipping a beer and watching his wife dance with Drew Holmes. Marco spotted Tag and a woman he didn't know dancing in a cluster with Peyton and Maria.

He sank down into the chair, smiling at the two men.

"Welcome home, Captain," said Simons.

"Thanks, Bill." He eyed Danté. "Why aren't you dancing?"

Danté jerked his chin at the dance floor. "Because that's happening."

Marco looked to where Danté pointed and saw Bartlet trying to moonwalk and crashing into people. He crashed into Tag and she shoved him, pulling back her happy fist to sock him. Peyton grabbed her arm, hauling it down before she could let fly.

"I get it," Marco said, nodding.

As the party wore on, Marco wandered from group to group, talking to everyone. Awhile later, he found Abe sitting alone on a couch at the edge of the dance floor, sipping a drink and watching the dancers. Marco sank down next to him and Abe offered him a smile.

"Can you believe this party, Angel? All these people are here just for me."

"Well, you're sort of an important part of all our lives."

Abe smiled wistfully. "Fifty years. Half a century. You wouldn't think it to look at me, would you?" He nudged Marco with his arm.

"Not for a minute," Marco said.

Peyton danced into view with Maria and Bambi, shimmying and shaking her body to the music. Marco smiled, watching her.

"She's something special, our girl, you know that?" said Abe.

"I know it."

"It's funny," said Abe, crossing one ankle over his knee and smoothing down the faux fur. "I was pretty worried about turning fifty."

"I know."

"But sitting here, looking at all these people, I realize it isn't so bad. Not when you have the right people around you. You know what I mean, Angel?"

"I do."

Peyton disengaged herself and came over, stopping in front of them and fanning herself. "Why are you sitting here like this?" she said.

"Just contemplating life, sugar," said Abe. He patted the seat next to him. "Cop a squat, little soul sista."

Peyton wiggled into the spot between them, laying her hand on Marco's knee, and resting her head on Abe's shoulder. "You're not supposed to be contemplating. You're supposed to be partying."

"Oh, I am partying, sugar. I'm just doing it my way. Don't you worry none about me." He kissed her forehead. "I was just telling Angel that when all is said and done, my life hasn't been so bad, now has it?"

"No, not bad at all. Look at all you've accomplished, Abe."

"Well, I wasn't thinking of material things, toots. I was thinking of the people that matter most to me. I mean, look at this party. Look at all these people. And to think Jakey put it all together by himself."

"He did a good job," said Peyton. "He loves you. We all do."

Abe leaned his head against hers and smiled. "I know that. And that's what makes all of this so special – the love."

Suddenly the music stopped and there was commotion on the dance floor. Jake and Bambi wheeled out a gigantic cake and everyone gathered around. Abe sat forward as Jake motioned for him to get up.

"Come on, Abe," he said.

Abe clapped his hands and pushed himself off the couch. Peyton snuggled into Marco's side as they both watched Abe take his spot before the cake.

"Abnormally large cake," said Marco, shaking his head. "I should have known."

Peyton laughed. "Is it bad that I'm worried about how much that cost us?"

"Is it bad that I'm worried about what's going to come out of it?"

The *Happy Birthday* song rose from the people gathered around the cake. Abe bounced with excitement as they sang to him. When they reached the end, he leaned forward to blow out the candles, but the top suddenly exploded and Abe jumped back, clapping his hands wildly.

A handsome young man wearing a bowtie and black slacks popped out and the disco ball began to whirl as the music started again. Lifting himself from the cake, the young man dropped to the dance floor and began to boogie down with the crowd of people.

Peyton and Marco laughed as Abe and the young man began a contest to see who could go lowest. Curving his arm around Peyton's side, he drew her closer to him and he knew that no matter what the next few weeks might bring, right now he was about as happy as a person could be.

The End

Now that you've finished, visit ML Hamilton at her website: authormlhamilton.net and sign up for her newsletter. Receive free offers and discounts once you sign up!

The Complete *Peyton Brooks' Mysteries* Collection:
Murder in the Painted Lady, Volume 0
Murder on Potrero Hill Volume 1
Murder in the Tenderloin Volume 2
Murder on Russian Hill Volume 3
Murder on Alcatraz Volume 4
Murder in Chinatown Volume 5
Murder in the Presidio Volume 6
Murder on Treasure Island Volume 7

Peyton Brooks FBI Collection:
Zombies in the Delta Volume 1
Mermaids in the Pacific Volume 2
Werewolves in London Volume 3
Vampires in Hollywood Volume 4
Mayan Gods in the Yucatan Volume 5
Haunts in Bodie Volume 6
Menehune in Kauai Volume 7

Zion Sawyer Cozy Mystery Collection:
Cappuccino Volume 1
Café Au Lait Volume 2
Espresso Volume 3
Caffe Macchiato Volume 4

The Avery Nolan Adventure Collection:
Swift as a Shadow Volume 1
Short as Any Dream Volume 2
Brief as Lightning Volume 3
Momentary as a Sound Volume 4

The Complete *World of Samar* Collection:
The Talisman of Eldon Emerald Volume 1
The Heirs of Eldon Volume 2
The Star of Eldon Volume 3
The Spirit of Eldon Volume 4

The Sanctuary of Eldon Volume 5
The Scions of Eldon Volume 6
The Watchers of Eldon Volume 7
The Followers of Eldon Volume 8
The Apostles of Eldon Volume 9
The Renegade of Eldon Volume 10
The Fugitive of Eldon Volume 11

Stand Alone Novels:

Ravensong
Serenity
Jaguar